Also by Karen Dales

THE CHOSEN CHRONICLES

Changeling
Angel of Death
Shadow of Death
Thanatos (forthcoming)

For Cheri
Keep out of the
shadows!

[signature]

Fan Expo
2011

shadow of
death

book two of
the chosen chronicles

karen dales

Dark Dragon Publishing
Toronto, Ontario, Canada

This book is a work of fiction. The characters, incidents, and dialogue are drawn from the author's imagination and are not to be construed as real. Any resemblance to actual events or persons, living or dead, is entirely coincidental.

Shadow Of Death:
Book Two of the Chosen Chronicles

Copyright © 2011 by Karen Dales

ISBN: 978-0-9867633-2-8

Cover Art, Design and Author Photo
© 2010 by Evan Dales
WAV Design Studios
www.wavstudios.ca

Dark Dragon Publishing
313 Mutual Street
Toronto, Ontario
M4Y 1X6
CANADA
www.darkdragonpublishing.com

For more information on the Author,
Karen Dales and The Chosen Chronicles
www.karendales.com
www.thechosenchronicles.com

acknowledgements

There are always many people to thank and if I named them all it would fill a book unto itself. If I did not mention you it is not because you have been forgotten, it is because there is not enough ink in the world to express my gratitude.

First and foremost I must express my profound love for my husband, Evan, who has always been a support to me, sacrificing so that I can follow my dreams.

Mike Winkler, thank you for helping me with the German and lending me *Subtle Persuasion*, you and your wonderful wife, Stephanie, do prove that Vampires can love.

Adam, if it were not for you my French would be a mess!

In my journey as an author I have made some wonderful friends, none more so than Violette Malan and her husband, Paul.

To my fans I have made, thank you! It is because of you that this book was finished.

Karsha Pearce won the right to have a character named after her. I hope you enjoy!

For my son...

prologue

Multitudes of snowflakes stuck together in the cold, damp night. Filtering down from silver laden clouds they formed misshapen globules that impacted silently upon their fallen, earthbound brethren. No sound existed in the forest. Any animal daring to venture forth would find itself a-swarm with sticky snow. Instead the smart ones stayed huddled in their warrens and holes waiting for the brunt of the gentle snow storm to abate, leaving the forest as quiet as a grave.

Fernando de Sagres, the last heir to the title Fidalgio de Sagres and now Master of the Chosen of the British Isles, did not count himself as one of the smart ones. Standing on the side of the cart track, he ignored the puff of vapour his annoyed huff left to gradually dissipate before his face.

"Are you sure this is the place?" he asked his companion.

"This is where the man from the livery said they delivered their things." Bridget, Mistress of the Chosen of the British Isles, turned up the fox fur collar of her ermine coat in an effort to keep the chunky snow from finding its way down the back of her neck. Hindsight proved that she should have left her golden tresses to flow naturally, rather than bind them tightly in a matron's bun. She peered into the dark forest, trying to find any sign of where they next had to go.

"This doesn't make any sense," fumed the Master. "Are you sure you got the correct information? I couldn't make heads or tails of what he was saying." Fernando placed his hands in his coat pockets. The cold did not bother him. It was standing out in the middle of nowhere on a godforsaken night, obviously at another dead end in their search. He could not count how many times they had sensed their quarry only to realize they were well off their mark.

The Mistress scowled at her Chosen and took a step closer to the edge of the track. The livery manager had succumbed to her charms easily enough without having to Push him for the information, but finding the path through the snow laden trees in the middle of a snowfall would not be easy. Ignoring Fernando's irritation, Bridget stepped onto the edge of the track and then took a step towards the trees. It was supposed to be on this side, right here, if the livery manager was correct. She grimaced as a clump of snow slipping from a bent branch made its way down the back of her neck. Despite the discomfort she stepped further under the skeletal umbrella of trees.

Through the dark Bridget watched the silver and white mix with the blacks and greys that painted a haunting picture. What she found strange was that there seemed to be equidistant space between what appeared as two rows of trees. Bridget's pulse quickened.

Hearing his Chooser's intake of breath and sensing her sudden excitement, Fernando took the crunching steps through the ankle deep snow to stand beside her. "What do you see?" He gazed into the woods, trying to discern what Bridget had discovered and failed.

"A path." Bridget's smile lit up the night, her summer sky blue eyes twinkling. "Over there. Can you see it?"

Fernando carefully walked to where Bridget pointed. When he stood between the rows of trees he returned her smile and nodded. "Have I told you lately that not only are you beautiful, but you're a genius as well?"

Stepping in her Chosen's footsteps, Bridget came to stand before the man she loved and placed a cool hand on his cheek "You often tell me that I'm beautiful." *You've never told me the other,* she Sent.

Emitting a growl at the intrusion in his mind, Fernando backed away. "I agreed to only remain myself open to you insofar that this damned situation with the Vampires is dealt with. You know I don't—"

"I know, Fernando," sighed Bridget, as she turned to follow the tree-canopied path. Brushing past the Noble, she turned as his hand suddenly grabbed her arm.

"No. You don't." Releasing her arm, he stepped to her side as they continued up the path. "And I'd rather I kept it that way."

"I know that too," snapped Bridget, expecting the same argument that they nightly engaged in since he came back with the Angel three months ago.

She had gotten her way in making sure that Fernando did not sever their mental link with one another. This time her arguments did not fall on deaf ears, but he still resented the bond when Bridget used their Chosen talents, allowing unspoken communication between Chooser and Chosen. Allowing the matter to lie, Master and Mistress walked along the path in mutually agreed upon silence.

Every so often a sloughing of snow would fall from branches too weak to hold their load, adding to the whiteness camouflaging the path. The only sound came from their leather booted steps, crunching and squeaking in tattoo. Any mortal human would never have found the path, let alone be able to traverse it, but to Chosen sight, the night was lit up in a spectacular array of glimmering diamonds against a backdrop of grey and silver.

Farther on, the trickling sound of a stream filled the silence, adding its natural cadence to the crunching of immortal feet. Neither Chosen could see the river far off to their left, but its melody added a mysterious otherworldly air. Quickly glancing at one another, they continued their pace until the bells of the stream turned into the bellows of a rushing of a river.

The path twined until it ran parallel to the river, its bank becoming a precarious edge to the path. Halting their progression, they stood in awe of the river as it flowed thunderously over rocks, muddying the banks and swallowing snow unfortunate in its landing. The thaw of the week before had raised the water level to nearly equal to the path. The shimmering waters pulsed with the promise of a spring reborn despite this late winter storm.

Threading her arm through Fernando's, Bridget and he continued on until the path opened up onto a snow covered field that ended against a bluff that rose high into the sky. The river, off to their left widened and was dusted in a haze of mist created from the foudroyant waterfall. In the middle of this majestic scene stood a tranquil sight – a simple stone cottage with a thatched roof. Gloaming windows and a puffing chimney indicated that they had found what they were looking for.

With a determined nod of his head, Fernando led Bridget to

the weather worn wooden door, ready to do whatever he must to bring back the Angel. Sensing and matching his determination, Bridget squared her shoulders.

Father Paul Notus threw another log onto the fire, stirring it to flaring life with the iron poker. Standing, he held out his ink-stained hands to savour the heat and rubbing them together before turning back to his desk on the opposite wall. The cottage was small and cozy. A threadbare loveseat lined the wall underneath the blown glass window that gave fish-eyed views of the cliff face, waterfall and the dark recess of an ancient cave. No kitchen or bathroom was present in the small cottage. Only a ladder beside the hearth reached up to the high rafters and the loft where two pallets stretched out beneath the blackened ceiling. It was a perfect home built by two Chosen as a retreat from the world.

Sitting at his desk, Notus adjusted the oil lamplight and picked up a fine four haired brush, dipped it in russet and mixed it with crimson before applying it to the illumination set before him. Jeanie's smiling face, framed by cinnamon curls, laughed at him as he stroked the brush to quell an errant lock. The green of her eyes could not compare to the light that had emboldened her gaze before death had taken her. Placing the brush down on the edge of the paint pallet, Notus sighed.

He still missed the girl and mourned the loss of the only reason for learning the culinary arts. She was always so willing to help him, and over the five years in his employ Jeanie had become more daughter than maidservant. Notus had not expected that and was shocked to find a rift that Jeanie's passing had rendered within him. It was even more unbelievable the devastation that her loss had created upon his son. It was for him that they had quickly packed their belongings and moved to the only place that gave solace, the place where Notus had found the boy so long ago.

It was the only property they owned, purchased half a millennium ago. In a strongbox tucked into the thatch where ceiling met loft, the original deed curled tightly with age, its scribing faded and difficult to read. The cottage was as old as the ancient vellum. Its upkeep was provided by the two Chosen who called it home.

Notus picked up the brush and readied it for another detail when a knock resounded through his home. Stunned at the intrusion, he placed the brush into a shallow water dish and stood up. No one knew where they were. The boy would just walk right in, having no need to knock.

A nervous shiver flowed over him with the imaginings that Vampires were at the door ready to capture and hold him hostage again, exsanguinating him against his will. Try as he may, Notus still had difficulties in coming to terms with what had happened to him and his son not so many months ago. The boy's scars and injuries, both physical and emotional, were still raw, and so, it seemed, were Notus'.

Taking a cautious step closer to the door, the monk closed his eyes and listened, popping them open at the gentle rapping and a female voice he recognized as the Mistress'. Without a moment's hesitation, Notus lifted the latch and opened the door to see Bridget and Fernando standing on his doorstep.

"May we come in?" asked the Noble, eyebrow raised in annoyance.

Shocked out of his reverie at seeing the Mistress and Master of the Chosen of Britain, Notus stood back and let them enter, marking their high fashioned winter dress. Fernando stomped off the snow that clung to his black leather boots, while Bridget daintily tapped the toes of her heeled boots against the threshold.

"I'm sorry that our appearance here surprises you," remarked Bridget as she allowed Fernando to take her fur coat. "That was not our intention." Her sapphire dress lined with fine white lace hugged her petite frame.

Notus closed the door against the abating snowfall and turned to watch the Noble remove his long coat, placing both winter attire on the short couch.

"I am at a loss," admitted the monk. "However did you find us here?"

Glancing around for a place to sit, Fernando pulled out the old wooden chair from the desk and sat down as Bridget sank into the couch. "With a lot of detective work and frustration," stated the Noble.

Bereft of a seat, Notus stood, bearing their scrutiny. He was much older than they, but they had, or at least the Mistress had, counted his boy a friend. That eased his mind but did not halt the expectation of why they would have gone to all this trouble to find them. He stated such as he crossed over to his desk and covered the illumination with a protective cloth.

Fernando had turned as the monk stood beside him and caught a glimpse of what could only be an amazing rendition of Jeanie. Their eyes met briefly and the Noble cast his eyes forward in awkward silence at the mournful expression of the ancient Chosen.

"We have come to take the Angel back to London," answered Fernando, his voice gruff.

Somehow Notus was not surprised and he let out a slow sigh as his shoulders slumped. "What for?"

"He's to stand before the Grand Council and testify." Fernando watched the monk walk to the other side of the small home to lean against the wall next to the hearth.

Notus shook his head. "You're condemning him to death."

"No!" Bridget's response raised her from her seat as she rushed over to the Angel's Chooser. "Never that. Please believe us. We need him. The Chosen need him."

Notus met Bridget's blue eyes with his sad hazel. "He cannot. He's not well enough." Realizing what Fernando had said, he turned to face the still seated Chosen. "A Grand what?" In all his centuries, Father Paul Notus had never heard of such a thing.

"A Grand Council has been asked for but Hugo of France, Hilde of Germany and us, to discuss the genocide that the Vampires would have all Chosen fall to," replied Fernando. "Franco of Spain, Alfonsina of Italy, Sigbjörn of Sweden and at least four others will be attending in London in a week's time to discuss the Vampire threat and what we need to do about it."

"But why do you need my boy?" Notus' anxiety geared up several notches. For his son to stand before so many Masters and Mistresses when he was still recovering from his wounds would instantly mean Destruction regardless of what promises Fernando and Bridget had made to the contrary.

"Because he's the only one they will believe," stated Bridget, calmly. "He's also the only one who can tell the difference between who is Chosen and who is not. Already incidences are arising and we are woefully lacking in our knowledge about our Vampire enemies, even if we try and read all the pulp that is published."

"No. No. No," Notus shook his head, brushed past Bridget and began to pace. "I won't allow it."

"It's not for you to decide," replied the Master, succinctly, bringing Notus to a halt.

He could not believe what they were asking of his boy.

"You're asking him to place his neck on the chopping block for you."

"Not for me." Fernando frowned, huffing his exasperation. "For the Chosen."

"You want him to die." Notus' eyes widened further.

"Never that." Bridget came to her Chosen's rescue. "Paul, the Angel can do things we can't." She placed her hand on the monk's rough spun woollen robe. "We need his help."

"Let him decide for himself." Fernando stood, the chair grinding into ancient floorboards. "If he chooses to stay in seclusion, hiding from the world and his responsibilities, then we will leave, but it will be on his head if this war against the Vampires sours terribly and all that remains of the Chosen is left in this cottage."

"We are already at a great disadvantage," continued Bridget. "Though we have halted some of the supply of the spice, it is still being imported across Europe. Chosen are still dying. In some areas there already has been open fighting between Vampires and Chosen, with us losing badly because of their infiltration into our societies."

"The Angel and I only took out the head of the snake," said Fernando. "The rest is still thrashing. We need to kill the rest before more heads grow."

Hating the truth of their words, Notus slumped onto the couch and rubbed his face before glancing at Bridget and Fernando in turn. He did not know what his boy could do, but they believed he could help save the Chosen. Maybe it was true. Maybe not. It was the boy's decision. He nodded his head. "You may ask him."

Smiling sadly at the defeat written over Notus' visage, Bridget asked, "Where is he?"

"He's out back." Notus stared at the flickering fireplace. "He's training."

Confused and intrigued, Fernando walked over to the window and looked out upon a winter wonderland and gasped.

The snow landed upon the Angel's bare shoulders as he stood with closed eyes facing the waterfall. Each clump of snow was noted as it touched his silver striped skin. The ice crystals did not hold its integrity for long. His slight body heat was enough to destroy the perfect little stars, forming them into trickles of water that ran down his back, chest and arms. The snow that touched his hair merged and disappeared into the white silk of the strands. If they melted, he took no note.

Standing statuesque, he slowly inhaled the cold night air, feeling the freshness fill his lungs before he exhaled a gradual cloud warmed by his body. Again and again he did this, taking in the night and releasing it as the sound of the waterfall rushed over him.

Clad only in black trousers, he felt the cold of the snow under his bare feet and the smooth wood grain of the *naginata* in his grip. The muscles in his wrists jumped at the painful position and he quelled it with another breath. Standing posed, ready to strike, was excruciating to his healing body, but the physical pain of practice was easier to endure than the tight band forged around his heart.

He could not stay in their cabin doing nothing while his Chooser dealt with his grief through artistry. The image Notus rendered from paint and brush was too painful a memory of what he had lost, and so he would come outside with *bokken* or *naginata* in hand, to force his healing body into exercises that over four months ago would have been child's play. Now, just holding the *naginata* his muscles trembled, threatening his body into a seizure that came only when he pushed himself too far.

Notus had begged for him to take it easy, to let the ravages of Violet's torture with knife and steel scourge slowly mend, but he could not allow himself the luxury of contemplative penance for failing Jeanie so completely. Instead, each night, he would come out and force his damaged body into relearning what torture had taken away from it. At first holding a weapon was impossible. His hands and fingers convulsed with the simple exertion. In the early days, even that would lead him into paroxysms of pain that would send Notus running to his aid as his body betrayed him with pain-racked spasms. Notus would help him, bringing him in from the cold, to force him to sit before the fire and let its warmth relax muscles twitching in expectation for more agony.

Tonight he held the *naginata*, all seventy-six inches of it, and his muscles relaxed beneath his measuring breath. Taking the risk, he raised the bladed staff into a defensive block. Holding it there, he panted with exhilaration and opened his eyes.

The mist on the waters danced like fireflies, flitting around or blinking out as the snow gently descended. The muscles in his left hand twitched, threatening to release the weapon but he stilled it with an exhalation. Closing his eyes once more, he willed his shoulders to relax and decided it was worth the risk.

Slowly pivoting on his left foot, he began the *kata*. His muscles twitched at the movements, his fingers and wrists promising the *naginata's* release, but he continued the flow, ever mindful of his breathing. He turned and spun, striking an imaginary foe before parrying and blocking. Each movement tortured his left leg and at one point he had to hop to his right, abruptly taking the pressure off that damaged limb lest it crumble beneath him. Hissing, he halted, the bright twenty-one inch blade on the end of the fifty-five inch handle gleamed above his head, holding the *naginata* straight up.

A few more regulated breaths quelled the tremors and allowed him to explode into action. This time he did not hold back. He led the deadly dance with the weapon, knowing he would pay dearly for this exertion. He did not care as he flowed from one move to the next, knowing the fluid grace that would normally be present was not evident to his tutored eye. Still he spun and moved each strike, each block, issuing from him an eruptive breath that rang off the cliff face.

Taken by the trance of the *kata*, he did not note the sense of awe that flowed towards him until the practice dance was ended and he held the *naginata* end down in the snow, the blade sparkling in level with his shoulder. Chest heaving in an effort to put down the tiny spasms trying to collate into a paroxysm, he turned to face Bridget and Fernando staring at him through the window.

He met their surprise with irritation and watched Bridget pull Fernando away from the window. Unable to fathom how they found him, he swept his long stray hairs from his face and sighed. He could feel their need pulsating towards him, beckoning him and he resented, again, this new ability to sense what other Chosen felt and for them to do the same with him. It presented an incredible lack of privacy and it was yet another reason for their retreat from London. No matter how much Bridget worried over him or Fernando's irritation peaked, seeing his own pain reflected back at him in their faces was unfair to them. His mourning was his own, shared only with his Chooser because they had both loved Jeanie in their own ways.

Resigned that the Master and Mistress of Britain had discovered him, he knew no other recourse and went to meet them, feeling their need to talk with him.

The snow crunched under his bare feet as he walked around the cottage to the front door, using the *naginata* as a walking staff. His leg throbbed as he limped, protesting the abuse he had caused it. Thankful for the tight wrappings around his forearms and wrists, he managed to hold the shaft of the *naginata*, but his fingers twitched in rebellion for their misuse.

He opened the weather worn door, and ignoring Fernando's annoyed expression and Bridget's smile, he met Notus' eyes before giving him the weapon.

Why are they here? he silently queried his Chooser.

They want you to come back to London to stand before a Grand Council of many of the Mistresses and Masters of Europe, replied Notus. The monk took the *naginata*, the blade shimmering above his head, and placed it against the wall. Before his son could ask the next obvious question, he replied in the manner that all Choosers and Chosen benefit from. *They do not mean to see to your Destruction.*

The idea of a Grand Council terrified him, but he still could not expect reassurances that he would not be taken captive, dismembered and left for the sun. He tried to repress a shudder and failed.

"No," he whispered without turning to face the Master and Mistress. Good intentions or not, he refused to go back to London. He stared at the fire, ignoring Bridget's warning gasp or the flicker of anger the surged through the Noble.

"No?" replied the Master. "No? I don't think so." Fernando grabbed the Angels scarred arm and turned the tall pale Chosen to face him and nearly caught his breath at the fury behind the garnet gaze. "Do you know what's happening out there? Do you even care?"

Fernando did not smile at the Angel's grimace.

"Leave off, Fernando," interrupted Bridget. Her blue eyes gazed up at the Angel. "It's clear that he does not."

Bridget's harsh tones and hurt feelings discomfited him and he looked away. It was Notus who came to his rescue. "Leave him alone. Hasn't he suffered enough?"

It was the wrong question. Fernando's anger flared. "He's not the only one who has suffered," stated the Noble, his sun kissed skin still bronze from his escape from *Le Jardin*. "Chosen are dying while he hides here, licking his wounds."

The venom in the words stabbed at him, but he could not deny the truth of the Noble's words. Turning back to face the Mistress and Master, he did not endeavour to hide the pain their emotions caused him. "What would you have me do?"

The three Chosen gasped at the misery he projected and he turned away to stare back into the flames. It was proof enough of why he could not be around other Chosen. His wounds still bled, infecting others.

He felt a tremulous hand alight on his bandaged wrist and he felt the pity flow from Bridget and hated it. She snapped her hand back.

"We need you," she pressed. "The other Masters and Mistresses need someone to guide them in this war." He shook his head in denial that it could possibly be he. "We don't know who is or isn't Chosen. They have so befuddled us that we're probably killing our own as well as the Vampires."

He groaned. Turning around, he sat on the worn couch, his leg throbbing in relief, and buried his face in his hands. He knew their need. He could almost taste their desperation. The Vampires had effectively confounded the Chosen from within, causing distrust as to who is or is not Chosen so as to affect their genocide. Fernando was right. No matter all else, Fernando was right. But could he accept that? He looked up at the three Chosen, his eyes falling upon Fernando's deep brown. "This Grand Council, who does that entail?"

Fernando told him the names, leaving Hugo's for last, and he groaned. Hugo, no doubt, would demand that Fernando and Bridget put him to death. There was no love lost between the new Master of France and the Angel, having had the Angel defeat him in battle and then being kicked off the rooftop. No. Hugo would demand his Destruction.

Dropping his gaze back to the gloaming hearth, he shook his head. "No."

This time he expected the rush of anger directed at him and he closed his eyes in regret, wincing at Fernando's rant. "You care more for your own blessed secrets than to help those who hold those secrets?"

Implication's dart hit true and his head shot up, eyes wide in disbelief of what Fernando was threatening. But it was the Master of Britain who spoke them, glaring down his disgust. It was

Fernando and Bridget's call whether or not he would be Destroyed for his differences. Some part did not believe it, but then again he had never imagined another Chosen, besides Notus, would keep his deadly secrets.

As Chosen, they had left him a choice: to be Destroyed by their command or to stand before the Master and Mistresses of almost a dozen countries and proclaim his differences so as to possibly help fight this war against the Vampires. He very much doubted that any of the others would grant him clemency, but what choice did he really have? He glanced over to Notus and a wave of despondency overwhelmed him and he knew that the monk could not save him. Notus' head bowed under the belief that his only son would be Destroyed before his eyes.

"I will go," he acquiesced. Refusing to meet Bridget's relieved smile and Fernando's smirk of victory, he stood with great difficulty. "I will go and stand before them. I will do all of what is asked of me so long as Notus remains shriven of responsibility for my differences." Notus' raised his gaze to meet his son's, surprise written over his features. "But understand this; I will purge this Vampire threat for you, but they will not see the Angel standing in their midst. They will only see a shadow."

Í

London, England - Christmas

Sitting at the medieval style kitchen table, he held the thick pencil meant for a five year old and began writing on the lined sheet of paper. He had not intended to stay as long as he had, but Gerry and Donna's insistence, coupled with their children's enthusiasm, made it impossible to leave at sunset. Carefully making each stroke of the pencil, the words of gratitude began to take form. After over a century, writing was still one of the greatest difficulties he had to overcome. Thankfully, Rory's school pencil was laying on the coffee table in the living room.

Concentrating on forming the words, he only heard Gerry's approach when the mortal descended from the stairs. He looked up at his friend and noted the tired circles and dishevelled dark hair. The lights from the Christmas decorations and tree were illumination enough, casting the open home in a cheery light, giving Gerry just enough to see where he was going.

Wooden chair sliding against the tiled floor, he stood at his friend's approach, letter forgotten. "I'm sorry," he said. "I did not mean to wake you."

Gerry covered his yawn with the back of his hand and waved dismissively with the other before walking to the kitchen counter to pour himself a stale cup of coffee. He pulled out a second mug and lifted it in offering.

Recognizing the offer, he smiled, shook his head and sat. It was nice to be himself with Gerry and his family. He had forgotten what that was like. Amongst the Chosen he was on guard, defending his emotions from leaking to others or shielding against them. Here, with Gerry, he could relax. It had been so long since he opened up like this to a mortal, despite Gerry not knowing his true nature.

He had met Gerry six years ago, several years after returning to London. It was Bridget's insistence that he find something to do. Since he could not properly use his sword because it was not light enough for his damaged wrists to manage, he knew she was right. Geraint's sword was relegated to being a wall decoration while he honed his skills with lighter eastern weapons. It was in search of a smith to fix some of time's damage to Geraint's sword that he met Gerry.

He had liked Gerry instantly and it was the man's curiosity as well as his enthusiasm that suggested that the ways of the forge might be of interest. It had been centuries since he had taken up learning anything new and Gerry's authentic friendliness and willingness was enough. He became Gerry's apprentice and friend, ever keeping his Chosen nature away from the mortal. It was enough that his appearance marked him different, he would not bring a mortal into the world of the Chosen ever again. He would not risk it.

Gerry sat down across from him and sipped the bitter liquid that steamed before his face. "You're heading out already?" His grey eyes landed on the long wooden box bisecting the oblong table.

Both knew that his Masters' piece was in there. He opened up the metal latches with two successive clicks and lifted the lid. "I was supposed to be home this morning."

"May I?" asked Gerry. Placing his mug down, he picked up the hilt of the sword; its silver pommel and guard plain against the ebony grip. Four feet of finely honed steel flashed red in the gleaming decorations as Gerry lifted it to his face and whistled. "She's a beaut and the balance is perfect. You did a brilliant job. I don't think I could have done any better," he offered, placing the sword back into the case.

Embarrassed by the praise, he closed the lid, locking it into place.

"So," continued Gerry, renewing his interest in the contents of his mug. "Are you going to come by before you and Paul head across the Pond, or is Donna going to have to drag you back by your ear for one last visit?"

The image of Donna doing so lit a grin to his face and he shook his head, sending long white locks swinging. "I will come by for a visit."

"Before the kids go to bed," interjected Gerry, matching his smile.

Standing, he lifted the box as he turned towards the front door. "I promise."

Gerry followed him, mug in hand, and handed the leather coat from the coat rack to him. "Rory and Jenna will miss your stories."

Slipping into the coat, careful not to get the black braces on his wrists stuck in the sleeves, he shrugged into its weight. A century ago he would not have endured the pressure against his back for even a minute. It is said that time heals all wounds. That was mostly right.

"I will miss them too." He had not expected to fall in love with Rory and Jenna, but their childish wonder and acceptance drew him into their trusting world. For the short hour between his arrivals to their bed time he had unwittingly became part of their night time routine and thus their lives. He had never been called Uncle before and knew he would miss it when he left. "I will send letters."

Gerry lifted the long wooden box by its leather strap and handed it to him. "We'd all love to hear them."

Slinging it over a shoulder, the sword case settled against his back and he smiled. "Thank you for everything, Gerry."

Dismissing the appreciation with another wave of his hand, Gerry blew through his pursed lips and shook his head. "Thank you. It's been a long time since I had such a talented or enthusiastic apprentice. And since I still have to be Santa Claus and get the rest of the presents from the back of the closet before the kids wake, I suggest you'd get going."

He opened the front door and both of them stared in surprise at the winter storm.

"Or maybe not," added Gerry as they both watched coagulated snowflakes fall in tiny balls with nary any space between them.

Spotting his motorcycle, his shoulders slumped at the sight of it buried in half a foot of white fluff. There was no possibility of driving it through this weather. Even with his Chosen sight it was difficult to see across the street.

"I guess the kids are going to get their wish," smiled Gerry.

"What was that?" he replied in sincere curiosity.

Gerry looked up at him, his grin broadening to show his perfect white teeth. "A white Christmas."

Turning back to the storm, his lips quirked into a smile, he could imagine Rory and Jenna in their snowsuits building snow forts and throwing snowballs at each other. It was a sight he would never see.

"I guess I had best get going." He took the couple of steps, white flakes swirling about him and halted at Gerry's voice.

"You could stay until the streets are clear."

He turned and looked at his friend standing in pyjamas, mug in hand, with a red glow spilling from the warm interior. "I appreciate the offer. I truly do. But I should get back."

"Okay," nodded Gerry. "But how are you going to get back?"

He would use his Chosen abilities to move faster than a mortal, but he could not tell his friend that, and then he remembered. "The train station is not far from here. Hopefully it will still be running."

Gerry sipped at his mug. "Alright. But if you get stuck there, come back. The kids and Donna would love having you for Christmas too. If you don't return, I'll put your bike in the shed once I can see where I'm going. Call us tomorrow to let us know you got home safely or Donna will skin my hide for letting you out in this."

Though it was a saying, having lived through such barbaric torture, it was difficult to repress a shudder as he turned to follow the dip of the walk where it met the street. "I will."

"Merry Christmas, Gwyn," called Gerry, closing the door.

He turned the corner, knowing that even had Gerry stood on his porch, his friend would not have seen him speed up his pace. Even for a Chosen it was difficult to tromp through half a foot of snow while it continued to accumulate. Blinking away large flakes of snow, he put his hand up to shade his eyes. If it were not for the street lamps he would not be able to see the station ahead of him. Tonight, being Chosen would not help him except to ensure he did not freeze to death.

Hoisting the box higher on his back, he approached the station, finding it deserted and locked. Alone in the middle of the night with the silence of the snowstorm he debated going back to Gerry and Donna's. He had inadvertently spent the day with them when he had intended to leave before dawn, but the work on the sword was incomplete and by the time it was done the sun was rising, making his skin prickle and forcing him to make a mad dash from the forge to the home.

Gratefully, he accepted the hospitality of a hot shower and a bed, but sleep eluded him in the forms of two young children. Rory and Jenna, thrilled that he was staying, had jumped on him while sleep slipped its arms around him, jerking him awake to their laughter. He did not remember the last time he spent the whole day awake, but Gerry's kids made it fly by.

He had to get home. He knew he would not be able to survive Christmas Day without collapsing from exhaustion or having his hunger flare up.

Resolved, he followed the chain-linked fence and glanced up at the ice-covered barbs. He had to be careful not to get caught on them. He was scarred enough from the damage that iron weapons and torture devices had wrought upon him. He did not know what more he could take. With that, he made sure that his feet would not slip and gracefully jumped over the barbed fence, landing in a puff of snow that cratered around him. Glancing around to see if anyone saw him, he settled the box on his back and found the train tracks.

The snow's consistency changed from loosely packed globs to smaller, ice laced ones as the wind picked up, swirling the top layers of snow into devils that danced around him. Blinking into the growing storm, he brushed his long hair from his face to no avail. The wind whipped up strands, entangling them in ice. Every time he tried to move preternaturally fast, the snowfall would become a wall, forcing him to slow down. His pace was still faster than a mortal's but nowhere near what he could have managed if the weather had co-operated. At this rate it would be well after midnight when he returned.

Flipping up the collar of his leather coat, he began the journey to the two-story flat he and Notus rented in Westminster.

The wind whipped around him, stinging exposed pale flesh with needles of ice, forcing him to keep his head down. The train tracks, buried beneath the snow, were hardly discernible and he would have walked off of them several times had there not been guiding posts and the fences to either side. Lone iridescent lights heading poles offered scant illumination as the buzzing of millions of snowflakes flittered around them before descending to add their small worth to the increasing girth of the white blanket.

Each step was fraught with the potential of slipping and falling. One misplaced heel, one overzealous push off could send him into the white fluff. No matter the powers of a Chosen, they were nothing when pressed against the ravages Mother Nature presented. Still he kept going, the plodding pace in a world a-swirl in white pulled him towards the lassitude of trance. No sound abounded except what wind and snow plucked at the immobile harp of a land asleep. Despite the storm and the attention it demanded, he found his mind slipping to other things.

Two decades had passed since the Mistress and Master recalled him back to Britain, his work complete, with the profound gratitude of the Grand Council that was formed to settle the issue of the Vampires. Settle it they did, by using him as their weapon. He was as much at fault as they, for he had given them no choice that night nearly one hundred and thirty years ago.

Bridget and Fernando had set the stage and he and Notus had worked out the finer details. It was no longer an issue of his Destruction, it was now a matter of the survival of the Chosen, and Bridget was right, only he could tell for certain who were Chosen and who were not.

His mind slipped to the past through a trance of snow and ice.

íí

He stood outside the old abandoned theatre, wearing only a cotton shirt and black trousers in the cold wind. He refused to glance in the direction of the puddle of light spilling from the lamppost where he had discovered Jeanie's corpse. Even within its proximity, the memories of finding her supine form, her hair a copper halo giving the illusion of spilled blood and a Vampire's mark upon her neck, threatened to fell him. Instead he stood in an attempt to still his tremors before it was time to re-enter the world of the Chosen.

Notus' hand alighted on his crossed arms and he opened his eyes to look down on concerned hazel staring back at him. He tried to offer a smile of reassurance, but failed, his crimson eyes filling. His Chooser knew what this cost him and what payment that could still be demanded. Taking a shuddering breath, he swallowed. He did not need to open himself further to Notus. It was hard enough seeing the monk so concerned.

Soon they would enter the building that had held Notus hostage, exsanguinated and crucified. Where Bastia, Mistress of Vampires, had fooled the Chosen into complacency as Katherine, Mistress of the Chosen of Britain, all the while exacting genocide on those she ruled. It was the place that had started the quest that had bound Fernando and he into discovering the deadly spice and the truth that Vampires did exist as a separate species from the Chosen – that Vampires sought the death of every Chosen. It was this circumstance that thrust Jeanie further into his life, uncovering his true nature, yet still accepting him enough so that love finally took root. It was here that sparked nightmares of his own torture at the hands of Violet, and worse the despair of Jeanie's murder by a Vampire.

Staring up at the theatre that was now the Courthouse of the Chosen of Britain, he tried to collect the tattered remains of what he was – the Angel. He squared his shoulders as best as his ruined back could allow and nodded to Notus.

It was time to stand before the first Grand Council of the Chosen in remembered history and give testimony to the truth that Vampires did exist and how the Chosen had foolishly believed that they had been the ones labelled as such by the mortals. Uncrossing his arms, he carefully walked up stone steps that threatened to buckle his left leg from under him and entered through the large double doors.

Several Chosen milled in the antechamber, their surprise and curiosity flowed over him as he and Notus entered. He did his best to quell the anxiety that promised to spill out to encompass them. This newfound ability, borne from his torture, was difficult to master, no matter how Notus tried to help.

Silence befell the large room lit only with gloaming candlelight from the chandelier. The gruesome paintings that had hung when the Vampires had ruled over the Chosen were now gone, leaving darkened patches against mahogany wainscoting. Only one canvass remained – the depiction of a devil subduing an angel with his wing horribly ripped off and terror written across his beautiful face.

His attention caught by the painting, he heard, rather than witnessed, the other Chosen move through the oak doors into the audience hall. Their nervousness scraped at him, adding to his anxiety.

"It's almost time, my boy," whispered Notus.

Unable to relinquish his gaze, he could only nod. Fernando, Bridget, Notus and he knew what most likely would occur if everything went well, but if it did not, then it was up to him to show the true damage the Vampires had caused to the Chosen. He also knew that if it came to pass, the other Masters and Mistresses would demand his Destruction and it would be Fernando and Bridget fighting to keep him alive. It was a responsibility that he never wanted them to have.

Are you sure that you wish to go through with this? sent Notus.

A frown turned down the corners of his full lips. *I don't have a choice.*

The monk caught his worried gaze. *You always have a choice. You are Chosen.*

"Am I?" he replied and then turned to enter the theatre and the Grand Council waiting within. He did not wait to hear Notus' reply, but he felt his Chooser's despair.

The small theatre was much as it was not too long ago. The red runner lining the space between the large double doors and the stage still remained. No seats were left for patrons of the arts. Instead, where once sat the Mistress who deceived them all sat fourteen Chosen in plain and simple chairs. In the centre sat Fernando and Bridget, as was right and proper for the Master and Mistress of Britain hosting such a historic event. Both were splendidly attired; Fernando in a black tux with tails and Bridget bedecked in diamonds, in a sapphire gown.

Making his way down the sloping rug, he felt Notus' presence tinged with worry. Other Chosen were in the room. Emotions flittered to him of awe, fear and curiosity. It was the absence of feeling, or rather the sense of cold voids from several individuals that made him clench his jaw in an effort to repress his anger. One thing he knew, Vampires left this chilly absence of space whereas mortals were warm beacons.

A tendril of concern touched him and his eyes met Bridget's blue eyes. No words were needed, her expression held the question she and Fernando dared not to ask out loud. He gave a slight nod that sent both of them into ridged tension. They had expected to have the Grand Council infiltrated by the Vampires, but having confirmation of the fact gave truth to their fears. Behind him the large oaken double doors closed with an audible thunk, followed by a ringing bang as the doors were locked. Jonathan placed the iron key into his breast pocket and nodded to his Mistress and Master. The large room settled into expectant silence.

It would have been perfectly natural for all eyes to fall upon the grand display of power sitting upon the stage, fourteen Masters and Mistresses of the Chosen, the largest number ever assembled. Instead all eyes fell onto the Angel.

A kaleidoscope of emotions bombarded him, setting off a mild headache that threatened to become more. He wanted to close his eyes and take a gulping breath in an effort to contain his tremulous emotions but knew he could not for it would only signify weakness. Raising his eyes from the base of the stage, he found Bridget smiling, belying the concern she held in her gaze. He knew she was worried about him, worried that his secrets were about to be ripped open for all to witness, thus forcing her and Fernando to present a sentence of Destruction against the Angel. It was a fear he had lived with through the centuries and standing so close to the precipice of its reality he could only drop his gaze back to the floor.

"First of all, I would like to thank the Mistresses and Masters who have graced us with their presence for this historic occasion," stated Fernando, breaking the awkward silence. His natural brass nature was replaced with a Fernando who had been reared to rule from a young age. As heir to the Fidalgo de Sagres Fernando knew diplomacy even though he rarely chose to use it. Now he wielded it with the finesse of a true Lord. "The Chosen are in precarious position. We are not the Vampires that mortals write about. Indeed, we have been deceived and reduced to victims by those that are Vampires - they who have started genocide against us for some unknown reason. All of us up here have communicated back and forth for several months on the issue, and Bridget and I are grateful for your attendance. We know how hard it must have been to leave your lands during this stressful time to come here and discuss how to unify against such a threat lest we become extinct."

"And how do ve know vat you say is true?" asked Gennadiy, Master of Russia, his chair creaked as he leaned his prodigious form forward so as to gaze over at Fernando. "*Da*, ve have written, ve have spoken, but ve still have no proof. None of zis is happening in my lands."

Bridget turned in her chair to face Gennadiy, her face lit up in a smile and tilted her head. "Then indeed you are luckier than most. As all of you know, here in Britain, as well as France, Germany, Spain and several other countries, the spice that the Vampires have created are still being bought, sold, and consumed by mortals. Our food supply is being poisoned. Already there are losses. Already there have been skirmishes between Chosen and those we believe to be Vampires. That is the problem. We do not *know* who is and is not Chosen."

"*Ich stimmoz mit dem Master Russlands übervin,*" Hilde of Germany stated. "*W' ist der Beweis, dass Vampire besteren?*"

"English, Hilde, English," sighed Alaric of Austria-Hungary.

"It was agreed upon."

Hilde's red painted lips twisted in an ugly sneer and turned her head away, setting strawberry blond locks bouncing.

"*Oui*, you have promised since our meeting in Calais, to share this information," sneered Hugo, Master of France.

"Actually, it wasn't my agreement on this," countered Fernando, his brown eyes blazing into Hugo's grey. "It was the Angel's decision to share this information. God knows why after you tried to kill us."

"You know why," countered France's Master.

"*Oui, parceque votre Maîtresse a succombée à l'épice et votre Maître l'a suivie, en vous quittant comme le Maître de la France,*" replied Bridget, her ire up.

Hugo huffed and turned his burning glare down upon the Angel.

The hatred Hugo directed at him eradicated all of the other's jumbled emotions, forcing an involuntary gasp from his pale lips.

Notus, sensing his distress, glanced up at him, concern flowing from his tense features. *Are you all right?* he Sent.

He had not been all right since Notus' capture by Katherine/Bastia and her Vampires, but he knew that was not what his Chooser was asking of him. Despite the pounding headache he nodded, keeping his gaze ahead of him. He just wanted this debacle over with so he could leave.

"And this is why you wanted us all together. To hear what *el Ángel* will tell us?" stated Franco of Spain, his dark eyes squinting in contemplation. His soft friendly features held no animosity, only genuine concern for the well being of the Chosen under his authority.

"Yes," stated Fernando.

"So stop your bickering and let us learn from *de Engel,*" piped in Jorge of the Netherlands. He offered the Angel and Notus an apologetic smile and shrugged.

Notus smiled back at his friend of many centuries and opened his mouth to begin his part of the tale that he and the others had planned, only to be cut off.

The Angel watched as a gentleman, wearing a simple tux, step across the stage, his shoes ringing off of the varnished wood, to bend down and whisper into the Master of France's ear. Message delivered, the dark haired man stepped back, resting his hands on the back of the chair. No emotions flowed from this man, only a cold void.

"Before we begin," interjected Hugo with false pleasantness. The malevolence that flowed from the Master of France changed subtly, adding an overlay of amusement. His steel grey eyes locked onto the Angel and he smiled.

All other emotions from the Chosen subsided beneath the barrage Hugo sent and it took everything the Angel had to keep from shivering under the Master's glare.

"There is one who, I know, was witness to the Angel and the Master of Britain," continued France's Master, nonchalantly. "I wonder why she was not called?" His smile broadened as he set the barb in the flail. "Where is your mortal whore, *l'Ange*?"

The question blindsided him, evoking the grief he had bottled in since the night of Jeanie's murder. He barely contained his shock at the flooding emotions battering against the surge of Hugo's vindictiveness. Surrounding it all was the confusion from the others as they sought to deal with the sudden grief thrust at them. It took Notus grabbing his arm and turning to face tearful hazel eyes to break the contact with Hugo's bombardment.

Stop this, Sent Notus, his thoughts raw with grief – his and his son's. *You need to take control otherwise this council will fall apart.*

Ripping his gaze away from his Chooser, the Angel shook the tears from his eyes. Hugo's triumph pelted down on him and he knew Notus was right. Several of the Masters and Mistresses had tears in their eyes, some, like Bridget, wept. Fernando seemed immune, his face tight with fury. He had not meant to rend his wounds open ever again, and never had he planned to do so in front of others.

"Where is your whore, *l'Ange*?" pressed Hugo, enjoying the discomfort the Angel appeared to be in. His assistant behind him snorted a laugh and fell quiet.

Hugo's abuse of Jeanie's memory rang in the Angel's mind, igniting the anger he had once felt when Hugo was just Aimeri's second and he had first named Jeanie a whore. The Angel had punished Hugo, ejecting him from the roof of a warehouse after fighting him while holding onto Jeanie with one arm. The fact that Hugo was referring to Jeanie in such a manner sent heat though his body.

"Jeanie is dead," stated the Angel through clenched teeth. Oh how the words knifed him to the core. He ignored the nervous chatter as grief turned to an anger the other Chosen easily picked up upon. Notus laid a hand on his arm in an effort to calm him, but he shrugged it away. The plan laid out no longer applied and he no longer cared about the consequences.

"You asked for the Angel to stand here and testify to the truth. Here I am." Barely contained rage tinged his words. "Jeanie is dead. Killed by a Vampire."

"Zis is preposterous!" shouted Gennadiy. "Ve all know ve are za Vampires."

"That is not so," interjected Notus, in an attempt to keep the Angel's rage from lashing out. He had never seen his boy in such a state. Notus pressed on despite the disquiet in the room. "I was their victim. I saw how they fed, for they fed on me."

The admission stunned the council into silence. Even Hugo's eyes went wide at the revelation. They all knew about Father Paul Notus' harrowing detention by the Mistress Katherine. It was still hard to believe she was another creature who had subsumed the identity of a Chosen so at to manufacture the genocide of the Chosen. The idea of a Chosen exsanguinating another to a hands breath of death was unheard of.

"Despite our many centuries of friendship," commented Jorge. "I, too, must admit that the whole concept that Vampires are different from us, and are the ones poisoning our food supply is hard to swallow. It is more likely that mortals are doing this."

The declaration erupted a heated argument between the Chosen on stage, raising voices in the debate of the truth of what the Master of Britain had told them, what the Good Father and the Angel stated, and their own choice to refuse to believe.

The Angel watched the Masters and Mistresses give voice to the anger he felt. Notus was right, the Council was falling apart and it galled him. Jeanie was dead and buried because of Vampires. He was called to stand before this Grand Council because of Vampires. Hugo incited his anger because of the Vampire who obviously now stood second to the Master of France. All that he had endured that made it impossible to be around other Chosen was because of Vampires. The cold voids that stood scattered around a room filled with frothing emotions were the reason why he was here.

If the Chosen could not see it, he would open their eyes. *To Hell with the plan*. He would wrest control whether they liked it or not, whether he was sentenced for Destruction or not. His life no longer mattered without Jeanie. If this one rash act brought unity and a chance of surviving this war against the Vampires then so be it.

Closing his eyes, the Angel took a deep breath and slowly let it out as he opened his eyes. The ancient words of Summoning that Auntie had taught him as a boy came to mind. He did not care that the theatre became cooler, damper; a sure sign that the white-faced demons were coming.

The shouting between the Chosen infected those witnessing the debacle and they too joined into the debate. None paid any attention to the slow rising mist swirling around their ankles.

Anger begat fury, feeding a cycle between the Angel and the Chosen. His Chooser was right, he was in control and it was up to him to do something.

Over the din he shouted, "Be quiet!"

His desire and anger washed over the others, immediately halting any further vociferous debate. All eyes turned to him and he knew what they saw: the Angel of Death standing in their midst. The throbbing headache was gone, leaving a sense of detached anger and he knew at this moment that if he wanted to he could eradicate all the Chosen in this room. The thought humbled him but still he did not relinquish the mists.

"You wanted proof. I'll give you proof. Proof of your blindness to the reality that Vampires stand here in our midst, spying on the Chosen to find out what we know and what we'll do about it. Proof that their sole purpose is the destruction of the Chosen." The Angel turned his burning gaze down onto each of the Masters and Mistresses.

Bridget ignored his stare, instead she clutched Fernando's arm. It was clear she was communicating with her Chosen and Fernando was rightly concerned.

Movement at the back of the theatre snapped the Angel's attention around. A null void in the shape of a red headed youth was trying his hand at the locked door. The Angel's lips twisted into a sneer as his fury at the creature unleashed.

"What are you doing?" demanded Notus, confusion filling his words.

His Chooser did not know about this new ability, but he was about to find out.

"Halt!" ordered the Angel. A thick rope of mist rose up from the floor, twirling itself around the double doorknobs and lingered. The Vampire snapped his hand back as if bitten.

Relieved that the creature would not be leaving, the Angel finished the spell and watched the fog churn and boil until it was level with his chest.

Shouts of terror from the Chosen and the sound of flesh boomed against wood as some beat against the thick oak doors in a vain attempt of escape. Somewhere within the din the Angel heard Fernando issue an order for everyone to stay still.

He met the Master of Britain's dumbfounded expression with cold fury. Today the Chosen will know him for what he was and he did not care. Bringing his attention back to the swirling mists he watched as faces and figures coalesced. Vacant black eyes in skeletal skulls cloaked in mist stared at him expectantly.

What is thy bidding, Sire? asked the one floating in front of the Angel, its mouth a putrid maw.

No longer afraid of the creatures that tormented him since childhood, the Angel now controlled them. *Take all but one of the Vampires. The one on the stage must not be allowed to leave. You are not to touch the Chosen,* he ordered in the dead language that Auntie had taught him.

As you will it, so shall it be done. Its ruined mouth opened further into a gruesome smile and swam off as the mists boiled up, filling the theatre from floor to ceiling.

Silence reigned but a moment, belying the fear and confusion that flowed through the mists towards the Angel. Then the sounds of terror erupted.

Screams and crying pierced the veil. Whether they came from the Chosen or the Vampires it was hard to say except that some were cut off in mid cry. Others gurgled into oblivion. Panic struck footsteps disappeared, leaving others to run blindly. All this the Angel listened to as he unleashed the white-faced demons to reap his revenge.

Eyes closed, he felt the savage satisfaction that the white-faced demons revelled in as their jagged teeth ripped into dead immortal flesh. Every so often one of those under his command would swim by to caress his outstretched hands and face. Each time brought a surge of energy. This was part of the pact, a part that his mind recognized. It was a symbiotic relationship that meant he could go without feeding for extended periods of time, but if he did not allow the demons to feed, then he would need to feed and they would feed from him. Tonight there was more than enough for all and he shuddered as another demon caressed his face before floating off for another victim.

Notus could not believe what he was experiencing. He tried to cross himself, but that did not abate his fears. Shuddering, he glanced up at his son's face. He did not know how this could be happening, but the look on the boy's face ignited a seed of fear that he had refused to believe was always there.

"Stop this, please. For God's sake, Gwyn, please stop," begged Notus, pulling at his son's arm.

It was not the fear and desperation from his Chooser that opened his eyes; it was the use of that name. The Angel of Death glanced down at the cowering monk. How could he tell the man he has known for centuries the sense of exhilaration and power he felt as the demons captured their prey? He sadly shook his head. Notus would never know.

At last the cries of the slaughtered ceased and a white-faced demon presented itself to its master.

Terrified, Notus clung to his son, eyes wide at the creature.

"As you so ordered, so has it been done," reported the creature. Its black maw tinged with red dripping blood.

The Angel felt his Chooser shudder at the sight of the creature that once haunted his nightmares and felt his anger reduce. *"You have done well. Return until next we meet."*

The apparition completed what could only be construed as a bow and slowly the mists receded, revealing the residue of chaos.

Some chairs on the stage were knocked to the floor, leaving those Chosen to stand, pinned to their spots in terror. Other chairs held Mistresses and Masters curled into themselves in an attempt to make themselves small against the rising of the demons. None knew that they were safe from harm. Only Fernando and Bridget stared at the wreckage of frightened Chosen who tried to hide in corners or had cracked the oaken door with bloodied hands. Only the Master and Mistress of Britain had ever experienced the mists before and to have survived it a second time still filled them with fear of their friend.

The theatre reeked of terror and blood and the Angel breathed heavily of its scent, his face a cold mask barely containing his disgust at the Masters and Mistresses. Too much focus on internal politics and too little on the realities surrounding them, that was what allowed for the Vampires to twist and warp the Chosen away from what they were meant to be. It was that weakness which opened the floodgates for genocide.

Blood red eyes roamed the wreckage until he found what he was looking for.

There, laying beside the red velvet curtain draped innocuously at stage right was the body of the Vampire who had stood at Hugo's side.

Uncaring that he limped, the Angel strode over to the stairs that lead to the creature. He did not care that the Chosen watched him with fear and loathing. Their emotions flowed over and around him, but he held his in check. They would feel nothing from him.

His footsteps rang in the silence as he climbed the steps. Notus' sandaled feet scuffed behind him in an attempt to keep up. Both halted at the top as they stared down at the man who stood second to the Master of France. It was Notus' sharp intake of breath that alerted the others to follow until they all stood in a horseshoe around the creature.

There, laying face up on the varnished wood, the Vampire growled and hissed, exhibiting its dual fanged teeth for the Chosen to witness. Hilde of Germany gasped at the sight. It was not just because of the teeth, but also at the reason why Hugo's second lay trapped on the floor. The creature's limbs had been removed as if bitten or chewed off, leaving oozing stumps.

"What the hell did you do to Degare?" demanded Hugo as he pushed through the throng; only to come up short at the sight of the one he had believed could be Master after him. Brown eyes widened at the sight of the man he once trusted with the operations and management of the Chosen of France.

Ignoring the accusation, the Angel refused to look up from the writhing Vampire. He could feel the hatred for this creature tightening his jaw. His hands attempted to mimic the movement but only weakly clenched at his sides.

"This is what the Chosen are up against." The Angel's whisper carried to the back of the theatre. "This is what is killing the Chosen."

"What are you saying l'Ange?" sneered Hugo, disbelieving his own eyes.

"This is a Vampire, Hugo," replied Fernando, pushing to stand next to the Angel, followed by Bridget. The smug tones were not lost on all present. "You were duped by a Vampire, just as we were."

Hugo snorted. "Answer this ridiculous accusation, Degare,

and I will ensure you have a quick release."

The Vampire flicked his gaze from the Master of France to the Angel and back and began to laugh. "It is the Vampires who are supreme and we will make a wasteland with your corpses."

"But why? Why do this?" asked Jorge, confusion lighting his fair features.

The laugh came again, this time ending with coughing. "You call yourselves Chosen, but you do not know for what or why. *Vous êtes dépassés. Vous êtes des imbéciles. Les Vampires vont dominer et toute l'humanité sera à nos pieds.* You cannot save them or yourselves."

"You are wrong." The finality of the Angel's conviction snapped the Vampire's gaze back to him. "Vampires have confused the Chosen for centuries, fooling them into forgetting their humanity, but no longer. Now they will remember what you have done to them and they will regain what they lost."

Turning to Notus, the Angel sent, *Now. Do it now.*

The monk took a deep shuddering breath at what he was asked to do, but that, at least, had been part of their plan. It was difficult to see one of the kind that had captured and drained Notus dry lying there helpless. No matter what had happened to Notus, he still felt the need to help, to heal, to save this creature, but underneath it was the anger and humiliation for what he had endured.

Taking the silver flask from between his robes, he uncorked it.

"You do not believe that it was Vampires, not Chosen, that is behind the genocide," said the Angel, his voice so low that the others had to strain to hear. "If his words do not convince, and the teeth not convince, then let this imprint on your mind, for Chosen do not burn under the Cross nor when blessed with Holy Water."

Comprehension widened the Vampires eyes until they were ringed with white. "No! No! Please, no!" He writhed on the ground in an attempt to move away from the monk.

Notus hesitated and glanced up as his son. He could not believe what he was asked to do, but the need to do so filled him with conflicting horror and relief.

With his free hand Father Paul Notus invoked the Cross, *"In nomine Patris, et Filii, et Spiritus Sancti,"* while he upturned the contents of the flask over the head and torso of the creature before him.

The Vampire began his screams of pain at the first stroke of the Cross and well before the first droplets of Holy Water fell upon his body. As the liquid impacted, the creatures' panicked screams escalated with the tendrils of smoke ascending from his body. It was quick and it was gruesome as the Holy Water ate through the Vampire like hydrochloric acid on paper. Flesh bubbled and ignited, burning and liquefying, searing the skin from his body only to eat deeper into the muscle and bones. The gurgling cry was cut off as the Holy Water made quick work of the skull, adding its own bloody mess to stain the wooden floor. It was a surprise to the Chosen, forcing them to take a step back, when the remains ignited to leave only black powder on the stage.

Silence thundered down. Notus was horrified at the reaction his precious God blessed water had created, but there was no dispute now. Vampires were as real as the Chosen, and as different as day was to night.

Slowly all eyes descended upon the Angel, who could not tear his gaze away from the remains.

"Crediamo. Caro dio nel cielo, crediamo," gasped Alfonsina. She halted in the middle of crossing herself, eyes wide. She found Notus' sad hazel and dropped to her knees. *"Per favore, padre."*

"Sì, la mia figlia," replied Notus, tears filling his eyes. Carefully, so as not to step on the blackened smudge, the monk came to stand before the Mistress of Italy. Laying one hand upon her head, he made the sign of the Cross once more with the other, *"In nomine Patris, et Filii, et Spiritus Sancti."*

The Angel turned away from the display and the tears that ran down the Mistress' face. There could no longer be any doubt about the existence of Vampires. Now it was up to the Grand Council to decide what to do.

Carefully the Angel made is way down the steps, intending to leave the Council to their heavy responsibility. He halted as Hugo called out.

"L'Ange, you have proven your point and you have proven mine."

Turning, the Angel faced the Master of France.

"What are you talking about, Hugo?" asked Bridget, worry widening her blue eyes.

"L'Ange is clearly not Chosen," sneered France's Master. The others murmured their surprise at the accusation, but the evidence could not be denied. Too many irregularities through the centuries

set the Angel apart no matter where he and Notus travelled to, leaving the question opened.

"If *l'Ange* is Chosen," continued Hugo, "then it is clear he must be Destroyed."

The murmurs became shouts of protest mingled with agreement. Not all were friends of the Angel no matter their feelings for his Chooser.

The Angel looked up at the Chosen, his face blank of all emotion. It was a gamble he took when he summoned the white-faced demons and he could feel Fernando and Bridget's panic about what they may be forced to declare.

"Before any sentence is carried against the Angel," shouted Fernando over the din, "Let his Master and Mistress ask him this: What are you?"

If he had not been expecting this from his friend, the Angel would have declared himself a fool. He had spent too much time with the Noble and been asked that same question over and over through the ages. Never before stating that he was Chosen was enough to dissuade the speculations. Now he knew he could not stand here before the Grand Council and claim to be one of theirs. Again, he was outcast, different, set apart.

Straightening his stance, he pulled on the glamour that had always fit him and felt so right. Fear percolated through the Chosen and he knew now how to answer. Allowing his burning gaze to slide from one to the next, he settled onto Notus for it was he who deserved the truth more than the others.

"I am the Angel of Death."

ÍÍÍ

ather Paul Notus carefully turned over the vinyl long playing album, gently blew the minute particles of dust from the other side and placed it back down onto the turntable. It was his favourite Christmas album, a collection of crooners from the early part of the last century whose voices plucked warmth into his body with each note. It was a Christmas present from the boy when the album was first released decades ago. Notus played it every year and though the vinyl was beginning to wear, creating static to mix with the songs, still he played it.

Checking the needle for fuzz, he placed it down onto the large black disk. Expectations of *Frosty the Snowman* sung by Sinatra made him smile. First the silence, then the scratching that picked up in volume until finally the smooth voice of the long dead singer mingled with the static, marking that all continued to be well with his antique turn table.

"Ugh. If you won't get an iPod or at least a CD player, I swear I will," complained Fernando, Master of Britain.

"Oh, quit your complaining," countered the Mistress of Britain. "I think it's nice."

"If you're a mouse."

A smile tugged at the corners of Notus' face and he turned around to face his houseguests. It was the same thing year after year, but only when Bridget and her Chosen deigned to join them at his place.

Fernando lounged in the large green leather chair, its ottoman tilted to one side under the crossed Italian shoed feet of the Noble. For the umpteenth time he pushed away one of the pine branches from sticking out close to his head. Again the tree snapped back the decorated limb, making the whole tree wiggle and the lights flicker.

"If the tree is bothering you, then move." Bridget sat at the end of the matching green couch closest to Fernando, her slim pale legs curled under her despite the blue sequinned dress that hugged her body. Her long blonde hair curled loosely around her shoulders.

"No," harrumphed the Noble. A dying tree gaudily made to twinkle at him would not force the Master of Britain from his spot. He grabbed the offending branch and twisted it away from him. The snap as the wood gave way under the Chosen's strength surprised the Noble as he came away with the decorated limb.

Bridget sharply exhaled through her nose and shook her head. Fernando was, typically, being Fernando.

The smile on the monk's face fell for a moment before turning into a grin at the shocked expression on the young man. Walking over, Notus took the branch from Fernando and gave it a look over before giving it back to the Noble.

"You broke it, you fix it," grinned Notus.

"And how, pray tell, do you expect me to do that?" Fernando's brown eyes glared up at hazel.

"Oh Fernando, it's easy." Bridget uncurled herself and took the branch in her small delicate hand and started to pick the decorations off of it. Gliding around the tree, she found areas on it where greenness outweighed gaudy. With artistic precision she added to the tree's bulk until the broken branch laid bare in her hand.

"Ah, my dear, you are ever able to bring beauty to every occasion," remarked Notus as he took the naked branch.

Bridget smiled and sat down, resuming her curled position.

Since his and the boy's return to London about a decade ago, Notus enjoyed having Fernando and Bridget over for the holidays. It was nice to finally settle back into a life of peace after over a century of moving from one country to the next as the Angel was called to hunt down and exterminate the Vampires.

It had been hard on the boy. Notus could see and sense it. At first, when the Grand Council declared that the Angel of Death was to be their instrument to clear away the threat of genocide by the Vampires, the boy had accepted it with relish. It was the perfect opportunity to exact his revenge against those that had done so much harm to the ones he loved. It was also a way to make sure that no matter where he travelled, no Master or Mistress would seek his Destruction. Even Hugo, Master of France, had relinquished his demands for the Angel's execution for being different.

It was after the third encounter with a group of Vampires in Italy that the Angel began to lose heart. It was not so much that he no longer wanted to exterminate the Vampires, but they were now placing their mortal servants into the mix and the Angel was reluctant to kill these innocent humans. His sentimentality nearly killed him in Germany, when the humans outnumbered their Vampire masters, but kill them the Angel did. It was then that his slaughters, using those demons, became more prominent. The regret in the Angel's soul blossomed.

Notus knew what made the Angel hesitate, what ate at him even as he killed Vampire and mortal alike. It was the understanding that when the Angel looked at these people, he knew that his lost love could have ended like any one of them. The boy would look into the crowd and see people that had mothers, fathers, sisters, brothers, children, turned into mindless slaves by creatures bent upon their dominance and the Chosen's destruction. His heart broke every time he killed them as they were forced to try and kill him.

Nearly a century of scouring Europe clean of the Vampires had darkened the Angel's soul and both were glad when they returned to England where friends awaited them. The condition for returning to London was that the Angel would not go to the courthouse again to stand before the British Chosen. If they wanted to talk with him, they would have to move to a new location. The agreement Notus had to make was to ensure they would not move back to the district where they had once lived and Jeanie had been their maid and the Angel's beloved.

It was said that time heals all wounds. It was true, but only if one did not constantly pick at them.

Notus placed the naked pine branch under the tree next to the presents expertly decorated in a myriad of tasteless colour combinations. He would have to figure out what to do with the limb since his two bedroom flat did not come with a fireplace. Modern technologies and conveniences lent towards the diminishment of simple heart warming experiences, and it seemed that fireplaces were one of the first things to go in tenements such as this.

Frosty the Snowman had given way to Bing Crosby's *White Christmas* and Notus sat down in the matching green lounge chair at the other end of the couch. The night was perfect except that the boy was, as usual, late.

"So when do you expect him?" asked Fernando, checking his gold Gucci wristwatch. Snapping his arm down so as to allow the black and silver pinstripe Armani shirt to flow over his wrist, the Noble settled himself with a disgruntled smirk.

Notus glanced at the clock beside the front door and grimaced. The boy had called before morning to say he was staying the day. Despite the monk's protestations the Angel said he would return shortly after sundown to see Notus off for Midnight Mass. It took another call from the boy to say that he would be back after Mass, but that was now over an hour ago.

"He'll be here," offered Notus, silently wondering if the boy was trying to evade being around his friends. It was common. Fernando and Bridget understood it to a point. The Angel still found it uncomfortable to be around other Chosen even though he had mastered his empathic abilities. It was his otherness that kept him apart. Even after all these decades it was still hard for the boy to accept that others did not see him that way – much.

"Have you decided whether you and the Angel are going to join us for New Years this year?" asked Bridget. She shifted on the green leather, making it squeak, so that she could see her host.

"I hope we do, my dear, but I want to let the boy decide. It's never gone well when I've thrust him into the spotlight."

"Tell him that it's an order from the Master of Britain," grumbled Fernando. The Noble knew how well that would go over with his tall pale friend, but the Angel would do it nonetheless.

"Fernando!" exclaimed Bridget, pushing back loose locks behind a diamond-studded ear.

"What?" replied the Noble, innocently. "It's going to be the first and only New Year's party he'll be attending before he and the Good Father head off to the colonies, which, by the way is the stupidest move I've ever heard any Chosen making in their lives! What the hell were you thinking when you decided to go there?"

Notus huffed. He had been expecting it from his friends, but did not think it would come up tonight of all nights. Then again, the piles of boxes with permanent marker scrawled over them would make anyone question this move.

"Fernando," warned Bridget. Regardless of the fact that they were

Master and Mistress they also knew that the Good Father was the oldest Chosen they knew of. It was never a good idea to berate one's Elders.

"No, seriously," replied Fernando, his ire up. It was a topic he wanted to bring up for some time, but never had the opportunity since the Angel would not talk about it. Instead, he closed up and shut down as was usual for him. "He's done his work for the Chosen. He's forced the Vampires from Europe, killing as many as possible. There's an uneasy peace now between us. They have the Americas and we have the rest of the world. Don't either of you know what you two can cause by going there?"

"Fernando." Bridget's warning tones grew louder.

"No, Bridget," snapped the Noble. "If they go, they will make themselves targets of the Vampires and we will not be able to help. You weren't there last time."

Silence reigned down upon the Christmas revellers. There was no escaping what Fernando was referring to.

"I was there when you brought the Angel home," whispered Bridget.

"But you weren't there to take him down from the manacles that shredded through his wrists. You weren't there to see his back flayed open with scorch marks and..." Fernando shuddered involuntarily. "You didn't see. What you saw was two weeks of recovery. Do you think that the Vampires will do any less than that to him after all he has done to them in the last century?"

This time Bridget had the wherewithal to stay quiet. Silently she knew Fernando was right. She just did not like the way her Chosen was handling the situation.

Notus understood where Fernando's concerns came from and he frowned. The images that were invoked through the Noble's description of the boy's torture were as difficult to face as seeing the boy's scars.

"I know that you both are concerned," began the Good Father, slowly. "I greatly appreciate it. Never before has the Angel and I had such friends–family if you will. We know what potential dangers we may face, but my work with the British Museum has tied my hands and offered me an opportunity of a lifetime and for me to say such a thing is, well..."

"You're Chosen, you don't have to follow human conventions," rebutted Fernando.

"True," nodded the monk. "But I have the opportunity to see

how my own works through the centuries have fared and to properly restore them."

"You don't have to go to North America for that," commented Bridget.

Notus turned to face his Mistress. "I do. The whole collection is going on tour. They want me to go with it to make sure everything is treated properly and to fix anything that may be damaged during the travels."

"Can't someone else do this?" beseeched Fernando.

Notus pursed his lips and shook his head. "Dr. Mark Preston was supposed to go on tour with the collection, but his skiing accident last week in Switzerland has left him wheelchair bound for at least two months and he'll be in therapy for at least two more. I only agreed to cover the tour until he was able to resume his duties. I didn't realize that the tour was through the United States and Canada. I said yes before I knew. Now I'm stuck and the Museum is stuck." Again Notus shook his head. "We'll come straight home as soon as Dr. Preston can take over. I promise."

"And who knows what will happen in the mean time," grumbled Fernando, knowing he had lost the argument.

ÍƱ

The darkness of the tunnel into Victoria Station gave way to the dull illumination of the platforms in the distance. Drips of water untainted by the blustery cold above ground echoed through the abandoned tunnels mingling with the occasional squeak from a rodent in search of Christmas dinner. It was not long before the Angel squinted up at the gloaming lights of the sleeping station. No trains ran during the storm. It would not only be from the inability of the trains to plough through the snow at the open air stations, but the fact that the conductors of the trains would be hard pressed to get to work.

It was odd to see the place vacant. Usually this hub was chaotic in its flurry of activity. People moving from here to there, unaware of those that brushed past them, all eager to remain solitary as they sought connection with those they journeyed to, while others, usually teens, chatted loudly, sang along with music only for their ears, or called to each other as they jumped from tube to tube. Above it all would be the static calls from the overhead speakers indicating which trains would be coming in and where they would be going.

Tonight the only sounds were the squeaks of the mice and rats that inhabited the tunnels, runnels of water and the soft footfalls of feet moving preternaturally fast.

The damp tunnels were a relief from the snowstorm that raged outside, allowing for the Angel to make up the time lost as he struggled against winter's onslaught. Occasionally he would sight a homeless individual huddled in the darkness. Tonight they were lucky as there were no bobbies to come and remove them.

The officers of the peace would be keeping to their precincts unless absolutely necessary.

Hefting the strap that held the sword length box higher up on his shoulder, the Angel was careful not to step on the third rail as he bounded up onto the deserted platform. Even though no trains rode the tracks the electric hum of the third rail spoke of a sleeping monster that would attack any trespasser.

With a quick cursory glance around, which was more habit than required, he followed the signs to the escalators that would take him to the large open station that served to tie the Tube's intricate network with that of the National Rail. The escalator remained stationary. There would be no relaxing while the mechanical stairs lifted him to ground level, but that was no problem for the Angel who quickly bounded up the metal stairs three at a time.

Emerging from the entrance of the Tube, voices filtered to his sensitive ears before he saw them. He knew he should not have been surprised, but when he rounded the corner to see so many homeless in the make-do shelter his eyes widened. The large open area that normally would be bustling with people desperately trying to achieve their destinations was replaced with makeshift sleeping arrangements for the dozens of homeless that trickled in from the storm.

The scents of bitter hot coffee and sweet hot chocolate mingled with the cold damp sour smell of unwashed bodies. A few volunteers handed out hot beverages and blankets; while others helped those with steaming mugs to find a place to get comfortable.

This was not a place for the Angel. It would be impossible to keep out of notice.

Sticking to areas least populated he sought his way out of Victoria Station. It was more difficult than expected as more homeless came in through rotating doors that were filled with slush and ice.

Keeping to the far reaches of the wide-open space, the Angel measured his pace to that of a mortal lest someone see him. It still surprised him that in an age of such magic and ingenuity there were still so many who had nothing. Some things did not change.

He turned a corner finding an exit. The wind howled against the glass door, rattling it as if to say he were not allowed out on a night when the storm ruled. Giving the door a firmer push than normally required he stepped into the storm, the wind whipping his dishevelled hair in punishment. Snow blasted, his face and eyes stinging, he stood outside in the midst of the storm at full force.

The Angel hunkered under the onslaught as he tried to regain his bearings. Their flat was not far from the station. Normally it would take but a moment to get there, but the foot of snow on the ground and the wind whipped ice crystals would prove difficult. The snow that had melted on him during his underground jaunt began to freeze and he could feel the runnels of water down the back of his neck grow colder. He tried to repress a shudder and failed. It would not take long before strands of white hair froze into icicles.

He lifted a hand over his eyes to shade them from the heavy snowfall and picked out familiar sights. Bearings received, he turned and trudged through the snow towards home, damning himself for not having worn boots.

The moaning sound of the wind screamed on occasion as faster flows chased after slower plodding downpours. The sad little trees, interspersed upon his route home, creaked and bent under the onslaught. The only cars on the road were buried in parking spots, their drivers wise enough not to drive on a night like tonight. Occasionally the Angel would see a brave cabby endeavour to force his car in the hopes of finding a stranded fare. One such individual slowed its approach upon seeing him walking and then realizing no fare was forthcoming began to spin its back wheels as it caught on some black ice under the snow. It slipped sideways and slammed into a parked car with a sickening crunch.

Shaking his head, the Angel continued on. A dogsled would be more apropos on a night like this than any modern convenience, except, of course, a snowmobile, but they were not a popular buy here in Britain.

The sound of voices in anger followed by glass bottles clinking and crashing into fragments caught the Angel's attention and he glanced down the darkened alley to his left. Halting, he saw a scrubby old homeless man failing in his attempt to fight against two ruffians similarly dressed. It was not clear to the Angel what they were fighting for, but whoever it was landed blow upon blow upon the grizzled man as he succumbed to the strength of the other two men.

Tonight was supposed to be a night of brotherly love, not violence. Saddened by the sight, he shook his head and entered the alley.

The two ruffians did not hear his approach. Their first and only comprehension of the danger they were in was when the Angel grabbed the one in a long brown trench coat by the collar and with one easy movement threw him into the brick wall. A thud and a crack as body and head impacted mingled with the whistle of the wind. The Angel did not turn to see what had become of the man who slid down the wall to settle into a heap, but rather focused his attention on the other assailant who had pulled a knife.

Silver flashed as the man slashed at him.

It was easy to dodge the attack. With one hand he used his assailants momentum to trip and spin the man head first into the wall next to his cohort. He winced at the wet cracking sound so similar to his partners before the second assailant landed face down in the snow covered filth.

No wisps of breath emanated from the two, and the Angel knew they were dead. Sighing at the useless waste of life he turned his attention to the old man attempting a futile escape from the scene.

Grey against white, the beggar stumbled down the small alley. His skin was tinged blue against the cold. Blood shot bruising eyes attempted to keep open against the inevitable permanent slumber his injuries and the cold teased him with. The creature stumbled on until he tripped over something in the snow and crashed sideways into the wall. Sliding down, the only indication that the man was still alive was the little clouds arising from his bearded mouth. In his hand he held a bottle in blue and blackened fingers.

The Angel watched this from where the other men had died. He had seen this scenario played out hundreds, if not thousands, of times in his long life, and he knew his role in it.

Taking the steps required towards the man, he found it a relief to feel the wind diminish and the constant pounding of snow lessen.

With the Angel's appearance, the dilapidated man's brown eyes widened. "'Ere wot?" He tried to regain his feet but could not. Instead he lay there huffing.

The Angel came to stand before the battered creature covered in grime and snow. If he allowed himself he would feel sorrow for this man and his wasted life. Instead he stood there with a decision to make and a choice to present. Placing the sword case down onto the snow covered alley, he knelt, his knee sinking deep into the fluff to pull unexpectedly on the ragged scar along his thigh.

He was tired, but he was not all that hungry. It had been a very long time since he last fed from a mortal in the manner of a Chosen, but he could smell death creeping up the homeless man's limbs and that was what drew him. Months could pass before the stirrings of hunger made itself present. The times between feedings could be even longer depending upon his interaction with the white-faced demons. During his century of Vampire slaughters using the demons he had not needed to feed once. He only did so to keep up the pretence with Notus and the other Chosen they encountered.

Now, without the need of the white-faced demons, the hunger slowly blossomed and he sighed.

"Wha–what are you?" stammered the man. He tried to bring the bottle in his left hand to his mouth but failed, the cold seeping his strength.

Recognizing the man's need, the Angel helped him drink from the neck. The pungent smell of whiskey permeated the snow swept air.

"Ye've come to take me, eh?" coughed the man. "I thought so."

"Who do you think I am?" asked the Angel. He knew he did not need to. No matter how much time had passed between inhabitations of a particular place, the locals, especially on their dying beds, would know him. It still disturbed him.

"The Angel of Death," stated the man, matter-of-factly.

"And you wish to die?" he asked in all curiosity.

"No." The man sighed. "But it's now a toss up between cancer, the beating those two sons of a whore gave me or the cold. Which would you take?"

The Angel inhaled sharply through his nose and then slowly let it go. No puff of warm air condensed about his face. The man had made his choice. Taking the man's hand in his own, he could feel the calluses of someone who had worked hard all his life. It was always a shame when people were felled low by circumstances beyond their control. Resting his eyes once more on the man's bloodshot brown eyes, he spoke with the rhythm of the man's heart.

The man sighed and closed his eyes. He would feel nothing except peace.

Lifting the hand to his mouth, the Angel gently bit into the vessel deep within the wrist. Cool sluggish blood flowed.

*I*t was not the blast of wind that halted the Angel in his tracks and nor was it the pelting of snow and ice, it was the sudden awareness of another Chosen nearby. Normally this sensation would not hinder him from climbing the steps to the flat he shared with Notus, but he had forgotten that there would be two other Chosen awaiting him.

He grimaced at the realization that the Master and the Mistress of the Chosen of Britain were sitting in his home waiting for him to join in the Christmas celebrations.

It had been Notus' idea to invite them over since he and the monk were leaving in a couple of months. The Angel had acquiesced after Notus had threatened to accept Bridget's annual invitation for Christmas at the House. He had done that once. Only once. It had been enough to send him fleeing back to the quiet confines of his flat. Who knew that so many Chosen could be so rowdy when given the opportunity to party? But it had not been that. It had been the bombardment of so many Chosen's feelings that sent him back into the night with a throbbing headache. Of course Bridget understood, Notus placated and Fernando, well, Fernando complained. Since then quiet Christmas get-togethers were fine, but this time he had forgotten.

Taking a deep breath of cold air, the Angel closed his eyes before allowing his breath to slowly steam from him. It had taken several decades before he was able to master this newfound empathy with the Chosen. Gradually the sensations flowing from the flat decreased until there was nothing. He hated to do this with Notus because it also meant that they could not communicate as Chosen and Chooser aught, but he knew how Fernando disliked the emotional connection between him and others. Bridget would not go into details, but left it to say that the Noble preferred, for his own valid reasons, to keep disconnected, and though she hated it, she let her Chosen have as much privacy as their connection allowed.

Calm, grounded and centred, the Angel opened his eyes and climbed the half dozen stone steps. Fishing the keys from his pocket by way of the chain attached to his belt loop, the Angel opened the outer door of the walk-up. Yellow and brown tiled floor stained with grey melt water proved that other tenants had made their way to their flats. Water dripped down the stairs in the middle of the lobby.

With a sigh he turned and placed his key into the lock. The action was automatic and unnecessary; Notus had left the door open for him. On well oiled hinges the fibreboard white door opened and he stepped from a cold winter wonderland to the warmth of Christmas lights and music. He could not have stifled the small smile even if he tried. Closing the door and throwing the latch, he met Bridget's sparkling blue eyes as she peered over the couch.

"Well, it's about time you showed up," complained the Master of Britain as he came to his feet, a smile belying his own irritation.

The Angel placed the wooden box down to lean against the wall as he began to remove his long black coat.

Rising from the green chair, Notus' expression did not match with his guests. "Don't move!"

Surprised at his Choosers reaction, the Angel complied and watched as Notus moved preternaturally fast into the bathroom and brought out a large white towel. It took but a moment for the monk to stand by his side offering the large swatch of terrycloth to him.

"You're soaked," stated Notus. "I don't want you dripping all over the floor."

Surprised at what his Chooser seemed to be insinuating, his eyes widened at the sound of Bridget failing to hide her laughter.

"Oh good grief," sighed the Monk. "Just dry off and come join us. We've been waiting hours for you. What took you so long, boy?"

The Angel hid his smile as he took off his coat and hung it up on the hook beside the door. Notus' irritation at his lateness coupled with him calling him "boy" made it even more heart warming. Turning around, he kicked off his shoes and grimaced; his socks were soaked. They too came off, leaving his feet cold against the laminate floor and he accepted the towel.

Realizing how soaked his Chosen was, Notus' eyes widened. "What did you do? Fall into a pond?"

Fernando snickered as he sat on the back of the couch watching the spectacle. A sound of flesh hitting flesh resounded in the room coupled with his bark of surprise made it all too clear that it was Bridget who smacked him. "What did you do that for?"

"Because you're enjoying his too much." Bridget slid off the couch and came around to kiss Fernando's cheek.

Removing the black braces from his wrists, the Angel placed them down on the tea table that sat beneath the draped window and began to dry his long white locks. The edges of his shirt and his trousers would have to dry in their own time.

The silence in the room was broken only with the static analog of an ancient Christmas carol. Pulling the towel down around his neck, the Angel ran his hand through his tousled locks, away from his face. The motion was not as effective as he would have liked, the tangles twisted his hair into non-compliance but he could still see that the three Chosen awaited his explanation.

"I would have been here earlier," his soft melodious voice filled the flat, "but I had difficulty getting through the snowstorm."

"Snowstorm? What snowstorm?" countered the Noble as he made his way over to the window. "There was no snowstorm when Bridget and I..." His protestation slid away as he took in the sight of the now uncovered window. White and green brocade creaked in his bronze grip. "Where's my car?"

"Dear heaven on earth," gasped Notus, his hand slapping his forehead as he stared at the blustery weather just inches from his face.

Bridget pressed her slim body against Fernando's back, her head peeking around his shoulder. The expression of her face matched that of the monks.

Notus placed his hand against the snow dotted windowpane and drew it back, leaving a faint condensation impression behind.

"When did this start?" Notus turned to his son who only shrugged.

"What I want to know is *where is my Ferrari?*"

The Angel stepped over to stand behind his friends. His height made it easy for him to have a clear view of the storm.

Scanning the street below he pointed at a large blob of snow sitting near the wind battered stop sign. "Is that it?"

Fernando groaned, his shoulders slumping. "Tell me I didn't leave the roof down?"

"You left the roof down," stated Bridget matter-of-factly. "I told you to put it up, but no, you said it was a nice night despite the fact people were staring at us driving like we were crazy."

Another groan escaped the Noble's lips and he turned away from the scene. He did not want to calculate the damage that the snow had already done.

"How are we going to get home, Fernando?" Bridget crossed her arms and glared up at her Chosen's stricken face. "I'm not walking home in that. I wore straps."

Quick to divert the oncoming fight Notus offered the only solution he could think of. "You two are most welcome to spend the day here. I'm sure by nightfall tomorrow the storm will have passed and the streets will have cleared."

Surprised at the offer, the Angel regretted not being open to the emotions of the Chosen. "Notus—" he began but was quickly cut off.

"The two of you can take the boy's bed."

Knowing where the next sentence would lead, he headed the monk off at the pass by walking over and collapsing onto the sofa. "I'll take the couch."

"Are you sure? We don't want to put you out." Bridget walked over to sit back onto her spot forcing the Angel to take up residence at the other end.

"She might not want to, but a bed is preferable to sharing a couch." Fernando closed the drapes, cutting off the horrendous view and returned to his chair next to the tree.

"Then it's settled," declared Notus as he went to change the album on the turntable.

"I'd better let Juliette know that we won't be coming back to the house by dawn."

"You'd think she'd figure that one out on her on," muttered the Noble.

Silence reigned as Notus picked out the next record to play and Bridget closed her eyes in concentration. Her communication with her Chosen was completed as Notus lowered the needle onto an old 78 of Fats Domino.

"So, has the house been destroyed yet?"

Bridget glared at Fernando. "The house is safer when you're not there."

"Now, now, it's Christmas," entered Notus. He sat down in the chair at the other end. "Truce everybody, truce."

Swivelling in his spot, the monk turned to face his wayward son. "Now where were you? You said you'd be home by dawn this morning, but you didn't show. Do you know how much I worried?"

The onslaught from his Chooser caught the Angel off guard. He opened his mouth to reply but no words were forthcoming. Even now, when he was over fifteen hundred years old, Notus still could make him feel as if the monk had just found him in that cave so long ago. Chagrined, he let his eyes fall to the floor. He had tried to reach Notus, but by the time he had done so the monk was asleep so he opted to leave a message on their answering machine. In soft tones he said as much.

"We have an answering machine for the telephone?" responded the monk, incredulously.

A groan answered from the other chair. Fernando slumped further down; finding it even harder to believe how technologically backwards his host seemed to be.

"So where did you spend the day?" asked Bridget, intrigued. She curled her legs up under her and propped her head on her hand as her elbow rested on the back of the sofa. Her smiling eyes landed on the Angel.

With all eyes uncomfortably upon him he explained, to Fernando's dismay, that he had spent the day at Gerry and Donna's because he inadvertently stayed later to finish a project and barely made it into their home as the sun was cresting over the horizon.

"You stayed the day at a mortal's house?" asked Fernando. "Do they know what you are?"

The questions should not have surprised the Angel, but it did. "No, they do not know I am Chosen, just that I prefer the night. They have a north facing guestroom and offered it to me. With the drapes pulled it was fine." A sudden yawn made his eyes water as he covered his mouth with his hands.

"It seems that you didn't get much sleep," smiled Bridget.

"I didn't," admitted the Angel as another yawn overtook him. "I was just about to fall asleep when Rory and Jenna jumped on me."

"Who are Rory and Jenna?" asked Fernando, his face darkening with concern.

"Gerry and Donna's children," answered Notus, a smile lifting the corners of his lips.

Fernando's shocked expression caused Bridge to hide a laugh behind her small delicate fingers.

"They insisted I play with them and help set up for Christmas." The Angel basked in the memory of the two pulling out games and puzzles, stuffed animals and action figures, fighting and laughing as he did something he had never done before – he played like a child and enjoyed every moment of it. They were the reason why he was happy to have stayed awake the whole day and into the next night, sharing a space at the Christmas Eve dinner but hiding the fact he did not eat and then helping to get the kids off to bed with his traditional story from his life, fictionalized, of course. It was the closest to a normal human life he had ever come to and he loved it and them. A smile caught the Angel's lips.

He did not realize that the others were waiting for him to continue until the music seemed louder to his ears. A sudden flush of heat radiated upwards and he ducked his head, letting the curtain of white obscure the blush.

Noticing his son's embarrassment Notus cleared his throat. "Did you leave their presents under the tree?"

Relieved at his Choosers rescue, the Angel nodded. "Mortgage papers stating that it is paid in full, their car loans and debts are paid off, and the legal papers for the trust funds for Rory and Jenna are all there. They will never have to worry again."

A large part of him wished he had stayed as Gerry had offered. It would have been wonderful to see the look of surprise as Gerry and Donna found the manila envelope and took in its contents. It was rare for the Angel to dispense joy, so when the opportunity presented itself he would attempt to witness it. Then again, not being there meant that Gerry and Donna had to accept the gifts.

There would be a phone call, of course. Gerry would try and refuse the gifts on a matter of pride, but what was done could not be undone. The Sanders' would never have to worry about their children's financial future ever again, nor their own.

"I'm glad to hear that," beamed Notus. "Now," he clapped his hands and rubbed them together, "that everyone has finally arrived; I believe that it's that magical time."

"What? To turn off that scratchy excuse for music?" mumbled Fernando.

They all looked over at the Noble. Being Master of all the Chosen in Britain had not smoothed his rough edges, only dulled certain ones while making others sharper.

Recognizing everyone was staring at him in either disbelief or hurt, Fernando sat up straight. "What?"

Not wishing to ruin Christmas with a fight between his guests, Notus signed and shook his head. He redirected the evening back to his question, this time answering it himself. "It is time to exchange gifts."

"Why didn't you say so in the first place," countered Fernando. A gleam of excitement grew in his dark eyes. "Presents. I can definitely sink my teeth into that!"

The monk's incredulous bark was accompanied by Bridget's laughter. The Angel did not join in, but his smile widened.

It was amazing that no matter how old they all were gift giving and, more importantly, receiving, still kept them young. Notus fondled the brown leather travel journal the Angel had given him, flipping through the decorated pages one by one, all the while the new point and shoot camera Bridget had bestowed, sat on his lap. The state of the art laptop, given by Fernando, lay by his feet.

Fernando sat on the dark laminate before the tree reading the manual of the large projector and sound system that would be installed in his home before New Years. All his attention was honed onto the fact that he now had a home theatre. It also explained why Bridget had been adamantly against him purchasing one. The Noble glanced up from the print and smiled at her. Bridget beamed back, her fingers playing with the four-carat diamond ring on her left hand.

The Angel unwound the white wires that ended in ear fobs and placed it in his ears. Manipulating the screen of the IPod he was surprised at the quantity of music listed. He knew it was Fernando's idea for the device, but it had been Bridget who had filled it with his favourites.

"Thank you," He found a suite written by *Hans Zimmer* and pressed play. Soft melodious music filled his head before he turned it off and took out the fobs. Winding the wires around the device he looked up at his friends. He would listen to the rest of the powerful suite later. "Thank you both."

"Well, we figured you'd need a distraction on your long flight." Bridget turned to face the Angel at the other end of the couch. "The Atlantic is the biggest crossing you'll have ever made."

He grimaced at the thought. He had acquiesced to Notus' desire to go into the Vampire-infested region for one reason – to protect his Chooser – but only if Notus agreed to stay the shortest time possible. This meant the scholar Notus was covering for had better heal damned fast. Notus had agreed. Now both would be traveling over deep water at high altitude and neither knew how the Angel's differences would be affected. At least if he were to fall ill he would be in first class and it would only be eight or so hours – he hoped.

Requiring a distraction from his worrisome thoughts, the Angel rose from the couch in one fluid motion. The three other Chosen halted in their admiration of their gifts, respective frowns forming on their faces. All knew the Angel well enough to recognize his agitation as he paced the length of the room.

"What's the matter, boy?" Notus gently closed the journal and placed it on his lap. His eyes never left the Angel.

Halting in surprise, the Angel frowned. He knew it was not the concept of being in a giant steel tube propelled at high velocity and altitudes across the Atlantic Ocean that bothered him. He also knew it was not the danger presented by being Chosen in Vampire territory. He had proven his reaping capabilities over the last century. For the life of him he could not pin down the root of his anxiety when the trip to North America came up in conversation.

The Angel shook his head in dismissal, refusing the attempt of a lie. Damp white locks were sent swinging against the nearly dry linen shirt. A distraction would be better. Taking the few steps to the front door he retrieved the case that held the sword. He needed to feel something solid, something tangible. Holding it lengthwise by two hands, the Angel frowned a moment. It had taken him months of painstaking effort to create the blade that slept in its case, but he never knew what to do with it until now. It was now or never.

"This is for you." The Angel stepped over destroyed gaudy paper and placed it on the floor before the Noble. The box thunked against the floor.

Surprise lifted the Noble's brows. Relinquishing the manual, Fernando eyed the long yellow wooden case decorated with four brass latches and then glanced up at the Angel. The two locked eyes for a moment before they broke away, one from embarrassment and the other shaken by the Angel's intense scarlet irises.

Fernando placed his sun kissed hands on the case and frowned down at the striations in the maple. "What is it?"

"Open it and find out." The Angel stepped lightly over the refuse and resumed his seat on the green leather sofa. A hint of a smile touched his eyes but not his lips, witnessing the concern on the Noble's face. He did not doubt that Fernando was wondering what the catch was. For a brief instant the Angel contemplated relinquishing his controlled block on his abilities just to sense at this moment what Fernando may be feeling, but squashed it. Opening that door would probably ruin the evening for everyone.

"Are you sure you want to do this?" Notus leaned forward so as to come closer to his son. He knew what was in the case and what it had cost the boy to make it.

The Angel met his Choosers gaze. "I do." The sound of four clicks in rapid succession brought his attention back to the Noble. "It's too cumbersome for me to handle. Fernando would do better with it."

Notus did not need further explanation. Ever since the boy's torture at the hands of the Vampires his ability to use the heavier European blades was near impossible. Any attempt, even after all this time, could cause the Angel to lose his grip on the blade as a spasm took hold and thus have disastrous results in a fight. Only the lighter Eastern blades could be used and that had taken nearly a quarter of a century for the Angel to master without suffering from the paralysing spasms.

Even still, the Angel worried that he would drop the blades at the most inopportune moment and so devised that the pommels of the blades be connected to his bracers by a thick steel linked chain. It was an ingenious invention by the boy; one that saved his life several times and required him to develop a new form of swordsmanship.

"Holy Mother of God!" exclaimed Fernando as he lifted the hand and a half sword from its case. He laid it by the flat of the blade across his left forearm as his right held the grip so as to ensure no fingerprints etched the mirror sheen of the steel.

The Angel's smile reached his lips as he watched Bridget

slide down from her end of the couch near the tree to kneel beside her Chosen. Both were held enraptured.

Lifting the blade to point towards the plastered ceiling, Fernando held the grip in both hands, testing the weight. The steel guard extended well past his curled fists, ending in identical tear-drops of jet.

"This is what you've been working on, haven't you?" Bridget relaxed her pose to sit before the tree, her pale legs curling around her. A smile lit up her face.

"You *made* this?" Fernando lowered the weapon and settled it back across his arm, his brown eyes never leaving its sheen.

The Angel nodded. It was not often that he was able to surprise the Noble in a positive way and his smile broadened. "I hope you like it."

"Like it?" Fernando stared incredulously at the Angel.

Bridget laughed. It was a rare occasion when her Chosen was made speechless and it was even rarer for the Angel be the cause. "Like it? He loves it!"

Fernando turned his attention to Bridget and growled at her amusement. Placing the hand and a half back into its case, he gently closed the lid, keeping one hand on the case, his thumb stroking the smooth wood. This time he forced himself to meet the Angel's disturbing eyes. At least this time there was laughter in them rather than the boiling dark emotions that resided there. "Thank you."

Hitching a shoulder, the Angel leaned back and broke eye contact, suddenly uncomfortable at the intensity of the Noble's reaction.

"I hope that you wield it with honour and purpose," said Notus. He was always intrigued at the friendship the boy had made in the Master of Britain. It confused him to no end since they always seemed to distance themselves from each other the closer they seemed to get.

"Of course." Fernando offered a mischievous smile.

Talk shifted to ordinary topics as the night wore on. Finding his eyes closing on their own accord, the Angel could no longer suppress his exhaustion. He enjoyed listening to the rolling conversation, establishing his standard role as observer rather than participant. A gentle thumping against the couch at Bridget's end caused him to open his eyes.

The Mistress smiled and tapped the couch seat again. "It's

alright. Stretch out."

He did as he was told; his feet came to rest in her lap. A sigh escaped unbidden as Bridget applied her hands to his feet, rubbing them with a strength belied by the daintiness of her digits.

"You never do that for me," whined Fernando. He sank down in his chair.

"You never ask," countered Bridget. The corner of her lip lifted a fraction.

"You never offered."

"I offer plenty." Bridget's smile widened.

Fernando returned it but added a suggestive glint in his brown eyes. "That you do."

The conversation that followed was lost on the Angel as he slipped into sleep; the padded armrest became his pillow. Contentment and the warmth of friendship became his blanket.

"He's asleep." Notus did not need to state the obvious. The sudden wave of fatigue that washed over the three Chosen was enough proof that the Angel had released his conscious control over his empathic abilities.

Fernando and Bridget yawned in unison, gazes snapping to one another. Glancing the time on his Gucci, Fernando levered himself to stand. "We should get going, Bridget."

She nodded, slipped out from under the Angel's bare feet and came to stand next to the Noble. "You're right. We may have stayed too late already."

Notus rose and watched the Angel sleep. "Though I would have to say you could never outstay your welcome here, it may be time to wish each other a good morning. If you remember, there's a storm outside."

"Oh, I forgot." Fernando's shoulders slumped.

Bridget yawned once more as she walked to the window. Dawn was at least an hour off, but the storm outside was proof that neither the sun nor the Mistress or Master of the Chosen would get through this storm unscathed. She groaned at the sight of Mother Nature's savage attack on Christmas morning as She threw more and more snow at the trapped populace.

"As I mentioned earlier, you are most welcome to stay the day." Notus took the drape from Bridget, closing it, cutting off the white frosted blur. "The Angel will be fine on the couch and you two can take his bed." The monk turned to face both his guests. "The only thing you need to know and do is to barrier your minds, if you can, while you sleep."

"Why's that?" asked Bridget, blonde brows furrowing.

"Nightmares." Concern darkened Notus' gentle features.

"Still?" Fernando scowled.

"Always."

There was no need to say anything more. They had all witnessed the Angel in the throes of a nightmare, and after over a century the fodder for them had only increased. All knew which angel he was named for. There was only one person who took it harder than the rest – the Angel himself.

Notus signed, glanced one last time at his sleeping son, and walked up the stairs to the bedrooms above. The Mistress and Master of Britain followed closely behind.

VI

arkness encompassed him.

It was not the gentle buoyant void that precipitated his visits with the Three Ladies in the Grove. This was harsh. Cold. He could not move.

He tried to curl into a ball but was held spread-eagle. Anything to hide. It was not the white faced demons he hid from. He would have been happy had they came to surround and embrace him. He was their master now and fear had turned to begrudging acceptance.

Here was a place where memories unfolded, twisted and pulled him to a past he refused to resolve.

A nodule of pain ignited in the centre of his wrists and began its pulsating fire outwards. Its tendrils snaked up to blossom in his hands, setting them ablaze as the flow of fire cascaded down his arms to mix with the inferno that was his back. Attempting to draw his arms closer to his body only excited the flames to burn brighter.

A shock of fire sliced across his back forcing a grunt from his throat. He knew where he was. He knew when he was. He was in his self made purgatory for the deaths of those innocent he could not save as he slew those who attempted genocide against the Chosen. It was his self made Hell for the death of Jeanie. He whimpered, refusing to release himself from damnation.

Light sparked in the distance. A pinpoint ahead steadily grew an explosion of brilliance with each increase of diameter. With each nova a slice of pain slashed through his back until the void brightened.

*   *   *

He was back, hanging by iron shackles facing a wall littered with strangely shaped steel instruments. All appeared deadly and well used. Bits of dried flesh and splatters of congealed blood marred the mirror sheen. He had returned to the chamber that had scarred him body and soul.

A cold metal rod stung his chin as it lifted his head up, forcing his eyes to meet with blue ones so pale that they were violet. Raven black hair spilled around a white heart shaped face, locks curling on shoulders clad in crimson.

It was the eyes that held his soul prisoner as the shackles held his body in fiery torment. A sinister smile split her bloodied lips, revealing canine teeth extended to deadly points.

"You are my prisoner, now and for always," she purred. "In death I have become more than I ever could have in life. For that I thank you with a kiss."

She leaned forward, pressing her corseted clad breasts against his sliced chest. Even through the layers of blood red cloth the chill of her undead flesh extracted the inferno of his fevered flesh, sending him trembling. Cold kisses trailed down from his jaw to settle on the great vessel in his neck. It took all his effort not to vomit. It took everything else to stay perfectly still.

He knew what would be next and even knowing it as a dream he would not stop it. Hot tears spilled from his eyes, making trails in his blood bespeckled face. A scrape of teeth against his skin precipitated the biting cold as her Vampire fangs ripped into skin and meat to create the fount of blood flow.

He cried out against the pain, against the ecstasy that her kiss elicited from him. Tears of humiliation and loss flowed faster as convulsing sobs shook him.

He did not know when she had ceased feeding, but her body stayed pressed against his. Her putrid breath tickled the quickly closing wound. It was the change in her voice that snapped him from his torment and settled a boulder in the pit of his stomach. A chill washed through him, extinguishing the blazes of his tortured form.

This was new. Reliving the torture at the hands of Violet had become par for the course, but this, this was new. He tried to turn away, ignoring the shocking pain through his wrists and arms. Pain erupted across his back and chest but the shackles held him firm. He needed to flee. He could not take what was to happen. Locked in the misery of his own making his ruby eyes widened as the woman pulled away.

No longer was her hair a black curtain. Now it flowed, twisting and curling with cinnamon, auburn and chestnut. No longer were her eyes the blue of flowers. They had become the green of grasses and leaves in summertime. A dash of freckles across cheeks and nose replaced a cold porcelain face. The only thing that remained the same was her mouth. Vampire fangs dripped his blood as she smiled triumphantly. He desperately desired to scream but terror closed his throat. He could not believe whom he saw.

Jeanie stood before him, dripping his blood from her chin. Jeanie, whose smile had torn down the walls around his heart and had taught him how to love. She was the only one in all existence whom he had fully opened himself to and had been returned in kind. She was the woman of his heart whom he had failed so miserably, for she lay six feet under in a grave Notus had refused to reveal.

Jeanie was over a century dead. Her corpse was nothing but rotting flesh and mouldy bones, but here she stood, in his nightmare, dripping his blood from a mouth he longed to kiss. Now it was twisted with rage and loathing.

"Ye broke yer Oath," sneered Jeanie. She leaned in close and brushed back his long white hair to whisper in his ear. He failed in his attempt to squash his tremors. "Tis time t' pay."

A shaft of pure molten pain shot into him just below his left ribcage and exploded through his body. The last image to fill his vision before the scream tore his throat was Geraint's sword impaled through his body, the hilt held fast in Jeanie's hand as she laughed.

"No!"

He did not know if he heard the shout or it was a product of his nightmare, but it had bolted him upright. Shudders rocked him and he allowed his waist length white hair to veil his face. He could not bear to see the cheerful Christmas decorations mocking his torment. Tears flowed unhindered and he buried his face in his hands, pausing for a fraction of a second to glance at the old silver scars ringing his wrists and the starburst pattern in the centre that was mirrored on the other side. He bit his lower lip in an attempt to keep his pain silent. He did not want to wake Notus yet again.

Another bone wracking sob tore through him. He had brought so much pain to so many and the worst always befell the ones he loved. He knew Notus worried about him but nothing could be done to relieve the guilt and sorrow he used to rebuild the wall around his heart.

A hand alighted on his shoulder, startling him. It moved down his arm as a weight settled on the sofa beside him. It was too light to be Notus and the concern that radiated towards him was too intense. Wiping the tears from his eyes with his fingers he felt the curtain of hair part and he gazed down on Bridget's beautiful face. Sky blue eyes shimmered with unshed tears.

He gasped at the realization that she and Fernando were witness to the nightmare. He could feel the Noble's worry mixed with annoyance coming from upstairs and Bridget's feelings flowing beside him. It was not right what his dreaming had done to them and he failed miserably at his attempt to place the blocks on his newest abilities.

Bridget's hand cupped his cheek, thumb wiping away the moisture with her gentle touch. He closed his eyes, releasing a new wash of tears. He could feel her need to alleviate his self induced torment and what it cost her not to be able to help.

"I'm sorry," he whispered, his voice rough.

Bridget sighed and dropped her hand onto her lap. It was only then that he noticed she wore only a sheet wrapped around her petite form. He averted his gaze.

"Oh, Gwyn." Her hand was back, finding his and twined her fingers with his until they held each other firm. Bridget's hand felt cool against his.

The touch exacerbated the empathy between them and he failed in his attempt to disentangle them, her hand clenching hard in response to his attempt to pull away. He could feel her desire to comfort and console him, for her to drive away the nightmares that had plagued him since he found himself naked and wounded in Bridget's bed over a century ago.

"Bridget, please." He pleaded, once again attempting to remove his hand from hers. This time he sent back through their connection his desire for her to back away. He did not want her to feel what he felt no matter how often she tried to help him.

With a sigh, Bridget released their grip. "Notus said you were still having nightmares. He didn't say how bad they were."

The statement surprised him. The fact that the three of them were talking about him behind his back rankled. He never wanted to be the centre of anyone's attention, except that of Jeanie's, but that would never ever happen again. He grimaced at the thought.

Picking wounds he would not let heal, the Angel stood and strode to the other side of the living room in an attempt to find solitude. Bridget's gaze lingered on him for a moment before she rose to her feet, a determined air surrounding her. He closed his eyes knowing what would be next. It was a dance they had done for decades. It was one of the reasons why he tried to stay away from his friends yet inextricably what pulled him closer.

He sighed at the touch of her hand on his crossed arms, but he did not open his eyes. He could not bear to see the look on her beautiful face.

"You can't keep running, Gwyn." Bridget gazed up at the Angel. His beautiful face was pinched with pain.

It was an old argument and his shoulders slumped. "What do you want me to do?"

"I, no, you, need to let go of Jeanie," Bridget said softly. It was something she had tried to tell him before, but he would always run away, finding excuses to flee the conversation by the time it got to this point. This time she pulled no punches and went straight for the jugular. Her friend needed it whether he realized it or not. "You need to let go of your guilt. You need to move on with your life."

He gasped at the sudden attack, his eyes popping open to look down at his Mistress in horror. He could not – no, he would not – ever let Jeanie's memory float to the past and nor would he ever forgive himself for getting her killed. His life had stopped that night; giving birth to an existence where he delved so deep into the Angel of Death that if Notus had not been with him he would have truly lost himself and his soul.

He shook his head. "It's not possible."

"Only because you don't want to let go," stated Bridget. She huffed her exasperation. Had anyone told her that the Angel could be like this she would never have allowed Fernando to let the Angel into her home that night so long ago.

He frowned at her irritation. He was not expecting that and was immediately sorry.

"Would you just stop that?" snapped Bridget. "No matter how I feel about how you're acting I still care about you. Fernando still cares about you in his own bizarre way. Hell, Notus loves you and aches that he can do nothing to ease your soul."

The admission punched him hard in the gut forcing a grunt. Bridget's battering against his carefully crafted walls forced him to turn away. He knew how they felt about them. How could he not? If not for the arduous process of learning to shield his new abilities he would know all the time. He did not need to be told. He also knew the secret emotions they held for him, not all of it nice. Awe. Jealousy. Lust. Fear. Only in regards to Notus was Bridget right. Oh sure the Master and Mistress of Britain cared about him, but those feelings were entangled with ones he had grown accustomed to through the ages with everyone he knew – except Jeanie.

Sitting back down on the couch he raked his hands through his hair, pushing the long white locks from his face. Settling his hands to drape on his knees he caught Bridget's fuming gaze with his own.

The pain flowing from the Angel was tangible, but Bridget would not let it stop her from doing what needed to be done. The Angel had eradicated the Vampire threat in Europe after over a century of slaughter. It did not take a genius to figure out that he had used that quest as a distraction from healing the wounds of his heart. Now that the fighting was over he was affecting the Chosen around him with his melancholy no matter how infrequent he interacted with others of their kind. This time she would not let him run.

"Did you know that Juliette agreed to be Chosen because she loves you?"

The admission stunned him to the quick. He knew the girl cared about him, but she would always run from the room when he went over to the House. He also knew that her love was entangled with the myth that was the Angel. Juliette did not know him and he grimaced at the thought that she had agreed to be Chosen because of her puppy love. It was one he could not ever return. *And thus the Angel causes more suffering,* he thought.

He did not realize he was shaking his head in denial until Bridget stood before him, her hand cupping his chin, halting the motion.

Bridget did something very few could do; she gazed directly

into the beautiful ruby eyes of the Angel and did not balk. She did not need to see the sadness there. His emotions rolled like thunder into her, through her touch, causing her to catch her breath. She immediately squashed it, but her heart ached to comfort him, as she always did when she saw him this way, in the only way she knew how. Leaning ever so slightly forward and down, Bridget captured the Angel's lips with her own.

He had felt her need to help him, but when her lips met his, the Angel's eyes widened in surprise before closing at the passion she sent towards him. He had always found Bridget beautiful and kind hearted, but he never considered her in this way. They were friends, but her desire flowed into him and, surprisingly, he found himself responding.

Her lips were soft, made for kissing, and he felt them part as she pressed firmer. It had been so long since he was kissed this way; to be desired and wanted for who he really was. Bridget's tongue caressed his and he felt his arms go around her petite frame, the sheet falling from her body to leave her gloriously naked between his knees. Her cool white flesh pressed against him with only his cotton shirt and trousers between them. The thought made him harden, as did her tongue to trail down the side of his neck.

He moaned as her tongue darted between succulent lips to play with his pale skin. He felt her hands roam down his chest and then the angle of the kiss changed. Bridget was now on her knees before him, fumbling with the button of his trousers. His breath caught as the pressure she applied in her attempt to undo the button brushed against him, causing his hardness to leap in anticipation.

A part of him knew he should stop this, but her desire to consume him had breached a hole in his wall he did not know he still had. It was his need to be needed, loved and cared for that betrayed him. He found her mouth as she undid the button and began to work on the zipper. His hand enclosed around her small breast, the nipple hardening instantly as his thumb brushed against it.

A flood of anger crashed down on him, slicing his head as if hit with a pickaxe. It was all he could do to remain vertical as he grabbed Bridget and set her back from him, ignoring her shocked expression. Pinching the bridge of his nose he could feel Fernando's jealousy and hurt under the anger. It was then he realized what he had almost done.

"Go," he ordered Bridget as his guilt rose to meet Fernando's feelings.

Everything had been going so well. Better, in fact, as she had always wanted to bed the Angel, even from the first time she had met him in her parlour all those decades ago. She had felt his need and desire match hers. Confused at the sudden turn around, she picked up the fallen sheet and hastily wrapped it around her. "What's wrong?"

His breath caught and he shook his head, sending white locks floating. "Fernando."

Realization dawned in Bridget's blue eyes. Fernando was now closed to her since the end of the Vampire threat. It had been the agreement they had originally made so as to make sure each was safe or to offer help if needed, but it was clear that it was not only she who was distinctly aware of the Angel's feelings.

"Fernando won't–" She began to explain that even through her relationship with the Noble, she still worked at her profession and he did not mind. It was her best way to feed herself. She did not understand why it would matter now.

"He does," stated the Angel, matter-of-factly. "And I…" His voice trailed off as he broke eye contact to stare at the floor beyond Bridget. Guilt tightened his throat. "I don't want to hurt my friends. I've hurt enough people."

He came to his feet, causing Bridget to stumble back, and walked to the other side of the room, his back to her. "Go back to Fernando, Bridget. He loves you. I never want to be the cause of any harm   between the two of you."

Bridget wanted to touch him, to let him know he could never do that to her, but she knew that the Angel was right about Fernando. She lowered the hand she had inadvertently outstretched towards the Angel and turned to go back up to the Angel's bedroom where Fernando waited.

She halted before she took the first step. "No matter what happens, Gwyn, we still love and care for you."

He pinched his eyes closed and hugged himself as he heard her ascend the stairs. A door opened and then closed, releasing a wash of relief that he matched with his own.

Alone, he walked over to the window and opened the drape. True dawn had occurred hours ago, but pregnant clouds kept the world in darkness, leaving a thick blanket of beauty in its wake.

SHADOW OF DEATH

Staring at the intricate patterns of frost on the window he took a deep shuddering breath as he contemplated what would happen when the clouds separated.

VII

Toronto, Canada – April 3rd

Well that went better than I expected." Notus hoisted the brown leather valise to hang by its strap over his shoulder as he settled the matching suitcase onto the floor next to him. Pressing the button, he extended the hidden handle that allowed for the case to easily be guided along the ground. The weight of the luggage would be of no hindrance to the ancient immortal but even Chosen had only two hands.

The Angel watched the metallic conveyor belt slowly move luggage around the baggage collection as more decorative and drab suitcases slid down the chute to land unceremoniously next to the ones waiting for someone to claim them. He already had his suitcase but he was still waiting for the most precious item he possessed – Geraint's sword. Nervous butterflies flitted in his stomach at the thought that the airline had lost it.

No matter Notus' excitement of their first transatlantic flight, it was one the Angel was not looking forward to repeating, even if it would take him home. In some ways he would rather spend a couple months on a ship. There at least the sensations would remain the same. But no, that was not the case with flying. Over land he was fine and thrilled at the sights of city lights beneath him lighting up the earth more spectacularly than all the stars in the sky. Witnessing clouds floating nonchalantly beside and below excited him. It had been so incredibly long since he had such a new experience move him. It was when the plane abruptly left land to fly over water that everything plummeted downwards to misery.

It was not long after takeoff from Heathrow that the bottom fell out of his stomach, sending his head spinning. When he thought he was going to pass out the sensations abruptly ceased. At first he and Notus thought he was growing accustomed to flight when, without warning, he passed out. It was only when they flew over Greenland that he woke, feeling fine, realizing that his sudden reaction was due to the fact that they had left Ireland for the deep waters of the Atlantic.

Watching the digital image of the plane inch forward on the GPS monitor hanging from the ceiling of the plane, his fingers made dents into his armrest. A groan escaped him as he passed out again. The last image was of the plane once again heading for open water.

That had not been the worst. It was when they reached Canada that the torment truly began. Who would have thought that land could hold so many bodies of water? It had given the Angel a deep appreciation of what it would be like to ride a roller coaster for hours at a time. Never was there a body of water they flew over that was big enough or deep enough to cause him to pass out, but there was enough to keep his stomach roiling and his head spinning.

It was only when they landed at *Toronto Pearson International Airport* did he finally breathe a sigh of relief. Their steward was happy to see his flight sick attendee pull himself off the plane. Notus' face, pinched with worry, had eased into a grateful smile. Never before had the Angel wanted to kiss the ground when they exited the plane for the boarding ramp.

His eyes widened as the long black case slid down to join the increasingly empty baggage conveyor. He stepped around a couple of backpackers as they hoisted their burdens, and ignoring their gasps at his sudden appearance he grabbed the strap of his case. It swung high, narrowly missing the girl before he settled it on his shoulder.

Her mouth dropped in indignation, ready to rip a strip off of him, but then she noticed his height and his looks and closed her jaw with a click. Barking an order at her male travelling partner they turned to leave.

The Angel sighed before a small smile lifted his lips. He knew he was an intimidating sight dressed in black jeans and his favourite motorcycle boots. The white dress shirt open at the top to show the white t-shirt underneath was innocuous enough, but add that to the black leather vest and leather vambraces that covered his hands in an imitation to the braces he usually wore, he knew that he appeared menacing. He was also grateful for the dark wraparound sunglasses he wore. Had they seen his true eye colour the situation could have been worse.

Returning to Notus he shrugged nonchalantly as his Chooser just shook his head with a smile. He too wore dark sunglasses. They both needed them in this overly lit place. Having shucked off the trappings of a cloistered monk, Notus wore dark beige cargo pants and a blue and white striped dress shirt. He also wore his most comfortable shoes – a pair of brown loafers that had seen better days. Modern times meant it was difficult for Notus to continue as a Priest when such things could be easily checked upon.

Turning from the conveyor belt and the people still waiting to retrieve their personal belongings two Chosen headed towards the exit's sliding doors all the while ignoring the stares and comments from mortals around them. No matter where they went the Angel always attracted undue attention.

The Chosen had come to Canada.

Dr. Elizabeth Bowen stood nervously outside the exit for the international flights in Terminal 1 of *Toronto Pearson International Airport*, waiting for the man renowned for medieval religious art history and restoration to meet her for the first time. Soft light fell from fluorescents anchored in the ceiling two stories above. The open concept of the airport, with its art deco designs of spirals hanging from the same ceiling set a welcoming tone. People, even at this late hour, went from one destination to the next ignoring her as she stood in front of the cafe offering late night java to those who still had further legs of their journey.

Taking a last sip of tea from the brown paper cup, she walked over to the recycling bin and tossed it out, all the while keeping her eyes on the large sliding frosted doors that would open for each traveller as they entered Canada. When she was informed that Dr. Preston had an accident, making it impossible for him to join the collection Elizabeth was heartbroken. After all their emails and telephone conversations Elizabeth felt sure that they would work well together and to throw a new person into the mix this late in the arrangements would only make things worse. It was when she heard that Paul Nathaniel would be accompanying the collection that all her worries fled. She had heard of Mr. Nathaniel and seen his astounding works on the reproduction and restorations of ancient manuscripts and paintings. When the *British Museum* informed her that it was he who was taking Dr. Preston's place with the project Elizabeth did not know whether to jump for joy or become nervously giddy like a teen expecting a celebrity to visit.

Glancing at her watch she stifled a yawn. It was late. Mr. Nathaniel's flight landed forty-five minutes ago and she was wondering what was taking so long. Normally she was tucked in her bed, fast asleep at one in the morning, not cavorting around the Greater Toronto Area. She contemplated calling home to see if her daughter, Vivianne, was fine, but dismissed the idea. She did not want to wake her sixteen year old, if in fact the girl was in bed and not watching horror movies.

The sound of the sliding doors snapped her attention back to excitement, but at the sight of two backpackers walking out and down the left ramp Elizabeth's shoulders slumped. She was starting to wonder if he had made the flight.

The doors opened again, admitting two men walking side by side. They were as different as night to day in their appearance. The older gentleman, who appeared to be about her age, had a relaxed and peaceful air about him. His dark brown hair was peppered with silver and pulled back into a short tail, and his smile softened his smooth features. Handsome in a classical way Elizabeth had to note that he was short, probably not standing more than five and a half feet, but up against his partner he appeared tiny.

Her eyes widened at the man's travelling partner. She had never seen anyone like him before. Tall, even taller than her own five foot ten, she was sure that he was at least a head taller than her, but it was not just his height that pulled her attention, it was his perfectly beautiful pale face and his long white hair, also pulled back into a tail. If she had been up on her runway models Elizabeth would probably recognize the man, as it was, even with the sunglasses and his obvious youth, he was the most beautiful man she had ever seen.

Completely enraptured by the way he moved, Elizabeth startled when the shorter man beamed a smile and made a beeline down the right side of the ramp straight towards her, the taller man following.

"Dr. Bowen I presume?"

Elizabeth pulled her focus from the young man to the gentleman before her. His hand outstretched in expectation to meet with hers. Slipping her hand into his she was surprised at the coldness of his firm touch. "Mr. Nathaniel."

They shook briefly before he let go of her hand to settle the strap on his shoulder that had slipped. His smile never left his face. Elizabeth wondered what colour his eyes were beneath the sunglasses and whether they were as kind and soft as his voice.

"It is wonderful to finally meet you," beamed Mr. Nathaniel. "I do apologize for being a bit tardy, but it took forever for the baggage handlers to relinquish their treasures."

Elizabeth blinked realizing she could sit and listen to this man talk about books and art all day long, to be held captive by his British accent. "That's alright, Mr. Nathaniel."

"Paul," he interrupted. "Please call me Paul. All my friends do."

She matched his smile, his happiness infecting her and she nodded. "Paul it is." She turned her attention to Paul's travelling companion who watched the introductions without exhibiting any emotions. It was like watching a live statue stand witness to the world around it and she immediately wondered what would cause a person, especially one so young as he, to have created such a mask to keep everyone at bay.

"Oh, I'm being rude," piped Paul, noticing where Dr. Bowen's attention landed. "Dr. Bowen, may I please introduce to you my dear, dear friend and ward..." Hesitation halted his melodious voice.

Elizabeth watched as a momentary frown washed away Paul's smile as his travelling companion's jaw momentarily tightened in obvious anger. Elizabeth wondered at the reaction.

"You can call me Gwyn."

If she had thought Paul's voice was delightful to listen to, hearing the tall young man speak stunned her; soft yet firm, the sound plucked through Elizabeth, sending a shiver down her back. He had a voice that matched his physical beauty.

"It's Welsh for white or blessed, isn't it?" said Elizabeth, congenially. She offered her hand and looked up at the young man.

A flitter of disconcertment passed across his pale features

before he propped his black suitcase to stand without support and released the handle. He slipped his hand into hers for a brief shake before he pulled away.

It was enough contact for Elizabeth to note that his hand was as cold as Paul's but that he had the long graceful fingers one would find on a master pianist; strong, alluring. A momentary vision of how those fingers would feel in a caress caught her breath before she realized that their palms had not touched at all. It was then she noticed the leather bracers fitted snugly on both his arms, coming down to cover his palms and held in place by an opening for his thumb and two middle fingers. She had seen similar garb before, in her time during the *Society for Creative Anachronism*, when archers practiced their craft. It was odd to see someone wearing something so out of time as if it were a normal piece of clothing.

A fine white eyebrow lifted above the wraparound sunglasses at her observation of his name. She did not understand its meaning, but without receiving a reply to her question Elizabeth turned her attention back to Mr. Nathaniel.

"I'm sorry about my son, my dear," said Paul. "It was our first transatlantic flight and it was not as enjoyable as we had hoped."

"That's alright. I don't fly well myself," smiled Elizabeth, taking note of what Paul had called the young man. "Shall we get going? I'm sure that you would like to settle in before you start work tomorrow evening."

"Oh, most definitely. It's not every night where we get five extra hours. I've never experienced jet lag before, but it never sounded pleasant to begin with." Paul inclined his head indicating for her to lead on.

Taking the cue, Elizabeth led them up a set of escalators and onto a carpeted bridge that kept pedestrians safe from the traffic below and any possible inclement weather. They walked high above taxis sitting dark, their drivers resting or talking quietly with co-workers. A few privately owned vehicles were stopped at the side to allow sleepy travellers off for their journeys. The sound of luggage wheels mingled with their footsteps over the grey fabric, adding its notes to the quiet cacophony of the early morning.

"I must say, I am a bit confused as to why you would insist on working only at night," she ventured as they entered the parking building. It had been a strange request from the *British*

Museum but the *Royal Ontario Museum* had to oblige if they wanted the exhibit. Elizabeth took out the parking ticket and placed it into the kiosk, paying for the parking before leaving.

"Ah, that's easy to explain, my dear." Paul walked by her side once she had taken the ticket back, his suitcase squeaking as it rolled along. "Night is the time when mysteries abound, when the ghosts of the past can come to whisper in ones ear, bestowing inspiration and teaching the ways of God."

The seriousness of the answer surprised Elizabeth. She quickly glanced at the man the *British Museum* sent to her and noticed his smile was gone. She also noticed that even at night he still wore the sunglasses.

Conversation quickly turned to the exhibit they would be working on together and Elizabeth dismissing the strange comment from her co-worker she dove into descriptions of some of her favourite items that would be placed on display. Even approaching her dark blue *Honda Accord* she kept up the conversation until she pulled out the keys. With a press of the button on the fob the car's lights flashed and the sound of unlocking doors echoed in the nearly deserted place.

"Here we are," she announced, popping open the trunk. "It's not a limo but it works."

She watched Dr. Nathaniel gracefully lift his suitcase and place it into the empty space. "My dear, it is not the ride that matters, but rather the company that makes a voyage enjoyable or not." He flashed a smile before his face pinched with concern as she watched the tall young man place his cases in the trunk as well. "Though for some of us, even with company as gracious as yours, the ride will be, unfortunately, uncomfortable."

Closing the trunk with a thunk, Elizabeth went to open the driver's door and stared at the interior of the car. She glanced at Paul's friend and then back at the inside. Understanding blossomed. Offering an apologetic smile, she looked up at the man who introduced himself as Gwyn. "If you don't mind riding in the front and push the seat all the way back you may be okay."

The tall pale young man turned to face her and she could feel his eyes bore into hers even though she could not see them behind the glasses. With a curt nod of his head Elizabeth almost thought she saw the pull of a half smile on his face and wondered what he would look like without the shades and a real smile.

"You don't mind sitting in the back, do you?" She asked Paul, but realized it was not necessary as he was already settling himself in the back behind her seat.

She blinked in surprise and followed suit.

Having the young man crouched beside her and Dr. Nathaniel behind her, Elizabeth locked the doors and started the car. Adjusting the rear view mirror she noticed that Paul had taken off his sunglasses. Her breath caught at the sight of his large expressive eyes that twinkled in amusement. Checking her side passenger, she noticed that he left the glasses on and seemed disgruntled. Shifting into drive she drove them out of the airport and into the city.

Shifting in the bucket seat proved that no matter what he tried there was no possibility of getting comfortable. Legs pressed the underside of the dash, and even slouching, his head still pressed the ceiling of the small car. This was why he preferred motorcycles.

The Angel could feel Dr. Bowen's attention descend upon him every so often as she drove them onto the motorway – correction; they were called highways, here – that would take them into the heart of Toronto and to the condominium they rented. He hoped the trip would not take long. Even after all these centuries he still became uncomfortable at prying eyes. In this day and age cloaks were no longer fashionable and wearing one would draw even more stares. With the invention of electricity and the advancements of fashion the Angel was now more exposed than ever. It is also what drew his attention, ignoring Notus' animated conversation with Dr. Bowen.

Light posts flickered past as they drove south to connect with the expressway that would take them into the core of the city. The Angel watched illuminated billboards selling expensive wares mingling with low rise buildings. Lights dotted his view until they turned onto the expressway.

Eyes widening, he was about to remove his sunglasses for an unimpeded view when he felt Dr. Bowen's attention fall on him again. Lowering his hand he tried to sit up straight only to find his head pressed against the ceiling, making him feel boxed in. This time he ignored the uncomfortable state of his body and took in the sight.

Ahead skyscrapers, lit up like Christmas trees huddled together, evoked an image of a giant spaceship against the blackness of eternal night. The greatest of these was the world's largest freestanding object, the *CN Tower*. Its needle lit up in purples and greens, giving colour to a monochromatic scene.

"Beautiful," sighed Notus, memorized by the site.

Dr. Bowen smiled, proud of her city. "And this is only the downtown core. The city stretches out far past there to the east and far to the North."

The expressway rose higher and the Angel noticed the absence of light to his right. In the far off distance he could make out a string of pin lights shimmering against black waters.

"And that's, of course, Lake Ontario," offered Dr. Bowen, noticing where his gaze landed. "On a really clear night you can see across the Great Lake. The best view is, of course, from the top of the Tower."

The Angel continued to take in the view while Notus quizzed Dr. Bowen on the history and the sites as they drove past them. Once in the belly of the core, the view of the lake was cut off by towering lakeside condos and office towers. All around them steel and concrete were illuminated by white and yellow.

The off ramp and the ride north sucked them further into the heart. Here was where Toronto appeared most similar to other world class cities, except for one thing – the proliferation of green trees studded in a concrete forest. Newly budded branches stretched high in competition against the high rises.

Even at this late hour people were out enjoying the night life. The Angel watched as they drove past groups of young people cavorting and laughing, couples walking hand in hand, and individuals striding with purpose. On occasion he witnessed a vagrant tottering down a street or sleeping in a darkened corner. Relief washed over him in the realization that nourishment would be easily obtained. Despite being a metropolis Toronto was the cleanest city he had ever seen.

"There is the ROM." Dr. Bowen pointed out as they were about to turn right onto Bloor.

Gazing past the doctor, the Angel saw a large stone building with yellow floodlights illuminating the carefully crafted brick and the large posters announcing the upcoming exhibit. It was a stately mansion until he saw the protrusion on the north side of the building.

"What is that?" asked Notus before he could ask the same.

Dr. Bowen sighed. "That is the Michael Lee-Chin Crystal."

"It's as hideous as the Pyramid at the *Louvre*! Who would do such a thing?!" The monk's outrage at the architectural vandalism brought a small smile to the Angel's face as he successfully squashed the laughter that threatened to burst out. It was so like his Chooser. Always stuck in the past, barely keeping up with these fast changing times, Notus preferred the beauty of old things even though when they were new he had raged like this.

"It's not funny," stated the monk in response to his son's emotions.

It's just a building, sent the Angel, amusement setting his tone.

"Building or not, it is hideous," growled Notus. He folded his arms across his chest, more indignant about how his outburst must appear to Dr. Bowen than the disfigurement of the *Royal Ontario Museum*.

They drove in silence. The Angel glanced at Dr. Bowen and noticed a small frown marring her full lips. Not one to pry he returned his attention to the road ahead of them.

It did not take long before Dr. Bowen pulled into the condominium's circular drive. Shutting down the engine, she leaned over to press the lever that popped the trunk open. "We're here," she announced.

"Thank you, my dear," replied Notus as he opened his door.

Following suit, the Angel gratefully exited the cramped confines of the small vehicle and went around back to retrieve their belongings.

Dr. Bowen opened her door and stood to lean against her car, watching Mr. Nathaniel and his travelling companion. "I'll pick you up tomorrow night, say around eight."

Startled, Notus peeked around the lifted trunk. "Whatever for?"

The Angel settled the wooden case across his back and closed the trunk with a clunk. A sense of foreboding tightened his gut.

"For the press conference, of course." Dr. Bowen smiled. "You do remember, Mr. Nathaniel, do you not?"

It was not often to catch his Chooser off guard, but this woman had done it. Lowering his head, the Angel hid his smile. The sharp look Notus sent him was felt rather than seen.

"Of course," replied Notus, searching his memory and looking for words. "But will it be night here at that time?"

It was Dr. Bowen's turn to look confused as she nodded.

"Then it's set," declared the monk as he pressed the button

that extended his suitcase's handle. "Eight o'clock. You have our information. I look forward to beginning our working relationship. Good night, my dear."

Turning towards the glass doors, the Angel held one open for Notus to enter first. They did not glance back when Dr. Bowen drove away.

Didn't you remember about meeting the press? sent the Angel.

No, pouted Notus. He pressed the button to call the elevator. *I packed the file that holds the itinerary in the suitcase.*

So what are you going to do? The Angel stepped into the elevator and pressed the button that would send them to the eighteenth floor.

I guess I'm going to have to grin and bear it.

We had better hope that the Vampires here don't read the newspapers.

Notus paled as he glanced up at his son's serious expression. *I hadn't thought of that.*

The elevator door closed and began its ascent. The Angel did not know whether the sudden fall of his stomach was due to the speed they travelled or to the fact that in about forty-eight hours the Vampires of Toronto may possibly know that the Angel of Death was in their territory.

Elizabeth frowned as she made her way back home following Kingston Road. The encounter with Paul and his tall pale companion rattled her. She could not put her finger on it, but certain things between them raised red flags with her intuition despite how likable Mr. Nathaniel appeared to be. It was Gwyn, who sat quietly, nary saying a word throughout the whole evening except for his introduction, which drew her attention. Shaking her head, she turned right into the residential area that would lead her home.

ⅦⅠ

omewhere in the back of his dreamscape he heard a knocking, but since it did not bear any relevance to the nightmare he was having he disregarded the interruption. Floating into a lucid state, the dream of Jeanie with his sword in her raised hand dissipated until all he was left was the darkness of the back of his eyelids and his fear driven heart. Burying his face into the pillow he attempted to slip into a peaceful slumber he knew was out of reach. Arms clutching the down feathers encased in cotton, it was the sound of the condo door opening and closing that made him realize that sleep eluded him.

Pushing himself up, he sat on the edge of the bed and brushed his sleep dishevelled white locks from his face, glanced around at his new bedroom and sighed. The tapestry drapes hung from ceiling to floor cutting off all views of the large pane of glass and its picturesque landscape of this young city. Even without any light he could see the details of the master bedroom quite clearly. The black stained oak dresser, night tables and wardrobe stood dark against the white of the walls. His king sized bed, dressed in white, stood in stark relief. Reaching over to the digital clock radio on the night table, he turned the glowing red numbers towards him.

Eight o'clock he grimaced. Notus and he had stayed up until dawn setting up the condo. Notus called it nesting. The monk could not abide in a new home until he had taken out all his paints, inks and tools of his trade, setting up a corner where he could work in peace.

Rising to his feet, he found his black denim pants where he

had left them on the dark hardwood floor and pulled them on, leaving the top button undone. A quick glance around and he found the white dress shirt hanging crumpled on the edge of the laundry hamper in the opened closet. The undershirt was not to be seen and he figured that he had had better aim with that when undressing that morning. With a shrug he slipped into the shirt, buttons undone, and walked out of his room and into the living room.

He halted dead in his tracks.

Dr. Elizabeth Bowen stood with her back to him as she studied something on the dining table. Completely oblivious of him, he was instantly aware of her beauty. Dressed in a black business skirt suit, Dr. Bowen now towered over six feet in her black leather heels. Her dark brown bob swept forward exposing the back of her pale neck, sparking a hunger he immediately squashed. It was when Dr. Bowen lifted his sword, chandelier light reflecting off of the ancient steel, that his breath caught and his heart hammered in his ears.

"Put. It. Down," ordered the Angel, teeth clenched as he strode towards the mortal.

Elizabeth stared in awe at the object laying securely in its case. She could not believe what her eyes beheld and she reached out to touch a sword that should be crumbling from age. Her fingers came to rest on a dragon's face that made up the tip of the guard. The details were smooth. Only slight indents and dark tarnish where cleaners could not reach delineated the creature's features. Caressing her fingers along the dragon's back to wrap around the black grip, Elizabeth lifted a blade that was witness to numerous nicks but still retained an edge. The blade was well taken care of.

The details, weight and even the texture and appearance of the metal revealed its origins. There was no doubt in Elizabeth's mind that what she held was the most perfect example of a sixth century British nobleman's sword she had ever seen. Jaw slack and eyes wide, excitement shuddered through her. *Such a find should be in a museum!*

"Put. It. Down."

The venom filled voice spun her around.

Elizabeth realized she still held the sword when its point floated an inch away from a muscular pale chest. Lifting her head,

Elizabeth's eyes widened at the sight of blood red eyes menacing down upon her. There, before her, the sword pointed at his chest, was Paul's companion appearing as if he just climbed out of bed, beautiful as an angel with demon red eyes.

She noticed his jaw clenched and his eyes harden a fraction of a moment before he lifted his arm. Catching the flat of the blade with his forearm he swept the deadly point from his chest. His other hand clasped around her grip on the sword, his icy fingers forcing hers to relinquish the blade. Stepping out from between this strangely alluring young man and the table behind her, Elizabeth caught a glimpse of a thick white silver scar slicing diagonally across his right breast before the white cotton shirt obscured the view.

Following his fluid movements with her eyes, Elizabeth noticed his fingers trembled as he placed nearly five feet of sword to rest in its wooden case. It was the thick band of scar tissue around his wrist that caught her breath.

Lowering the gold velvet lined lid, the Angel gently secured the sword into its resting place with the sound of the clicks of the latches. Witnessing the woman handling his precious belonging startled him, but it was seeing its point so close to his chest the rattled him. It was too much like his recurrent nightmares.

He rested both hands flat on the wooden case, its texture smooth despite the visual grains. Simple in its construction, the maple had been carefully sanded down to belie the fact that it was made of wood and not of silk. His hair swooped forward, obscuring his face, as he bent his head and closed his eyes in an attempt to push down the surging emotions that her act had evoked in him. Taking a deep breath and releasing it, he stood back and swept his hair from his face, letting his eyes rest on Dr. Bowen. He did not care if she grew uncomfortable with the scrutiny of the Angel upon her.

"What are you doing here?" he demanded. His arms crossed his chest as he glowered into her ice blue eyes.

His gaze penetrated and caused Elizabeth this shift in her stance. She did not like how this young man made her felt. Not one to back down, she lifted her chin and met his eyes. He was the first man to truly force her to look up at him. "To pick up Paul and take him to the press conference, as I explained last night."

"That does not explain why you felt the need to pry into an individual's private property." His eyes narrowed as he spoke through a clenched jaw.

Surprise washed over Dr. Bowen's features. "The sword is yours?" incredulity coloured her intonation. "I don't believe it."

"Believe what you will, I care not." He brushed past her in an attempt to go back to his bedroom. With his sword secure, he could try and catch up on some sleep.

Elizabeth was taken aback by the young man and shook her head. *Nobody talks like that anymore, and no one owns a sword a millennium and a half old.* Emboldened by her own rising irritation at this strange young man a thought exploded into her mind, the corner of her mouth lifting in a smirk. "Then you wouldn't mind if I borrow it for the museum exhibition."

Almost to the hallway that led to his door, he spun around, shocked at what Dr. Bowen was asking.

"It would be a perfect addition to the exhibition," continued Elizabeth, her heels clicking against the hardwood floor as she came to stand before the stunned young man. "I could guarantee its security and it would return to you at the end of the exhibit, if in fact the sword does belong to you."

"I think that is a marvellous idea, my dear." Notus walked out of the other hall, fumbling with the adjustment of his green and yellow striped tie.

You cannot be serious, sent the Angel to his Chooser. He could not believe what he was hearing. Notus understood, more than any other being on the planet, what that sword meant to him. He could not let it go to be an object for people to stare at.

Why not? Notus tucked the gaudy tie into the waistband of his brown wool slacks and then buttoned the single breasted matching jacket. *You carry it from place to place. You cannot use it any more. I'm sorry, my son, but I think that for our duration here in a land populated by hidden Vampires, having the blade securely ensconced in a high security venue such as the ROM is an excellent way to keep it safe. Elizabeth, without knowing it, may have solved this dilemma.*

Dilemma to you, maybe. I disagree.

Chooser and Chosen stared at each other, one calm and patient while the other stood with folded arms, clearly not willing to acquiesce.

Elizabeth stared from her co-worker to his travelling companion. She knew something was going on between the two. It almost felt as though it were a contest of wills.

Notus lifted a brown brow and tilted his head. *And what would you do? This flat is not nearly as secure as the museum. What would you do if a Vampire came here and tried to take away what they believe holds your power to destroy them? You can't carry a sword around with you everywhere you go. Not anymore.*

The Angel broke eye contact with his Chooser and glared at a nondescript spot on the floor. He hated to admit that Notus was right. Carrying a sword around wherever he went would invite more trouble than negate it, and leaving it here unprotected on occasion would be nerve-wracking. He should have left Geraint's sword in Fernando's safekeeping just as Notus originally suggested. He knew that as he had always known it, but he had never gone anywhere without it before. It was too much a part of him.

Raking his hair back with both hands, he let out a huff. "Fine." He turned around to head back into his room. "But I am going with you tonight."

Notus smiled warmly up at Dr. Bowen, triumph written over his gentle features. "I wouldn't have it any other way."

Confused, Elizabeth shook her head. "What just happened?"

"You won the battle without having to lift a finger, my dear." Paul turned around to walk into the living room and sat down on the brown leather sofa.

VIII

The soft cushions of the chocolate leather sofa sighed as it accommodated his weight. Leaning back, eyes closed, he released the breath he held and inhaled the luxuriant scent of leather polish that helped keep the cow hide newborn soft. It was his daily ritual, a way to begin in calm serenity before delving into the chaos of death and wrought emotions that was the nature of his business. He sat there, meditating upon the silence of peace, waiting.

A new scent floated to his sensitive nostrils, sparking his hunger. He opened his dark brown eyes to see Godfrey walking towards him, a delicate China tea cup and saucer, decorated in hand painted roses and gold filigree, carefully held between his large hands. The contents wafted translucent steam and he knew that his servant had heated the contents to perfection. He waited until Godfrey's bulk stood in front of him before he outstretched his hand to take the drink.

"Thank you, Godfrey," he said, sipping the contents and leaning back against the cool leather.

The young man solemnly nodded his short cropped blonde head and backed up. "Did you wish to see the paper, sir?"

Tilting his head to gaze up at Godfrey's impeccably tidy appearance, he nodded. "Why not? It has been a while since I peeked into the goings-on around me. Maybe there will be some good news for a change."

"Yes, sir." Godfrey backed up to the doorway before turning to leave the parlour.

He relaxed into the sofa's comfort and sighed. When returning home he would repeat the ritual before turning in. Taking another sip of the dark liquid, he surveyed his surroundings.

Cathedral ceilings played in shadows with the decorative plaster swirls and mouldings. Books in ceiling high mahogany shelves lined the opposite wall where a small fire flickered in the grand hearth; its orange gloaming married with the soft electronic lights ensconced between the ceilings patterns. Dark cherry stained the ornate wainscoting that blanketed the walls, lending the room its sweet warmth.

It did not take long for Godfrey to return with the newspaper.

Placing the teacup and saucer onto the mahogany side table, he took the paper and shook it out to its full length. He ignored Godfrey's departure as he thumbed through the news print. It was much of the same, he noted, skimming past article after article. Politics, murder and mayhem ranked top, pushing uplifting stories of simple folk to lines of text that were lucky to be inked. He sighed and pulled out another section of the paper, this time taking pleasure in reading articles that lay black against the white. Science was a love he caressed as often as he could and reading about new discoveries and inventions always uplifted his heart. He sipped away at the teacup's contents until the dregs lay thick and cold at the bottom, enraptured at what visions the print opened to him.

Finished the section, he placed it back onto his lap and pulled out another section. The one that was local to the city, explaining the intimate goings on for individuals in search of culture and entertainment. It was this that caught his attention.

Ignoring the placement of the saucer, he clunked down the cup, unaware that it toppled onto its side. A small pool of dark fluid dribbled out of the now chipped China, marking the tea cup's demise. He was unaware of the mess, his eyes widening at the sight of the photo on the front page and he laid it on his lap, smoothing out the wrinkles until the image was as clear as the newsprint could allow.

Staring at it, through black and grey rasterization stood Father Paul Notus and the Angel beside a tall smiling woman in the *Garfield Weston Exhibition Hall* of the *Royal Ontario Museum*. His jaw dropped in reading the bi-line and he carefully looked at the photo. There, on the table, was the Angel's sword laying securely in an open case. Scanning the image to the Angel he could see that the Chosen was none too pleased even with the sunglasses obscuring his eyes. The monk seemed happy yet there was a disturbance in his features. It was the woman, the curator of the event, who was unaware of their discomfort and was positively beaming.

"I–I can't believe it," he exclaimed as he quickly read through the article. No matter the names the Chosen used, he knew them upon sight.

Lifting his gaze from the paper to land upon an empty room, he had thought that not much could surprise him or elicit a response that electrified through him, but this had proven his assumptions wrong.

Another look at the photo and he shook his head.

"Are they crazy?"

íx

he music pounded through her body, its rhythm vibrating through every cell as the volume made it nearly impossible for anyone to speak to each other. Then again, this was not a place for conversation. Flashing strobe lights of black, green and purple tainted the darkness. Each danced to the beat, changing and modulating as the music flowed, catching individuals unaware in sudden illumination before plunging them back into darkness, never knowing when next they would be thrust into the light. It was a place where one lost oneself to the throbbing pleasure the trance provided. It was her place and she revelled in it.

She kept her eyes closed as she moved her body on the dance floor, allowing the beats to lead her body as the scents around pressed and caressed. So many mortals came to this place, to her place in hopes that she would join them for just one dance. If they were lucky she would invite them for a second and then they would be begging for the joy of pressing themselves up against her as she undulated to the nightclub's heartbeat. Men and women flocked to her, some brought by others she had kissed so that they too would understand the rapture she bestowed. Little did they know with each sip of their blood they became more and more hers, and she revelled in it.

Hot hands pressed against her belly, drawing her closer until a mortal's heat fired along the length of her back. For any other she would have turned and sent the offender fleeing into the night. No mortal touched her without her permission save one. She leaned her head against his shoulder, their bodies moving together in time with the music.

Opening her eyes she smiled up into Terry's blue sapphire eyes. There was a hunger, a longing that pained his features, widening her smile. She knew what he wanted and she was more than willing to give it to him. Terry was hers as completely as any mortal could ever be. She was his drug, and at his pitiful young age of seventeen she was hoping she would eventually be given permission to turn him.

His long corn silk hair and a face and body of an angel had drawn her to him the instant he had tentatively walked into *The Veil*. His tall, slim swimmers body titillated her and she knew she had to have him. That night she had danced the whole night with him, ignoring the rest. It was not long before he would come back almost nightly, dancing with her, letting her drink from him. She had read the Vampire stories and knew the terms mortals called such creatures; *pomme de sang, Renfield,* and others. The true word was *slave*.

She felt his need rise, pressing hard against her and she turned to face him without losing the beat. His breath came fast and hot on her face and she luxuriated against it, throwing her head back to expose the length of her pale neck and the full mounds of her breasts that pressed up from the leather bodice. The invitation was clear and he lowered his head to kiss them, his hands resting on her hips.

Opening her eyes, she did not care what occurred in the middle of the dance floor. Other Vampires took their pleasures as did mortals, though there were more private rooms for those more squeamish about voyeurs. She brought her head up and watched him enjoy himself. No pleasure stirred within her. That part was dead. It was the intoxication of aroused blood that lengthened her fangs.

Fumbling with the buttons of his leather pants she managed to free his stiff member. Its heat scalded her as it jumped to her touch. She would never let him enter her. Her body was her own. It was the taste of his orgasm enriched blood that drove her to sweep her fingers against him, making him dance to her beat.

A groan escaped him as he pressed close. Her hand found his sack and played with the delicate balls within before rising to find the tip of his shaft. He was closer, oh so close, and with her other hand she gripped his hair and yanked his head away from her breasts. His gasp of surprise coupled with the beginnings of his shuddering release. Her teeth set into his jugular as the first spill of his seed washed over her hand.

Sweet, sex flavoured blood pounded into her, riding out the music's pulse. Only Terry's orgasmic heart satisfied the longing in her soul. Each pulse, each spill, he gave everything he could and she received it. It was only when the throbbing of his member ceased that she pulled out, a rivulet of blood leaking from the two puncture marks next to all the old and new scars. All came from her. He was her property and all the other Vampires knew it.

Terry wobbled, his breath coming in quick shudders and he smiled at her as she licked his blood from her red stained lips. With a glance at his now flaccid member, his eyes following, he tucked himself away. He had done well, and as with any dog she threw him a bone. Leaning close, she pressed herself against him, depositing a kiss on his smooth cheek before turning away to lose herself in the rhythm of a new beat.

The tempo accelerated into a new song, sending the dancers into a frenzy of movement. With Terry's blood warming her, she took up the dance once again. She did not care with whom she shared the dance, her body moved as her mind set itself free in ecstatic rapture. This was freedom. This was the life she was born to live and she excelled at it.

An unexpected tap on her shoulder brought her out of her trance and she looked behind to view the offender. If it had been most anyone else, she would have ripped out their throats. No one interrupted her dance. Lips drawn back, her fangs fully extended, she hissed at the man who had interrupted her pleasure.

"Give it a rest, Rose," stated Brian Haskell, shouting above the din. His short dirty blonde hair was gelled back into a slick style and his storm grey eyes appeared bored. Dressed in black slacks and t-shirt, his muscular pale arms crossed over his chest, straining the cotton.

Halting her dance, Rose brushed her stray copper curls from her face before resting her hands on her leather miniskirt covered hips. "What does he want now?"

Brian crooked a finger at her and motioned for her to follow.

Huffing her displeasure at the interruption, Rose set her jaw and followed. The crowd parted to allow their exit. The music was too loud to converse over so she had no recourse. Brian had always been in her life since her birth over a century ago. Her initial memories had him holding her first meal. She had remembered how the creature had screamed before giving way to her feral need for food. It was only after she had wiped the blood from her chin that she realized it was a child. A part of her knew she should have been upset at the revelation, but the blood had tasted so good and its heat had enlivened her newborn body.

Brian was the first person she saw that night. His strong square face held a business like seriousness. It was he who had given her the handkerchief to wipe her dripping chin. No smile, only calm as he pointed with his chin to the one responsible for her birth. Now it was Brian who led her back to him, to Corbie Vale, the Father of her soul and the ruler of the Vampires since his own Mistress died at the hands of the despised Chosen. Of course, that was before her time. Curious about the strange creatures that threatened their very existence she would ask for more details, only to be told to hold her tongue.

Corbie had fled Europe, taking her, Brian and a few of his coterie to the New World, settling in Canada's largest city whose inhabitants were ripe for the picking. He had hated his craven retreat, but word spread quickly amongst his kind and no matter where he ran the Angel followed. Each battle line he created, the creature decimated until nothing was left, not even bones. Even when Corbie ordered his coteries and their coteries to use their mortal slaves as a first line assault, it did not deter the Chosen. City after city, country by country, until backed against the Atlantic with nowhere else to go, Corbie had ordered her into the wooden freight and locked her in, doing so with each of his treasured first coterie until he was left. It was he who brought them to the New World, setting the Vampires free to be themselves without the threat of the Angel and his Chosen to descend upon them.

She did not know the reasons behind the war or why they lost, only that the vile Chosen had discovered that they were not the real Vampires and took out their vengeance upon them. The young ones, born during the war and after knew one thing only – all Chosen must die. It was the precious few who made it to the Americas that held the secret of how it all started and no one was going to say anything to her.

The line in the sand was made in the depths of the Atlantic and that was good enough for her.

Through a hidden door at the back of the nightclub that led to a back door exit, Brian paused long enough on the landing for the door to close and then led her down a stairwell painted in black.

Black floodlights illuminated their pale flesh and the faint outlines of the rickety old steps leading to the basement. She always hated the sudden reduction of sound and the boom of the solid steel door as it vibrated through her causing a pressure in her ears that quickly disappeared. Her thigh high black stiletto boots clicked against the wood while Brian's black dress shoes whispered.

She knew better than to ask Brian why she was being summoned by the Lord of Valraven who was now known as Mr. Vale, owner of the Vampire sex club *Beyond the Veil.* Brian would ignore her as he always did unless he was ordered to involve himself with her, and then the condemnation and disgust written on his face was always evident. She wondered why Corbie kept him around.

It did not take long to find themselves at another solid steel door with a punch code security device beside the wall. She knew the combination but let Brian do the honours. The lock gave way with a clunk and Brian pulled it open, standing aside to let her enter. Beaming a smug smile up at Brian's stoic countenance, she walked past him and entered another world.

Where the club was dark with splashes of electric light, the lobby was filled with gold reflecting candlelight. Honey sweetened the air, hiding any taint that may have splashed upon the red laminate floor. A gold chandelier and sconces glittered in the brilliance with the assistance of melting beeswax. The walls were decorated with mirrors and paintings, many of them gruesome, depicting horrific images of the human psyche.

She smiled as she passed *Saturn Devouring His Son* by Goya. Ah now there was a man who could paint to warm the cold heart of a Vampire.

It was the door to the left of the painting that she headed towards. She did not need Brian to tell her where to find her Father and Dominus. Opening the dark stained wood, she moved from the past into the future. Here white walls, floors and ceiling made a stark contrast to the previous room. The silvers of steel bordered and delineated the white wood desk. On a white leather chair, Corbie sat, his feet crossed, on the desk next to the white keyboard that sat beside the matching computer monitor. He did not see her as he held the newspaper out in front of him, reading.

She walked to stand before him, ignoring the two matching steel chairs with white cushions that were placed equidistant from one another. Behind Corbie, an array of twelve monitors lined the wall, each one flickering from scene to scene of the goings on of his nightclub.

"Go wash your hands," ordered the Dominus of Vampires. He turned another page, refusing to look at her.

The door closed behind with a gentle click and Brian came to stand beside the desk, hands behind his back.

Confusion twisted her features at the strange request and she looked down at her hands. Strong, yet delicate fingers, nails painted crimson, appeared fine until she noticed her other hand. Sucking in her breath at the sight of Terry's release still on her hand, she turned and all but ran to the bar nestled into the wall opposite to Corbie's desk. Thankful for the white porcelain basin decorated with steel fixtures, she ran the hot water, scrubbing her hands until they turned slightly rosy.

Shaking her hands, she turned off the faucet and returned to stand before Corbie, her hands running through her hair to tame some of the curls. "I doubt that you called me here just to have me wash my hands."

With a flip of the paper, Corbie folded it. Removing his feet from the pristine desk, he sat straight and laid the newsprint down where his feet had recently rested. His dark eyes came to land on her, a slight smirk pulling the corner of his thin lips.

Rose sucked in her breath. She did not find her lord and master attractive, but he cut a nice figure in his grey turtleneck sweater and black slacks. His usually unruly black hair was styled back making his Roman features more severe. She hated it when he made her wait upon his pleasure.

"You know I wouldn't call you from your enjoyment without good reason," stated Corbie. He leaned forward, resting his forearms on the paper, his eyes penetrating her.

Resisting a shiver, she shook her head and glanced away, hitching a shoulder with her arms crossed. She knew that at this he was truthful. After all she was his little flower. He had done everything necessary so she could have her own playground. The only thing he would not allow her, the thing that wedged a gap between them, was that he held back his permission for her to form her own coterie. That meant until he did Terry would always be her slave and not her servant, just as she was Corbie's.

"Come here, Rose. I wish to show you something."

The order hardened his voice and brought out an accent she rarely heard and could not place. The commanding tone lent no question of his authority over her, over Brian, and over all other Vampires. It is what forced her to take a shuddering breath, drop her arms and meet his liquid brown eyes. She wondered at the origins of the man who was her father and what he had been before his own Vampiric birth. She would never ask. It was likely he did not remember, just as she could not recall who she might have been before waking in the oppressive womb of her coffin and clawing struggling through the earthen birth canal to the cold night and hot blood. The only hint she had to her own past was her fading Scottish lilt.

Taking the few steps towards the desk, Corbie leaned back, turning the newspaper around for her inspection. Her eyes landed upon the half page photo, her cinnamon brows furrowing.

"I don't think this is a good idea," muttered Brian.

Corbie shot the Vampire a look to kill before returning to study his little flower.

Rose found the photograph pulling at her, tightening a knot in her belly. The image was of three individuals. The tall woman, dressed in what Rose would call corporate Goth, was smiling as she stood before a table with a sword lying propped up in its wooden case. It was the short man beside the glamorous lady that tugged at her, but it was the very tall young man that stood statuesque behind the shorter gentleman that stripped the breath from her body and nearly doubled her up in heart wrenching pain. She had never seen anyone so beautiful. Even Terry's beauty paled against this man. In that instant Rose knew she had to have him.

"Who is he?" She glanced up, fevered eyes meeting ones cold as the grave.

A growl emanated from Brian and it snapped her attention to the normally emotionless man. She wondered what could draw such a vehement reaction.

"Do you recognize anyone in the photo?" Corbie's insistent voice drew her back to the photo.

A part of her wanted to cry out that she knew them but it was impossible. She had never seen them before. She read the bi-line. *"Dr. Elizabeth Bowen, curator at the ROM, and visiting Art Director on loan from the British Museum, Mr. Paul Nathaniel, presents new discoveries that will be on display at the* Medieval Arts of Britain and Europe Exhibit *set to open at the end of the month at the Royal Ontario Museum."*

There was no mention of the man standing in the back. She shook her fiery mane. "I ken none of them."

The sudden thickening of her accent shocked her and widened Corbie's eyes.

"I told you it was a bad idea." Brian's smug tones tore their gazes to Corbie's second.

"I didn't ask for your opinion, Mr. Haskell." Corbie's voice darkened with the threat of violence.

"No, you didn't, but you should have." The blonde Vampire uncrossed his arms and came to stand beside his Dominus. Placing his large hands on the white melamine desk he leaned down to match Corbie's glare. "Having the Chosen come to our shores is one thing. Having the Angel and his sire publicly declare themselves is another matter."

"You think I don't know that?" spat Corbie, leaning back in his white leather chair. "This is the perfect opportunity to take my revenge."

"Don't you mean 'our revenge'? We both lost many friends."

"Fine. Our revenge."

Brian stood straight. "What do you have in mind?"

Corbie's dark gaze fell once more on Rose, a malicious smile forming his lips. "The Angel and his sire are outnumbered and are in our territory – a territory they have no knowledge of. We are going to hit him where it hurts."

"Lady Bastia tried that and look where it got us," stated Brian, matter-of-factly.

Corbie ignored him, but the twitch at the corner of his mouth belied the control over the fury that was bubbling forth. Rose knew that if Brian did not halt his nit picking he would be staked out on the roof to await the sun, no matter the history between the two Vampires.

"And for that and countless other reasons I want the Angel on his knees, before me, begging for his life as Rose slaughters him."

"What?" exclaimed Rose and Brian in unison.

"It begins with the Angel's sword." Corbie tapped the photo, drawing their attention to it again.

Rose's eyes did not fall on the blade indicated, but to the one that could only be the Angel. She had wanted to possess him. But if he was truly the one that had decimated her kind in Europe and forced the Vampires to flee, then Corbie was offering her an honour undreamt of.

A frown pulled her full lips. There had to be a catch. "What do I get out of it?"

Corbie's smile blossomed. "Your dream come true, my little flower."

"You don't mean...?" Hope widened her eyes.

"You will have my blessing to spread your seeds and start your own garden," nodded Corbie.

The shout of joy ripped from her throat as she launched around the desk to hug her father.

"I'll do it. I'll make the Angel bleed and wish he was never Chosen," she whispered into Corbie's ear, hugging him tight.

X

team billowed, fogging the glass doors of the shower stall and every other surface in the chrome and black tiled master bathroom. He stood there, under the large showerhead that hung from the ceiling, as hot water pelted down on him. The jets that sprayed from the corners of the stall pounded his body, to mingle with the rains from above before swirling down the drain set between his feet. Tilting his head, the flush of heat washed over his face before he bent his head forward to let the water beat down on his neck and shoulders, his long white hair hanging heavy and lank under the barrage. If he opened his eyes he would still be in darkness but it would not be as complete. After an hour of Tai Chi and then another in seated meditation the shower was pure luxury and added to his relaxed sense of being.

Streams of heat flowed over him, merging with others to form giant rivers only to break apart into waterfalls cascading from his body. Many things had changed in the short time of human progress but this was pure heaven. He thanked the Gods for modern conveniences. When he and Notus returned to London he was insisting on installing one of these magical stalls in their home.

His hand found the controller and pressed another button, changing the steady streams into rhythmic pounding. The heated water massage forced a sigh and he wondered how much more relaxed he could possibly become.

Three weeks had passed since their arrival and he still could not believe he had agreed to let Dr. Bowen have his sword for the exhibit. The first few days after the dreaded meeting with the press had left him unable to sleep. He hated to admit it, but having the sword around was a comfort blanket, making him feel secure in his ability to defend himself no matter what may come. Now it was gone, or to be precise, on loan, and he missed its presence and what it represented.

Notus said that he could have it back whenever he wished it, but he had given his word. It would stay with the exhibit while they were in Toronto. When it was time to return home, or Gods forbid, they were forced to continue onto the next city for the exhibit's tour, then the sword would return to him.

In the meantime, he had managed to dodge Dr. Bowen's prying questions about Geraint's sword. After the night of the press conference and the car ride with her there and back, she had learned that grilling him for information was just burning her. In the end she apologized and insisted that he call her Elizabeth, just like Notus did. He refused. He preferred not to be around when she was, but this was not always the case.

Since Notus worked nights, Elizabeth shifted her work schedule a couple of days a week so that their hours overlapped. It meant that when he drove Notus to work on the motorcycle he had delivered four days after their arrival; she was there, getting ready for home. Sometimes she stayed a little longer to work with Notus or to stay and chat.

He tried to ignore her and leave, but she was Notus' colleague and that meant she was also the monk's friend. It even got to the point where on the evenings Elizabeth stayed late Notus insisted on stopping off to pick her up a coffee or some other such beverage. It also meant that for the first couple failed attempts, Notus had to figure out the best way to carry a hot beverage while being a passenger on a very expensive and very fast motorcycle. Those were the evenings where the Angel spent the rest of the night cleaning the spilled drink off the bike and then off him. Notus somehow never got spilled on.

Once the monk had perfected the skill of carrying a beverage with one hand and holding on with the other, Elizabeth was always thrilled with her evening treats and her partner's consideration. The way the two talked made the Angel wonder if something more would come from their working relationship, but quickly dismissed it. No matter the times, Notus would always be a monk, even if it was at heart and not in practice. In any case, Elizabeth's eyes always would alight onto him and follow him around until he left for the evening.

The worst was when her car broke down and he had to give her a lift home. Riding a motorcycle was not the issue. Elizabeth was excited by the prospect of being on one since the last time was before her daughter was born. It was when he walked her out to where his bike was parked and handed her the helmet that she balked. He had to call for Notus to help cajole her that she was safe with him driving his *MTT Turbine SUPERBIKE*, most commonly called the *Y2K*. Being on a jet with two wheels was a bit much for her as he barrelled through traffic. Elizabeth clung onto him with closed eyes. By the third night she was relaxed enough to enjoy the ride, but her hands never let go of their death grip around his waist.

Despite her every effort to get him to warm to her he still remained remote. It was better this way. Better for him and especially better for her.

Pressing another button changed the massaging waters back into a steady stream before he found the faucet and turned the handle, cutting off the flow of water. The absence of falling water amplified the sounds of water racing down the drain and the water droplets falling from his body to be swept away in the drain's whirlpool. He stood there for a moment before releasing a sigh, and opening his eyes he slid the shower stall's door open.

In the total darkness of the bathroom he could see everything coated in moisture. Condensation formed droplets on the black sink and ran down the tank of the black toilet, creating streaks in the midst of smaller drops that were already coming together for their gravity assisted journey. The wall width mirror over the counter was completely obscured.

Stepping out onto the cool black floor tiles, he noticed that they were dulled to grey with condensation. He reached to the chrome towel bar and grabbed the white terrycloth towel before wrapping it around his slim waist. Streaks of red, silver and gold ran riot through the black marble countertop as he picked up his hairbrush. He was tempted to turn on the lights just to see if the brilliance would be increased but decided against it. The colours were spectacular enough.

Pulling the bristles through his hair, he stared at the obscured mirror and stifled the urge to swipe his hand through miniscule beads to reveal the glass below. He knew what he looked like. He did not need a mirror to reflect back at him the differences that had caused so much grief in his lengthy lifetime. He did not want to see the scars that remained of his torture under a Vampire's hand. It had taken him a long time to be able to brush his own hair without his hands twitching painfully.

He released his breath in a huff and placed the brush back down. Its wooden handle clicked against the stone. Running his hands through his wet hair, he felt the drape slap against his back and he stiffened. Even after all these decades it was little things like this that could evoke memories he wished would stay buried, and he turned away from the mirror.

Tonight he would do the same as every night since arriving to Toronto. He would get ready, take his Chooser to the museum and then enjoy the rest of the night exploring the city. Sometimes he would walk for hours, other times he would get on his motorcycle and ride the wide straight highways, amazed at the breadth of the metropolis. It was these times, when he opened up the engine and let fly that he could really feel part of this new land. Of course, police would pull him over for his excessive speeding, but with a little Push he was off to repeat with the added benefit that if the same police officers ever saw him they would ignore him.

On nights when it rained, making the roads too slick for the expensive bike, he would walk Notus to work and then catch a show or two. It was in the darkest hours of the early mornings, when he would return home after feeding, if he felt so inclined, go up to the roof and practice his forms. Here he pressed his body to move in ways they used to. Some took more concentration than others, some were easy, allowing his mind to let fly and his body explode with action. Many nights, Notus would find him up on the roof before dawn. He did not require his link to his Chooser to know that it was those times that Notus truly worried for his son.

He would press the time he stood outside waiting for the dawn before Notus would reign him back inside. The monk need not worry, but having him do so told him that he was cared for, that his life still had meaning. That he was still loved.

A twinge in his stomach yanked a grimace from his face and he placed his hand on the doorknob. Closing his eyes, he turned around and leaned his back against the cool wood. The summoning raced into his mind, voicing silent words that were ancient in origin.

Pressure began to build in the room, its moisture seeping into every pore of his body, and he knew he should not have called them in such a small area. It was too confined. On the rooftop they would have more space to fly free, appearing to those below as nothing more that wisps of mist. But here, in the master bathroom, they drew upon the condensation to give them form.

His chest felt heavy as if something or someone sat on it and he opened his eyes to see one of his white faced demons pressed up against him. Others, obviously distressed at their limited mobility, tried and failed to swirl in the darkness. The sudden sense of danger pressed him further until he gasped. He had made a mistake.

You have sssssssssummoned us, sssssire. The one before him whispered. Its voice a rasping of autumn leaves against concrete. *We are hungry, sssssssssire. It has been too long. Much too long.*

"I know." Shame filled him. He had not fed nor alleviated their need for sustenance since before his flight to this land. A part of him did not know if they would be able to follow, but a larger part was afraid to find out. Now that they were here and hungry, he knew he was in a precarious position. If he did not give them what they wanted, they would take it from him, raping his body of the life force they needed to survive by sinking their putrid maws onto his body until there was little left. He had survived many encounters with them before he had mastered him. There was no way he was going back to that nightmare.

Trapped by his own unthinking actions, his hunger having called out to theirs, he did what he could only do. Swallowing down the ache in his gut, he tried and failed to calm his breathing enough to slip into that other realm. There he would be able to drink from the Lady's Well, sipping from the silver chalice, and transform that energy into something the creatures before him could suckle.

Unfortunately, it had been too long and his body cried out for blood, distracting him from shifting his consciousness. His own assumptions about whether or not he could reach the sacred grove had cut himself from it. Now, seeing and feeling the white faced demon's needs, he knew how wrong he actually was.

Raising his hands, he watched the creature before him fleet back, its black eye sockets widening in surprise before its mouth split into a smile glittering with sharpened teeth. With a nod to it, it and its brethren descended upon him.

A gasp tore through his throat as they sank their incorporeal teeth into him, suckling him. He tried not to fight. It was every nightmare that plagued him since he was a child. This time he was a willing participant.

He felt his energy lag as black spots popped in and out of his vision. A sense of vertigo overwhelmed him and he slid to the floor. *"Enough!"* he ordered.

Gratefully, they relinquished their suckling and backed off. One floated down to his level, its head cocked to the side. *Remember, sssssssire,* it hissed.

A cough of laughter caught him. *"How can I ever forget?"*

Its smile broadened.

"Go back," he whispered, suddenly tired and famished. *"I promise I won't forget."*

Nodding its diaphanous head, it turned, disappearing with the others.

It was then that he heard the pounding on the door, the vibrations rattling up his spine. Climbing to his feet, all the benefits of the hot shower were doused away and he opened the door to see Notus standing, his fist upraised for another barrage against the wood.

"I'm alright," he sighed and then knew it for a lie when the world tilted and he had to grab onto the door jam or fall over.

"You are *not* alright," stated the monk, taking his arm and leading him to the bed.

The sudden soft support beneath him rushed a sigh out of him and he closed his eyes.

"What in God's name were you thinking, boy?" Notus grabbed his chin, forcing him to gaze into worried hazel.

"They were hungry." He winced at the lame excuse. He knew how the demons unsettled the monk and how Notus despised the strange symbiotic relationship, but he had accepted it as a necessity in the Angel's battles with the Vampires. The demons were one thing no one could stand against.

Notus released his jaw in a huff. He walked two paces, as if ready to flee the room, and turned on his sandaled heel, placing his hands on his brown robed hips. "I don't want to hear it. There was absolutely no reason to call them and let them have their way with you, hungry or not. What if they hadn't stopped?"

Guilt and shame flushed through him at the thought of making his Chooser worry, but Notus did not know all the facts and it was better that way. Halting his feeding of the demons would only mean they would come to him in his dreams again and take what they needed, rather than be tamed by his controlled feeding of them. The only difference this time was that he lost control because he had waited too long.

"It won't happen again," he murmured. He would never let them gain the upper hand again.

A cool hand landed on his shoulder and he looked up at his Chooser, a wry smile on the monk's face.

"What am I ever going to do with you, my boy?" smiled Notus, shaking his head.

He shrugged, offering a lopsided smile of his own. "Keep me around?"

"Of course!" exclaimed his Chooser. "There's no question of that! But, my God, lad, if I could get drunk you would have driven me to drink long ago."

"I think with that we're in mutual agreement, old man." His smiled widened, offering Notus a rare glimpse of the man behind the Angel.

Notus patted his shoulder. "That we are, my boy. That we are."

It was then that the Angel noticed something oddly familiar. Notus was back in plain brown monastic robes, cinched in the middle by a knotted white cord on which hung a rosary. His salt and pepper hair hung loose and sandals adorned his bare feet. Having seen him wear such over the long centuries of their relationship it should not have been a surprise, but after another century of Notus doffing the attire for something more modern it was an odd sight.

"You're wearing your robes, and they are *new*," he commented, his fine white brows furrowing.

"Of course I am," announced Notus, plucking at the wool fabric. "It's the opening gala tonight."

It did not make sense. If it was such a special event, would not Notus wear something more appropriate? He shook his head.

The monk huffed in exasperation, obviously having read his thoughts. "It's a costume, boy," and then muttered, "unfortunately."

Realization dawned on him and his crimson eyes widened.

"The ROM, under Elizabeth's advisement, has announced that tonight will be a costumed event where medieval attire is the code," explained the monk.

"And you're going like that?"

The wry smile came back. "Why not? I spent the entirety of

those tumultuous years wearing this. The question you should be asking is what are you going to wear?"

The hunger that smouldered in his belly was replaced with a cold stone. He had conveniently forgotten that the invitation had both their names on it and that Notus had R.S.V.P.'ed the positive on his behalf as well.

He shook his head, his white hair whipping around him. "No. You did not?" He did not need to read his Chooser's mind, just the man's face and he groaned. "You did."

Standing up, hand holding the towel in place, he strode past Notus, out of his room and found the offending material draped over the back of the couch. He closed his eyes, took deep breaths, counting to ten before turning around to face the culprit. "I am not going to wear a houppeland again."

"But you looked so good in it last time," countered the monk.

"That was eight hundred years ago! And we both know how well that evening went." He did not attempt to keep the accusatory tones from his voice. The last time he wore something so *festive* was the night he first met Fernando de Sagres, saving the mortal man from drowning in his own vomit.

"Then what will you wear?"

Matching his Chooser's frown he tried to think. No matter the time period he always tended to wear similar things. An idea came to mind. Sweeping back into his room with Notus on his heels he found what he was looking for. "How's that?"

A smile blossomed on Notus' face at the sight of the black leather trousers and white laced shirt dangling from their respective hangers. Close enough in style, it was still modern. "That'll do."

Shaking his head in amused disbelief, he laid the clothing on his dishevelled bed. "Let me get dressed so we can eat first before the party."

Notus turned to leave but halted at the opened bedroom door. "Elizabeth is having a limousine sent to pick us up in half an hour."

"What's wrong with my bike?" he asked, scooping his long hair out from under the white shirt that he now wore.

Notus glanced down at the lengthy robe and an image of the monk sitting astride on the back of the *Y2K*, the robed hoisted around Notus' waist with bare legs enjoying a very brisk breeze blossomed in his mind. His bark of laughter was enough to bring a rush of red to his Chooser's face. "Okay. Fair enough."

Turning around, Notus left him so that he could change for the party.

It was when he was strapping the black leather bracers onto his forearms did he realize that for the first time he did not balk or attempt to back out of going to such an event. Sitting down on the bed, he felt it sink under his weight. More dismayed than anything, he was surprised at his own lack of trepidation and that in itself slicked the cold stone in his belly in ice.

XI

The limousine drive to the Royal Ontario Museum was blissfully uneventful. Unfortunately there had not been enough time for either of them to slake their thirst before the condominium's security officer informed them that their ride was awaiting them. Gritting his teeth at the blood scent wafting from the mortal driver, the Angel sat in the back, lounging on the black leather as Notus played with the buttons that erupted music from unseen speakers, turned on and off the television, and opened and closed the fridge and cabinet that held many treats for a mortal to savour. It did not do him any good, for what he craved sat in the driver's seat guiding the incredibly long vehicle through the busy roads. The saving grace to the whole experience was that Notus agreed to him wearing his sunglasses.

Uncomfortable at the confined surroundings, he took a deep breath through his nose and released it in a huff, instantly regretting the action. Releasing a groan, he closed his eyes but not before catching the driver's blue eyes in the rear view mirror as the scent of mortal blood filled his senses. He had not felt this famished in a very long time and he wondered how he would manage through an evening surrounded with delicious unsuspecting prey without giving into his cravings.

Are you going to be alright? sent Notus. The monk's worried hazel eyes descended upon him from across the seat.

I'll be fine, he replied, doubting his own truth. He rolled his shoulders and looked out through the shaded glass window, ignoring Notus' snort.

City lights flickered by, slowing down and speeding up dependent upon the driver's expertise. It was when the conveyor belt of images ceased to flow past for more than a minute that he realized they had arrived at their destination.

Leaning forward, his hand was poised on the lever to open the door when it was ripped from his grasp. The limo door opened at the expert hands of the chauffeur and the Angel looked up to see him standing at attention, black gloved hands on the door, refusing to meet his gaze. Uncertain whether the driver's apprehension was due to fear of his appearance, or some sense of the danger he was in, fear permeated through the mortal's pores, spicing the blood that raced through his body.

A hand lowered on his shoulder. "You are not alright."

Ignoring Notus' observation, he stepped out of the car before instinct would overcome control. He witnessed blue eyes dart at him before fixating upon the monk climbing out of the car, believing if he dismissed the obvious threat it would go away. The perspiration from the man's temples proved otherwise, as did the thudding vessel of the carotid artery.

Straightening his robes, Notus grabbed his elbow and forcibly turned the Angel. It was then that he realized how close he had been to losing control. To do so, in public, would have been a disaster.

A breath escaped him in a shuddering sigh. Notus was correct. He was not alright. He was hungry.

"Get a hold of yourself," hissed Notus as he guided them both into a throng of event goers that lined up to enter into the Michael Lee-Chin entrance beneath the crystalline structure attached to the ROM.

Scents of perfume mingled with flowers and spices, flavouring the scent of blood that permeated off of the mortals. Placing a hand over his mouth, he closed his eyes trying to gain control. With so many mortals, their effervescence sinking into his senses, he did not know how much more control he could muster. Every cell in his being cried out to grasp at the first unsuspecting mortal and devour them. He had made a mistake, a fatal one if he could not get a hold of himself.

He felt a cool hand encase his free hand and the grip tightened. The sudden sensation of the monk's flesh against his own was enough for him to draw strength. He could sense Notus' desire for him to reign in instincts he had been trained centuries ago to over ride with willpower. Taking a gasping breath, he consciously pushed away the desires of his body for sustenance. His body would be succoured, but not until after the party, he promised himself. A few more breaths and he lowered the hand from his mouth and nose. Opening his eyes, he gazed down at his Chooser.

Thank you. He gave Notus' hand a squeeze before letting go.

"It won't last long," sighed Notus. "But it may last long enough."

Nodding, he stepped up to the doorman holding the guest list. Notus gave their fake names and they entered into the ROM.

Colourfully decorated marketing posters lined white painted walls in the hopes to entice museum goers to pay the extra to descend to the lowest level of the building and be given the treat of seeing works on display that had not been seen in hundreds of years, if not millennia. Little did any of the guests know that standing in their midst were two individuals older than most of the exhibit, and that one of them was responsible for more than half of the scrolls and manuscripts protected in their environmentally controlled glass cases.

The ROM was a dichotomy of old and new, clashing in a way that one either loved or hated. Regardless of one's personal tastes one thing was certain, the new addition meant greater floor space for the exhibits.

Walking past the line up on the left for the coat check, the two Chosen emerged from under the white angled ceiling and walls of the Crystal and into the spacious *Hyacinth Gloria Chen Court* that bridged the old yellow bricked building with the stark drywall of the new. The differences were always jarring to the senses.

Tonight more couches and chairs filled the court, allowing for party goers a place to relax and enjoy the cocktails before heading into the *Samuel Hall* beyond the five display pillars further into the building. There, in the long hall, boarded with medieval frescoes on the walls, modern tables dressed in white linen patterned the hardwood floor. A dais dressed with a table for the guests of honour blocked the entrance to the *Philosopher's Walk Wing* and its ancient Eastern treasures.

Men and women costumed in middle aged garb and holding modern cocktails drifted around the great room. Their conversations mingled into a drone occasionally punctuated by a laugh or a click of glass. Servers in page costumes and fake livery moved from group to group offering appetizers that would never have been known or tasted hundreds of years ago. Drinks as diverse as the riotous costume colours passed from servant to fake lord or lady with nary a thank you.

Stringed music floated above the murmur of conversation. It was when a young woman, not more than twenty, dressed in purple livery, came up to the Angel and Notus to offer fluted glasses of champagne that they realized they stood in shocked silence at the spectacle. Her question broke their reverie and the Angel took his eyes off the medieval menagerie to watch fear blossom across her young face. Ducking her brunette head, she scurried towards a more amenable cluster of patrons.

A deep chested chuckle swung the Angel's attention to Notus, whose face lit up in a smile. Unable to contain his mirth at the sight, Notus erupted into peals of laughter.

Heads laden with conical hats topped with colourful veils and floppy hats stuck with fake ostrich feathers turned towards the monk. Mortal faces twisting with disgusted curiosity only encouraged the monk to laugh even harder until he was bent over and tears streamed down his face. Through the halls his laughter rang until even the music halted and all was silent except for him.

Surprised at the outburst, the Angel could only stare at the monk's bent over form. It was their connection that explained it to him. Images of a past these mortals tried to emulate over lapped with the gaudy spectacle in front of them. The absurdity of it all hit him and he bit his lip in the successful attempt not to join his Chooser.

He was saved just in time by Dr. Bowen's appearance.

Dressed in a long black velvet gown hemmed with silver vines, Dr. Bowen could have stood model for a portrait of *Morgan la Fay*, except her brown hair was cut into a pixie bob, exposing her long pale neck, yet covering her ears with longer hair in the front. Black eyeliner accentuated her pale blue eyes. The silver girdle emphasized her willowy curves. Mouth suddenly dry, he tapped Notus on the shoulder.

"Oh my dear, Elizabeth," managed Notus as he strained for breath and brushed the tears from his eyes. "What a delightful party!"

"I'm so glad that you're enjoying yourself," smiled the curator. Her blue eyes still queried the true culprit of her co-worker's outburst.

Aware of Elizabeth's discomfort, Notus smoothed the wrinkles from his robe. "Ah…yes…well," he attempted. "It is that this party has brought back some old memories."

The Angel shook his head at the statement. His memories did not elicit such mirth. Already the murmur of renewed conversation accompanied by ethereal music filled the hall.

"I'm happy to hear that." Dr. Bowen turned her attention up at the Angel. "And do you find the party equally enjoyable?"

He could feel Notus' gaze, the monk's curiosity touched his flesh evoking a shiver. Under it was concern in how he was to answer. Taking a breath, he dragged his attention away from her pale smooth neck to fix onto her wide mysterious eyes.

"We've just arrived, Dr. Bowen," he answered, his voice barely above a whisper.

His non committal answer raised a fine brown brow and he quickly amended, "So far it has been quite impressive."

The answer did not alleviate the sudden tension that tended to develop between them.

Dr. Bowen gave him the once over, a flicker of disapproval crossed her features before her eyes caught his. It was strangely uncomfortable to have someone match gazes with him. Most kept their eyes diverted, but after the encounter at the condo where he was forced to relinquish his sword into her care, she never backed down. In response, he adamantly refused to call her by her given name.

"I do believe that sunglasses are a modern affectation," she said. "Why not take them off?" Her long, graceful hands lifted to remove the offending plastic.

His hands reached up to grab hers before he could be exposed. "No," his voice harsher than intended.

He lowered her hands, only to release them when they were far away from his face.

"You'll have to excuse the lad, my dear, but it's better for all if he keeps his glasses on," interjected Notus.

He Sent a thank you to the monk for the timely rescue and received a curt nod tinged with disappointment.

Unhappy with the obtuse reason, Dr. Bowen shrugged a shoulder and smiled. Taking Notus' hand, she slipped it through hers to lead him into the Samuel Hall.

Dining tables dressed in white and accompanied by black

chairs held conversing patrons patiently waiting the time when dinner would be called. The Angel turned to glance over his right shoulder as he followed, taking in the medieval suit of armour that stood behind the ancient halberd, partisan and two handed sword in one of the five display cases that marked the entrance into the Hall. It was only due to his Chosen sight that he was able to see the rampaging lion imprinted in the blade of the sword. Overhead theatre lights dressed in coloured gels aimed at the head table while florescent light illuminated the rest of the grand hall.

He followed Dr. Bowen and Notus as she turned left to proceed into the *Rotunda*, the original entrance to the ROM. Their scholarly conversation flitted to his ears only to be ignored. There was only so many times he could hear the same thing. This was their passion and he did not share it.

Past the dual staircases, one to the left and to the right, each adorned with gigantic Haida totem poles, one larger than its brother, he noticed that Dr. Bowen steered Notus to a small group of elaborately dressed men and women standing in the centre of the rotunda, conversing.

They were nearly there when a shout from above rang through the beautiful room, before thunderous feet echoed down the stairwell.

"Mom!" cried the voice again.

The teenage girl nearly crashed into him.

Placing a hand on the girl's shoulder to prevent her from falling backwards, he drew back as her robin's egg blue eyes widened at the sight of him.

He took in the bizarre combination of ancient and modern dress that the girl wore. A black gown similar to Dr. Bowen's was short enough to show off fish-net black stocking legs and Doc Martins boots. Her long black hair was tied up into a mass of curls and a black headband sporting white skulls kept stray hairs from her pale face. Dark eyeliner swirled at the corners of her eyes in intricate patterns. Her ears were littered with silver rings and studs. Even her nose held a glittering ring.

A smile lit up her face and he snatched back his hand. He had also seen that smile over the ages.

"Vee, watch where you're going." Dr. Bowen's voice was stern. She turned to face him, Notus beside her. "This is Paul Nathaniel and his friend, Gwyn. This is my daughter Vivianne."

"Vee," corrected the girl. She drew her gaze away from him just long enough to take in Notus' robed figure with a nod before returning to smile up at him.

"Vee," amended her mother as she came to stand beside her daughter.

Standing side by side the resemblance between mother and daughter was striking. The only clear differences were that Vee was shorter and more roundly built, giving the teen greater curves.

"How wonderful to meet you, my dear!" Notus approached the girl with a smile and took her hands in his, much to her chagrin and the Angel's relief. "Your mother has told me much about you. You are as lovely as she said."

Vee gave her mother a sideways glance as if to ask what was wrong with this guy.

"Thank you, Paul. She is a gem." Dr. Bowen's tone slightly soured in recognition that her sixteen year old was about to say or do something inappropriate. "What was it that required you to shout at me from the second floor?"

"Oh, Mom! You didn't tell me you got more amethyst geodes for the Gold and Minerals exhibit!" Vee's face completely changed, brightening with excitement, her fixation on the Angel broken.

"I didn't know, sweetie. That's not my division."

"They're awesome! You so need to come and see them!" She took her mother's hand in an attempt to guide her upstairs.

The corner of Dr. Bowen's mouth tightened as she stood her ground. Vee glanced back when she realized her mother was not following. "Not now. I've got guests and I want Paul to meet a couple of people."

Vee's shoulders slumped, disappointment written across her pale features. "Okay." She turned to head back up the stairs.

Recognizing the despondent tone, Dr. Bowen called to her daughter before she alighted up the stone steps. "We'll go together after dinner. Just the two of us, okay?"

Vee nodded. All that was left of her was the sound of her heavy boots echoing in the stairwell. Once she was gone, Dr. Bowen sighed and turned back to her guests. "I'm sorry about that. Vee has been going through a hard time since her father passed away nearly a year ago."

"Oh, I'm sorry to hear that," offered Notus.

Dr. Bowen shrugged. "He was a good father even if he was a lousy husband. We amicably divorced when he came out of the closet. Vee was very young at the time. Anyway, that's the past." She turned to Notus with a smile. "Before dinner is called I'd like to introduce you to a few people."

The idea of being introduced to even more strangers did not sit well with the Angel as the mingling scent of blood touched his senses, sparking the hunger that had been held at bay with the help of Notus' control. It was clear that it was fading, as he knew it eventually would. He needed to get away before he did something both he and the monk would regret. "If you'll excuse me, I'm going downstairs to check on my sword."

"The exhibit isn't officially opened until after the dinner," remarked Dr. Bowen. She tilted her head as she gazed up at him.

"It's alright, my dear." Notus patted her hand as he held it through the circle of his arm. "The boy's been missing it." Shifting through the leather pouch hanging from the cord, Notus plucked out a security card and gave it to him. *Go and get your head cleared. If you can, please feed. I'll see you upstairs for dinner.*

The Angel nodded his thanks and took the card. As he left the *Rotunda* to head to the stairs that would lead him to the second basement level and the exhibit that held his sword he heard Notus explain, "He's not good in crowds, my dear, though he's much better than he used to be."

He shook his head, sending his long white hair swinging. He was not denying Notus' explanation. He was getting better, but that was a matter of degree. In the past he would have balked at coming to such a party. The gazes of the women and men would make his skin crawl and the whispered comments would entice him to flee. His reaction to crowds was even worse amongst his own kind because too many of them debated amongst themselves whether he was Chosen at all. If the answer was yes, then his differences would be argued as to whether or not he should be Destroyed. It was one of those differences that kept the Chosen from being annihilated by the Vampires and for that reason alone, he gathered, he was still alive. It was probably a matter of time before even that would no longer be a barrier to the day where he would be drawn and quartered before being left to the sun. A shiver ran up his spine as he descended two flights down the *Stairs of Wonder* in the Crystal portion of the building.

The entrance to the exhibit was off to his right as he left the stairwell. No one was around and he inhaled the scents of paint and glues mingling with the clean air forced through the vents. Behind it all was a trace of the blood scent of the mortals above as if it had followed him down into the bowels of the earth to entice him to return to the surface. Without a second thought, he slipped the card through the reader, heard the click and opened the doors.

He stood at the entrance to the exhibit. The cash and ticket taker's booth was to the left, but it was the wall before him that captured his attention. Illuminated texts masterfully recreated, their words translated into modern English and French, stood testimony to Notus' magnificent expertise. He could see the style of his Chooser in every brush stroke and it was clear the monk had outdone himself. It was no wonder that Notus would come home elated from working most of the night. He had never before been given the opportunity to ply his talents onto such a large canvas.

Following the guiding ropes, his white fingers absently trailing the black fabric, the Angel finally came to stand before the artistry. He laid a hand on a bestiary that included a medieval monk petting a unicorn, its horn foiled in gold. Of course it was not real gold, but whatever Notus had done made it appear as if it were. The length of the wall was just an introduction, a mood setter for the general public, so as to transport them back into a time they could only read about or imagine. For the Angel it brought memories of blood and pain sporadically peppered with peace, an era when the Angel of Death truly took form. A frown pulled his full lips as he moved on.

It was in the next section, as he slipped around the wall, that artefacts of paint brushes and pots found in archaeological sites were now placed in glass cases to be illuminated from the vertical lighting from above. In other display cases, monastic robes and vestments from hundreds of years ago went on to help explain life within the cloister. Bi-lingual panels beside the artefacts described pieces of history illuminated by what lay contained behind glass.

He moved through the gallery, taking in the sights as a melancholy flowed over him. It was bizarre to see that what had once been new to his eyes now held mystery and antiquity for those who live so briefly upon this earth. Taking a shuddering breath, he felt very old indeed.

Through the maze he travelled, moving deeper into the past until he found what he was looking for. There, in the middle of the fourth gallery, large cases containing ancient manuscripts and scrolls were stationed around a tall central glass case holding Geraint's sword. Illuminated by a theatre light pointing directly down upon it the sword glowed white. Held point down in a special stand made just for it, the sword seemed to float in the case. It now appeared to be something of fantasy rather than the scythe of the Angel of Death who had claimed hundreds, if not thousands, of lives. No sign that it had ever been drenched in red flowing blood tarnished the brilliant glimmer of the ancient steel.

He had not seen his sword since he had reluctantly given it into Dr. Bowen's care and seeing it thus deepened his frown. No longer did it appear the reaper's blade he had carried through the ages, using it to defend Notus and himself and eventually the rest of the Chosen. Here, beneath the lights, it looked old, worn and very tired beneath its reflected light.

His steps rang out as he crossed the distance to stand a hand's breath away from the glass. There was no doubt that it was well cared for. In fact, whoever was in charge of metallurgy at the ROM did a wonderful job in cleaning up parts of the hilt that he could never fully do himself. He laid his hand on the glass, a sudden need to feel the sword's heft and balance filling him. It was the sight of the black leather bracer descending down over his wrists to encircle his hands up to his fingers and thumb that made him relinquish the cool glass.

Four black benches squared the case and he backed up to sit on one, never breaking his gaze from the sword. When did his past become an archaeological curiosity? He sighed, gazing up at his sword turned relic.

Ever since the Vampires fled Britain and the rest of Europe he did not have much to do. No longer were the lighter *katanas* necessary except for practice. Death had followed him wherever he went but for the last decade or so it was no longer the case. An ironic thought flitted through his mind. Was the Angel of Death obsolete? Staring at his sword, he frowned, disturbed by the question. If that was the case what did that mean for him?

Footsteps sounded through the gallery, but it was the scent of young blood that brought him out of his contemplations to see who was coming up behind him. He turned his head to watch Dr. Bowen's daughter tentatively walk through the gallery, her eyes wide as she took in the sights. She had not noticed him, but her smell stilled him except for his predatory eyes behind his sunglasses.

He studied her as she moved from display to display, bringing her luscious blood closer. It was when he swallowed in expectation of what her hot blood would taste like as it poured down his throat that he came out of his reverie. He had not realized how hungry he was. The girl was in danger and she did not even recognize it.

Her boots rang out through the desolate space, bouncing off the walls to echo through the gallery. The smell of soap tinged with sandalwood mingled with bloodscent making his mouth water in anticipation. Cocking his head to the side, his white hair falling to brush against his thigh, he opened his mouth and inhaled her scent as if she were a bouquet of flowers. Every rational thought in him screamed that he should leave as his visceral instincts stilled his body with the promise of a kill. He was a guest in a private party and to sup from the hostess' daughter would not go over well with his Chooser, but it was the throbbing need within his own body that tore through logic and forced his nose to flare, drinking in her scent.

Blue eyes caught the sword in the case and she whistled. The sharp piercing sound was enough for him to gain trembling control. If she came any closer, he knew that the last vestiges of that control would leave him. Instead she stood gawking at his sword suspended and lit up like a Christmas ornament as he watched her as a cat with a mouse.

It was when her eyes slid off the blade and onto him that she started. Recovering quickly, Vee smiled and strode over to him unaware of the immediate danger she placed herself in.

Backed by the bench, he could not move away without brushing against the girl. Instead he chose to be rude. Swinging his long legs over the bench he stood behind it, the black length acting as an artificial barrier. It was not enough to decrease her scent, but it gave him a false sense of security – a line drawn in the sand. He trembled as he felt his control slowly fray, his rational mind praying she would leave.

It was clear by the frown on her face that she was aware of his avoidance tactic. Of course she could never know the true reason why he retreated when all he wanted to do was lunge onto her, devouring her to the last drop. The thought sent a tremor through him.

"Mom told me you'd be down here," she explained, tilting her face so that her querulous eyes could pierce his behind the sunglasses. "Everyone is being called to dinner."

He clenched his jaw, grating his teeth in an effort to control his blood lust at the images her statement inadvertently evoked.

When he did not reply, Vee stuck out her pierced lip in a disconcerted pout. With a shrug and a shake of her head she turned and walked away. He only released his guard once the ringing of her boots mingled with the clunk of the door opening.

The scent of the girl still lingered in the large room, but without her presence it was manageable. Closing his eyes, he released the breath he had unwittingly held in a tremulous huff that slumped his shoulders. It had taken every ounce of control but he had managed it. Turning around he sat down on the bench. With elbows on his knees he placed his head in his hands in an effort to still his shaking.

A pop, followed by a series of pops, filtered to his preternatural hearing and he lifted his head at the faint sound of screams. A sense of dread overwhelmed him and he cried out to Notus.

Stay down stairs! Notus replied harshly. Panic and worry filled the monk's emotions.

What's going on? sent the Angel. A couple more pops and then, closer than he would like, the sound of a girl struggling with someone.

The party is being by robbed by a group of gun men, sent Notus. *I'm fine. Just keep safe.*

I'm coming. He rose to leave the exhibit.

No. A few of the guests have been shot. You are in no state to be around spilled blood.

He frowned and knew the truth of the matter. He had nearly lost control with Vee. Going into a room where violence had already shed blood would be too much. *What are you going to do?*

Whatever I can. Now stay safe.

Groaning with the need to do something, he walked to the doors that acted as both exit and entrance and instantly pulled back into the shadows before his hand could alight on the bar.

The door swung open. Vee stumbled in, a mask of terror on her face before a man all dressed in black, even to the balaclava covering his features, strode in training an UZI submachine gun upon the girl. His black gloved fingers held ready on the trigger.

"Move it!" he ordered, nuzzling the barrel into the girl's back.

"Take me to it!"

Whimpering, Vee shuffled forward, too scared to move.

The prodding came again and she stumbled with a cry. Black streaks tarnished her pale face as paint coloured tears trailed down her cheeks.

The Angel backed further into the darkness and watched as another, a woman, dressed and concealed like the male, followed.

They have Vee, he Sent Notus, never relinquishing his sight of the thieves.

Shock came as his reply. *Do whatever you can, my son. Memories can be dealt with afterwards.*

He slipped further into the darkness, keeping his eyes trained upon the criminals and their hostage. They did not appear to notice him as they followed Vee through the maze of artefacts. It did not make any sense as to why they were ignoring so many priceless items until they halted before the case that held his sword.

Cold dread filled him as he watched the two study the design of the case. Vee's fear spiced blood could not elicit the hunger he had felt moments ago. The realization that it was his sword that they had come to steal set his heart hammering in his ears. There was no way he was going to allow anyone to take his sword without his permission.

Relinquishing the shadow, he stepped into the light. "You do not want to do that," he stated, his quiet command filling the exhibit area.

Vee spun around, eyes holding fear and hope in equal measure, before the man yanked her into an awkward embrace. His strong arm held her tightly around the midsection while the UZI's nozzle dug into her ribs. The woman looked up long enough to take note of the situation before returning to the quandary of how to get the case open. A smile lit her full lips as she drew back her fist and hit the thick glass square on.

The sound of shattering glass mingled with the panicked breathing of the girl. It was then the Angel realized he could hear no heartbeat from the perpetrators. Despite how famished he was, there was no choice but to rescue Vee from the Vampire's clutches.

"Uh, uh, uh," tisked the man, digging the UZI into Vee's chest. "You don't want to do that, Angel, or your little girlfriend is going to become an early evening snack." He tossed the submachine gun over his shoulder by its strap and grabbed the sobbing girl by the throat, exposing her neck with his grasp of her hair. Exposed, the vessel danced a frantic beat beneath pale skin.

Gritting his teeth, he began the Summoning. He would feed, but not from the girl.

The male caught sight of a wisp of white oozing across the floor. Anger and fear mingled in his blue eyes as he clutched the mortal girl closer, forcing her head back onto his shoulder. When he spoke again, the glistening of white fangs were now the deadly threat.

"Call it off, Angel, or she dies now," he ordered. The girl sobbed louder as he shook her in a demonstration of ownership.

The Angel cut off the spell that would bring forth the White Faced demons. His hands locked into fists. It would not take much. He was faster than a Vampire, but the female now held his sword, twisting and turning it to catch the light. He took another step forward.

The male Vampire growled, licking the girl's neck but never breaking his gaze with the Angel. The promise was sincere and no matter how fast the Angel could move he could not move fast enough to halt the Vampire from ripping Vee's throat apart.

Impotent to help and incapable of stopping them from taking his beloved sword, he followed them, always keeping his distance, as the Vampire carefully backed away.

Chosen and Vampire, their eyes locked on each other. The male carefully followed his female partner, never relinquishing the girl. It was when the female opened the door to allow her and her partner out that the Angel knew it was now or never. Silently, he leapt forward only to find Vee stumbling into his arms. Stabilizing her, he watched in growing horror as the Vampires bounded up the stairs, his sword in their possession.

Setting the girl aside without a thought of her well being, the Angel sped to follow the two Vampires. There was no way in hell he was going to allow them to steal his only true possession. Up he followed, past the glittering rocks, the feathered birds, and other artefacts that bequeathed the stairwell its wondrous name. He heard a door opening and came upon it before it was closed half way. Glancing to his right, it was the fast footpads to his left that told him in which direction to follow. Turning down the hallway he ran from the *Crystal* and into the second floor of the *Hillary and Galen Weston Wing*.

Ignoring the glassed in displays, he could see the Vampire ahead turn right. The sound of ringing steps told him that he was on the Rotunda's stairs, the same stairwell that Vee had descended from earlier. Turning to follow, he halted at the stone landing to listen before sprinting up the steps three at a time.

The third story was as far up as the stairs would manage, but there was another level above, one that could only be accessed by an elevator. He got to the lift just as the doors closed and in his frustration he punched the metal door, denting it. It felt like a century had passed before the door opened at the button's call and he rode it to the top. It was then he realized he had done something completely stupid – he had allowed himself to be boxed in.

Glancing up, he saw the escape hatch and knocked it open in time to jump through the hole as a rain of bullets peppered the car.

As suddenly as the UZI fire started it halted. The Vampire who had held Vee hostage carefully entered, checking for wounded. The female was nowhere to be seen. With preternatural speed the Angel slipped through the hatch, swinging with enough force to expel the creature from the car as his feet caught the Vampire square in the chest with a sickening crunch.

Dropping down, the Angel followed the path of destruction the Vampire's flight had caused and swore when he could not find the man. The smoking UZI was left in the litter of destruction of broken glass and slivered wood.

A shadow shifted on the floor of the *RBC Glass Room.* Instinct and centuries of training took over. Spinning around he blocked the round-house kick, curling his arm around the limb while his other hand struck the knee. The Vampire howled in pain as the kneecap was shattered. He twisted around to yank his leg out of the Angel's grip. Once out of reach of the Angel, the Vampire fled across the room, his knee cap almost healed.

The Angel gave chase. He needed to capture this Vampire to find out where his female accomplice had disappeared to, taking his sword with her. Through the fire doors and onto the rooftop he was surprised at the vicious storm that pelted rain and marble sized hail. Screaming wind whipped his white locks, obscuring his view.

Squinting into the tempest, he caught sight of the Vampire on top of the wing they had just occupied, running north along the roof. The Angel followed with a running jump that landed him on the slippery stones that covered the flat roof. Lightning flared overhead, followed directly by a crashing boom that cancelled out all sound for a brief moment. With his balanced restored he sped after the Vampire through the curtain of rain and ice.

Lightning halted as he moved with preternatural speed. He could see the Vampire glance back at him before racing over the peaked roof in the centre of the Wing. For a moment the Angel lost sight of his quarry as he too scurried over the glistening shingles.

The storm lashed him with its full fury as he halted for a fraction of a moment before continuing his pursuit along the west side of the wing. Again the storm paused as he ran to catch the Vampire that now stood motionless at the edge of the roof.

Turning to face his hunter, the Vampire pulled off the balaclava, his dark blond hair plastered to his head. A smile crossed his ruggedly handsome face. "And let the games begin!" he shouted above the storm. With a salute the Vampire jumped over the edge.

The Angel slammed into the concrete edge of the guard and watched the Vampire slide down the outside of the Crystal. Lightning flashed as if the sky were taking photographs of the event, the thunderous booms were nature's shutters.

The Vampire landed without any mishap. The police that were called shouted to each other, pointing at the fleeing perpetrator with their guns and calling him to halt and put his hands up.

Without a second thought, the Angel stood up on the concrete guard, preparing to follow. Everything moved so slowly, the sudden sense of static filled the air around him as he shifted to the balls of his feet to propel him forward, and then there was white brilliance.

XII

emi-automatic gunfire took everyone unaware. Many screamed and tried to flee only to find black clad gunmen blocking the exits. Other party goers ducked, hitting the deck to fearfully peer up at their assailants. The scent of terror and spilt blood filled the air as Notus crouched beside Elizabeth behind the dinner table he had thrown onto its side, the expensive china and crystal broken, lying mixed with silverware. Of course such a flimsy piece of metal would not stop a bullet, but it did help to provide a hiding space. He held onto Elizabeth, forcing her to stay hidden as she attempted to find her daughter in the chaos.

Trying to still her shaking, he wrapped his arm around her waist, holding her close. He had Pushed her to keep quiet, her rising panic would have been detrimental in finding her daughter, possibly getting one, if not both, killed. Risking a peek around the side of the table, Notus watched as four gunmen herded several partygoers into the Samuel Hall. A man dressed as a courtier clutched his arm as it dripped red jewels onto the ground. At gunpoint they were forced face down on the wooden floor to then have their valuables plucked from their persons. Shouts and cries resounded off the brick walls, occasionally punctuated by gunfire. So far only one or two had been hit.

It was the sound of rubber soled feet that turned Notus to stare up the length of a barrel. Elizabeth began to sob. It was so tempting to just grab the barrel and rip the gun from the man but Notus stopped short, his eyes widening at the sight of the fanged smile on the Vampire's face.

"Looky here," drawled the Vampire, his accent pure southern gold. "What do we have here?" He motioned with the nozzle of the UZI for Notus to stand.

Ignoring Elizabeth, Notus slowly stood, never removing his eyes from the plain brown of the Vampire's; the rest of the face hidden by the same styled black balaclava as all the others. There was no doubt in Notus' mind that all the gunmen were Vampires and he was at a great disadvantage. Despite being able to heal from such things, the unloading of a clip from an UZI would leave him incapacitated to the whims of the Vampires. He wished he had not told the boy to stay away. For the first time Notus wanted to see those horrific ethereal creatures his son could call.

Other Vampires turned, some smiling at the luck that befell them. To have captured the Angel's Chooser was even better than what they were sent to do. Their predatory gazes would have sent a shudder up the monk's spine had he not squashed it, returning tit for tat. The only thought that flickered into mind was that he should have agreed to let the boy train him in some basic self defence. That way he would be able to create some sort of distraction, allowing the mortals to flee.

He was about to ask the Vampire what he and his cohorts wanted when another Vampire appeared from the *Stair of Wonders* waving his boy's sword in triumph.

"I've got it!" shouted the female thief. "Let's get out of here!"

The Vampire in front of Notus cocked his head to the side and gave a little nod, his gaze landing on Elizabeth. "Better luck next time. It's too bad; she looks to be a delicious cow." With that, he turned and followed the woman down into the *Canadian Court*. The four others turned in different directions and fled with their stolen treasures.

It took but a moment before a new type of chaos to descend. The emergency doors in the Rotunda exploded open at the same time the main entrance and after hours doors opened to allow a stream of Emergency Task Force police in to secure the building. Regular uniformed officers followed, accompanied by blasts of cold damp wind.

Notus helped Elizabeth to her feet, calming her with his preternatural abilities, wishing someone could do the same for him. When her tears ceased to flow, they turned as one as Vee came flying into her mother's embrace. Standing back to give mother and daughter a moment, Notus realized that the boy had yet to make his entrance. He was about to say something when without warning the ROM's lights blackened out, white light poured in the doors, and a crashing boom set the building to shudder as agony ripped through his body.

Collapsing to his hands and knees, Notus fought to regain his breath against the intense pressure on his chest, his heart beating erratically in his ears. The dark spots that littered his vision were made more pronounced once the lights flickered back on. He felt a hot hand on his shoulder and somewhere in the muffled sounds his ears picked up the slow speech of Elizabeth asking him what was wrong.

He shook his head, trying to clear it and surprisingly the pain receded, as well as the spots and stuffy ears. Taking Elizabeth's hand in his he stood, his body creaking and groaning like an old man's.

"I'm alright," he lied, his voice quavering as he refused to look at Elizabeth's mascara smeared face even as he dropped her hand. No, something was definitely wrong. Closing his eyes he Sent to his son and received – nothing. He shook his head at what that could possibly mean. He needed answers to the boy's whereabouts and the only one who could know that was standing next to her mother.

"What happened in the exhibit, Vivianne?" asked the monk, his voice shaking.

Vee looked up to her mother. Elizabeth nodded and the girl matched worried gazes with Notus. "I went down to tell him that dinner was called, but he didn't answer, so I left."

"What happened then?" pressed Notus, impatience tingeing and strengthening his tones.

The girl, her face smudged as much as her mothers, told Notus what happened down in the exhibit, how the gunman called Notus' friend "Angel" before the woman broke the glass case and they fled with the sword. Notus could tell that Vee omitted some details, but he did not feel the need to push right now. It was when Vee told him that the boy chased up the stairs after the male that he broke off listening, a new fear clutching his gut.

Turning around, he made to go up the stairs only to be halted by talk meant for police ears. It seemed that someone had fallen from the roof, possibly struck by lightning, and that EMS personnel were onsite performing CPR. A pit of foreboding gripped Notus. Shaking his head in disbelief, Notus rushed through the throngs moving in and out of the main entrance to stop short in the slowing rain outside of the *Crystal*.

There, under the protection provided from the protrusion of the structure, lay his son on damp concrete, his long white hair splayed on grey as paramedics worked to revive him. Notus did not need to be told that the boy no longer breathed and that his heart no longer beat. The silence was deafening. Though a Chosen could consciously halt these functions without any detriment, Notus knew that this was not the cause. In a daze he stepped forward, watching as a paramedic pumped oxygen through a mask as the other compressed the boy's chest. It was when they brought out the defibrillator, ripping the shirt and placing the pads on the scarred pale chest, that the reality of what he felt during the lightning strike, hit him

Shaking his head, tears filling his eyes, Notus did not care about his preternatural speed or strength. Only one thought drove him forward, pushing him past frightened guests, police and reporters. In a haze he heard the paramedics call clear and watched the boy's body jerk to the current. Notus should have felt something through their connection but there was nothing.

He came to the ring of police providing a barrier to the onlookers, halting his mad rush on the hand now pressed against his shoulder. Breaking his gaze off the boy's supine form, Notus looked up into the firm features of a police officer.

"I'm sorry, sir. You are not allowed further."

"He's my son." Notus did not intend to Push. The weight of his need overrode the officer's will. His glazed brown eyes proved no resistance as Notus slipped past him and into the circle provided for the paramedics.

Notus arrived in time to watch the boy's body lifted as another wave of electricity slammed through his body. This time it was rewarded with the jumpstarting heartbeat. The paramedic on bag duty quickly glanced up at the intruder before checking to see if his patient's breathing became stabilized. "Who are you?" he demanded.

"I'm the boy's father." The words slid out without a thought. The medic made a face as if he did not believe him. "Adoptive," amended Notus.

The medic nodded, returning to the care of his patient as his partner brought the gurney and lowered it as far as it would go. Notus did not require any other invitation to kneel at the boy's side, taking his warm hand in his own.

The sensation widened his eyes and deepened his disbelief. It was not possible!

The second paramedical mumbled an "excuse me" as he took the boy's other hand, a long needle connected to an I.V. bag. It dawned on Notus a fraction too late what the medic's intention was. His order for the man to stop came too late.

The needle pierced into the back of the boy's pale hand, the bracers having been removed and laid on the ground. Three pairs of eyes grew in horror as black tendrils serpentined through the vein viper fast, branching up into the vessels. Notus could not believe what he witnessed. Never before had the boy had such a sudden onset from even a small piece of iron. He watched the toxic spider weave a disjointed web, sending the boy into convulsions.

Having dealt with these attacks early on in the boy's healing from the Vampire's tortures, Notus threw himself over the boy in an attempt to still him before he could do damage.

"Take it out!" he cried.

The medics scurried to follow protocol. One brought out a syringe filled with a clear chemical.

His declaration ignored, Notus angrily yelled, "He's having a reaction to the iron. Take out the I.V.!"

"It's surgical steel," snapped the one with the syringe. "He can't react to it."

Gritting his teeth, Notus Pushed, "Take the I.V. out *now*!"

Dropping the syringe, the medic grabbed his patient's arm and took out the two inch needle. Within a few moments the black tendrils broke apart and began to fade, taking the paroxysms with it. Carefully, Notus sat up, his hand resting on the boy's shoulder, listening to the boy's ragged breath.

Everything was wrong. The boy should have woken up by now. Instead he lay on the concrete, his white hair splayed in soggy ropes around his pale face. What was most disconcerting was that Notus felt nothing, absolutely nothing, from the boy. No pain. No emotion. No thought. The implications drove him to his feet at the same moment the boy was lifted onto the gurney.

They should not be taking him to the hospital. He should stop them and take the boy home for his eventual quick recovery. Against all reason, Notus allowed the paramedics to take his son.

A hand alighted on his arm and he turned to peer up into

Elizabeth's worried blue eyes. "They'll let you ride with him," she said softly. "I'm finished speaking to the police, for now. We'll follow."

Numb, Notus could only nod. He followed the paramedics to the ambulance, its lights flashing blue and white. Somewhere in the back of his mind he noticed it had stopped raining.

XIII

The stark white hall lined with the occasional occupied gurney and sporadic plastic moulded chairs echoed voices that called out in pain or in stern directives from medical personnel. Underlying the cries were the shushed voices from those across the hall, hidden by drapes concealing patients under care in bed sized cubicles and the machines that monitored them. In a blue plastic chair Notus sat, elbows on his knees, resting his chin in his hands, fingers covering his mouth and nose. To any passers-by he appeared the concerned family member. Little did they know how right and how wrong they were.

Notus watched a gurney, carrying a motor vehicle accident victim, wheel past. Blood splattered across the young girl's damaged face and chest. Cuts oozed their precious liquid, staining the sheets and blankets that failed to keep her shocked body warm. Frantic emergency crews ran along, their expert hands already at work. It had been a very long time since Notus had been around such a strong scent of fresh blood. He also realized, too late, that he had not fed as efficiently as he had thought. Trying not to inhale too deeply, the monk watched the unconscious girl be whisked down the hall. Her sporadic and failing heartbeat called to him to follow. Releasing a shuddering breath, Notus closed his eyes in prayer both for the young woman and for the boy who lay in the bed curtained off across the hall.

It should not be like this. Everything was going wrong. He witnessed the shocked expressions on the nurses' faces; one so shaken that tears fell from her eyes. He knew what upset them and had the boy been awake he would have been ashamed into anger. Notus tried to ignore the scents of blood, pain and fear. What he could not ignore was the evidence placed before him, no matter how unbelievable it seemed.

A hand alighted on his shoulder and he glanced up at Elizabeth and Vee. Taking the cup of coffee she offered, Notus sat back. Her presence was strangely comforting.

"Any word?" she asked, sitting in the vacant seat beside him.

Vee slid down the wall to sit on the floor beside her mother, her knees bent to act as a table for her cup of steaming liquid. Her gaze fell onto a spot in the middle of the floor, a sad frown on her face. It was clear to Notus that the girl was well versed with waiting in hospitals. He also noticed that they had taken the time to clean up their faces, but they were far from perfect.

Notus shook his head; his brown and silver hair fell into his eyes only to be brushed back by hand.

Elizabeth accepted the news with a nod and sipped her coffee.

The three of them sat there in silent concern. It was when Notus watched a doctor and nurse enter into the draped cubical the boy lay in that the monk sat up in expectation. Several more minutes slowly ticked by until the doctor left the boy, the nurse closing the drapes behind them and pointed towards the monk. The doctor nodded and walked across the hall. The nurse walked down the hall to enter into another curtained off cubical.

"Mr. Nathaniel?"

Notus placed the untouched coffee on the floor and stood up to greet the man, slipping his hand into doctor's dark hand.

"I'm Dr. Thompson," he introduced. His voice held the hint of the Islands in it, as did his dark skin and nearly black eyes. "Your son has a concussion, some bruises and a burn on his right shoulder. He is a very lucky young man to have survived not only a lightning strike, but a fall from the roof of a building. From what I was told, he slid most of the way off of the side of the ROM's *Crystal*."

"Will he be released soon?" asked Notus

Dr. Thompson shook his head. "He hasn't awakened yet. We're going to keep him under observation until he does."

Notus frowned at the news and sat down. He could Push the doctor to release the boy, but at what cost? If he was wrong about what he suspected – and by God he wished it so – then he could reconstruct the doctor's memories if necessary. The other aspects, such as the medical records would be trickier to deal with, but placing Dr. Thompson under control would help ensure the records' destruction.

Dr. Thompson glanced at the two women beside his patient's father. "Mr. Nathaniel, may I have a word in private with you?"

The question surprised the monk and he nodded. He had a feeling what was coming. Turning to Elizabeth he did not need to say a word. With a pat on his knee, she stood. "I think it's time for me to take Vee home. Please let me know how things go."

Notus nodded and watched Elizabeth and her daughter walk down the hall. When they were far enough away, he motioned for Dr. Thompson to take the vacant seat. "What is it, doctor?"

Dr. Thompson frowned, trying to find the right words. "I've been a doctor for over twenty years and I've never met a patient like your son."

"He is unique." A sad smile lifted Notus lips and was rewarded with a nod.

"We managed to get an I.V. line into him. It was difficult. I've never seen anyone who had such a reaction to surgical steel before. I'd like to run some tests, with your permission, of course."

The request was not what the monk expected. It was out of the question and he told the doctor, reinforcing it with the Push.

"The other issue I'd like to ask, and if you do not wish to discuss it, I'll respect that," stumbled Dr. Thompson, his eyes lowering.

Ah, here we come to it, thought Notus.

"It was a shock to see such scars on him." Dr. Thomson shook his head, obviously disturbed by what he witnessed on the boy. He did not need to verbalize what was clearly written on his face.

Notus sighed and hoped what he had to say would be accepted as truth. "The boy is unique, Dr. Thompson, and for some people that gives them license to believe they have ownership to do what they will because of those differences."

Brown eyes widened in understanding. "But those scars – it is clear what someone did to him."

Notus sadly nodded, remembering the boy's slow recovery. "One hundred and fifty, even two hundred years ago, on this continent, your people were treated similarly just because of the colour of their skin. Differences are differences. For many that is enough to dehumanize another."

Dr. Thompson sighed shakily, clearly disturbed. "He must

have been young."

"Younger, yes," nodded the monk, sadly.

A couple of orderlies walked up to the cubicle and pulled the drapes back, exposing the boy's unconscious form on the bed. A tube provided oxygen to his nose, electrodes monitoring his heart connected to the machine behind him and an I.V. was hanging on the opposite side. The scar on his chest paled in comparison to the ones that covered his arms, especially the right. The sight of the boy in such a state yanked at the monk's heart.

"We're moving him to a private room," mentioned the doctor. "It's better for all concerned. You have a couple of minutes before they take him up."

Notus stood and watched the doctor stand and walk away, presumably to his next patient, before crossing the hall to stand by the boy's bedside. Placing a hand on the boy's upper arm, he frowned at the warmth and leaned in so that his forehead pressed against the side of his son's. The intoxicating blood scent arising from the boy tightened his gut.

Please answer me, he called, closing his eyes against the tears that threatened to spill. He doubted that he would ever hear his boy's thoughts again. Pulling back, he ran his fingers through his son's long white locks, noting the dampness. He did not know whether to be elated for his son or to be devastated for him. All Notus knew was that a hole was rendered in his heart at the impossible truth – his boy was now mortal.

XIV

ose held the sword across both hands as she waited for Brian to input the code that would open the back door to *The Veil* and the steep stairwell that led to their Dominus. Brian's coterie – five Vampires of various ages – animatedly talked behind her, victory filling their elation. She heard the Angel's Chooser's name mentioned a couple of times and how it would have been so easy to finally kill him had they not left when they did. Rose frowned and gazed at the sword.

It was familiar to her, but she could not place it. The photo in the newspaper article Corbie had shown her paled in comparison to the gleaming steel lying on her hands. What was even more disconcerting was that the Angel had been in the exhibit when they stole the sword. If it had not been for that mortal girl there was no doubt in Rose's mind that she and Brian would be dead.

Flickers of memory caused her to frown. She had tried not to glance at the Angel as she worked to free the sword from its case, but her eyes kept alighting upon his predatory features. Each time she had to yank her gaze away lest she become ensnared by his pale beauty. Terry was as beautiful as an angel but what had stood in front of Brian as she shattered the case *was* an angel. A knot had wound itself around her belly at the sight of him, tugging her to remember something she knew was important.

"Let's go," ordered Brian, taking her by the arm.

Reverie broken, Rose looked up at Brian. He was always stoic, as if emotions never played a part of who he was. Deciding that it was not worth the fight, right now, she followed Brian and his coterie down the dark steps, through the candlelit parlour and its gruesome artwork, to halt in Corbie's white office.

Corbie sat in his usual place behind his desk, his hair dishevelled. His dark attention did not move to his new guests, but stayed fixated upon the man standing in the centre of the room. All of the anger permeating through the office came from Corbie. The stranger appeared annoyed, but otherwise undisturbed.

Brian quickly walked over to take up his guardian pose next to his master, eliciting a raised brown brow from the guest. Corbie glanced up at his second and Brian ordered his coterie out of the room.

"Not you, Rose," snapped Corbie as she turned to leave.

Turning back to face her Dominus, Rose swallowed. Taking the steps further into the office, she gently placed the Angel's sword onto the desk. "I did what you asked."

Corbie nodded satisfactorily, sparing a glance at the sword.

The dark haired man in the charcoal business suit scowled as he walked over to examine the sword. Rose backed away from him. She had never seen the man before, but his presence filled the room, even to the point of making Corbie appear small. Rose thought it better than to venture her master's permission to turn Terry.

The stranger picked up the sword, turning it this way and that, before placing it back on the desk with an expletive. "I'm saying this one last time, Corvus Valerius Tertius. Leave him alone."

Roses' eyes widened at the revelation of Corbie's true name. Glancing at Brian, it was clear by his frown that he knew; causing Rose to wonder what was their real relationship.

Both had retained their mortal birth names. That in itself was enough evidence of their age. Vampires, upon their birth, were now bestowed new names, their Dominus or Mistresses Domina ensuring the break from the past was complete. It also allowed for that Dominus or Domina complete control over the development of the new Vampire, moulding him or her without reflections of the past life imposing upon the new. Many new Vampires' memories tended to be a mystery and their original names were a key to them. Rose knew her name was not the one bestowed upon her by mortal parents. It was a gift given by Corbie and she treasured it. Whoever she had been as a mortal was left behind in the shredded coffin at the bottom of a filled in grave half a world away.

"It's too late for that," snapped Corbie, leaning his elbows on the desk so as to hunch over them.

"It is never too late," replied the stranger. Weariness slouching his slim shoulders. "You need not walk the path Bastia set upon all those centuries ago, Corvus. You can choose another way."

"You sound like one of them," spat Rose's Dominus. His shoulders shook in contained rage.

The stranger released a sigh and shook his head, ignoring the threatening pose of the Vampire. "You are playing with fire. Bastia did the same and now she is ashes in the wind."

Corbie bristled at the mention of his Domina's demise. "That fate will not befall me. I have…insurances."

The stranger turned to face Rose, a scowl on his handsome face. He appeared to be in his mid to late twenties. In the suit he could easily pass for older, Rose noted. His nearly black hair was gelled back from a broad face. Large dark eyes rimmed with long lashes were striking, taking away from a nose that was a shade too large for his face. A full generous mouth made Rose wonder what it would feel like to have them on her neck as he fed off of her.

The thought was jarring and she took a step back from the man who measured her own height.

"Insurances," repeated the stranger, his eyes locking onto hers but clearly his words were for Corbie. "It's often better to provide a reason *not* to require insurance." He turned to face Corbie once more. "You play a dangerous game, Corvus. Do not make it necessary for me to intervene. The Angel is mine. Leave him alone."

Without waiting for a reply from Corbie, the stranger turned and strode past Rose. In that brief moment of passing, his eyes caught hers, sending a shiver of guilt down her back. She did not know why he would look at her in that manner, but as soon as he was through the exit and the door closed her anger surged to replace the unwanted emotion.

"Who was that?" she snapped. Striding over to place her hands on the desk, she glared at Corbie.

He matched her anger with a sardonic smile. "That, my dear little flower, was Thanatos."

XV

otus' hand lingered over the light switch before allowing his arm to fall. The darkness was preferable to the light of truth. Stepping into the confines of the condo, he closed the door, locking it with a click. Every movement was slow, methodical, as if he had to think to make his body move. That was not the case. The monk walked in a stupor, allowing his body to navigate mundanity on its own as he tried to process the impossible.

A red blinking light caught his attention and he shuffled to the answering machine that sat on the black leather sofa's glass end table. The boy had insisted on getting one. It was supposedly easier than the ones that local telephone service providers offered. The boy had shown him countless times but his finger hesitated, unsure of which button to press, before pressing the black playback button.

Fernando's gruff tones filled the room. "God damn it! Pick up … I need to speak with you – now! …Fine. Call me as soon as you get this." A click was followed by a beep, plunging the room into deafening silence.

Picking up the receiver, Notus dialled the number from rote. He knew to whom Fernando wished to speak. Instead the boy lay in a private hospital room hooked up to monitors and tubes.

"Hello?" said the feminine voice on the other end.

Notus inhaled sharply, wondering at the intelligence of calling the Master and Mistress of the British Chosen. He was about to hang up when he heard Bridget call his name. He lifted the reliever back to his ear.

"Paul? What happened? What's wrong?" Worry brought out her slight French accent, combining with her South London accent.

Shutting his eyes in pain, he could not speak the words. To do so would shed more than a million suns upon a truth too difficult to bear. He heard a muffled argument on the other end and the phone was passed.

"What the hell is going on, Notus?" growled Fernando. "I've been getting calls from Masters and Mistresses all over the EU – like I have any clue – as to why we all nearly passed out earlier tonight."

Notus' breath caught at the revelation. It was not supposed to happen like that. Only the Chooser or Chosen would suffer if the other died. That was what happened to the boy and explained the sudden pain Notus had felt, nearly felling him at the ROM. How the boy was killed after so many centuries remained a mystery, but if the emergency doctor was right, then it still did not explain it. Then again Notus had never heard of any other Chosen having been hit with lightning. It was a fluke. It was also a miracle that the paramedics were able to revive him. What could not be denied was the boy was no longer Chosen.

"So are you going to tell me or do I have to speak to the Angel like everyone's been demanding me to do?" threatened the Noble.

Swallowing the stone that had formed in his throat, Notus barely recognized the voice as his own. "The Angel is gone."

"What are you talking about? Gone where?"

A click and Bridget joined the conversation on another handset. "Paul, what is going on?"

Closing his eyes did not help assuage the lump in his throat or the tears that threatened to spill. "The boy—" His voice caught in an attempt to halt the truth that when spoken could no longer be denied. "He died. He is no longer Chosen."

The dam broke releasing a flood of tears.

"What?!" came the unified response.

"What happened?" asked Bridget.

"What are you talking about?" yelled Fernando.

Slowly, through a halting description, Notus explained the events of that evening, ending with the incredible revelation that the boy, after a millennium and a half, was once again mortal.

Silence filled the void, allowing Fernando and Bridget the ability to digest the news.

"That's not possible," whispered Bridget, finally breaking the silence.

"Everything about the Angel is impossible," remarked Fernando with a snort. "You will fix the problem, won't you, Notus?"

The question caught the monk unaware. "What do you mean?" he asked cautiously, afraid of the answer.

"You will Choose him again?" Fernando's question was more a statement of fact.

Notus released his baited breath in a huff. "No," he whispered into the receiver.

Shocked responses travelled the line to his ear forcing him to pull the handset away.

"Fernando! Fernando. Calm down!" Bridget's voice filled the air.

"Calm down? Don't you realize what that idiot monk is condemning him to?"

Notus sighed as he listened to the banter between Master and Mistress.

"He'll be eaten alive, literally, by the Vampires, once they find out!" continued the Noble. "They'll make what Violet did to him look like a fucking day at the fucking beach! He has to come home, now."

"To what?" replied Bridget, hotly. "Once the news is out that the Angel is no longer Chosen, what do you think the other Masters and Mistresses will demand? He'll either have to be Chosen again or put to death, and we know how most of them will vote. Notus, you *must* Choose him again before anyone finds out."

"I can't," replied the monk. Hating himself he placed the receiver to his ear. "God gave the boy a treasured gift. He's done his work in saving the Chosen and this is his reward."

"That's bullshit and you know it, Paul," spat Bridget. "What's the real reason?"

New tears trailed down the monk's face. How could he tell them that he wished that it had been he and not the boy to have been given the blessing of mortality? Jealousy percolated up to join with the desperate loneliness that filled him. He should be happy for the boy, but he could not find it within himself to be so.

He shook his head, knowing that they could not witness his denial. The boy had been Chosen accidentally – an Oath broken unwittingly. Notus cared for his charge, growing to love the boy and eventually believed he was blessed with someone to walk eternity with. It was no longer the case. The boy had received what Notus had always hoped to attain, and now he was asked to consciously break his Oath never to Choose another, thereby insuring his search for mortality was a failure.

"I'm so terribly sorry," he whispered. "I *can't.*"

Notus lowered the receiver until it fit into its cradle, cutting off Fernando's protestations.

In the darkness, Notus made his way to his bedroom. Despite the newness of the building the door creaked on its hinges. It was then he realized it was not his room, but rather the boy's.

The unmade bed awaited the boy unknowing that he could never return. A book lay open, its spine cracked despite Notus' constant insistence to treat them with more care. A black wooden stand on the dresser displayed the boy's *wakizashi* and *katana*, and on the wall behind hung his *naginata*. All appeared expecting the return of their master, unknowing that the boy's life among the Chosen was over.

Turning away from the weapons, Notus walked to the open closet, running his hand over the white cotton dress shirts, their textures soft to the touch. The scars the discipline, a scourge made of steel chain and barbs, had left on the boy's back were sensitive to the touch. Only the finest clothed his boy. But the boy was no longer his.

Pain gripped the monk around the chest and he spun to face the empty space.

The boy was no longer his!

Notus had been in a stupor, even when he spoke to Fernando and Bridget. Having spoken the words to them and witnessing the desolate room sloughed off the shock, permitting reality to crash in.

The boy was no longer his!

On unsteady legs, Notus barely made it to the dishevelled bed before his legs gave out. The scent of the boy on the bedclothes was strong in his nostrils. Lifting the expensive down pillow the boy used, Notus hugged it to his chest, tears flowing to moisten the pillowcase. For the first time since he was Chosen, millennia ago, Father Paul Notus wept.

XVI

nipping the last suture closed, Thanatos leaned back on his heels to observe his work and sighed. It was not his best, the irregularities in the sutures' spacing was evidence to this fact. It did not matter. There would be no healing, no scarring, only decay. Thanatos placed the tools of his current trade on the stainless steel tray, the clatter resounding off the concrete walls, and cocked his head to the side as he took in the nude form of the corpse before him.

He had found the cause of death in the stomach of the too skinny woman. A condom filled with crack cocaine had burst. There was a word for her kind - a mule - and her blue horsy features fit the bill perfectly.

He had seen these things over the ages. Death came to all mortals, some by choice, some by accident, some by genetics and bad luck, but most by stupidity. It was clear by the tracks in this woman's arms which route she had chosen.

Snapping off the latex gloves he hit the stop button on the recording device that had to be on during autopsies and removed the gore stained apron over his grey-green medical uniform. He would leave the body for the individuals responsible for taking her back to the freezer but before doing so there were notes to make and forms to sign off on.

The desk housing the computer sat in the corner and was splashed with cold illumination from the old CRT monitor. It was the chair that offered succour to his tired body. A couple of clicks with the mouse and the program providing him with the basics of the woman's existence came to life. Her first and last name was listed simply as Jane Doe157. No birthday, no address, no other information was filled out except for her height, weight and colouring. An estimation of age was listed, but it was always so hard to tell with heavy drug users. They always appeared much older than they were, the drugs sloughing off years the harder the drug usage.

Typing in his findings, he filled out the online form. Computers made life easier and more complicated at the same time. One of the best things he had ever done was to have Godfrey go and purchase him a typing tutorial. Now his fingers flew over the keyboard until the computer could no longer catch up. Lifting his hands, Thanatos watched the screen magically display the words he had written, his brown eyes widening at what was revealed.

Instead of his autopsy observations and conclusions the words "The Angel" repeated themselves over and over, filling in the lines of text meant for the deceased girl.

Dumbfounded, he knew he had not typed those words, or had he? Highlighting the text he hit the delete key and watched the pixels disappear. It did not erase them from his memory.

Releasing a huff, he leaned back in the chair and ran a hand over his brow before letting it fall to the armrest. He was shaken. That was the feeling he denied himself. Having seen, let alone touched the Angel's sword was the closest he had ever come.

He would have approached the Angel earlier, but fear of what to say to him, what to ask, curdled in his stomach. All his hopes were pinned upon the Angel, but what Bastia had done shattered any possibility of approaching him. He had only to watch from the distance as the Angel summoned the Dragon's Breath to eradicate the Vampires of Paris to prove that it was better to watch and to wait. After all, he had waited all these millennia; a few more centuries would not hurt if it meant that Thanatos would finally find the answers to the questions that plagued him.

It seemed now Bastia's first born would continue where she was forced to leave off. If only Thanatos had enough sway over the pup to convince him to leave the Angel alone.

It had been centuries since he stood before a Vampire. The last was when Bastia yelled at him over his obsession with the Angel and the Chosen, before she rushed out in a huff never to be seen again. His beautiful Priestess of Bast had twisted into something he never had intended to see. Now Corvus was taking up where she had left off. Corvus, the first Vampire Bastia ever created. The mortal Roman general who had been her plaything, her slave, bending to her will as she supped upon his blood. The same one who had proven that the curse continued onto the next generation, and who was now Dominus of all Vampires and set to destroy Thanatos' only chance for redemption.

Thanatos frowned. The idea of being placed in the middle of the Vampires and the Angel seemed more promise than threat. Removing the small plain metal phial that hung around his neck, Thanatos clutched it in both hands, his eyes closed in fervent prayer.

XVII

Somewhere in the distance the sound of organized chaos mingled with metallic calls to order permeated the shroud that darkened his consciousness. Computerized sounds superimposed themselves over flesh and blood voices, yanking him further into his body until pain washed away the external noise as his breath caught. Aching all over he tried to retreat into the void that succoured him, but to no avail. The pain, throbbing in time with his pounding heart, pulled him further into his body. He did not realize his groan until the sound hammered his brain, sending a wave of nausea to crash in. He was going to be sick and it took the tattered shreds of his will to push it down. Mouth dry, he wished for something to wash away the metallic cobwebs.

A familiar voice caught his attention and yanked his focus away from the bone deep ache that throbbed in time with his heart.

"Are you sure of your findings, doctor?" The familiar voice sounded weary despite the tinge of surprise. "I informed you that I did not want further tests to be done."

"I understand that, Mr. Nathaniel, but the blood tests are routine and were ordered before your request. No further tests were done in accordance to your orders." Slight annoyance coloured an Island accent. "Regardless, the findings of the blood tests have prompted me to ask you to reconsider your decision."

Tense silence masked the distant cacophony.

"What…what did you find?"

"There were many irregularities, things that registered outside the normal levels." The doctor's voice dropped into a drone. "His white count is nearly triple while his platelets are well below normal. Despite the glucose levels being normal, the HDL, LDL and triglycerides were all over the place. There was also an irregularity to the shape and colour of the red blood cells. I would like to have a full genetic profile done on your son, Mr. Nathaniel."

There was a sharp intake of breath and a subtle change in how the familiar voice spoke. "Dr. Thompson, you will cease and desist any further investigation into my son's health. Furthermore you will do whatever is necessary to delete, destroy, erase, and remove all physical and all electronic evidence and all records of my son within the hospital and any networks this hospital shares. Since my son is now awake, you will give orders for his immediate release and then you will carry out my orders. Once complete, you will forget that my son has ever been a patient of yours and you will forget having ever met me. Do you understand all that I have stated?"

Quietly, in a voice sounding drugged, the doctor repeated the instructions without any faults.

"Good," replied the voice. "Now you may leave. As you pass the threshold you will not consciously remember this conversation and nor will any attempts to retrieve this memory from your subconscious find success."

The shushing sound of rubber soled feet disappeared into the chaos of the hospital floor.

Fatigue bit at his aching muscles and he felt the darkness close around his consciousness, buffering him to sleep.

Icy tendrils snaked down the side of his face before resting on his cheek, burning the warmth away and draining his awareness from the nightmare that clutched at him. Again Jeanie thrust his sword through his body, his blood on her twisted full lips. His gasp at the fiery sensation startled the cold touch on his face, allowing heat to rush in where the tendril had been. The conflicting sensations, both real and imaginary, were enough to snap his eyes open.

The alien room was awash in gloaming darkness. A beige curtain cut off his view of most of the room. The ceiling was striped with large rectangular fibrous tiles intermingled with darkened clear plastic that housed slumbering fluorescents.

Everything appeared off, fuzzy and too dark for the yellow

light that splashed across the lower half of the ceiling near the source of the distant, yet hushed, sounds. Blinking did not alleviate the bizarre images his eyes sent to his brain. Raising his hand in the hopes that rubbing his eyes would return the world into brilliant detail, he was surprised to see a thin plastic tube disappear beneath the white tape stuck to the back of his left hand. He followed the line with his eyes until it led him to the clear liquid suspended in an intravenous bag. Eyes wide he closed his dry mouth with a click and nearly jumped out of his skin as something cold grasped his invaded hand.

"Let's get this thing off."

He turned his head to see Notus carefully remove the I.V., bending the plastic back on itself so that the clear liquid would not leak onto the floor. White brows furrowed, increasing the headache pounding in his temples. Something was very wrong.

Where am I? What's happening? he Sent, worry blossoming to constrict his chest.

When no voice replied in his mind he took a closer look at his Chooser. In the dim light he could barely make out Notus' red rimmed eyes in a face drawn and haggard. The monk's eyes slipped away from his as Notus continued to remove the wires leading to quiet monitors. Notus' silence sent his heart racing in fear and he grabbed the man's cold hand in the process of removing a padded wire from his chest. Hazel eyes glanced sideways up at him and he dropped his grip. There was no doubt that something was terribly wrong. He had no awareness of his Chooser beyond what his regular senses told him and they were woefully lacking.

"What—" he began, his voice dry. He swallowed the dust in his mouth and tried again. "What's wrong with me?"

He did not intend for his voice to rise in volume but the panic strangled it out of him. It grew when Notus frowned and turned his head away to stare at the curtain.

"Notus." His voice, constricted in fear, was barely audible, but he knew his Chooser heard him and chose not to respond.

"Paul," he whispered, hating how small his voice sounded. "Tell me."

Notus sighed. His shoulders dropped in resignation and began his quiet retelling of the events leading to their current situation. Straining to listen to the whispered narrative, it provided more evidence to the situation he currently found himself. His ruby eyes widened throughout the retelling, his ears unbelieving. It made no sense. The last he remembered was preparing to jump after the Vampire responsible for the theft of his sword.

His sword!

They stole it!

"My sword!" he gasped. He made a move to get out of the short bed only to find a cold hand on his chest, pressing him to be still. Notus met his gaze, holding each other still.

"Did you not hear, boy?" Hazel eyes welled with unshed tears.

"I heard," he replied, confused. He did not understand.

"I don't know how it's possible. A miracle, maybe." Notus' eyes bore into his own.

For the first time in their lives he was the one to look away. He had never seen Notus in such a state. A new thread of panic twined around the others and he frowned. Daring Notus' burning gaze he was frightened to see tears trailing down the monk's face.

"You are no longer Chosen. Gwyn, you are mortal again."

The words, at first, made no sense. Disjointed sounds strung together to imply meaning slowly coalesced and he sucked in his breath, comprehension punching his gut.

"Tha—that's not possible."

Notus lowered his eyes and stood. "Possible or not, the fact is for some reason you are once again mortal."

Disbelieving shock filled the silence. It was impossible!

It also explained why the room should be brighter, the images sharper. It explained so much, but even more, it explained why the I.V. puncture was still there and why he could feel nothing from the monk. He shook his head, denying the truth the facts pointed towards.

"I must go," announced Notus, sadly, as he turned to leave. "I've stayed far too long. The sun will rise shortly. I've arranged for Elizabeth to pick you up in a couple of hours."

He could not believe what he was hearing. He too should be able to sense dawn's approach but the absence was yet further proof he was no longer Chosen. Then the thought struck him - Elizabeth will expect him to go out into the sun. Mortal or no, he could not do that! He had not been able to go out during the day since he was a child beaten and left for dead by other children because they thought him Fay.

"Notus. Wait!" he cried out, but it was too late. In a blink of an eye the Chosen was gone. The only evidence of his departure was the curtain swinging as if a breeze had blown through. Staring at the beige fabric he took a shuddering breath.

This cannot be happening.

XVIII

ain slithered down the window, obscuring the steel grey that enveloped the view from the hospital window. Lightening flared a spectacular display that cut across the leaded clouds before the booming thunder rattled the window. He stood there, watching the show, his hands clutching his elbows in an effort to hold himself to the reality that presented. He wanted to run from what he witnessed. He should run. He would have fled had he been Chosen. Now he was able to stand here at the window, the sun well over the horizon, even though obscured by the thick clouds. Another flash of lightning cut off his vision of the sliver of city the window allowed for and he closed his eyes, waiting for the rumble that quickly followed.

After Notus left, he had laid there in the hospital bed too stunned and too afraid to move. Almost every cell in his body protested the truth except those that proved his mortality. For the first time in over a millennium and a half his bladder screamed at him for release. Disgusted and ashamed, he had managed to rise unassisted from the bed and use the facilities in the water closet attached to the room.

In private, he found clothing left for him in the crude armoire across the bed, and dressed. He did not know when Dr. Bowen would come to drive him back to the condo, but it was better than standing around in hospital garb that was far too small. Now he stood in black jeans and an ebony dress shirt, the top two buttons undone to show the white surgical tape that bound the gauze pad to the burn over his shoulder. His black leather coat still hung in the closet in expectation for the time of departure. The sound of someone entering his room turned him to face an Asian orderly carrying a breakfast tray. It was clear that the young man had not expected the patient to be out of bed, nor to be so strange in appearance.

"I'll just leave this here," he murmured. He placed the tray on the rolling table, turned and fled.

A frown furrowed his pale brow. Some things never change.

The scents arising from the tray drew him over to inspect the contents. Lifting the cover revealed runny scrambled eggs, oily sausage and over cooked chunks of potato. Despite the disgusting appearance of the food his mouth watered in anticipation. Horrified by the mortal need for sustenance he dropped the lid to cover the sight. This was not the nourishment he should crave as his body cried out for the meal denied.

"Hospital food has a reputation for being unpalatable for a good reason."

He spun around to see Dr. Bowen standing in the doorway. He whould have known she was there had he still been Chosen. The lack of preternatural senses unnerved him, knocking him off his centuries old balance.

Dr. Bowen took the few steps into the room to stand before him. He was surprised to see her in blue denim trousers and a cream coloured sweater. The casual attire transformed her appearance to that of a younger woman. She looked up at him and for the first time he realized that she never balked at meeting his gaze.

"How are you feeling?" she asked, concern filling her ice blue eyes.

The question cut to the heart. He knew what she was really asking but the truth made him turn away to walk to the closet to grab his coat and the small suitcase that Notus had brought over earlier.

How was he feeling?

His hand gripped the edge of the fake wood melamine as his stomach clenched and his head swam. He felt mortal and the loss of being Chosen cut him deeper than any blade had ever done. He needed Notus. He could not continue to live like this.

A hand alighted on his back. "I'm sorry. You must be furious with me. If I hadn't convinced you to trust me with your sword all of this wouldn't have happened."

He closed his eyes and failed to keep the shudder from his

sigh. Everything that had made him who he was had been stolen that night by monsters who probably did not fully comprehend the damage they had done. An icy fear crawled up from his belly, cancelling out the hunger and thirst that cried out for mortal fulfilment. Did the Vampires know his current state? He needed to see Notus.

"Gwyn?"

The hand left his back and she stood beside him, staring up at him, and he knew that the silence he had left was a poor answer.

"I'm not angry," he replied, lowering his hand and turning to face her. "It's not your fault." *It's mine.*

She frowned, peering into his eyes, searching for any lie in his words until he glanced away.

"Come on. Let's go. We'll stop off at Timmy's for breakfast," smiled Dr. Bowen. Concern still etched the corners of her eyes. "Unless, of course, you want to stay and eat that?"

He glanced back at the table and shook his head.

Gingerly he slipped on his coat, feeling the burn tug with the movement, and grabbing his suitcase, he followed Dr. Bowen out of the room and into a hallway bustling with activity. Teeth clenched and head down so as to allow his long white hair to veil his features; he ignored the stares and surprised exclamations as he walked towards the elevators. He did not need the senses of the Chosen to hear the comments or feel their eyes land upon him. He was almost relieved when the elevator door opened, but the sight of the nearly packed car made him nauseous. If it were not for Dr. Bowen, he would have waited for the next car or, better yet, have taken the stairs. Instead she led him into the elevator cab, their bodies pressed against each other for the few moments it took to reach ground level.

It was only when the doors opened and they exited that he realized he had forgotten to breathe and now found himself panting for breath.

"The car's this way." Dr. Bowen led him to the right, past the café that served as a refuge from the hospital food served on the upper levels and towards the back of the building. The scents wafting from the café and the coffee stand gripped his stomach and made it rumble in anticipation. Ignoring the need for food, they passed the escalators and the Admissions office to stand before the revolving door.

Outside the rain had tapered off, but lightning still flashed high above, occasionally washing the view in momentary brilliance. Even through the heavy clouds enough sunlight filtered down to sting his eyes. Fear wound tighter with the realization that he would have to step outside, during the day, for the first time since he was a child.

"Are you okay?" asked Dr. Bowen, sensing his trepidation. "The car is in the garage across the street. If you're worried about getting wet, I have an umbrella, or I can bring the car here."

"I'm fine," he lied.

He patted his pockets until he felt a familiar bulge and pulled out the broken and slightly melted sunglasses. He stared at them and realized there was no way they would be of any use. Walking over to the trash can he threw them in with a sigh. They had been his only pair.

Mustering his resolve he followed Dr. Bowen through the revolving door and under the shelter the building provided. Dr. Bowen paused long enough to open the umbrella that hung from her purse strap. The black nylon offered basic protection from the rain as she stepped off the curb to cross the street. With no other recourse he followed and she lifted the umbrella higher to accommodate his height.

Eyes burning in the subdued sunlight, they began to tear and blur. When he raised his hand to wipe his eyes he felt a tingling along his skin as it reddened. The sensations vanished once under the protection of the garage. Flesh and eyes relieved, his trepidation increased as he sat in the front seat of Dr. Bowen's car.

Uncomfortable in the small sedan, he closed his eyes as she pulled out of the parking spot and drove to exit. The sound of rain hitting metal and glass mingling with the steady beat of the wipers told him that they were outside.

He knew he should express his appreciation that she was taking him back to the condo when after a quick ride she pulled into a street parking spot next to the police station.

"Look, I'm sorry," said Dr. Bowen, shifting her position to face him. "I don't know what's going on between you and Paul, but he's asked me to take you in."

Confusion crashed down, making his head swim. It did not make sense as to why Notus would want him turned over to the police. He was about to say so when Dr. Bowen realized her mistake.

"Oh, no! You've got it wrong!" she exclaimed. "I didn't mean for it to come out that way. Paul wants you to stay at my home and I agreed to the favour."

"Then why have you halted here?" he ventured, squinting out the window to the building beyond. Her explanation still did not alleviate his confusion. He should go back to the condo and to Notus.

"Detective Donaldson needs your statement regarding the events three days ago," she replied.

He turned to face her, their eyes connecting briefly before he leaned back with a sigh. Three days unconscious. Notus had not told him that. He stared outside the windshield and the rivulets running down the glass. What could he possibly tell the police?

"I told Detective Donaldson I would bring you over before taking you home."

He closed his eyes, digesting what she was requesting of him. The silence stretched, waiting for his response and before too long Dr. Bowen spoke up. "It wasn't just your sword they stole," she said quietly. "They robbed the guests, hurting some of them. Vee hasn't been able to sleep without nightmares since the incident, though she would never let on as that being the cause of her sleeplessness. If what you tell the police can put these people behind bars and get your sword back, wouldn't that be reason enough?"

Her pain and worry struck him. She did not know how right she was in calling them evil, nor did she fully comprehend the truth of their vile nature. If he could get his sword back it would be worth it. He nodded and heard her relief.

"I'll do this thing you ask if you answer me one question," he replied.

"What is it?"

He opened his eyes and gazed into hers, unable to keep the frown from his face. "Did Paul say why and how long he wanted me to stay with you?"

Her hand came to rest on his and she shook her head, sending short brown hair swaying. "No, he didn't. He just brought over your things, including a couple of cases. I hope you don't mind, but I peeked."

Pulling his hand away, he ran his fingers through his hair to spill in a white veil across his shoulders. His hands twitched and his wrists throbbed. The fact that Notus had sent over his weapons disturbed him greatly. He did not know what the monk was thinking but the allusion was there – Notus was expecting him to stay at Dr. Bowen's for an extended period of time.

Agitated by the revelation, he opened the car door and stepped out into the easing downpour. The daylight immediately stung his eyes, and despite the cooling effects of the rain, he could feel his skin prickling with heat. Ignoring Dr. Bowen's rush to follow, he quickly made his way to the front doors of the white box shaped building. Once inside, the burning sensation receded, leaving his flesh tender and his eyes sore. He hated to imagine what it would be like to go out on a sunny day.

Water dripping to form small puddles by his feet, he walked with Dr. Bowen to the front desk and had to catch himself on the edge as the world suddenly tilted sideways and the knot in his stomach tightened nauseatingly. Dr. Bowen slipped him a worried glance before returning her attention to the officer managing the desk.

"We're here to see Detective Donaldson," she announced.

The officer did not hear her, his surprised Italian eyes were caught on the strange young man before him.

"Excuse me, uh, Officer Giglio." Dr. Bowen snapped her fingers, reading his name badge.

The man blinked and turned his attention to her. "How can I help you?" he asked snidely.

"We're here to see Detective Donaldson," reiterated Dr. Bowen, brushing her soggy hair from her eyes.

Officer Giglio took a moment to consider the words of the tall sultry woman before him. A sly smile forming on his thin lips betrayed his thoughts and Dr. Bowen huffed in annoyance, plainly used to such treatment. Picking up the phone beside him, the officer punched a couple of buttons.

"You've got guests," he announced into the receiver, his eyes roving up and down Dr. Bowen before placing the receiver back onto the cradle.

It did not take long for Detective Donaldson to approach her guests. The short woman clad in a dark grey pin-stripe business suit held out her dark brown hand. "Dr. Bowen. Thank you for coming." She turned her attention to him, her fine black brows rising beneath long neat dreadlocks that were carefully styled.

"I appreciate you taking time out of your busy day to come over," said the detective indicating that they should follow her to the back of the building. He ignored the gawks and stares that the police and suspects threw his way. Never to be truly used to it, he was glad when Detective Donaldson opened a metal door and allowed them all to enter the small interrogation room.

The lights were subdued against the plain grey of the walls. In the centre a table and three chairs awaited expectantly. Off to the right, the wall exhibited a large mirror that was obviously meant for one way viewing. He took it all in, failing to keep the frown from his face.

"Please have a seat. I'll be right back with the file and recording device."

Following her invitation, his hand twitched painfully as he attempted to pull out the heavy metal chair and then everything went black.

Hands on his arms gently settled him in the seat as he focused on his breathing to push down the sudden vertigo. He had not felt this ill since flying over the Atlantic. Sweat dampened his skin and he grimaced.

"Maybe we should do this another time," he heard Detective Donaldson say in a far off voice.

"No," he croaked, his throat parched. He closed his eyes against the spinning room and hated himself for being so weak.

"Are you sure?" Dr. Bowen's whisper floated close by.

He nodded his head and instantly regretted the motion. Placing his elbows on the table, he held his head in his hands, his long white hair draping the grey tones that crept into his pale face.

A hand took his and placed something cool in it. Sweetness wafted to his nostrils.

"Here, drink this," offered Dr. Bowen.

He did not want to bring the contents to his lips but he could not deny the cries of his body. Hand shaking, Dr. Bowen assisted him. Citrus and sweetness exploded across his palate. The taste was unlike anything else he had ever had, yet it still paled against the drink of choice that had kept him alive over the ages.

"Small sips," she murmured.

He slowed his gulps and followed the suggestion when the coldness reached his belly. The sensation made him wince at the strangeness. When the contents were gone he lowered the paper cup and frowned at the orange dregs. Already the orange juice was working its magic. The shaking had subsided and the room no longer spun. All that remained was the fierce hunger he had kept at bay.

"When was the last time you had anything to eat?" asked Dr. Bowen. She offered him a small opened packet of crackers.

He wanted to laugh at the absurdity of the innocent question. How could he tell her that he had not eaten food in over fifteen hundred years? Maybe the question should have been when was the last time he had anyone to eat, and even that was a vague memory. Taking the offered cracker he did something he had not done since before he was Chosen – he ate mortal food.

The salty crunchiness exploded the saliva in his mouth and he quickly consumed the cracker, ignoring the question. Once all four crackers were gone and Detective Donaldson had been kind enough to procure him more orange juice, he felt physically better though the hunger cried out for something more substantial. He hated the feeling and attempted to push it down in an effort to ignore the truth of his new state of being. The desperate need of his body for mortal food shook him more than the lack of sustenance had done.

"Better?" inquired the detective.

He looked across the table at her pleasant dark features, slight concern pinching her large brown eyes, and he slowly nodded.

"Then I'd like to ask you some questions about your involvement with the robbery at the ROM." Detective Donaldson opened the manila folder and laid it on the desk before her, pressed record on the digital recorder and lifted her pen.

Over the next hour and a half he was riddled with questions. Why was he in the exhibit? How did he come to own the stolen sword and did he have proof that it was his? Describe what happened. Describe the two thieves as best as possible. Question after question, each seeking out minutiae for any possible evidence until finally the last question – Why did he jump? Through it all he tried to concoct believable lies in an effort to conceal an unbelievable truth, all the while wishing Notus were here to weave the web of deceit with a Push here or there. Several times Detective Donaldson stumbled him over his half truths; her dark eyes penetrating him, making him feel that she knew he lied. He knew he was a horrible liar. It was when he started to hear only half her words, making her questions disjointed and her statements obtuse that he realized that the juice and crackers had lost their efficacy.

Detective Donaldson was in the process of asking yet another question when Dr. Bowen cut her off. "Excuse me, but are you implying that he's a suspect?"

Detective Donaldson sat straight, her dark face hardening into a stony mask. "At this time we cannot rule anyone out."

"Then I think it is time we leave," Dr. Bowen stood up and place a hand on his shoulder. The firmness surprised him but he did not look up, instead he held the detective's gaze until she lowered her eyes.

Rising on unsteady legs, he turned to leave but halted.

"If there is anything else I can help with, Detective, please let me know," he offered, turning to face the officer. "I want my sword back." Compliance tended to alleviate suspicion and he hoped that would be the case here. He just wished he knew why he was a suspect.

"Thank you," replied the detective with a nod. "If we need to contact you, where can we do so?"

The question caught him off guard and he floundered.

"He'll be staying with my family and I," announced Dr. Bowen. "I believe you have my address on record."

Detective Donaldson made a note in the file and then stood. "Yes, thank you." She walked around the table to the door, blocking the exit. "I appreciate you coming in today. I'm sure speaking with the police was the last on your priorities, but the information you provided was very helpful."

She stepped back, revealing the exit and he walked through with Dr. Bowen behind him. Again the hum in the precinct diminished as he and Dr. Bowen walked to the front doors. The only benefit he found to being mortal was for the first time he could not hear the whispered comments that his presence always generated. He opened the door and stepped into the brightening day and he winced, thus eradicating any positive thoughts about being mortal.

Head pounding and eyes burning, he gratefully collapsed into the front passenger seat once Dr. Bowen opened the doors using her key fob. Despite the cramped space of her Honda he closed his eyes and rested his throbbing head in his hand. He felt a hand on his upper arm.

"Do you want me to take you back to the hospital?" Dr. Bowen's concerned tones filled the cabin.

The implication snapped his head up, surprise seeping into his pained eyes. "No." His voice came out in a rasp. "I just need to get out of the daylight."

Dr. Bowen's frown turned into a studious gaze that blossomed into realization. "Oh, I'm sorry. That's why you always wore your sunglasses and why Paul worked at night."

He did not know what she understood but did not rise to the bait. No longer Chosen he still had to be a creature of the night.

"We'll stop at Timmy's drive through on the way home." She started the car, worry still creasing her brow.

Closing his eyes, listening to the nauseating throbbing that echoed in his skull, he knew one thing as Dr. Bowen slipped the car into traffic – he desperately needed Notus. He could not live like this.

xix

Elizabeth sat at the large oak desk that had been her grandfather's and where she had fallen in love with the ancient world as she sat astride his knees. The half foot stone *Sheila-na-gig* still sat on the left corner of the desk. Grandfather Davies had given it to her the day she toddled in and stared slack jawed at the figurine. Over the years of living with the old man after the deaths of her parents, Elizabeth had learned not only the love of archaeology but the myths and legends of the Europeans which eventually led her to find spiritual fulfilment as one of the Hidden Children of the Goddess.

Elizabeth did not know whether her grandfather would have approved of her growth away from his atheist views, but her gut suspected he was pleased with the choices she had made, especially in following in his professional footsteps. The only thing she was sure of was that he would have scowled at all the redecoration she had done after inheriting the house in the second year of her Bachelor's degree. The only room she left untouched by modern interior design was her grandfather's sanctuary – the same room in which she now sat, having claimed the memory infused room as her own.

Laying down the iron spearhead into its foam case, Elizabeth pushed the magnifying lamp to the side and rubbed her strained eyes. She really ought to get her eyes checked, but she did not want to admit that she was getting older. Having a pair of reading glasses displayed prominently on her nose would be too much. It was bad enough that she had to break the oath to herself never to colour her hair. Who knew that divorcing her husband and best friend to another man and then losing him to AIDS while trying to raise a teenage daughter could take such a toll? Now she had taken in a strange young man as a favour to a colleague and friend, unable to comprehend why Paul abandoned him.

She pinched the bridge of her nose and rolled the leather armchair back from the desk, sighing at the memory of Paul's distraught visage as he all but begged her to "take the boy." Ever the softy for a hard luck case, Elizabeth acquiesced. It was when she saw him standing at the rain slicked hospital window that she second guessed her decision.

It was not often that she truly had to look up into anyone's face. Rudy, her deceased ex-husband, had stood an inch shorter, and that was without heels. Now she was forced to tilt her head back to see the hurt and confusion in his exotic crimson gaze.

The flicker of fear that had sparked when she first saw him without the sunglasses still burned. Elizabeth chalked it up to her imagination at the notion his eyes glowed like embers, the anger of her holding his sword pointed at his chest being enough justification. Now the sword she had promised that would be safe was stolen, making her an unwitting oathbreaker. It was one of the main reasons she had agreed to Paul's pleas.

Her gaze lifted to the stucco ceiling, its swirling pattern around the central hub of the small unlit crystal chandelier ran riot with shadows. It was not so much the decorative elegance that drew Elizabeth, but rather who was above in the guest bedroom. A frown pulled at her face. She could not believe the radical change in him. No longer had the strong self assured young man who exuded a cold air of aloofness, Elizabeth now saw him shaken and uncertain – vulnerable. He had attempted the imperious glamour during the police questioning but it became obvious how much of that mask was a ruse.

His reaction to the sunlight was odd but answered the real reason why the night was preferred by Paul. It took all of her strength to assist her new tenant from the car to the guest bed. A slight tinge of green had seeped into his ivory skin and his face was pinched in pain. An offer of painkillers was ignored yet he gratefully grasped the damp cloth she placed on his forehead before leaving him to rest in the blackened room.

Closing her eyes, Elizabeth stretched her senses to encompass the goings on in her home. *Much Music* entertained her daughter in the family room below the study, the heavy bass beats travelling through the air ducts. Elizabeth knew she should go downstairs to tell Vee to turn down the volume but the sound of water rushing upstairs drew her attention to her guest as he ran the shower.

An unbidden image popped into her mind, filling her with heat as she wondered at the paleness of his flesh and how it would feel.

"He's half my age!" she admonished, eyes snapping wide at the attraction she felt. The rides on his motorcycle, clinging to his body, and now his vulnerability had only enhanced her desire.

"Stop it!" She slapped her forehead several times in an attempt to banish the feelings. *Goddess, it's been too long and too close to Beltain,* she thought as she stood.

A quick glance at her wristwatch told her that it was time to make dinner, halting her approach to the door with the ritual musings of what to make. A new thought came to mind – except for seeing him grudgingly eat the crackers at the police station, she had never seen him eat. The tuna sandwich she had bought for him on the way home sat untouched in her refrigerator.

Placing her hand on the crystal doorknob Elizabeth turned it and opened the door inward only to nearly jump out of her skin. There, before her, stood her house guest, his hand poised to knock on the door. Slowly, he lowered his hand and she noticed the familiar sight of the braces on his wrists. Not for the first time she wondered why he wore them.

Dressed in a black shirt with abalone buttons and black slacks he appeared stunning despite the pinched expression playing hide-and-seek beneath long wet white locks. Elizabeth noticed he appeared even paler and decided to apply a light hand.

"It's good to see you up," she said. She almost let her smile slip as he frowned and averted his glittering ruby eyes. "I hope you're feeling better." She was rewarded with a slight nod.

"I have to go out," he said softly. His eyes refused to meet hers and he stepped back, allowing her to exit the study.

Closing the door behind her, Elizabeth was surprised at his announcement. "Are you sure?"

She watched his partially hidden face as he frowned. He appeared so dissimilar to the young man she thought she knew. The strength and surety was now replaced by a fragile veneer where uncertainty and, dare she say it, fear showed through. It was incongruous to her daughter's description of the man that saved Vee. It was inconceivable that here stood the one who had miraculously eluded a hail of machine gun fire in the close confines of the elevator to manage a damaging blow on the escaping thief.

Walking towards the kitchen Elizabeth was aware of him following without answering. Elizabeth was still unsettled by his silences, but it was unusual for him not to answer a direct question.

Her mahogany and steel modern kitchen was thrown into brilliance from the antique styled ceiling fan as she flipped the switch on her way to the refrigerator. Navigating around the island counter that served as a preparation area, she opened the steel door of the freezer.

"I was just about to make dinner." She fumbled through the bags and boxes in an effort to spark an idea of what to make. Grabbing a bag of frozen vegetables Elizabeth turned to see him standing by the island counter, his long graceful fingers pale against the caramel granite. He absently caressed the cold stone, his eyes watching the speckled pattern. She wondered at his involvement and, biting her lower lip, she recognized a shyness she had only seen in young inexperienced men.

Elizabeth walked over to him and placed the defrosting bag on the table. "Is something wrong?"

He grimaced and dipped his head lower, his hair spilling forward to mask his discomfort. "I appreciate your kindness and help." He paused, searching for words until she thought he would not say any more.

She moved to grab the damp plastic bag but halted as he looked up, his crimson eyes arresting her. She never thought that eyes could really be that colour, let alone that beautiful.

"I don't want you to think I'm ungrateful, but I won't be coming back."

She sucked in her breath at the pronouncement and then realization blossomed. "You're going to speak with Paul."

He nodded and she smiled.

"That's good." She stepped closer. "I don't know what happened between the two of you, but if you and Paul can patch things up, that would be wonderful."

His thin white brows furrowed and she did not understand his consternation. Would it not be best for all concerned that the two of them patch their rift? "What is it?"

"My wallet, I can't find it, and I hate to ask after all your generosity."

It was clear to Elizabeth he was not one to ask for help and was deeply uncomfortable doing so. She knew well enough to be patient for him to continue.

"I have a taxi waiting and … well." He grimaced sheepishly.

"No problem." Elizabeth patted his arm before walking into the foyer to retrieve her black leather purse and matching wallet from within. Fumbling through the papers as she headed back to the kitchen, she held out several green bills.

"Thank you," he said, taking the money. He carefully folded them and placed the bills into his trouser pocket. "I'll pay you back."

Elizabeth had no doubt that he would keep his word as she followed him to the front door. Quietly, she watched him slip into his shoes and long leather coat, a nagging feeling percolating up from her belly. Without another word he left her home.

She watched as he entered the orange car and she closed her front door to the sight of retreating tail lights. Hand resting on the lock, she removed her hand, leaving the door unlatched. The sensation in her gut formed into a certainty. She would not lock her door for she knew he would be back. Sadly shaking her head, Elizabeth turned back to the kitchen to make dinner for herself and her daughter.

X X

He stood outside the condominium door, his heart hammering in his chest. He did not know what to expect but the sudden fear about what he was intending to do surrounded and encapsulated him. Regardless, he had no choice as he knocked on the locked door.

It had been disconcerting to find both his wallet and his keys missing from his belongings.

A faint reply bidding him entry floated through the wood. Spurred on by the inviting tone, he pushed the handle down and gave the door a shove inwards. Stepping into the condo he was surprised by the packing boxes stacked beside the door and a frown formed on his face as he stepped further in. There was no doubt Notus was preparing to leave. Closing his eyes he failed to connect with the Chosen, another damning piece of evidence to his mortality. It made the space increasingly uninviting.

"There's a couple of smaller boxes–" Notus instructions abruptly ended as he came into the hall and saw the boy standing by the door. Pain flashed across the monk's face before quickly retreating, leaving only blank coldness in its wake.

Unaccustomed to seeing the monk direct his stern stare at him, he spoke Notus' name as he stepped closer to the Chosen.

"What are you doing here?" Notus took a step back.

His jaw dropped and his eyes widened at the accusatory tone.

"You're supposed to be at Elizabeth's."

"I–I had to come." Confusion filled him. This was not the welcoming he had expected. He had assumed that Dr. Bowen had picked him up from the hospital because Notus could not have done so during daylight hours.

Notus lowered his hazel eyes and brushed by as he walked into the living room. He stood for a moment by the sofa, his pale hand, stained with ink, resting on the leather before turning around. "There was no need for you to come."

The proclamation and the matter-of-fact tone rocked him. He took a step towards the monk. "Of course I had to come," he implored. "How could I not after what has happened?"

"Do not come any closer," stated Notus as he retreated from the young man who had been his son for centuries.

He halted his approach, his gut twisting at the sudden distance between the two. "Notus?"

The Chosen shook his head, sadness filling his eyes.

He had to try again. "Paul, please," he implored. "I can't live like this." The monk's shoulders slumped as he pressed on. "This time it's my Choice."

Notus closed his eyes, grimacing as if in pain. "I prayed that you wouldn't ask. That you would joyfully accept God's grace that has lifted the curse from you and rejoice in being mortal once more, as I would have, as I have always prayed for." He opened his eyes to penetrate stunned ruby eyes. "You have a chance to live a normal life, finally. You no longer need to be the Angel."

Silence crashed down between them as the monk's words and their meaning seeped in. When they impacted, the force thundered his heart in his ears, making his head swim and his legs weak. He hated to beg but there was nothing left to do but to do so. "Notus, please, you don't know what you're condemning me to."

"But I do," replied the monk, his whisper barely audible.

"No, you don't," he pressed. "Being Chosen freed me to live fully in the night. Now it's all darkness."

Notus shook his head. "You can live your life in the light."

"No. I can't." He knew his voice was harsh. Fear twisted into anger, anger at Notus for denying him and anger at his differences that would always keep him in the dark. "That night when you Chose me, you saved me. Please, Paul. I'm begging you."

Tears welled in Notus' eyes before he brushed them away. "You don't know what you're asking."

"I do."

"Then you know why I cannot." Notus' voice was soft and filled with remorse. "You were an accident. I never Chose you. It was a mistake I had been forced to live with, an oath broken to

God. He has lifted your curse and forgiven me. I cannot – nay, will not – consciously break my oath never to Choose another. You of all people know this. Regardless of how I feel I cannot Choose you."

The words felled him to his knees as his legs failed and nausea rose. Eyes burning with unshed tears he could not catch his breath. He should have known. He had known. But he believed Notus would take him back, that somehow Notus' oath to his God would not encompass him.

He heard Notus' quiet approach and a blossom of hope filled him as the monk laid his cold hand on his shoulder. Reaching out, he grasped Notus' other hand and pressed his lips to cold flesh. It would be so easy to take the transformative substance from the monk, to take the Choice away from him, but he would not. It would be tantamount to rape and he had enough experience to know he could never do such a thing. The Choice had to be mutual. "Please," he begged, tears falling.

"I'm sorry, Gwyn. I cannot." Notus pulled his hands away. "I can only pray that through His grace you will finally receive the happiness you so richly deserve."

He heard Notus walk towards to door. With each footfall the numbness of shock swept away the anxiety of being denied. It was only when he heard the click of the doorknob that he found the wherewithal to quietly ask, "What am I to do?"

"Live, Gwyn. Live life to the fullest. Live the life Jeanie would have wanted you to live had you been mortal."

New tears welled in his eyes at the wound Notus wrenched open and the door clicked closed, leaving him alone in a place that was not his home. Rising on weak legs, he found his wallet and keys, minus the condo's door keys, laying on one of the boxes next to the door. They had not been there when he came in and could only surmise that Notus placed them there when he left. Opening his wallet he found it full to near bursting with cash and credit cards. A note on yellow parchment stuck out from between the bills. With shaking hands he opened the note.

My Dearest Gwyn,
I am so terribly sorry that we must part, but
our lives are now divided by what we are. Know
that though I cannot be in your life as you learn
to walk a mortal path you will never want for

*money. Your cards are your own and will
continue to be so, even down to your future
generations, which I pray will be many.*

*May the Blessing of God be with you
always,*

Father Paul Notus.

Neatly folding the note back into quarters, he carefully placed it back into his wallet. Numb from shock, he exited the condo with the certainty that he would never see Notus again.

The wind whipped the ends of his hair to smack against his back. Normally he would tuck his long hair into his coat before climbing onto his motorcycle but this time he did not care. It was better to be reminded of his past physical torture than to feel the ache in his heart and the desolation of his spirit. Still he rode on, the racing bike constantly bucking for greater speed which forced him to concentrate more on the manipulation of the machine. It would be exhilarating if not for the undercurrent of speculation of what would happen if he gave the bike full throttle.

He did not know where he was going and nor did he care. It was the feel of the machine beneath his body and the flickering lights sparsely illuminating retreating landscapes that kept the solid ball in his chest from exploding. Therefore a sliver of surprise wiggled to dull the numbness of his heart when he found that he was almost back at Dr. Bowen's home. He did not know how long he had ridden but as he drove up to her house he was met with darkness. Shutting down the Y2K, he walked it up the drive and kicked the stand to allow the motorcycle to stand on its own beside Dr. Bowen's *Honda*.

Removing the helmet, he gazed at the house he had believed he would not see again. The time bomb in his chest lurched and he grasped at the leather seat in an effort to diffuse the sudden emotions that threatened to overwhelm him. Willing away the tears that threatened to overflow, he released his grip and took a deep shuddering breath.

The house appeared foreboding as did the lack of colours the streetlight tossed everything into. The absence of colour and texture forced him to turn away. He could not enter this place. This was not his home. His home had always been with Notus and now the man who had always been more than a father to him for generations had turned his back on him, casting him out.

The knot in his chest expanded and he gasped. Try as he may he could not squash the bubbling emotions as the solid reality hit home with a devastating blow.

Notus had abandoned him!

The monk had turned his back, calling him an accident!

His legs failed to keep him upright and he slumped to the pavement as a light rain began to fall, slicking the tarmac and mingling with his tears.

Everything was gone.

Even the sense of who he was was gone. Notus had told him so.

No longer Chosen, he was no longer the Angel.

Jeanie was taken from him. Despite the years that pain remained as a dull ache. Now Notus had refused him and left him because he was mortal.

Sobs tore through him. He did not ask for this. Had he known that chasing the Vampire onto the roof would have resulted in his current state he would have gladly given that bastard his sword. Did not Notus realize, after all these years that to him, being Chosen was a blessing and not a curse? Had the monk never seen it?

The cold rain fell heavier as he wept.

Slumped on the driveway, he could not feel the chill seeping into his mortal flesh nor the rivulets running down his neck to soak his chest, shoulders and back.

Everything was lost.

Without a thought he sat cross legged, elbows propped on his thighs and hung his head in the palms of his hands. Despite the veil of his hair his tears mingled with the rain. This time he did not have any friends, no father figure, no one.

He wept until all that was left was a hollow where the ball had been in his chest. Lifting his face to the falling rain he closed his eyes as the water washed away his tears. Breathing in a deep sigh he felt the emptiness burn through him. There was no chance to become Chosen again. Even if he flew back to Europe, without Notus' protection, his life, mortal or not, would be forfeit. No Chosen would Choose him knowing that his differences would instantly target that individual, and him, for Destruction. It was only his usefulness as the Angel that kept him alive. Now that too was gone he had no doubt that someone, someone like Hugo, would take the opportunity to kill him. Then again being mortal and having knowledge of the Chosen was a death sentence. Of course he could go to England, but he doubted Fernando and Bridget could do anything more to protect him. As Master and Mistress of the Chosen of Britain they had pushed the limits with their acceptance of his differences. It would not be so this time.

The unbidden thought of staying in North America nearly made him laugh. That would surely be a death sentence. There was no doubt that the Vampires knew the Angel was in their midst and it was just a matter of time before one or more found him and exacted their revenge. He doubted that a quick death would be afforded to him. Then again they did not know that he was now mortal so it might be a quick death.

It was amazing how being mortal brought the inevitable thoughts of his own demise.

Lowering his head back into his hands, the tears all washed away, the wet chill made him shudder. He was back to where he was before his run in with the monk all those centuries ago. This time his sword was taken away.

His sword.

Geraint's sword.

The idea that it was now in the hands of Vampires twisted his guts. He knew the police were working to return his possession but he doubted they would be successful. They did not know what they were dealing with.

A sudden overwhelming need to feel the weight of the blade and to touch the ancient metal filled him, making him gasp. The sword, carefully cared for and used with reverence and respect held the last remains of his previous existence. The cloak clasp had finally succumbed to the ravages of time, having broken and fallen in a battlefield during the Great War. Now all he desired was to hold what had been given to him that connected him to a past where he was loved and cared for. New tears threatened to spill so he closed his eyes. He would have his sword back, the rest did not matter, not even his life, he told the gaping hole in his heart.

XXI

I t was not a sound that woke Elizabeth, though the pattering of rain on the roof made her feel cozy under her comforter. It was a sensation of unease, as if something was terribly wrong, that nibbled at her subconscious and made staying in bed uncomfortable. Turning over she glanced at the red glowing numbers on her alarm clock and frowned. A quarter to three in the morning glared back at her. Lying onto her back, Elizabeth closed her eyes and tried to settle back into sleep but to no avail. The uneasiness filled her until she threw back the covers with a groan. Something felt wrong and she had to find out what it was.

Slipping on her indigo terrycloth robe over her nude form, Elizabeth went to her window that overlooked the front yard. From her viewpoint she could see the back end of her car and beside it, the distinctive tail of a motorcycle. Her frown deepened.

Exiting the master bedroom Elizabeth carefully navigated the dark hallway past the circular opening in the centre of the second floor that housed the stairs to the first floor. Hand running on the railing that protected one from falling below; she paused at Vee's slightly ajar door. Opening it enough to peek in, she was relieved to find Vee asleep in her daybed, a menagerie of stuffed animals and wall posters keeping watch. Carefully closing the door, Elizabeth continued past one of the landings that were stacked full bookshelves, past another spare bedroom, and came to stand before the guestroom. The soft glow from the nightlight in the large bathroom that ran perpendicular to the guestroom was enough to show that no occupant was within.

She stepped away from the empty room, following her growing unease down the dark stairs. Alighting from the hardwood stairs to stand in the foyer, the conjoined living and dining rooms to her right and the front entrance in front of her, it was clear to Elizabeth that no one untoward was in her home. Instead of heading back up the stairs to climb back into bed, she frowned as her intuition beckoned her to the front door. It was still unlocked. Her frown deepened as she opened the dark oaken door and shivered as a blast of cold damp air flowed over and around her. Even in the dark she could see the rain easing to a fine mist, yet from her position she could not get a full view of the driveway. Damning herself for not donning her slippers, Elizabeth stepped out onto the concrete veranda, a shock of cold stinging her feet.

The cool breeze caressed her legs, evoking gooseflesh, and she pulled the robe tighter in an effort to keep the gentle wind from stealing precious heat. A few more steps, two down concrete stairs, dampened her feet and moistened her body. She knew she was an idiot to come out here in the middle of the night but she never dismissed her intuition, no matter the form it came in.

Past the garage wall she halted, blinking incredulously at the sight before her. There, on the ground beside the motorcycle, her houseguest sat, drenched through, oblivious to her presence. She took a step towards his hunched form and spoke his name. She did not need to see his eyes as he glared up at her, his misery arrested her until he lowered his head, shoulders slumping further. There was no doubt in Elizabeth's mind that things with Paul had not gone as the young man had hoped. At times like these she hated her intuition.

Taking the steps towards him, Elizabeth crouched down, running her hand through damp brown locks. "Come on, let's get you inside where it's warm and dry."

She placed her hand on his arm and he looked up at her with a nod. Rising to his full height, he shrugged off her assistance as she too stood. Dishevelled white hair partially obscured his morose features as she gazed up at him.

"Why didn't you come inside?" asked Elizabeth, trying to catch his eyes with hers. "The door was unlocked."

Fine white brows furrowed until a darker expression took over his young face. Elizabeth's gut plummeted and for the life of her could not fathom his reaction until realization hit. *He must think I knew from the start that Paul wouldn't have him back,* she thought. "I left the door open in case you needed to come back to get your belongings." The half truth came easily. She did not want to add to his misery.

His eyes fastened onto hers for a brief moment. "Then you weren't expecting me?" he asked, his voice rough with emotion.

She shook her head, afraid to be caught in a lie. "Let's go inside." She took his chilled hand in hers. "We'll catch our deaths if we stay out here any longer."

Turning back towards the house she knew he followed. What disturbed her was hearing him mumble, "Would that be so."

Lying on her back, staring up at the plaster ceiling above her bed, Elizabeth failed to recover a lost night of sleep, the night's events running over in her mind in a continuous loop. There was something intriguing about the tall pale young man and it was not just his incredible good looks. When he left her home earlier that evening there was something of the man she had gotten used to before his accident.

Before he was quiet – though that did not change – there was a solid inner strength she had never before seen in someone so young coupled with an emotional detachment bordering on coldness. Elizabeth had only seen the like when her ex-husband's brother came back from an extended tour of duty in the Middle East. Since her guest's accident Elizabeth had witnessed a gamut of emotions from the man, and none of them ever evoked a smile, only a frown. The tip of the iceberg was seeing him on the ground before his motorcycle. There had been no question that he had been crying. That evidence alone shook her and pulled on her heartstrings.

A deep sigh escaped her as she rolled onto her side, away from the glowing red numbers. She did not need to be reminded that morning was soon approaching, yet maybe that would be better than having her mind stuck on her guest. She could not deny that she found him attractive and nor could she turn a blind eye to the fact that he was much younger than she. His current emotionality had only enhanced her attraction.

Annoyed at her insomnia Elizabeth propped herself up on her elbow, grabbed her pillow with her free hand and punched the down filled case until it was an imaginary shape that would clear her mind and allow her to sleep. Flopping back down, she realized that she was irritated. No, more than that, she was angry at Paul for throwing the boy out, especially in a foreign country. If only she knew what was going on between the two of them then maybe she could do something to help.

Groaning at her stupidity, she rubbed her long fingers across her face. Meddling always turned bad for the meddler. No, she would not get in the middle but she had to do something to help. Whatever had gone on between the two of them she would not deal with, but having Gwyn as her house guest and in obvious distress, Elizabeth knew she could, at least, try and help him. After all, it was her fault that his sword was stolen.

Decision made, and resigning herself that sleep had completely eluded her, Elizabeth flung off her bedcovers and slipped back into the robe. This time she put on her fuzzy purple bunny slippers before exiting the room. Tea and paperwork would make a nice early breakfast as she padded towards the staircase.

Poised to assay the steps Elizabeth halted at the sound of a groan of pain coming from the guestroom. Mouth twisting in self-rebuke, Elizabeth shook her head and damned herself for a soft hearted fool. Quietly she walked to the guestroom, her slippers shushing over the broadloom, to find the door open. Fleeting moonlight cast short lived shadows across the room, mingling dark and light to give birth to silvers that illuminated before dying, only to be reborn in a midnight cycle of creation and destruction.

An exclamation followed by a whimper drew Elizabeth into the room, her heart hammering in her ears. There was no doubt in her mind that her guest was in the throes of a nasty nightmare. Intent to wake him from whatever gripped him, Elizabeth, shocked, stopped still, her hand flying to cover her opened mouth.

In the fleeting moonlight, snaking up and down his back in a tangled mass of silver, thick scars ran riot leaving no flesh untouched, his long white hair splayed against the bands. A shift of shadow turned her attention to his right arm that curled around his head, his face turned away and buried in the pillow. A rope of a scar slid from his shoulder to disappear into the crook of his elbow, marring the strong supple musculature and giving rise to a multitude of silver lines across his pale forearm. Elizabeth's gorge rose at the sight of the wide banded scar encircling his wrist and the raised white blossom in the center of the band. There was absolutely no doubt that he had been viciously tortured.

Swallowing the bile that threatened to overflow, Elizabeth's heart ached as tears threatened to spill. She could not imagine how anyone could do this to another being. A wisp of a thought entered her mind and she shook it away. No. She knew Paul well enough by now to know that he would never raise a hand to another. Working side by side for hours at a time and for several weeks could not hide the true measure of a man, yet doubt still lingered. Oh, the pain he must have endured, and probably at such a young age from the sight of the scars. Tears trickled down her face. It explained so much, and yet, created so many more questions.

A shuddering breath and a whimper made her jump. The nightmare was still upon him. Without a second thought she placed her hand on his cool shoulder and gave a shake. She had to save him from more pain. It was enough. With a gasp, he rolled over onto his back, eyes wide before freezing over as the dream left his vision and recognition seeped in.

Desiring to dispel the anger tightening his pale features, Elizabeth blurted, "You were having a nightmare."

The tension leaked out of him and he lowered his eyes. "You saw."

It was not so much of an accusation, rather a statement of fact. Elizabeth nodded. Glancing at the covers, she noticed they came to his midriff and for the second time she witnessed the scar on his breast, this time matched with the healing red of the lightning burn on his left shoulder. His every line was softly sculpted, long and lean. Her mind screamed at her that he was more of an age with her daughter and yet she could not deny the attraction she felt towards the young man. When her eyes found his face again, dejection turned his eyes away as he sat up, the comforter pooling in his lap. Sweeping the stray locks from his face, Elizabeth noticed his left forearm and wrist bore similar silver disfigurements as his right.

"May I sit?" she asked, her voice but a whisper to her ears.

He gestured with an open hand but did not meet her eyes. Accepting the invitation, Elizabeth sunk down on the mattress, keenly aware that he did not move when her hip rested against his covered leg.

"What do you want, Dr. Bowen?" he asked, sounding very tired.

"Elizabeth," she implored with a sigh. "I've asked you many times to call me Elizabeth. Why won't you?" It had always bothered her that he would not use her given name, she just did not realize how much.

Abashed, he met her gaze before lowering his eyes. There was enough of a wash of moonlight to catch his eyes, momentarily bringing out their crimson. His shoulders slumped in defeat and he sighed. "It's easier."

"Easier? How?" Not understanding, Elizabeth shook her head. Then it dawned on her as brilliant as the new moonbeam that illuminated his egregious scars. "You rarely use anyone's name. You do it to keep yourself apart from everyone so you cannot be hurt again," she blurted without thinking.

Her observation hit hard, snapping his head up, eyes wide with shock and fear. Even his mouth fell open and he closed it with a swallow. Pinching the bridge of his nose, he appeared defeated.

Elizabeth grimaced. She had not wanted to do this to him. It was then that she clued in. No longer aloof and emotionally unreachable, Elizabeth found she could read him as clearly as any book. She did not consider herself empathic but with him his emotions were written plainly across his face and body. It suddenly made sense why he always appeared closed off. It was another way to keep people out.

"I'm sorry," she said, realizing that she was banging on the thick walls he had erected.

"No, you're right," he whispered, dropping his hand to his lap.

His admission surprised her. Most would flee from her trebuchet personality. That was why she had only a handful of good friends. Could it be that he was not running when he, more than anyone she had ever known, had reason to rebuke her?

"You still haven't answered my question, Doct–Elizabeth," he sighed. He dropped his gaze with a grimace, clearly uncomfortable with the use of her given name.

Taken with his pronunciation of her name, his accent rolling it into something more, Elizabeth shook her head when she realized she could not recall his question.

A perturbed frown tugged at his full pale lips and he met her blue eyes. "What do you want?"

The question took her aback. "You were having a nightmare and I wanted to see if you were alright."

"Oh," he replied, discomforted by her answer.

"Are you okay?" She studied his youthful face as he frowned, wishing she could smooth such unhappiness away with the touch of her hand, but she kept her fingers entwined on her lap. It was clear he was not alright. Drawn by her desire to help, Elizabeth said, "You can talk to me, Gwyn. Whatever you tell me will be just between us."

His breath caught and sadness seeped into his eyes. His pain drew her closer and she did what she had unsuccessfully tried not to do, she caressed the side of his face, surprised at his smooth soft features. He raised his hand to capture hers and Elizabeth moved upward on the bed until she was right in front of him, their thighs touching.

Heart pounding with his touch, she followed his gaze as he lowered their hands to his lap. An unbidden thought blossomed about what lay directly under the covers, sending her heart racing to warm centres of her body that had not been kindled in a long while. Try as she might, she was desperately attracted this younger man.

"I appreciate your offer," he said quietly, still holding her hand. "I wish I could ..." He shook his head and sighed in resignation, his long hair tickling the back of her hand. Meeting her eyes once more, he let go of her hand. "You have been so kind to me."

Elizabeth froze, waiting for the "but" to tie his statement to something less pleasant, but when none was forthcoming she relaxed. "Whatever I can do to help, I'll do."

"I don't understand." His voice was filled with quiet misery.

"Understand what?" she pressed, concern tingeing her tones.

"Why you are so nice to me. You're Paul's friend."

She noticed the slight stutter as he mentioned her co-work and she frowned. "I'm you're friend too." She rested her hand on his muscular thigh, the covers soft beneath her fingers. "How many times did you bring me coffee, without being requested, when you visited Paul and I as we worked late at night to ensure the exhibit would be ready to open on time? When my car was in the shop, without me needing to ask, you drove me home, every night for a week, on that infernal machine of yours." Elizabeth was rewarded with a subtle rising of his full pale lips. It was the closest thing to a smile she had ever seen him attempt, and wondered how he would look if he truly smiled. "Of course I count you as a friend," she continued. "How could I not? I had hoped that you would have counted me as one as well."

He was about to protest when she impulsively laid her fingers across his mouth, halting him before a sound was uttered. She was struck by their softness and her boldness, and before she could repress the urge, she replaced her fingers with her lips.

His lips were softer than she expected. At first he did not return the kiss but as she pressed up against him, she felt him return the kiss. She opened her mouth in anticipation of his taste, her tongue running between his lips, seeking entrance.

Abruptly she was pushed away, his hands on her upper arms, holding her steady. The last cloud dissipated and the full moon's brilliance illuminated his pale physique. It was all she could do not to gasp at his pale beauty. Her rapid breath kept time with his and she could make out the mixture of fear and desire on his face. The idea that he was a virgin was dashed to the rocks as Elizabeth could not imagine someone so enticing to be chaste, especially not after that kiss. Yet confusion and fear pinched his brow.

"No strings," she smiled, hoping to assuage his concerns, and her own.

This is what she wanted, what she had craved since she first saw him walk down the ramp at the airport. Never had she offered this to a man. It was unlike her. Even in her university days there were no such thing as a one night stand because she was already married and a mother. Even when Rudy left her, Elizabeth only gave herself when a relationship was solid, and that was very rare. But with this beautiful man before her, his pain written with the ink of his scars and the sadness in his face, Elizabeth cast her inhibitions to the wind.

Leaning in, she kissed him again, slowly, gently, her heart racing in her ears. This time he yielded to her penetration and as their tongues caressed tension between them snapped. Suddenly, it was his tongue that thrust into her, tasting her.

Elizabeth was barely aware of anything except the heavy pressure of his lips as he sucked and pulled at hers, trying desperately to consume her as she tried to do the same to him. He tasted so good, their mouths finding one another over and over, greedily attacking one another and she wanted more, much more. The burning deep in her belly screamed out to be filled.

Hands, both hers and his, tore away her robe in desperate need. A gasp escaped as he trailed bruising kisses down her neck to suckle on her pulse. A groan of frustration vibrated against her skin before he found her mouth once more. This time she met his violent passion with her own. Grabbing his hair, she yanked his head back to deliver unto him what he had done to her, but stopped at the ferocity of his glare.

"Don't ever grab my hair again," he growled.

A tremor of fear fluttered through her, merging with the heated desire the press of his body created. Mutely, she nodded and let go, remembering his scars.

His hands came up and brushed her cheeks, pulling back her short dark locks before kissing her again. Sighing at the rough treatment, Elizabeth was vaguely aware of being lowered to her back, his smooth flesh against hers, as he left her mouth to encapsulate her nipple with his mouth. Sharp teeth scraped against the sensitive skin blossoming moist warmth between her legs. He sucked and flicked his tongue, teasing her to cry out for more.

Lifting his head back to her face, his hair a silver curtain around them, she kissed him again, penetrating and being penetrated, all the while keenly aware of the solid throbbing length that pressed against her thigh. Reaching down she grabbed his thick shaft, its length jumping at her touch. A groan escaped him as she caressed his smooth hardness.

It was not enough. Elizabeth needed to feel him deep within her. "Now," she gasped between their kisses.

Pulling back, with her hand guiding him, he slid into her. He was larger than her touch had informed her and he slammed into her, causing her to cry out.

Lifting her hips, she met him again. It was then she realized she lay on her shoulders, her hips lifted off the bed as he stood on his knees. His soft hair brushed against her legs as she entwined them around his slender waist. He thrust deeper, the new angle caressing her before pounding against her inner gates. The exquisite pain filled pleasure arched her back, tilting her hips with each intrusion.

Elizabeth watched him above her. Fantasy overlaid reality. Moonbeams invoked ethereal silver, causing her to gasp. Above her, within her, through her, this beautiful young man towered above like a Celtic god from her mythology books and she shuddered at the image, closing her eyes as he filled her again.

His long fingers dug into her hips as he held her to him and she felt herself tightening around his shaft. Spurred on, their pace quickened. With one hand gripping the edge of the bed behind her head Elizabeth ran her other hand over her breast, tweaking and pulling at the swollen nub. He thrust harder and she cried out.

Faster he pounded into her until the tension rolled her in convulsing waves. Within her depths she felt his pulsating release as her orgasm pulled at his, their cries mingling in their unified release.

After forever he sat back on his heels, maintaining his connection with her. Opening her eyes, Elizabeth could see the shimmer of sweat upon his skin making him glow in the moonlight, his breath coming in gasps. Surprised wonderment modeled his features. His long hair stuck to his face and body. With a shudder that she felt deep within her, Elizabeth watched him close his eyes as he folded to lay his head upon her chest. His arms slid up the sides of her torso in an embrace. Languidly she encircled him with one arm while her other played with his baby soft hair. Still deep within her, Elizabeth could feel his passion leave and wondered how much encouragement he would need to harden him for another go.

"I never knew it was supposed to be like this," he whispered against her breast.

Elizabeth halted her stroking of his silken strands, unnerved by his admission. Virgin he was not, but his statement sent a flurry of speculation as to what else he might have endured along with those scars.

Wetness trailed around her breast.

"Shhh," she susurrated, resuming her caresses.

XXII

 take it that Dr. Thompson is safely home." Thanatos sat in his high backed leather chair staring at the blazing fire in the hearth, the logs red and glowing as they were consumed.

"Yes, sir," came the reply from the blond major-domo who stood by the door.

"And he has no memory of our conversation?" Thanatos frowned.

"Only that he enjoyed meeting you and discussing the aspects of medicine that lead from his speciality to yours," explained Godfrey, his hard face clear of emotion. "Dr. Thompson was quiet elated at having made your acquaintance."

"You are sure he remembers nothing of the true aspects of our conversation?"

"I am sure, sir."

"Thank you, Godfrey."

The blonde man turned to leave.

"One more thing, Godfrey."

Godfrey halted at the door and turned back to face his hidden employer.

"I'd like you to track down the Angel. It seems he has been misplaced. Find out if he is staying with Paul Notus or if the lady who picked him up from the hospital has him." Thanatos absently turned the silver phial that hung from the chain around his neck. "Let me know immediately what you find out."

"You wish me to wake you, sir?" Godfrey raised a brow.

"Yes, I do."

"As you wish, sir." Godfrey turned towards the exit, baffled at the request.

"Thank you Godfrey. You are dismissed for the rest of the night."

"Thank you, sir," replied the manservant as he strode out of the room.

Thanatos frowned, his fingers plying the pendant. If what he had managed to get out of Dr. Thompson was true then every hope Thanatos had could be swept away. It had not been easy to untangle the carefully constructed glamour Notus had placed upon the good doctor, but once unravelled and the man's mind was pushed to remember, details that may have seemed insignificant became a glaring reality.

Once the ill gotten memories were gained, Thanatos craftily spun a new web tighter than Notus could have ever done. Dr. Thompson would have no memory of having met, let alone treated, the Angel and his Chooser. Thanatos' frown turned into a grimace with the addendum of the knowledge that the Angel was no longer Chosen. After centuries of watching and waiting, Thanatos was unsure if the opportunity he had sought was now past or forthcoming.

Releasing the silver phial to rest against his chest, he stood and walked to the fireplace. He tossed another split long onto the fire, sending crackling sparks to fly up the flue and he crouched to watch the dancing colours of gold, crimson and amber. Occasionally blue the colour of the daylight sky would kiss the other colours before disappearing in a brilliance of white. All the while the black of the wood was consumed by hungry heat in sun yellow.

He sighed, his breath stirring the flames. If only he knew what to do. Should he finally approach the Angel and talk with him about what he knew? Would he agree to help him attain his desire? Or more to the point – could he? Variables upon variables swirled into his mind, all leading to the question that held him prisoner since he found out about the Angel – could the Angel be the one to lift Thanatos' curse and restore the Chosen to what they once were?

Another thought crept into his mind. Scrubbing his face with his hands he stood. Closing his eyes before opening them with a sigh, Thanatos prayed that Corvus would follow his orders to leave the Angel alone. He did not want to contemplate what would happen if Corvus found out that the Angel was no longer Chosen. He also did not want to consider what he would have to do to the Vampires if they did something to the Angel.

Sitting back down in his chair, Thanatos watched the flames and waited for dawn.

On the rooftop of the condominium he had once shared with the boy, Notus sat with his legs dangling over the building's edge. He watched the lights below as tears streamed down his face.

The phone rang again in the condo until the answering machine picked up. "Paul. It's Bridget... Fernando and I are in town... Paul?...Are you there?...Paul, where's the Angel?"

XXÍÍÍ

scent, enticing rumbling from his stomach, pulled him from the depths of sleep. Eyes fluttering open, he instantly shut them against the bright daylight that poured into the guestroom. Panic caught him and he swept the covers over his head. It took a moment before he realized that his flesh had not ignited and he groaned, remembering the horrible truth that he was now mortal. The millennia born instinct to flee the light continued to grip him as he tentatively folded the bedclothes away from his head.

Yesterday the muted daylight had sent his head pounding and his skin prickling. What washed across the room was pure unadulterated sunlight that set his head throbbing through pain filled tearing eyes. The only sensation missing was the burning of his skin. Closing his eyes he took a deep breath to banish the nausea that came with the migraine and got off the bed, closing the distance to the offending window. It took a couple of tries and the drapes were set free, plunging the room into relative darkness.

On shaking legs he sat back down on the bed, his head resting in hands supported by elbows on knees. Mortal or no, he still maintained sensitivity to the sun that had been beaten into him as a small boy. Releasing a shuddering breath he waited for the agony and nausea to dissipate.

Too much too soon. His existence was changing too fast for him to keep up. No longer Chosen, he had pinned his hopes on Notus Choosing him again so that their lives would continue on together. A tiny part of him should have known Notus would turn him down. To be rejected, to be called an accident – that was not what he expected. His breath caught in a constrained sob and he closed his eyes against the tears that threatened to spill.

Pushing down the dejection that attempted to overwhelm him, he heaved a great sigh and sat straight, his hair falling to drape against his naked back. With that touch his eyes widened as the memory of what occurred between he and Dr. – no, Elizabeth – swelled to the forefront.

Oh my Gods, he thought, rubbing his face. Never had he imagined that he and Elizabeth would become intimate. Lowering his head he closed his eyes as the memories flooded back. He could not remember the nightmare Elizabeth saved him from. All he could recall was feeling vulnerable as her concern evolved into desire. He had seen that look on countless women, and men, in his earlier years, but this time it was coupled with the need to comfort.

The first kiss surprised him. Bridget had kissed him like that at Christmas and he had pushed her away not wanting to ruin the tenuous friendship he had with Fernando, but when Elizabeth told him there would be no strings something within snapped. He needed the touch, to be needed in return, anything to fill the incredible loneliness that clawed at him.

It was when he found her throat with his mouth that it hit him that there was no desire to pierce her flesh with his teeth and drink her blood. Instead he needed to devour her and in turn to be consumed. It was all he could do to constrain himself.

All was a blur of mouths sucking at each other until he felt her hand guide him. It was all he could do not to shudder his release before he entered her. Warm, moist flesh held him tight and even as he reached the ends of her depths he wanted to press further. Never as Chosen had sex felt this way, so centred upon his need to be taken within another, the encapsulating tenderness that stroked him as he pounded into her, taking all of his attention. There was no blood scent spiced with lust that teased him to drink. There was no strict control not to rend and tear flesh to reach that blessed font. Now it was all about surrounding him, pulling at him to drive deeper until her embrace threatened to never let him go and that intense pulsating release matched only by hers, sucking him further into her depths until he could go no further. He never knew it was supposed to be like that.

It should have been like that.

It should have been like that with Jeanie.

Releasing a shuddering sigh, he swept his long white hair back and attempted to remember he was in the twenty-first century, not the late Victorian Age. What he had with Jeanie was something he never had with another and a part of him would always mourn her. Now he was a guest in Elizabeth's home, and though she stated there would be no repercussions to their love-making, he could not deny the impact the act had wielded upon him.

It was an act of compassion and succour the like of which he had never experienced before. There was no love, not like what he had with Jeanie, but what was there was enough to take away the raw edges caused by Notus' abandonment. Closing his eyes he took a deep cleansing breath. Here he was, Chosen no longer, awake in the day, with a yawning abyss of his past behind him, and for the first time in a very long time, an unknown future was set before him. The question as to what to do made him frown. No longer the Angel and his sword in Vampire hands, the question he had denied himself for ages flourished in the absence of other persons perceptions. Who was he? And more importantly, what was he? Opening his eyes he knew one thing, he would not find the answers sitting naked on a bed.

Rising from the bed he went to the opened closet and knelt before his suitcase on the floor. Other luggage was tucked further in as well as a box or two. He wondered when Notus had arranged all this and shook his head, dismissing the thought. Lifting the lid he was surprised to find only the white tank top undershirt and a pair of black jeans he wore yesterday. The rest were gone. Taken aback at the missing clothes, he slipped on the shirt and pants, closed the suitcase lid and pulled the smaller case forward. He did not need to open it to know it too was empty. Disconcerted and with no other recourse he left the room, the cream coloured broadloom soft beneath his bare feet, and he went down stairs.

The scent of cooking became stronger as he touched the cool Spanish floor tiling. Unknowing of what to expect he nearly fell over the short haired grey cat that appeared out of nowhere to rub against his legs. Lest he trip, hurting it or him, he scooped the cat up into his arms and cradled the purring ball of fur against his chest, absently scratching it behind its ear as he walked to the kitchen

Standing at the gas stove, dressed in blue jeans and a purple t-shirt, Elizabeth flipped pancakes on the griddle. In the centre of the kitchen a table was decked out for a breakfast feast. With the bounty of eggs, bacon and juice, his mouth flooded and his stomach roared. Called to the table by his visceral needs, he was unaware of Elizabeth opening the curtain over the kitchen window. Sunlight splashed across the room, ending its spill just before his feet. Eyes burning at the sudden brightness, the cat yowled and fell as his hands lifted to shade his eyes to diminish the throbbing headache that exploded.

"Grimalkin, what are–" Elizabeth halted her spin around, her eyes wide at the sight of her guest standing just inside the kitchen wearing only black denim and a white shirt that exhibited the scars on his arms and shoulders. "Oh I didn't know you were up."

Blinking through tearing eyes he could only see Elizabeth as a dark blurry shadow. "Could you please…" He waved his hand at the offending window.

"What? Oh! Of course!" Without further direction, Elizabeth closed the blinds. "I'm so sorry." She turned back to her guest who stood with eyes closed, a slight green tinge to his fair skin. "After yesterday, I should have known better." She walked over to him and placed a hand on his arm. "Come on. Sit down before you fall down."

Swallowing the gorge that rose, he let Elizabeth guide him to take a seat in the colonial style chair. Head in hands it took several deep steady breaths before the nausea and the pounding migraine dissipated enough for him to open his eyes.

"You really are that light sensitive, aren't you?" Surprise widened Elizabeth's blue eyes.

With a sigh he closed his eyes and nodded.

"And it's always been like this?" she queried.

"It's much better than it's been in a long time," he replied unable to keep the harsh irony from his voice.

Elizabeth sat straight and blinked several times before closing her mouth, surprise slowly turning to revelation. "That explains why Paul works at night. He does it because of you."

The mention of the Chosen who had been with him than more mortal lifetimes than he could count caused him to grimace. Let her believe what she might. It was usually close enough to the lie of convenience that Notus tended to spin that it was best not to contradict Elizabeth's conjecture.

"Oh dear, I did it again, didn't I?" Elizabeth laid a hand on his upper arm. "I seem to be making things worse for you, rather than better."

"It's okay," he lied, shaking his head. Lifting his head from his hands, he sat straight. "I appreciate everything you have done for me. I truly do. There's nothing for you to apologise for."

A frown touched Elizabeth's full lips and she leaned forward, raising her hand to his shoulder. It felt odd to have another touch his scarred skin, yet at the same time it was comforting. "You are most welcome to stay as long as you need," she said solemnly. "Our home is yours."

Sincerity wrapped her words, piercing him with their strength, surprising him and filling him with a sense of unworthiness of her generosity. "Thank you," he said breathlessly.

Elizabeth smiled warmly. "Now, is there anything I can get you?"

His white brows furrowed. "Actually there is. I was wondering where the rest of my clothes are."

Surprise alighted Elizabeth's blue eyes before she let out a laugh. "You didn't look in the dresser, did you?"

Comprehension took hold and he groaned. No, he had not.

"I unpacked for you after we came back yesterday. You were asleep."

"Then where are the rest of the clothes I wore?"

"They're in the laundry. I would have taken the shirt and pants too, but I didn't have any more room." Elizabeth's laughter rang through the kitchen.

Chagrined, he was hesitant to ask his next question. "And my braces?"

"In the night table drawer," smiled Elizabeth.

Groaning at his own stupidity, he leaned forward, elbows on the table, and rubbed his face before covering his mouth and nose with a shake of his head.

"Don't beat yourself up about it." Elizabeth rose and went over to the stove, picked up the plate of pancakes and placed them on the table. "I should have told you, but I don't think that was foremost on either of our minds at the time." She walked out of the kitchen to the bottom of the stairs and hollered for Vee to come down to eat. Without waiting for a response, Elizabeth re-entered the kitchen and sat down beside him.

It was not long before the sound of a rampaging elephant crashed down the stairs and thudded across tiling before skidding to a halt at a vacant kitchen chair. Dishevelled from having just woken Vee sported a knee length black t-shirt with a happy bunny with fangs on the front. Her black hair was a wild halo that now held purple streaks. Devoid of all make-up, she appeared younger, more innocent than the first time he had seen her at the *Royal Ontario Museum*. It was clear from the shocked look on her face that she had not expected company at the breakfast table. With a sharp intake of breath Vee crossed an arm over her chest while the other attempted to pull down the shirt past her knees. The sudden modesty surprised him as did her blue eyes as they widened at the sight of him. He did not have to follow her gaze to know that she stared at his scars. Mouth dry, he empathized with her need to cover up and not having anything with him to do so, he averted his eyes and clenched his jaw.

Recognizing the origins of the sudden tension in the kitchen, Elizabeth started piling her plate with food. "Vee, when have you ever been modest? Sit. Eat. No one here cares how you look. It's breakfast." Elizabeth took the bowl of scrambled eggs and began scooping some onto the plate next to hers. "What would you like with your eggs?"

Attention turning to the yellow clods being deposited on his plate, he was about to deny he that he was hungry when his stomach growled. Elizabeth smiled, traded serving dishes and added bacon to his plate and then a couple of pancakes. Across from him Vee attempted to flatten down her hair as she sat, filling her own plate with what her mother passed to her.

Returning his attention to the food before him, he took a shuddering breath. He could not deny what the mouth watering scent evoked in him but the idea of finally eating a real meal like a mortal still remained foreign as did the use of eating utensils. Lifting the fork, he surreptitiously glanced up at Vee watching how she held hers. It was awkward and his hands rebelled against the fine motor movements as he went to stab at the eggs with the fork. Releasing the cutlery, it clattered against the ceramic and he placed his hands under the table clenching each wrist in an attempt to ease the sudden spasm. It was too long since he wore the braces.

"Is everything okay?" Elizabeth's gaze rose from his lap to his eyes.

"I'll be fine in a minute," he said. He watched a querulous brown brow rise. He did not want to explain so he picked up the fork again, scooping eggs onto it, only to watch them fall off as his hand shook.

Without a word Elizabeth rose, walked over to a drawer, pulled something out and gave it to him before she sat down. "Try that."

Lifting the tablespoon he scooped up the eggs again, this time less of them spilled before he got them to his mouth. Their softness surprised him, as did their taste, as he chewed and swallowed. The effect of real food settling in his stomach erupted hunger in him and he scooped up more.

It was strange feeling the textures and tastes of food. A part of his mind rebelled against the reality, screaming at him that it was not what his body truly craved, but he could not deny the new instincts riding him to rapaciously dig into the breakfast Elizabeth laid before him. It was a different need that this nourishment fulfilled in him. Picking up the bacon in his fingers, after seeing Vee do the same, he bit into the salty crispness that was so different than the sustenance he had craved for centuries.

When he was Chosen he did not consider what he had left behind. It was too easy to walk away from starvation and loneliness. Now mortality brought new experiences, but despite the fact he sat with others he still felt alone. Placing the half eaten bacon back on the plate, he sat back, surprised and concerned at what he was doing. There was no blood lust driving his hunger, only the need to eat dead flesh and consume plant material. His body no longer subsisted on what living blood gave him. Experiences that once held a connection with the consumption of human blood were now shed of that need, revealing to his senses other sensations. The visceral needs of his body were different than what they once were and the realization that he was truly mortal was no longer a mental recognition, but now was forcibly internalized.

"Is everything alright?" asked Elizabeth, placing her fork down on her plate.

Her concern was palpable and Vee's querulous expression as she chewed her mouthful made him frown. Picking up his bacon, he bit off another portion, chewing it slowly. No, he was not alright.

Silence descended upon the breakfast table.

"Vee, are you still going out with your friends tonight?" asked Elizabeth in an attempt to alleviate the tension around the table.

The girl nodded. "I'm meeting Shell at seven-thirty," she said around a mouthful.

Elizabeth frowned in contemplation and turned to face him.

"Do you have any plans tonight?"

The question surprised him and he laid the spoon down on the table as he shook his head, wariness tightening the corners of his mouth. After their encounter last night he did not know what to expect.

Returning her attention to her daughter, Elizabeth placed her cutlery across her empty plate. "Vee, I'd like you to take Gwyn with you."

"What?" exclaimed Vee at the same time he turned to face his hostess. To chaperone Elizabeth's daughter's night out was the farthest from his imaginings.

"You know better than anyone why we can't have guests in the house tonight," expounded Elizabeth.

"Oh, Mom," whined the girl. Slouching in defeat, she released a melodramatic sigh. "Fine. I'll call Shell and let her know." Rising from the table Vee grabbed the cordless phone from the counter's end and went into the living room.

Confused at what just transpired, he pushed his half filled plate away, a sense of dread filling his belly.

"I'm sorry to do this to you," apologized Elizabeth, her blue eyes seeking understanding. "It's just for a few hours."

Refusing to meet her eyes he stared at the partially eaten food and frowned. "Why?"

A hand alighted on his scarred forearm and he turned to face her. Indecision averted her eyes and she worried the inside of her cheek. He knew that whatever her reasons, they were important to her.

"It's okay," he said. "You don't have to say. You've been more than generous to me and my silences."

"Thank you," she said, relieved, and gave his arm a gentle squeeze. "I appreciate it. I'm just worried about Vee. Ever since the incident at the ROM she's been afraid to leave the house. Her friends convinced her to go out with them tonight but she's trepidacious. Having you go with her will make her feel better, more confident."

"She didn't appear to be happy at your insistence."

Elizabeth let out a chuckle. "I would have thought you would understand considering it hasn't been that long since your teen years."

Her observation surprised him. For all intents and purposes he was twenty-one. It was what seemed logical to place on his expertly forged passport, but in reality he had be eighteen or nineteen when being Chosen had halted his growth within the stasis of immortality. Even still, he was never a teenager as Vee experienced it.

"I guess you had a very different time being a teen," observed Elizabeth, noting his frown.

"You could say that," he remarked, wryly.

Elizabeth nodded. A flicker of a smile lifted a corner of her sensuous mouth while her sad eyes roamed down his scarred arm, landing to focus on the silver blossom that told the tale of the spiked manacle that had been driven through him. Uncomfortable, he pulled his arm away, hiding his hands under the table.

Her hand no longer resting on him, Elizabeth sat straight. "The fact that Vee didn't fight me on this just shows that she's happy to have you along. Just wait. You'll see. After all, you are the one who saved her from the thieves."

Memories of that transformative night filled him and he closed his eyes against the flood. He could see the Vampire's lengthening teeth threaten Vee's perfectly pale neck. The fear induced effervescence arising from her had almost released his carefully controlled hunger. If it had not been the other Vampire stealing his sword things might have gone differently.

Rising from the table he gazed down on his hostess. "I will go with Vee." He did not need to add that he would try and keep Elizabeth's daughter from harm. It was implicit in his tone, which was very much that of the Angel.

XXÍV

He hugged his motorcycle as he guided the machine along Queen Street. It was slow going at this time of night and it took all of his concentration to keep the Y2K from bucking its reigns. Unfortunately, Toronto's active night life meant that if he did so he would end up in an accident. Mortal or no, he had promised Elizabeth the safe return of her daughter.

The car ahead of him hit their brakes as an elegantly dressed couple mindlessly jay walked towards one of the fancier restaurants in the Beach. Slamming his breaks and releasing the accelerator the motorcycle came to a halt inches from the yellow Mustang's bumper. Once the oblivious couple passed between two parked cars he put the bike into gear and the motorcycle jerked forward in an attempt to run free. Gritting his teeth he could not deny that the Y2K had been easier to control when he was Chosen.

He hated being mortal. The positive aspects were greatly diminished by the new physical experiences that were natural to everyone else. It was the return of mortal limitations that made it clearer than before his need to be Chosen again. Maybe, if he could find the right way, he could accidentally convince Notus, again. *Probably not.* He frowned as the dull pain of rejection flared back into life. Distracted he almost ran a red light, the Mustang having caught the tail end of the amber.

The tightness around his waist increased as he sat up. "Let go," he said into the headset built into the helmet. "You don't have to hold on so tight."

The arms relaxed but did not release. "Sorry," replied Vee, her quavering voice blossoming in his helmet.

The light changed and he leaned forward, taking the motorcycle in hand. The tension around his midsection increased and he could hear her panicked breathing in the headset. "Try and take slow even breaths," he said, concerned that she would hyperventilate and pass out.

"Okay," she mumbled.

He could hear the elongations of her breathing as he drove. After a few minutes she relaxed her hold.

"This isn't so bad," said Vee. "As long as you don't go too fast."

A small smile lifted the corners of his mouth and he slowed the bike down.

"Thanks for coming with me," murmured the girl. "I really didn't feel like going out, even though..." She let the thought trail off with a sigh.

He did not respond. He figured silence was the best approach and he focused his attention on the packed road ahead of him.

"I want to thank you for saving me from that crazy thief," said Vee. "I'm also sorry that they took your sword and you got hurt."

Frowning at the reminder she presented he wanted to press the motorcycle faster but could not in the congested traffic. Stuck once again he sat up. The bike hummed beneath him as he planted his feet on the tarmac. He knew Vee was expecting a reply but there was none he could give. Hands free from the handlebars he squeezed his hands into fists as far as the braces would allow, and released the threatening spasm. This was yet another thing since becoming mortal he had difficulties contending with. The injuries of his body seemed to constantly ache.

"Are you angry at me?" queried Vee, her voice wary over the speaker.

Releasing his grip he stared at all the cars lined up with their left signal lights on. With the parked cars taking up the right lane there was nothing to do but wait. "No, I'm not angry at you," he replied. He wished the girl would settle into quietness, but that afternoon, hearing her monopolize the telephone, he knew that was beyond her ken.

"Are you angry at Mom?"

The question surprised him and he shook his head. It was not Elizabeth's fault that his sword was in the hands of Vampires and he was now mortal. That was all his doing.

"Then why won't you talk to me?" Hurt filled her tones.

The traffic moved ahead a few car lengths and he gentled the beast to glide into its next waiting position.

"It's because of how I stared at you at breakfast? Isn't it?" reasoned Vee. "I didn't mean to. It's just that I never saw anyone with so many–"

"Stop," he ordered, gritting his teeth.

"That's it, isn't it?" babbled the girl as if she had not heard him. "It's just that you're so different than anyone I've seen before and–"

"Vee, just stop." He relaxed his jaw and opened his eyes. He had not realized he had closed them. The girl was too accurate in her observations and he did not need to be reminded of things that had attracted too much attention to him, good and ill.

"Sorry." Her voice was small in the headset. "You probably don't want be with me and are upset that mom made you come with me."

The traffic inched ahead and he followed, wishing that the road would open up and he could put some speed on. It was better when she was afraid. She was quiet.

"If I tell you why you couldn't stay at the house, will you stop being angry at me?"

"I'm not angry at you," he stated unable to keep the coldness from his voice.

"Mom's a witch," bluntly stated Vee.

The declaration stunned him. "What?" Witches were both medieval women and men who were killed because they were singled out as scapegoats or for land grabs during a time of superstitiousness and idiocy, or they were Hollywood inventions to amuse the masses. To hear Vee talk about her mother that way was shocking.

"Actually, she's a Wiccan High Priestess and her coven is coming over tonight for one of their Circles," expounded Vee. "That's why we couldn't be there. I used to go to my father's before he got sick, but now I usually go over to a friend's or go out."

The revelation surprised him and it took the car behind him honking before he popped the motorcycle in gear and finally cut through the intersection. He had heard of this new religion when he returned back to London. It was all over the press with photos of naked women and ominous looking men. Notus just shook his head, ignoring it, but many of the principles of belief that he read about in the interviews were very similar to the ones taught to him as a child.

Moving past cars as he came closer to the centre of the city he caught the reflection of the full moon off of one of the glass covered buildings. Memories of a childhood with Auntie pouring libations and leaving offerings at the full moon flooded back, as well as times when he would wake afterwards to find the old woman not on her pallet but outside speaking the old words in ceremonies he was not allowed to participate in. She had never fully trained him in the religion of the Goddess Danu and Her Children. If this Wicca was some sort of recreation of that, then it made sense why he and Vee could not be in the house, but Vee should not have told him. That was for Elizabeth to do if she deemed fit, and he told Vee so. "Don't you think that if Elizabeth wanted me to know that about her she would have told me herself?"

Chagrined, Vee offered a hasty apology before uttering a squeak as he gunned the engine. The tightness returned around his waist as well as blissful silence. He would not tell Elizabeth what Vee had revealed, but it did explain her expertise in Celtic archaeology and the figurines and paintings adorning her walls.

Once past Spadina Avenue, Vee indicated where they were to stop. Pulling the Y2K into an open parking space on the street he shut off the engine and gave Vee a hand off the bike. She passed him her helmet, freeing her head with a savage shake of her head. Turning off the headset in the second helmet he dismounted, hauled the motorcycle up on its kickstand and turned as someone shouted the girl's name.

A group of teens dressed in black garb, some of it reminiscent of Victorian England, descended upon Vee who happily ate up the attention of her friends. One girl in particular leaned to whisper something in Vee's ear, her soft blue-grey eyes on him. A bright smile split Vee's black painted lips. Slipping her arm through her friends, she turned towards him. Wishing he could remain hidden under his helmet he knew he could not and proceeded to remove the black head protection.

"This is my best friend," Vee announced as an introduction. "Shell, this is—"

A gasp from Shell cut off the rest as she saw him reveal himself.

Placing the helmet next to the other on the seat of the

motorcycle he suppressed a sigh of annoyance and freed his queued hair from the inside of his black leather jacket to the widening of Shell's eyes. Vee's other friends shared Shell's surprise. Some even mingled their shock with longing. He knew that look. It was one that tended to get him into more trouble than those who gazed at him with fear and horror.

"You're the guy that saved Vee." Shell's question was more of a statement, her eyes wide in awe.

He scanned the group of five girls and two boys. One thing struck him. They all appeared so young despite their adult costuming and make-up. The sense of his own years overwhelmed him, making him feel very old.

His gaze descended lastly onto Vee's friend. Dressed in a black silk blouse cinched by a black vinyl corset, the ends draped over a black layered skirt that hinted at the knee high laced boots. If it were not for her hair being light brown with purple streaks Shell's appearance was almost identical to Vee's. The only thing out of place was the glasses sitting on the girl's small nose. There was no doubt that Vee and Shell were thick as thieves.

Knowing that Vee and her friends were expecting an answer he crouched down, turning his back on them as he proceeded to lock the two helmets to the motorcycle. "It could be said," he replied, quietly.

"Ooooh, he's got an accent," remarked one of the other girls.

He immediately closed his eyes and inwardly groaned, thankful he faced the Y2K. He used the seat to assist him to stand once the expensive helmets were locked into place. Not knowing who made the juvenile comment he looked down at Vee. Smiling, and with a better sense of decorum, Vee ignored the comment and introduced her friends. Each quickly met his gaze before sliding away. Once the introductions were made one of the boy's announced that they should head over to the club and the gaggle proceeded down the sidewalk.

He hung back and went to the parking slip dispenser to pay for the spot. Taking the white and green slip he turned to the motorcycle only to find one of Vee's friends waiting for him.

"Vee asked me to make sure you know where you're going," remarked the slender boy. "She noticed you hadn't followed."

Placing the slip onto the dash so as to be seen through the tiny windshield and still protected from blowing away he dismissed the comment until he witnessed the boy caress the tail of the

Y2K. A sudden sense of territorial proprietorship filled him and he turned to glower at the lad.

"Sorry, man," placated the boy with raised hands. "Didn't mean to dis your lady. She must be a sweet ride," he said, and added as an afterthought. "I'm Justin." The boy held out a black nailed hand.

It was a gesture of friendship that he was not expecting. Quickly he reassessed the teen all dressed in black leathers. His black hair, painted almond eyes and soft features were enough to declare Justin's Oriental roots. Slipping his hand into the teen's they briefly shook.

"We should get going," suggested Justin. "Vee'll bite my head off if she starts to worry where I am." He gave a grunted laugh and turned to take the same route the others had gone.

He fell in beside Justin, silently impressed that the boy easily kept up with his long strides. He was also appreciative that the boy did not succumb to idyll chatter. It was also clear that Justin enjoyed the ominous appearance the two of them made. Several passers-by stared wide-eyed. Only those similarly dressed to Vee and her friends smiled appreciatively as they passed.

It did not take long to arrive at the entrance to what could only be their destination. Black painted doors and frontage gave the false appearance of an abandoned building. Only the pounding music sliding out of the open doors and the small black and red Gothically painted sign above were proof of the building's true purpose. In front, a group of handsomely black clad individuals waited patiently to pass the large security guards checking identification. Their black t-shirts sported the club's name, *Beyond The Veil*, across their muscular chests. Frowning, he followed Justin to the group of friends. Unhappy with the prospect of being in a crowded group of youngsters, he slid his hands into his pockets and gazed at the ground.

"Isn't this exciting?" asked Vee. She pounded up to Justin and gave the boy a fierce hug. It was obvious that the two were an item. It also offered more clarity why Elizabeth had wanted him to go with Vee rather than going out on his own.

He did not know if Vee's excitement was directed at him or Justin but was glad when the boy replied with a smile and nod. "You have your I.D. ready?" asked the boy, pulling out a card from his front jacket pocket. He gave Vee a wink and she answered with a smile.

The subtleties between the youngsters were not lost on him as they moved up the line. He kept quiet as one by one the teens flashed forged identification and entered *The Veil* until he looked down on the burly security guard. The man gazed up at him, seeing him for the first time, and the guard's stoic visage broke into surprise.

"I.D?" the man requested his voice gruff.

"I'm well over the legal age," he replied, keeping his eyes on the man. It was not that he was trying to Push the man, but centuries old instincts still governed him. He only realized the futility of his action when the guard broke eye contact to give him the once over.

"You'll do," stated the guard.

Passing the threshold into the noise infested venue, he did not see the guard speak into the tiny earphone.

The first thing that struck him as he ascended the worn black linoleum stairs was the incredible loudness of the pounding music and how it was accentuated with the buzz of voices. Once at the top of the stairs he was in the club proper. Before him a bar, attended by exotically black clad women, served an extensive array of alcohol to clientele and wait staff. Despite the very low light the multi-coloured pot lights added enough to throw everything into shadow. He exploded a breath of irritation that his now mortal sight could not penetrate the darkness as his Chosen vision had. He heard a familiar voice call out to him through the cacophony and turned towards it.

To the left, booths of black vinyl seats and square marble tables lined the sides of the area. In between, black metallic bistro tables peppered the space. Repressing a shudder, he stepped into the crowd and walked over to Vee and her friends who had pulled together a row of tables.

"I'm going to dance," announced Shell. Grabbing two other girls, they got up. "Maybe I'll see Brian again," she said hopefully before she and her friends were swallowed up by the crowd.

He watched them until they disappeared on a dance floor framed with nearly nude dancers in brass cages and flashing lights. A sudden sinking feeling gripped him as he sat in the vacated chair. He ignored the idyll chatter that screamed back and forth over the table and watched the crowd.

Never at ease in a large group, or even a small one, he was

surprisingly grateful to be inconspicuous among the men and women dressed in Gothic fashion. The only accentuating colour seemed to be red. Many outfits were elaborate in their stylings. Some brought back memories of times he wished had never occurred. Uncomfortable at the clash between old and modern, he redirected his attention to the fantastical metal artwork and statuary that gave the night club a futuristic quality. Unease grew in him with the realization that this was his first time in a night club.

His musings came to a halt with the sudden silence around the table. Glancing from one astonished teen to the next, he realized they were not staring at him but rather at someone at his side. Swivelling in his seat he turned to find a very attractive woman standing beside him.

Smiling blue eyes were given greater prominence with her blonde curling hair pulled away from her face to play seductively on her pale shoulders. Dressed in a low cut black peasant blouse, the tops of her breasts prominently showed. The knee length layered skirt accentuated her perfect figure and shapely legs.

"My name is Orchid." She offered her black netted hand to him. The blood red of her fingernail polish momentarily caught the light from a flashing strobe. "You're new here."

He briefly took her hand in his, noting its chill.

"I'd like you to buy me a drink," she smiled, flashing the whites of her teeth.

He frowned at the sight of her elongated canines. A tingling spread up his back, forcing him to sit straighter. "No thank you," he replied over the music.

"Are you sure?" she purred, coming closer to him. "I'll make it worth your while."

"I said, no." Ice froze his tones as he gazed into her eyes.

A flash anger flickered and then was gone, replaced by a fake smile. "It's you're loss," said Orchid. With a dismissive wave of her hand she allowed the crowd to swallow her up.

"Are you crazy?" demanded Vee, her eyes wide with shock. "Don't you know who that was?"

He did not care. He was more concerned with what she possibly could be and what the night club was really for. The Chosen had similar places where they could feed from mortals without the concern of discovery. If this place was something similar for Vampires, then he was in grave danger. Not risking an answer he stood, ignored Vee and her friends, and left the table. Descending the steps to exit the building he did not notice Orchid speaking to two men sitting at the bar, no drinks in their hands.

Once outside the building he walked a few store fronts west before halting inside a laneway. Taking deep breaths he slowed his racing heart. One thing he did not need reminding of was now that he was mortal he could not defend himself as he used to when he was the Angel. There would be no preternatural speed and strength, and there would be no white-faced demons to call.

The sound of people entering the alley lifted his head. Two men of nondescript colouring and average height stood smiling maliciously. He did not need to see their fangs to know that two Vampires approached.

Standing away from the brick wall he glanced down to the other end of the alley and silently swore. He inadvertently boxed himself in a dead-end. The only thing he had in his favour was that if they knew him as the Angel then they would assume he was still Chosen. Then again, if that were the case then there would not be only two Vampires facing him. Regardless, he was in a fight for his life. If was extremely lucky he would come out of it alive, and with information about his sword's whereabouts. He turned to face the two Vampires, settling into a loose and ready stance. He would wait until they made the first move.

"You insulted our Lady," said the one on the right.

"She doesn't usually interact with the patrons," explained the other. A sneer twisted his plain face. "And you rejected the honour she was showing you."

He stood silently, not daring to reply. What was clear as they approached was that they did not know who he was. It also provided the explanation as to why only two Vampires sauntered towards him. They believed him to be mortal and thus had the advantage. In that they were right.

The punch from the one on the right was easily blocked and redirected while at the same time he landed a blow to the Vampire's nose. Cartilage imploded in a gush of blood and a yowl. The Vampire stopped to lick the blood from his lips and smiled, revealing extended canines. His partner shook out his hands in expectation as a sinister grin split his face revealing his elongated teeth.

Taking a cleansing breath, he eased the growing panic and waited for the inevitable to come.

The Vampires exploded into motion. Their speed was blurring as he tried to block their unschooled blows. Training and centuries of practice barely kept him apace in his mortal body. He met punches with blocks barely in place to be effectual and his strikes barely grazed their targets. His arms and legs ached with the impacts. It did not take long for one of the Vampires to slip past his defences.

Pain blossomed in his chest as he felt his body leave the ground. Agony slammed into his back, his sight blacked out as skull met brick. Nauseous and tasting blood he slid to the rubbish strewn alley trying to regain his stolen breath. He had to move. He had to get to his feet and defend himself but as his sight returned so did sensation. Gasping in pain, he cut it short as a stabbing sensation burned across his ribs. Hand on the wall he spat out the blood and watched liquid threads hang from his mouth before he wiped them away on the back of his arm. The cool leather gave some relief from the split lip he had no memory receiving. He attempted to stand but felt his body forcibly spin around as one of the Vampires grabbed a hold of him. Knocked to his knees, stagnant water seeped through his denim. A hand yanked his hair, forcing him to expose his neck.

He knew what they were about to do and long held memories surged forward from the time he had been a prisoner of a sadistic Vampiress. He tried to break free only to feel the connective tissue of his shoulder start to separate from the joint as his arm was pinned behind his back. He gasped and immediately regretted it for the renewed stab across his chest.

Facing the entrance of the laneway he watched, immobilized as the other Vampire came into sight. Panic stirred his heart and he could not catch his breath. He had to break free but could only anticipate the inevitable.

"Dyed hair and costume contacts," derided the Vampire. "The only reason I can think of for my Lady's interest in you is your pretty face."

The Vampire gripped his chin and forced him to meet the Vampire's eyes. The smile widened and the Vampire bent forward towards his exposed neck. His gorge rose as he felt dead breath tickle across his skin. Held firmly in place he could only wait for the slice of teeth into flesh.

*   *   *

Corbie sat with his back to the desk, his chin resting in one hand while the other held the remote control for the array of videos that spanned from floor to ceiling. His thumb absently hit the reverse button on one of the monitors and he watched again the entrance of the Angel to his club. A moment on fast forward saw the Angel leaving his establishment. Face twisted with growing anger Corbie hit the playback on another camera that showed the Angel sitting with well known patrons. Strange in itself, what was truly disturbing was seeing one of his coterie approach the Angel and then stalk off. Reversing the image, Corbie watched the unsuccessful interaction with growing anger. What if the Angel had run into Rose? Swivelling around, he punched a button on his desk.

"Mr. Haskell. Find Orchid and meet me in my office." The order spilled through seething lips.

"Yes, sir," came the static reply. The sound of Brian's infuriatingly calm tones were mixed with the beat of the club.

Releasing the button, Corbie raised his hand to strike the desk and thought better of it. He had splintered the last one and it took three months and an exorbitant amount of money to have it replaced to his specifications. Regardless, the Dominus of Vampires desperately wanted to hit something, or someone. How could the Angel saunter into his domain without Corbie having been notified? And then to have one of his coterie walk up to the Angel and speak to that damnable creature without his permission was downright insubordinate. One question exacerbated the situation – where was Brian when all this was happening?

A knock tapped at the door. Without waiting for an invitation Corbie's second walked into the white room with the seductive Vampiress on his heels. "You summered us, Dominus?"

Mr. Haskell took up a relaxed stance before the desk while Orchid curled up on the white leather couch against the back wall. She appeared dreamy and Corbie knew she had just fed. Returning his attention to his right hand man, Corbie went for the direct approach. "Why wasn't I informed about the Angel's visit here tonight?"

Corbie's anger grew at the confusion overtaking his second's usually emotionless face. Orchid's frown made her appear younger.

"I don't know what you are talking about, sir," stated Brian. "No one informed me of the Angel's appearance."

"No?" pressed Corbie. His hand lay flat on the desk as he rose like a vulture to peer at the man and was rewarded with Mr. Haskell's stumbling response.

"I–I would have been informed," said Brian, obviously flustered. "Becky would have told me."

"And what about you?" rounded Corbie, his gaze descending upon Orchid.

"I don't know what you're talking about?" replied the Vampiress. She nervously smoothed down her blonde locks.

Picking up the remote control Corbie set the video to play back her brief interaction with the Angel. He kept his eyes on her, marking her reactions as she watched the recreation. Surprise and disbelief widened her beautiful brown eyes.

"That was the Angel?" she asked, incredulously. "I thought he was just another kid in costume. Granted, he was a gorgeous looking kid,"

Corbie smacked the desk. The crack resounded through the room as well as the groaning sound as wood succumbed to force. He did not want to hear how attractive the hideous Angel was to the opposite sex. His strange allure was what caused Violet's demise. "I want to know what you did after the Angel rejected you."

"He–"

Corbie raised his hand, halting her excuses. "Rejection is not a word in your vocabulary. What did you do?"

Anger darkened her eyes. "I told two of my coterie."

"And?" He met her gaze.

"They went after him."

Corbie closed his eyes. Maybe if he did not look at her he would not be tempted to stake her. He only opened his eyes when he sat, the soft leather cushioning his body, the anger hardening his heart. His gaze fell on Orchid. "Get out."

"Get out?" she queried. Fury forced her to her feet.

A smug smile pulled at Corbie's thin lips. He loved it when he was proven right. "That is what I said." He allowed his anger to simmer. "If you do not wish to be transferred to Sudbury to rule rather than New York City I would suggest that you leave now."

Without a word of protest Orchid stalked to the door and left, her face marred by the twisting effects of restrained anger. The door closed quietly behind her.

Once the click died out, Corbie relaxed into his seat and

turned his attention to his second. "I want you to send the best four of your coterie to find Orchid's wayward sons."

"Yes, sir." Brian stood straighter.

"When they find them, stake them and then leave them for the sun."

"Sir?"

"If the Angel hasn't already killed them I want their deaths to help fuel my plans."

"Yes, sir!" Brian turned to leave but his Dominus' voice halted him as his hand touched the door handle.

"Two more things, Mr. Haskell." Corbie nonchalantly played with the leather of his chair as Brian turned back towards him. "There has been a significant break down in communications. Fix it. Secondly, the Angel has been here. He will be back. I was not expecting him so soon but I will not be caught off guard again." He patted the leather and stared into his second's blue-grey eyes. "You will immediately inform me of the Angel's arrival in or around *The Veil*. Are my orders clear?"

"Yes, sir."

"Good," replied the Dominus Vampire. "No more mistakes, Mr. Haskell. You are dismissed."

Corbie ignored Brian's departure and picked up the white telephone.

XXV

It was unexpected when death came. All he could do was stare in wide eyed shock at the sight of a ragged piece of wood jutting from the chest of his would be murderer. Thick black blood coated the wood, leaving trails and globules to drip onto the murky alley floor. The sight of the Vampire shrivelling around the stake was cut off as he was flung to the ground. Arm freed, he managed to lift his face from the puddle. Spitting polluted water he tried to focus on the fight going on nearby. His assailant and would-be saviour battled with blurring speed. He tried to watch but could not focus on the fight. Instead he attempted to stand only to fail. His ribs and shoulder stealing his breath, leaving him panting and kneeling in stagnant water.

Abruptly as it started the fight was over. His second assailant splashed to the ground in front of him, shrivelling despite the moisture. Dead wooden eyes stared up at him as skeletal hands grasped the piece of wood sticking out of the Vampire's chest. Relief washed over him at the sight.

"Holy fuck," swore his saviour. "I didn't want to believe Notus, but seeing you like this…"

The man walked towards him, haloed by streetlight. "Fernando?" he asked in surprise.

"Who do you think it is? The Tooth Fairy?"

He felt himself hauled to his feet and he gazed down on the Noble, a bronze hand holding him steady lest his legs give out. "How? How is it possible?" he asked, wincing at the pain across his chest.

Fernando cocked his head, listening to something outside

mortal range. Turning back, the Noble grabbed a bruised arm and pulled his friend into the street. "C'mon. My car's this way."

Gasping in the effort to still the pain while filling his lungs, he hugged his arms across his chest as he tried to keep up. It was not long before he was ordered into a titanium convertible *BMW Z4 Roadster*, its interior open to the sky. He groaned out a sigh as he let the fine leather take his weight. Beside him Fernando started the engine, pulling out of the parking spot with a screech of the tires in a tight U-turn. Gripping the door handle a flurry of questions bombarded his mind. He blurted out the most pressing one. "Why are you here?" He grimaced at the pain from his lower lip. Sucking on it, his tongue tasted blood from the split.

"Saving your sorry ass," replied the Chosen as he swerved the Beemer around a double parked vehicle, forcing the oncoming traffic to hit their brakes. "Shit," muttered the Noble. "Can't people drive here?" He gunned the engine until they were forced to halt at a red light.

Fernando turned to face his friend. A mixture of disgust and pity filled his dark brown eyes before facing forward with the turning of the traffic light to green.

Fernando's answer disturbed him and he frowned. He was already beholden to the Noble for saving his life and for ensuring he would not be Destroyed so long as the Angel served the Chosen in the capacity he had excelled in – death. He had been the Chosen's assassin. That was all over now. He could not even defend himself against two Vampires.

"How did you find me?" He hated how tired his voice sounded.

Missing the amber light Fernando had to wait to turn north on University. "By sheer dumb luck," answered the Noble. "I was out searching for a bite when I saw the commotion. I figured what a better way than with a ruffian. I wasn't expecting a run in with two Vampires about to make the Angel into a nice light snack."

He winced at Fernando's bluntness.

"By the way, you owe me a meal," stated the Chosen.

His eyes widened before he recognized the glint in the Noble's eye. "How do you—" His voice caught in agony as Fernando spun the car north before the oncoming traffic could register the change to green. Closing his eyes he gripped the door handle, the centrifugal force sending stabs of red heat. Once the car straightened out the pressure released but the pain did not.

"How badly hurt are you?" asked Fernando with a mixture of annoyance and worry.

"I don't know," he breathed. Each breath was agony.

"We'll be at the hotel soon." Fernando focused on driving. "When Notus said you were now mortal Bridget and I could not believe it. Once Chosen always Chosen. No one has ever been changed back, as far as we know, and we checked. We also knew we had to come. Ha, here we are." He pulled the car to the front door of a luxurious hotel that was across from the *Royal Ontario Museum*.

A valet opened the passenger door, his bored expression replaced with shock. Ignoring the valet he gingerly exited the low riding vehicle and stood on the sidewalk staring at the location that had changed his existence. Fernando threw the keys to the valet as he rounded the sloped rear of the car. Taking his arm, the Noble led him into the hotel, its grandeur lost in the rush to the elevator.

It was strange to be manhandled by the Noble and to suffer his silences but he was grateful to have an empty elevator and the time to try and catch his painful breath. It was also strange that even though he was no longer Chosen he could still sense the seething emotions from the immortal standing beside him. It was not as strong as before. It was more of an undercurrent that nudged at his consciousness. His attention was driven away from the sensation as the elevator came to a stop, causing him to wince. Panting in pain he followed the Noble down the brightly lit hall to a door that admitted Bridget.

"Oh my God!" she exclaimed. Tears filled her eyes as she sped over to him, appearing before him in a blink of an eye. "Let's get you inside." She took over from her Chosen, guiding him into a suite fit for royalty. He would have been impressed by the fine décor had it not been for Bridget guiding him to a tan brocade sofa.

"When Fernando informed me that he found you I was thrilled," explained Bridget as she helped him to sit. "But when he said you were attacked by Vampires I was worried."

Relaxing into the sofa, he gazed up at Britain's Mistress. Concern creased her pale brow. Her knowledge of the incident made it clear why Fernando had been so quiet in the car. Despite being mortal he was relieved to be with them.

"Let me see your neck," ordered Bridget. She walked around

to the back of the couch to stand behind him.

"They didn't bite me," he replied. The idea of how close he had truly come to having his life drunk out of him sent a chill up his spine.

Ignoring him, Bridget swept his hair to one side and turned his head from side to side. He suffered the inspection lest a greater argument ensue but it was the motion that made him wince. He knew better than to say no to her.

"That's a relief," she announced. She walked around to face him. It was then he noticed the simple style of a black and pink floral summer dress hugging her petite form. Blonde hair spilled in waves around her heart shaped face. Pulling the locks back, she magically transformed her appearance into one of greater efficiency and maturity as she twisted her hair into a self held bun. She turned to watch Fernando walk in with a bucket of ice and offered her Chosen a sad smile. He responded with a nod, dark eyes flashing in annoyance before turning towards the suite's hall to the bathroom.

"Where else are you hurt?" asked Bridget, returning her attention to her patient.

"I'm fine." He immediately regretted the lie when the Noble returned with a facecloth filled with ice. Taking it from Fernando, Bridget sat down on the couch and pressed the cold pack against his split lower lip. The sensation made him pull back. His ribs, protesting the movement, making him gasp.

"You're fine, my ass," muttered Fernando as he sat on the lounge chair across from him. "I've seen you worse, but you didn't try and lie about it."

The accusation stung. Having Fernando save him from Violet's ministrations forced him to reveal all his precious secrets to the Chosen. It was hard to lie about iron's effects on him when the evidence was carved, pierced and whipped into him. Now he sat before the Mistress and Master of the Chosen of Britain, his lip split and Gods know what else damage that proclaimed him mortal. Lifting a hand, he took the cold pack from Bridget and glanced at the blood on the white terrycloth before pressing it back onto his numb lip. The relief from the cold almost convinced him the wound was healed, but when he touched his tongue to the cut the pain flared back into life.

Bridget stood back, finger to her lip, as she studied him. Her scrutiny made him nervous and he stared at the find sand coloured broadloom.

"What happened to you, Gwyn?" she asked in all seriousness. She sat on the arm of Fernando's chair.

He knew the question was coming and grimaced. "I don't know." He closed his eyes to the memories. "I was on the roof of the museum, chasing the Vampire who stole my sword, when suddenly there was a tingling sensation and then nothing. I woke up, several days later, in a hospital with Notus saying I was no longer Chosen."

"Vampires managed to take your sword from you?" asked Fernando, incredulously.

He glared at the Noble. He knew what Fernando was thinking and sought to correct it. "I had lent it for the exhibit. Vampires stole it from there."

Fernando made a disparaging sound as he shook his head sending shoulder length brown locks to fall in his face. Gracefully, the Noble swept his hair back with a tanned hand. "What I want to know is why you are still mortal? You can't very well continue to be mortal. Just look at you. As the Angel you could have easily taken down two insignificant Vampires, but now," Fernando shook his head, "you're a target for every Vampire in the Americas. Why hasn't Notus fixed this problem?"

Always the one to cut to the heart of the matter, Fernando pierced his. Unable to match gazes with the Noble, he turned his head. "I asked him," he said quietly.

Silence impacted in the room.

"He denied you?" Bridget's stunned whisper grew in indignation with each syllable, forcing her to her feet.

Uncomfortable with her accusation and his surprising reflexive need to defend Notus, he rose from the couch with the intent to pace away his agitation. Ice pack discarded on the glass end table, chips spilled from the cloth. Pushing to stand, pain flared across his chest, stealing his breath and forcing him to hunch over.

"You're hurt," exclaimed Bridget, coming to his side.

Grimacing, he straightened in the hopes his lungs would pull in much needed air. Bridget tugged at his leather jacket in an effort to remove it. "Why didn't you say something?"

"He did," stated Fernando. He crossed his ankles, stretching out in the chair. "He just lied, and badly as usual. I don't know why you even bother."

He attempted to scowl at the Noble, but as he did Bridget

freed one arm from the coat with a jerk that caused him to catch his limited breath. He knew what was giving her difficulty – the braces on his wrists. She was right and he tried to assist only to feel another breath stealing stab.

"Are you just going to sit there," Bridget turned to her Chosen, "or are you going to help?"

Fernando crossed his arms over his muscular chest, the navy blue silk shirt whispering at the movement. "Do I look like a nurse-maid?"

Uttering a sound of disgust from the back of her throat, Bridget returned her attention to gingerly remove the jacket. Once relieved of the heavy weight, he found he still could not take a deep breath without pain. Concerned, he assisted Bridget with the removal of the braces. It was the first opportunity to study the bruises developing across his knuckles. Twinges radiated up and down his hands as he flexed them.

"Sit down," ordered Bridget as she placed the black braces next to the jacket now perched on the sofa's arm.

Carefully he lowered himself down onto the couch. The height difference allowed Bridget to unbutton his black cotton shirt.

The Master of London leaned forward, elbows coming to rest on his knees. "Why did Notus refuse you? And don't lie to me. We all know you can't lie yourself out of a wet paper bag. And don't make excuses for that monk in an effort to protect him. His denial already threatened your life."

The Noble stared at him, brown eyes smouldering. The points brought one more to mind. "Being Master of the Chosen you no longer have dominance over me since I am no longer Chosen. I do not have to answer you."

He realized his mistake too late. Fernando stiffened his body tight in controlled rage. Bridget turned to face him, hurt and anger written across her delicate features.

"No, you're right," she said cutting off Fernando's response. Her voice was succinct as emotion threatened to overtake her. "We're no longer your Master and Mistress. You are not beholden to us. I guess we were wrong all these years, protecting you from the other Masters and Mistresses from wanting to Destroy you because of your differences. That's all they ever saw. They don't know you. They only know the Angel, not the man behind him. Do you think we came all this way into Vampire infested territory because we were your Master and Mistress? We came here, searching for you, after finding out that you were no longer Chosen, not because of that, but because we thought we were friends."

He stared up in surprise into watery blue eyes, mortification twisting his guts. "I – I did not realize," he said lamely. He dropped his gaze.

"No, you didn't," said Fernando through clenched jaws.

"And that's the shame of it." Bridget sat down beside him on the couch, taking his scarred and bruised hands into hers flawless ones.

"Why the fuck do you think we came here?" accused the Noble.

Guilt and confusion flowed through him and he pulled his hand back, not wanting to see the effects of his thoughtlessness on her face. Now he was mortal, and stripped of that identity he did not know who he was.

Closing his eyes he could not believe how low he felt. Patterns of behaviour over centuries had taught him that there was only one reason for his worth – the Angel. He believed Notus had cared about him for himself. He was wrong. Notus had said so, denying him to be Chosen again by the man who had been more of a father to him than anyone in his life. Now he was mortal again and the truth had shown him the real reason. He had been an obligation due to a broken Oath. The truth of it slammed home and he had trouble forcing the tears back down.

He had used the word friend to describe Bridget and Fernando, but only now did the true extent of its meaning strike him. Where Notus had abandoned him, they had left their safe home to travel to a dangerous place to help him in the name of that friendship. "I'm so sorry," he said, opening his eyes to look at his friends.

"You bet your sorry ass you are." Fernando shook his head, a slight smirk marking his lips. "Now, if you're done with your standard melancholy, I'd like to get past the mushy parts. It's bad for my digestion."

Bridget smiled in agreement and brushed stray white hairs from his face with her cold hand. "Let's see what the damage is."

"I hope it hurts," muttered Fernando. "Too bad you left your paddles at home." The last was directed at Bridget.

"I didn't have room for them in the suitcase," countered Bridget, a golden eyebrow lifting.

"No, of course not. Shoes are more important than toys."

"We don't need toys," purred Bridget.

Fernando grinned back, his pointed Chosen teeth in full view.

He was not so sure whether or not it was a good thing when Bridget returned her attention to him. "Let's get you out of that," she said, helping him as he shrugged out of his shirt.

He did not know what to think when Fernando's brows lifted and Bridget's eyes went wide at the sight of his bare skin.

"Finally, you'll have some real colour," jovially remarked the Noble.

"Fernando!" admonished Bridget. Returning her attention to her patient she continued as she took in the scope of his wounds, "You're arms are going to be black and blue. What did they hit you with? A crow bar?"

"And red, don't forget red," commented Fernando.

"And is that the burn from the lightning strike?" she said, a look of awe across her face. "That's healing fast."

He knew they were just trying to lighten the mood but at the sight of the large welts running the lengths of his arms he was secretly impressed at how well he had defended himself against two creatures who were now stronger and faster than his mortal body. It was a miracle he had not broken an arm, or a leg. It was when he prodded the blossoming swelling down the left side of his ribcage that he realized he may have not gotten off that easily. "I think I have a broken rib."

"Let me see," ordered Bridget as she began her own palpations.

Each touch made him flinch eliciting more stabbing sensations. He tried to endure the examination with gritted teeth and was only able to relax his jaw when she finally removed her hands.

"At least two are broken that I can feel," she announced. "We can either go to a hospital to see what's really going on with an x-ray, or I can bind them and hope for the best."

"You do it," he replied. He gazed into blue eyes. "I trust you."

She rewarded him with a smile as she stood. Walking over to the stand next to the couch, Bridget picked up the mobile phone, punching numbers as she walked towards the window.

Left effectively alone with the Noble, he turned to see a thoughtful expression cross Fernando's face and was surprised when the Noble came to sit beside him on the couch. Uncomfortable with Fernando's proximity, he tried to back away only to have his left hand caught in a cold grip. A dagger with a white dot in the centre of a black teardrop decorated the pommel of Yin, one of a matching pair of blades Fernando was never without, pressed against the back of his pale hand. Anger blossomed at the attack and tried to pull away only to find himself in an iron grip.

"What are you doing?" he asked when he realized Bridget was out of sight.

"You're an ass, you know," stated the Noble.

"I thought that was reserved for you," came the automatic reply.

The pressure in the vice grip tightened and he felt his bones grate against each other causing him to wince.

"Were you like this before you were Chosen?" sneered Fernando. "Or because of being Chosen? Shall we find out?"

"What are you talking about?" His heart sped up.

Fernando leaned closer, his voice turning sultry like a snake oil salesman. "Didn't it occur to you that you could find out if the differences that marked you for Destruction as Chosen were because of an aberration in the blood you exchanged with Notus or because of something about *you*."

The query stunned him. It was not something that had come to mind since his return to mortality. He had had too much else to contemplate. Now with the question before him he frowned, staring at the bruising scars along the arm Fernando held fast. He did not recall having such reactions when last mortal, but could it be possible and if so what would that mean? Meeting Fernando's gaze with determination he nodded once. "Do it."

An eager grin lifted the corners of Fernando's lips, sending a chill to dampen the need for the truth. Before he could voice his concern Yin bit into the back of his left hand.

Searing pain spread up his arm as the scent of burning flesh wafted to his nostrils. He watched in growing horror the cautery the simple dagger had caused. It was the sight of thin black tendrils slithering up his wrist to his forearm that widened his eyes. Without warning the room began to spin and the bottom of his stomach dropped.

"You okay?" asked the Noble. Releasing the wounded hand, interest mixed with concern in his brown eyes, colouring his tone.

No, he was not alright. Perspiration dotted his forehead and he felt his gore rise. "Washroom," he croaked, scrabbling off the sofa. Somewhere in the background he heard Bridget call out to him as he managed to find the bathroom fixture before it was too late.

The poison in his body shook him, expelling everything from

his gut. He felt a blissfully cold hand on his forehead, supporting him, and one on his back. Another spasm rocked him and he felt the cracked rib give way with a snap. Agony stole his breath and his consciousness.

Bridget caught the Angel before he could add insult to injury by falling onto the toilet. Just as she hung up on the concierge she watched the Angel race on unsteady legs to the bathroom. Calling out to him garnered a sick reply and she raced to follow. She supported him as he vomited, his skin blazing at her touch. It did not make sense. One minute he was fine and the next she was holding him as if he were one of her prostitutes having had too much to drink. It was the audible pop and the intake of breath that confirmed the broken rib. The sudden unconsciousness alarmed her.

Standing up, the Angel's weight easily managed, she found it was his bulk that made things difficult. "Fernando. Get in here now!" she shouted.

"What? What did I do?" Fernando appeared in the doorway none too pleased about being called over. Fernando had been pleasantly surprised that the Angel decided to go along with the experiment. What had shocked the Noble was that the Angel's differences had nothing to do with having been Chosen. It was not what he expected, as well as witnessing Bridget's hand around the Angel's slim waist while her other hand held his arm across her shoulders. Never before was it so apparent the size difference between the two. It would have made him laugh, if not for Bridget's furious expression.

"Do?" barked the Mistress. "That's exactly what I'd like to know." She stepped forward. The Angel's lower legs dragged behind. An amused grin lighted the Nobel's features. "Don't you dare laugh," she sneered.

"No, of course not," chuckled Fernando. "I would never do anything so disrespectful." He broke into chest rattling laughter that brought tears to his eyes.

Petering off, Fernando wiped his eyes and cleared his throat, noticing Bridget's carefully contained fury. He was about to burst into new laughter when Bridget yelled and Sent, *"Don't you just stand there. Help me get him on the bed."*

The double onslaught rang painfully in his head, causing him to wince. "Alright. Alright." He stepped in to assist, taking the Angel's other side and was surprised at the heat radiating off of him. The touch of the Angel had not been this hot since Fernando released the Angel from the manacles from Violet's dungeon. "You didn't have to shout."

Bridget shook her head in resignation and led the way out of the washroom and into the suite's magnificent bedroom. The soft beige continued, blending with a soft rose and gold. The sand stained headboard was simple but lent austerity to the room. Simple brocade drapes, made from the same material as the sofa and chairs, hung to block out the night's jewelled lights.

Carefully laying the Angel on the king sized bed, Bridget rounded on her Chosen. "What did you do to him, Fernando? I turn my back for one moment and … What's this? You cut him! I can't believe you did that? You know better than anyone how iron affects him!" She placed the Angel's wounded hand back onto the bed and scowled at the blossoming bruise around the fractured rib.

"No, actually, we didn't," replied the Noble, dryly, his arms crossed over his chest. "He's mortal now, if you've forgotten."

Bridget frowned and studied the charred edges of the cut and the receding black poison twining up his arm.

"He agreed to it," he continued. "It seems that which marked him for Destruction had no bearing on the Angel being Chosen. In fact, being Chosen probably kept him alive longer had he been left to his own devices."

A knock at the suite's door raised Bridget to her feet. Jaw clenched, she did not realize she had moved preternaturally fast to the door until it loomed before her. Shaking her head, she knew she was angrier than she thought. The young man from the chemists appeared startled, his grey eyes wide as he handed her the shopping bag with one hand and a slip of paper with the other. Taking the paper, she signed it and gave it back with nary a word.

Gently closing the door lest she slam and break it, Bridget turned around and tossed the bag onto the table next to the door. "But cutting him?" She shook her head, sending blond locks bouncing. "You couldn't think of another way? One that wouldn't cause his broken ribs to fracture even worse?"

"I guess I could have, but where's the fun in that?" Fernando's grin melted into a scowl at how Bridget's disgusted expression twisted her beauty. Collapsing on the sofa he glared at her. "And pray tell what would you have done?"

"I would have waited until he healed." Bridget stood her fists on her hips.

Fernando snorted and rolled his eyes. "He's mortal now. How long do broken ribs take to heal? Bridget, be real about this. I'm surprised he hadn't checked this himself before now. Now we know and so does he."

"But you cut him. Doesn't he have enough scars that you have to give him one more?"

"Give me a break. How else could we have determined this?"

"You could have suggested having the Angel call his—"

"No. Absolutely not." Fernando repressed a shudder that threatened to rock him. The thought of being in the midst of the Angel's demons made his blood run cold. The Noble was not a fearful man, but having several times witnessed the mass murder those creatures caused, proved to him that the Angel was best under the control of the Chosen. That meant keeping the threat of Destruction away from his friend. If mortality did not change the Angel's abilities, then the Angel could be even more of a danger, but at least easier to kill if necessary. "It's all moot. The Angel's differences are not dependent upon being Chosen or mortal."

"What are you saying, Fernando?"

"Since his reaction to iron is worse, if these differences are consistent, then he can call those things. The question we have to ask ourselves as Master and Mistress of the Chosen is what to do about the Angel."

Bridget relaxed her arms, the anger seeping out of her face to be replaced with horror. "You're talking about killing him." She sat heavily into the opposite chair.

Fernando huffed through his nostrils. Normally he would have followed up with an impertinent reply, but the concern on her beautiful face made him reconsider. "What happens, Bridget, when a mortal finds out about the Chosen?"

"They're given the Choice – death or become Chosen," came the automatic reply.

"Not all are given the Choice."

Bridget stared at the coffee table between them. "No. Most are killed." She looked back up at her Chosen, piercing him with her gaze. "But he was Chosen."

"By an accident," countered the Noble. "Let's not forget that. He was never given the Choice."

"And because of that he should be killed?" Bridget leaned forward. "Let him have the Choice. Now. He can't continue like this. If he stays in the Americas he will eventually be killed by the Vampires."

"And if he returns to Europe, as a mortal, he *will* be killed by the Chosen, or worse, he'll be forcibly Chosen by someone who would want to control or abuse him," countered Fernando. "He's not under our protection anymore, Bridget. If he can still call those things then we're all at risk."

"So, he has to be given the Choice," she responded matter-of-factly. "We both know what he'll Choose."

Fernando steepled his fingers, index fingers pressing his lower lip, and nodded. "But should he be Chosen?"

"Fernando! I can't believe you'd say that." Outrage twisted her features and raised her voice.

"Listen to me," he countered, seriousness darkening his tones. "It's clear that Notus won't Choose him – why? If, Notus won't, then who will? Who will tie their immortality to the Angel's and place their head on the block? Only Notus has ever done so."

"We've done so."

Fernando scowled. "As Master and Mistress, yes, but that can change. It has changed."

"We have to find out the real reason why Notus won't Choose the Angel."

"And if he still doesn't Choose him?" queried the Noble.

Bridget let out a huff in resignation. "Then he must die or one of us must give him the Choice."

"I won't do that," said Fernando, darkly. "If it comes to it I will kill him, mercifully if you will, but I will not Choose him."

"Fernando, you're his–" Bridget's statement was cut off by a slicing gesture from her Chosen.

I will not have another's thoughts in my mind, he Sent. *One is already too much.* "Besides, after your shared kiss at Christmas you would be better suited."

Bridget frowned. It was unlike Fernando to be jealous. She could not deny her desire for the Angel, but she did not love him. She loved Fernando. "Fine," she agreed. "But find Notus first and see what he says."

"And what are you going to do?" Fernando rose.

"I'm going to treat the Angel's wounds," she sighed. Rising to her feet she followed Fernando to the door. "Bring Notus back so we can show him what mortality has done to the Angel. Maybe that will convince him if nothing else does."

Fernando nodded and opened the door, halting only when Bridget laid her hand on his shoulder, their cool touch separated only by a breath of silk. Turning around, he gazed down into two pools of water. He ran his hand down the side of her face, gold strands sliding between his fingers. Bending, he caught her lips in his and drove his tongue between them. She gave way as he pressed hard, her moan vibrating through them. Breaking off as suddenly as his stolen kiss had started, he caught her wavering body by her arm, steadying her.

You're mine, he Sent. *You Chose me, but you're mine. Don't ever forget that.*

A playful smile lifted her moist lips. "I love you too."

Fernando returned with a wry grin and a shake of his head before walking out of the suite and down the hall to hunt an immortal a thousand years older.

Closing the door, Bridget turned and leaned against it. She stared at the shopping bag filled with supplies to heal a mortal Angel and wondered if it was worth the effort.

XXVİ

He pinched the bridge of his nose and dared not close his eyes lest he succumb to Orpheus' call. Yawning wide and long, years of educated manners automatically raised the back of his hand to cover his mouth. Normally a yawn would be met with a closed mouth. Decorum was his livelihood and how he presented himself to the world directly affected his master – or so he had been taught from a young age.

Leaning his head against the head rest of the driver's seat, Godfrey relaxed but did not sleep while he waited outside the coroners building. It was two hours before dawn and Thanatos would be out shortly, expecting to go home to his mansion on the Bridle Path. If traffic was amenable Godfrey would be fast asleep before sunrise. Oh how he looked forward to lengthening days and shorter nights. It was only during the summer months that he saw the sun, sleeping the hottest part of the day before waking to enjoy several hours before sunset. Many times he would sleep outside, allowing the sun to bronze his skin before the shade from the manse cloaked him. Summer was a time when he had more time to himself. There were some advantages to working for the God of Death.

Stifling another yawn he sensed his master's approach. A quick check of his attire, straightening his black tie and driver's cap, Godfrey stepped out of the stretch limo and walked around to open the passenger side back door.

"Good morning, Godfrey." Thanatos stepped past and settled into the black leather seat.

"Good morning, sir," he said, closing the door.

Quickly, so as not to make his master wait, Godfrey settled into the driver's seat and started the engine. In the back Thanatos settled in with a sigh. Without further instruction Godfrey began the journey home in silence, a blessed change from the racket he had endured earlier.

"Did you find out anything, Godfrey?" asked Thanatos, his dark brown eyes closed.

Godfrey knew his master was listening for more than his verbal response. It was not that he would ever lie to the God of Death but Thanatos sometimes could read his answers more truthfully by the way his body responded. That was one thing that Godfrey had taken the longest to become accustomed to. "It seems, sir, that your concerns about the Vampire Dominus are well founded." Godfrey turned the limo onto Bloor Street.

"He's the one behind the Angel's transformation?"

"I do not believe he knows the true status of the Angel. The Vampires patronizing *The Veil* were very open in their communications with one another."

"Oh?" Thanatos opened his eyes in surprise and waited for his servant to continue.

"Yes, sir," nodded Godfrey, driving them across the Bloor-Danforth Bridge. "It appears that the Angel made a brief visit at the club earlier tonight and enticed two young Vampires into a fight in an alley close to *The Veil.*"

"Go on."

"A couple of Mr. Haskell's coterie found the staked bodies. I don't know what became of the Vampire corpses but I did find out that they were of Orchid's coterie."

"New York's Domina sent some of her coterie here?" Surprise filled the God's voice.

"No, sir. Orchid is here too," replied Godfrey. He dared a glance in the rear-view mirror at Thanatos' erect posture. A sense of foreboding filled him. He knew Thanatos would never shoot the messenger but the news he had to give could change that.

"What is it, Godfrey?" asked Thanatos, his voice abrupt at the pause of information.

"Stephanie and Michael are also here," replied Godfrey, his shoulders taught. His hands clutched at the steering wheel as he descended the vehicle down the on-ramp to the *Don Valley Parkway.* He did not need to peer into the mirror to know of his master's shock. "Others are due to arrive, sir."

"He's calling in all his Dominus and Domina?" whispered Thanatos.

"It appears that way, sir." Godfrey slowed down the speeding limo as they passed one of the well known sections where Metro's Finest lay in wait for unsuspecting law breakers.

"Corvus is consolidating his power," stated Thanatos before he gasped, "Oh no!"

"Sir?" queried Godfrey, worried.

"He's not heeding my warning. Damn!" Thanatos smacked the leather, the sound a large explosion that made Godfrey jump. "I'm sorry to do this to you, Godfrey, but I need you to find the Angel and convince him to return to Britain immediately."

The idea of confronting the Angel dried Godfrey's mouth to ashes. He would have to do it surreptitiously so as not to disclose his master and that may be near next to impossible. A new thought spilled from him. "Sir, is the Angel under that much of a threat?"

"Without the Chosen around him, yes," stated Thanatos succinctly.

"Sir, if you don't mind me asking," cautiously approached Godfrey. When he heard his passenger's grunt of assent he continued, "Would it not be in the Angel's best interest to take the opportunity to finally eradicate the threat?"

Thanatos sighed and shook his head as Godfrey took the Lawrence West exit. "He's too young."

"But sir, he's approximately fifteen hundred years old, surely–"

"At fifteen hundred years old, the Angel is only now just coming into his power," interrupted the God of Death. "Also, now that he is no longer feeding on human blood and without having Chosen of his own to feed on he is…well…Let's just say that any confrontation between the Angel and the Vampires would destroy my only hope."

Godfrey chewed on his lower lip as he navigated the roads that led to the mansion. "I will find him, sir, and will encourage him to return home."

"Good, Godfrey, very good." Thanatos relaxed into the leather upholstery, eyes closing in relief.

Frowning at his dubious assignment, Godfrey rolled the limo up the long drive, ending at the large two story mansion that was built in the latter half of the last century. Without waiting for him, Thanatos stepped out, closed the door and disappeared into the house leaving Godfrey alone once more. Shifting gears, Godfrey returned down the drive, his pillow's call unheeded. Stifling another yawn he went in search of an open coffee shop before beginning his quest to find the Angel of Death.

The ground was damp and littered with the crumbling remains of last autumn's fall. In the centre of the maple grove freshly turned earth darkened the silver illuminated place. High above diaphanous clouds languidly moved across a diamond studded sky. Far in the west a gibbous waning moon reached for the blanket of cold earth in an attempted to retreat from a sun that would soon rise from the other end of the blanket in an endless game of peek-a-boo.

Rising from her seat at the base of a large maple, Rose stretched her arms and hands to brush against quickening limbs and reborn foliage. Nobody had told her that this would be so boring. The first part had been thrilling. It had been so easy to convince Terry to follow her into the dark woods of the *Don Valley*. Easier was it to have him remove his clothing, his erection tight against his belly in anticipation of his lady's touch. She gave him his release, but not how he expected. His seed pumped from him one last time as she gulped hot red fluids from the deep wound of his femoral artery. Rose's eyes lit up as he arched his back in ecstasy, his beauty becoming increasingly paler under the watching moon until the last shudder of his release matched the one of his last exhalation.

Licking her lips, Rose had wiped her chin with the back of her hand as she stood up from the lovely corpse. It was before she had taken shovel to earth that she noticed his pale beauty, his body askew from the ecstasy of death. His long blond locks splayed around his head, the moon bleaching the strands to silver as its rays milked his skin to white. Rose had gasped at the sight. Never had Terry appeared so beautiful. She wanted to touch him and hear his melodious accent whisper his love as he touched her where she would allow no other man.

A shudder had run through Rose. Terry did not have an accent. The voice she had wished to hear did not belong to him. It was not his touch she craved. A pit opened in her gut. Vampires did not desire fleshly contact the same way as mortals. What was wrong with her? Shaking her head, she had dismissed the rising anxiety and dug Terry's grave with ferocity. She had placed him, his seed cold and dry still on him, into the grave, the black of the earth having bleached his pale beauty further beneath the moonlight before Rose dashed dark loam to cover him.

No mortal, save a few disturbed homeless, roamed these parts. This viaduct of thriving nature ran the vertical length of the city, allowing woodland creatures' access to its stony heart. It was not unheard of for a deer or a coyote to make its way down to the core of the city.

Silently, Rose walked the several feet to the disturbed earth and stared at the shallow mound. Nothing moved save for what the gentle breeze played with. Releasing a disgruntled huff, she nudged the earth with the tip of her black leather boot. Corbie had given her permission to turn Terry, but with a warning that not all will be born a Vampire. Sometimes their internment was permanent. Rose hoped it would not be the case with her beloved pet. She had already waited two nights. She had even picked out his new name, for once Terry rose reborn he would become Thorn.

Rose shivered at her own recollections of scrapping and scrabbling through silk, wood and dark earth to finally taste the blood scented air. It was the all pervading effervescence rising from the child that had eradicated the driving reason to liberate herself from an eternity of darkness.

A groggy moan filled the grove and she abruptly turned to the unconscious old bag lady tied to a tree. In a blink of an eye Rose crouched beside the crazy lady. "Shut up," she sneered as she banged the homeless woman's head against the bark.

A blossom of blood scent filled Rose's nostrils, exciting her hunger and lifting her lips in a ferocious smile. A scraping sound returned Rose's attention to the grave. Holding her breath, her vine green eyes widened in anticipation as pale worm-like creatures broke the surface of the dark loam. The unconscious hag forgotten, Rose found herself crouched a few feet away from the grave.

Time slowed. Fingers became long artists' hands. Dirt tumbled down to reveal dust coated paleness. Then a great heave, creating a mountain that fell away from Thorn's pale head and torso, causing Rose to gasp. Elation shivered through her as Thorn lifted his glorious nude body from the abandoned grave. Earth flowed down smooth pale skin, augmenting his toned muscles. Rose licked her lips, the remnant taste of Terry's blood a memory. No longer would she feed from him. Now they would hunt together for eternity.

His fine straight nose scented the breeze, new instincts asserting themselves. Rose smiled as Thorn found his prey and pounced on the bound woman. No screams pierced the grove, only the sound of suckling and slurping as Thorn's drank.

Walking over to her newly made Vampire, Rose knelt beside his feeding form and ran her hand through his dusted corn silk hair. "Pierce deep, Thorn, and drink immortality."

XXVII

otus sat on the couch, head in his hands and dreaded to answer Bridget and Fernando's question. Even to look at their furious expressions sent him into despair. He should not have agreed to go with the Noble, but he had no doubt that the Master of Britain would have trussed him up like a Christmas goose and hauled him away like one. Now he sat in the hot seat of their suite. Their burning glares cooked him in an effort to reveal the truth as to why he would not make the Angel Chosen once more.

"You're not making any sense," exploded Bridget. She stepped around the opposite seat and sat down, her eyes boring into the Monk.

"I told you why," implored Notus, refusing to glance at Bridget's angry blue eyes.

"An Oath! An Oath!" Fernando swore as he paced, hands gesticulating as if strangling someone. He halted beside Notus and stared down at him. "You swore some fucking oath not to Choose another."

Bridget laid a hand over her Chosen's tight fist as if to hold him back from pummelling the Priest. "We get it. We understand that."

"You might, but I don't," snapped the Noble.

Ignoring Fernando, Bridget continued. "But why? Do you not know what you've condemned him to?"

Notus flinched and pressed his hands firmly to his face. He knew. He had seen the boy's battered and bruised body lying on the bed in Bridget and Fernando's guest room. Hands grabbed his and pulled them away from his face. He could not hide the tears or the pain his decision created. Bridget sat back from what she revealed by taking his hands into hers. The anger melted away, leaving pity in its wake.

"Why, Paul? He was your Chosen – No, it doesn't matter if it was an accident or not – the two of you have been closer than any Chooser and Chosen in as long as anyone can remember. It's clear you love him still, so why not Choose him anew? What is your Oath in comparison with that?"

Bridget's words tore at him. It was the same question he fought against since the accident that left his boy mortal. He woefully shook his head. "I cannot."

"Cannot or will not," sneered the Noble.

Notus eyes widened at the unspoken threat and then lowered them in defeat. "Will not," he sighed.

"But why?" implored Bridget. "Just answer that one question. Make us understand, because right now we don't."

Meeting her concerned gaze Notus sighed and resolved to do what he never believed he would have to do – to cut into a long healed wound and let it bleed out once again. He leaned back in defeat. "What I am about to tell you I've not told anyone."

"Not even the Angel?" asked Fernando in disbelief.

"Not even him." Notus glanced up at the Noble and then at Bridget, searching their surprised visages for their judgement. Receiving none, he continued, "What I will tell you I pray you will understand, for I believe only a Chosen can. To explain, I have to go back to my beginnings."

Fernando and Bridget shared a look of surprise before the Noble sat on the end of the couch, both Master and Mistress waiting patiently as two children for a story to begin.

"I was eight years old when my father, a Bard, took me to the Holy Isle to begin my training," began the monk, his cadence turning to one well practiced in the art of storytelling. "I had an exceptional memory and a propensity for the retelling of stories I had heard even once. There on the magical island I learned first to become a Bard like my father. With my aptitude it did not take long. I was one of the youngest ever to be initiated to that grade, but it wasn't good enough. I needed to learn more.

"My voracious appetite for knowledge fuelled my studies up and through the grades until I was given the last initiation that made what came to be called a Druid. Don't appear so shocked.

Yes, I've always been a priest, but I came to Christianity as it was born. I was already Chosen, but I digress.

"During my years on the Isle I married a beautiful and exceptionally gifted Priestess. Our children, two boys and a girl were the holders of our hearts. All three were dedicated to the Old Ways...I have not spoken of them before." Notus voice choked with emotion. Wiping away an errant tear he cleared his voice. "I still think of them often. My memories of them are their immortality."

Notus cleared his voice of the strangling emotions that threatened to steal the story from being told.

"I was studying with our chief astrologer when the war came to our shores. I, like all the others, did not think it strange or unthinkable that the Astrologer kept to himself and only appeared hooded and cloaked when around others, and only at night."

"He was Chosen," stated Fernando, bluntly. Bridget shushed him and encouraged the continuation of the tale. Notus offered a flicker of a smile.

"He was a great and learned man, and not just upon the topic of the stars. He would have been High Druid, the leader of us all, but for his humility and insistence upon his station. No one remembered when he had arrived, only that he seemed to have been there forever.

"During my years under him I never once saw his face. Of course I wondered at his appearance for his voice belied youth. His reasoning for the darkness and his appearance were, at the time, logical. After all, his study was portends of the heavenly bodies and he needed to keep his night vision pure. No one suspected the truth and neither did I. I did find his predictions fantastical and incredible."

"Like what?" asked Fernando, completely drawn into the tale.

Notus glanced at the Noble and let out a small chuckle. "He was looking for a portent that would herald the Old Gods return to earth."

"Did he ever receive it?" asked Bridget, her eyes bright with wonder.

"I don't know," replied the monk. "He had been concerned about something that ate at his soul and tossed him into despair. It must have been serious as he went to the High Council with it. The night before the attack that destroyed the sanctity of our peace he had whooped and hollered in glee. I had never seen him so happy.

"It was just before dawn when Rome breeched our island. With shining metal and glistening steel they slaughtered. I tried to find my wife and protect my children, having spent the whole night with my mentor. To this day I am not sure exactly what occurred. One minute I was running, the Astrologer yelling after me and then waking up in dark woods, my body on fire.

"I could not move. I tried to call out, only to have a cold hand clamp my mouth shut. I did not know who it was or where I was but once I heard my mentors soothing voice I relaxed. In the light of a small fire I took my first sight of the ancient man. I was stunned. He appeared no older than I! Younger in fact! He spoke to me then. He informed me that I was dying, that my wounds were too grievous. I could not comprehend what he spoke of. All I knew was I was cold and I couldn't feel parts of my body. It was then that he gave me the Choice. I did not believe I was fully cognizant of what he was offering me. Had I known then what I knew later I would have begged for death, but life demands living and I agreed.

"My teacher put me through a rite the kind of which I had never experienced. He cleaned me and prepared my body, shaving my beard and leaving my face naked as it had been when I was a boy. I tried to protest but he assured me that it was better this way, after all he too was clean of facial hairs.

"The process took the rest of the night. Unlike today, there was more pomp and ceremony. In words ancient and unknown my Chooser beseeched the Old Ancient Gods whose names have been lost in the mists of time. The culmination of the ceremony was, of course, the exchange of blood. I do not need to convey to you the agony of my transformation, but I will state this – had my mentor not stayed by my side, lending his strength through his grasp of my cooling hand, I would not have survived the metamorphosis.

"When dawn approached he lifted me to stand and we entered the shelter he had constructed, there to spend my first day as Chosen. I had many questions and when I hungered he fed me from his body. Both he gave willingly, feeding my curiosity and satiating my physical being. The only answer he could not give was my burning desire to discover the fate of my beloved children and my darling wife. To that end I was forced to wait until the setting of the sun.

"I'm sure at some point I slept as memories of Rome's assault awoke me with such a terror that I startled my Chooser. Despite the incessant need of my body for fresh living blood my desire to discover the fate of my family burned more brightly. Knowing I could not move forward in my new state of being without learning my past, my Chooser reluctantly returned me to the only home I had ever truly known."

Notus closed his eyes with a shuddering breath as two thousand year old memories rushed forward, colliding with the present as if the occurrence happened just yesterday. Taking hold of the tumultuous emotions he opened his eyes, aware of his audiences' expectation, and continued, "What can I say? Everything was lost. My Chooser and I walked through a field of slaughter. My newly Chosen senses fed me more than what daylight could have to mortal eyes and nostrils. Death and decay walked the land and we immortals could only weep. Bodies of our beloved Brotherhood littered the blood caked land in grim mocking sacrifice. Children lay slain with terror as their final emotion etched on their faces as they clutched at siblings, parents or dolls. Pregnant women with their unborn babes sliced from their wombs. Their only touch was of cold earth. It was horrific, but none more than when I found them.

"Bryn and Rhia were sliced near in twain in defence of their younger brother and mother. It was clear they died first, and it was a long and agonising death. Little Gareth was unrecognizable for the sword slash that split his beautiful face. But it was what they had done to Gwendolyn that finally made me wish I had refused the Astrologer's Choice. In a fury of grief and despair I became senseless. I do not remember much after that except screams of terror, incomprehensible shouting, fire and the taste of human blood. It was the next night that sense returned to me and my Chooser informed me what I had done. I'm sure I do not need to spell it out to you."

Bridget nodded. Her blue eyes bright with unshed tears while Fernando's face darkened, hardening as if he knew all too well.

"My Chooser took me away from there. We travelled the land together as he taught me about what it meant to be Chosen and helped me in my mourning. Through the decades we watched our land invaded and transformed by foreign conquerors. I was introduced to the Master of the Chosen and was astonished at the immense reception and honour he did for my Chooser. I learned the Roman tongue and ciphers. In the process I was forced to leave behind my belief in the Old Gods, for fear of retribution.

"Oh how I hated to do that but to declare myself Druid would have been suicide. Regardless, my need to continue my knowledge of the spirit eternal led me to discover the teachings of a desert Jewish holy man sacrificed as the Son of God. Intrigued and desperate to find meaning in the suffering of mankind I eventually took up the mantle of Christian priesthood. It was at that time my Chooser left me, claiming that he would not continue as he was.

"You see, we had seen so much war, so much slaughter, my way of life was gone and all I loved had withered and died if not cut down before its time. My melancholy at being an immortal witness to such loss drove my Chooser from me. His parting words bid me to find solace in my immortality and a way to turn it to help others. As part of my Oath to follow this new Son of God I swore never to Choose another so as not to bestow upon another the misery of living past ones loved ones, ones people and oneself. It was an Oath that kept me sane so that I could help others in their short lives without allowing myself to become too attached to anyone that I may have wanted to Choose. It kept others safe from me."

"But what of the Angel?" asked Bridget. "His Choosing was an accident."

Notus nodded. "He was. He also never truly lived." Their scowls encouraged him to explain. "On the night he was accidentally Chosen, I can only say that his appearance startled and evoked a fear in me the like I had never known. It was only after I had realized what had transpired that I decided to follow him as he succumbed to the transformation.

"I have never seen, before or since, someone go through what he did. I believed, nay prayed, he'd slip into death. Please don't think me heartless. Between my Oath and his feral living I did not believe he should be Chosen. He was alone in the world. Abandoned and shunned because of prejudice. When I saw the elation in his soul that surviving the change had bestowed on him I knew I had failed to keep my Oath but I had to salvage what I could.

"He was terrified of me. I believe it was because of what I had inadvertently done, but no, his fear encompassed all people. It was difficult to bring him out of that existence."

"What was he afraid of?" queried Fernando.

Taking a bracing breath, Notus placed his hands on his knees.

"What does anyone fear? Rejection. Abandonment. Never to be loved."

"Why?" frowned Bridget. "We all suffer from these fears from time to time."

"His appearance," stated Fernando matter-of-factly.

Notus silently nodded. "Chosen or mortal he has always been a target, either as a possession to be owned or controlled."

"It was only with you that the threats diminished," observed Bridget.

"It was why Katherine kidnapped you," stated Fernando. "To attack a Chosen of your reputation and age is unthinkable. The Angel protected you from harm as your renown kept him from being Destroyed."

"And you became a buffer for him to function with others," continued Bridget. "But that doesn't explain why you won't Choose him again. Oh I understand why you made the Oath that you did, but isn't this different?"

Notus sighed and turned his hands over to look at his palms. "You only met him when you were thrown together to discover the subterfuge of the Vampires. You saw him like I had only ever seen him once, a very long time ago when he gave his heart to another, before and since he existed as the Angel. Societies through the ages never saw him as human. Can you dare say the same when you first met him, and even after? I know the rumours. I know the gossip. I also know that his detachment has kept him safe, at least until recently. Now we live in an age where his differences won't mark him for destruction. Now he can have the mortal existence that includes a family that won't abandon him and turn him out because of those differences. We live in an age where those who hopefully will share his blood won't hide in plain sight and pretend to be strangers for fear of prejudice. He can finally start to truly live the life his sister has hoped he'd find."

"What?"

Notus, Bridget and Fernando turned to see the Angel leaning against the threshold of the hallway. The pain lacerating his pale features turned the monk's stomach to lead, his hazel eyes and mouth widening in realization of what he had said and what had been heard.

*   *   *

It was not the excruciating pain that made it next to impossible to breathe that woke him, and nor was it the throbbing headache that subordinated his hunger. It was the voices floating into the room that forced him to pry open his eyes.

In the shadowed darkness of the bedroom he managed to sit, his hand pressed against bandages that bound his broken ribs. With slow movements he carefully slipped on his black shirt and jacket that had been left at the foot of the bed. He noticed the bandage on his hand as it shook, working the buttons. He wanted to stop and rest but the familiar voices drew him to stand, slipping on his black leather boots. Carefully and quietly he made his way out of the room and came to a frozen stance at the end of the hall.

Notus was there!

And was telling Bridget and Fernando stories he had kept from him!

Jealousy thudded his heart. *How could he?* he silently wailed. Why had Notus never told him? And now the monk was revealing all to others rather than to him. The pain of Notus betrayal cut even deeper as he stood still, listening to what other secrets his former Chooser divulged about him.

Shame and hurt filled his eyes with tears as coldness constricted his heart. He had thought that Notus stayed with him for love but the discovery of that lie choked him on bitter bile. It explained so much as to why Notus refused to Choose him again. It was when the monk mentioned a sister that he found his breath, anger fuelling him as he stepped into the room.

"Sister?"

The sparsely lit room dimmed except for the light around the monk who slowly stood, his face blanched with shock.

"I had a–a sister?" He advanced, ignorant to the pain of his broken ribs.

Bridget and Fernando rose in unison. Her youthful beauty marred with sympathy as her Chosen's twisted with wry amusement.

"You never told me," he cried, dismissing the other Chosens presence. "Why?" He did not need Notus to tell him. A sinking weight nearly drove him to his knees. *My mother had a son that died before the madness took her. I wish he could have been you.* He heard Eira's long deceased voice, the revelation driving the breath from his lungs in an exhalation of her name. He did not care that Notus winced at the utterance.

"I had a sister and you kept this from me?" Hurt and anger vied for supremacy.

"She swore me to secrecy," implored the monk.

"What else have you kept from me?" he demanded. Bridget stepped towards him as he advanced on Notus. She quickly backed away from his angry glare. Returning his gaze on the man who he had loved as a father, he witnessed Notus wilt in defeat.

Disgust filled him. He wanted to scream, to shout, to do anything to release the devastation and fury that clutched at his broken heart. Instead he made his usual decision. He raked his tear filled eyes over the immortals and fled, slamming the door behind him. The resonating sound boomed after him as he ran down the hall.

"Well that went brilliantly." Fernando collapsed into the soft padded chair, an annoyed smirk warping his face.

Notus sat stiffly, as if his body betrayed great age, and rested his head in his hands, elbows braced upon his knees.

"I think that persuading you to Choose the Angel again is moot," said Fernando sarcastically. "I doubt he'd even take the Choice again if offered. Well, monk, you got your wish. Your Oath is intact."

"Fernando!" gasped Bridget in response to Notus' pain ridden groan.

"What?" snapped the Noble. "What did you expect?"

Bridget frowned. "Fernando, go after him. Please."

"What for?" he demanded, crossing his arms over his chest. "I see no way to salvage this disaster."

"Because he is our friend and he has the right to know that *we* have not abandoned him."

The Noble closed his eyes to her worry and shook his head.

"Fernando," she continued, coming to stand before him. "You are his friend."

"And you think he'll listen to me?" He opened his eyes to take in her beauty despite her concern.

"We can only hope," she sighed.

"Fine," Fernando stood and added with a twisted smirk, "but you're putting too much faith in my powers of persuasion. They never really worked very well on the Angel."

"He's no longer the Angel," she said sadly.

Bridget's statement widened the Noble's eyes, the full implication of his friend's predicament finally driving home. It was Fernando's last chance, not only to maintain the second longest connection he had with another, but a last chance to recover a valuable ally and weapon. Slipping past his Chooser he made a sound of disgust at the sight of the monk before grabbing his black leather jacket from the closet. Before reaching the door, he Sent, *What are you going to do with him?*

I'm going to take a chapter from you and read him the riot act, returned Bridget.

Too bad I can't stay and watch. A glint of amusement lit his eyes. Opening the door Fernando followed his absent friend, not knowing what to say when he found the exAngel.

Emotions swirled in a convoluted mixture, picking at pieces of a distant puzzle that clicked quickly into place revealing a picture that had stared him in the face without its true meaning until now. With each added fact new tears of anger, frustration and hurt blurred the real world into which he fled. The one question that fuelled everything else was why no one had ever told him that he had a family.

He escaped down University Avenue, passing the precipice that had forever changed his life. Just a couple of short hours before dawn, the illuminated streets were virtually empty. He knew where his body went and left his mind and heart to piece together the truth about his past.

Eira was his sister!

That meant her children were his niece and nephew. She had also been in that grove when he was but a boy. Did that make his childhood tormentor and the others family? The thought made him sick, but it was the next piece that nearly felled him in the middle of the sidewalk.

If Eira was his sister then that meant Geraint was his father!

The realization stole a gasp as he bent over, clutching his burning ribs.

Geraint must have known but never told me. Why? he silently implored. Then another thought hit him. It was Geraint who had given him up to die that winter night when he was just a babe. Anger and hatred mingled with ancient feelings of love for the father of his mortal existence. Behind it all confusion reigned.

Why was he abandoned? Why was he never claimed or recognized by them? He knew the answer as plainly as if he stood in front of a mirror. If they did not want him why did Geraint agree to teach him the warrior's ways and why did Eira open her home to him and give him her father's sword?

His father's sword!

The sword that had trained him and had hung at his hip for centuries was his father's sword. The same sword that the Vampires had stolen because Notus had insisted they come to these cursed lands. Notus had convinced him to give up the blade for the exhibit. Notus had known all along that it was originally Geraint's and had kept secret the ties that bound him to a mortal life - that Geraint had been his father! The betrayal of both men, mortal and Chosen, burned but it was Notus' that seared his soul and invoked more hurtful questions.

"Gwyn!"

The name that his father had warned him about and the name that his sister had bestowed upon him spun him around to face the Noble. He could not recall coming to stand beside the monument on the north end of Queen's Park. Without a thought he wiped the tears away and demanded, "What do you want?"

Fernando halted, his eyes momentarily going wide before settling into a smoulder. "I want you to come back."

"To what?" The ludicrous demand surprised him, especially coming from the Noble. He turned to walk away only to find Fernando standing before him, arms crossed in agitation.

"You're being an ass," sneered the Noble as he gave him the once over. "Come back now and—"

"Come back?!" he exploded, bearing down on the Noble. All the anger he felt had found a target. He savoured Fernando's momentary flash of fear and stood to tower over him.

Recovering his composure Fernando matched his glare. "Back to the hotel, you idiot."

"What for?" he spat the words at the Noble.

Fernando pursed his lips in an effort to keep his anger in check. "So you can talk–"

"Talk?" he yelled. "You want me to talk with that man. You want me to listen to his lies? I lived with them for years and didn't know it! Now I do. I won't listen to his fucking excuses." He tried to brush past the Noble only to find a bronze hand gripping his arm.

"Let. Go. Of. My. Arm," he sneered through clenched teeth.

The threat hung in the suddenly chill air. When the cold hand released him he entered the treed park, leaving the Chosen behind him.

XXVIII

ernando took deep even breaths as he strode past the concierge and into an awaiting elevator. He did not even look at the tired bell hop that trundled a tray of breakfast edibles as they rose up the floors. It took all of his concentration to keep his rage under tight control. Fernando had expected a confrontation with the Angel, but he had wrongly assumed that he would win and the Angel would be with him now. He had also grossly underestimated the Angel since his new found mortality, yet it also proved another point. It was that fact that ignited fear in the Noble's heart that transmuted into anger.

Impatiently tapping his foot, he realized he should have taken the stairs. He could have climbed them much faster than this mechanical device and would now be at his hotel suite, safely able to explode his anger. He almost sighed in relief as the doors opened to his floor. Ignoring the fact that a mortal shared the elevator Fernando disappeared out of the lift and down the hall with preternatural speed.

With emotions boiling, Fernando slammed the door open, ignoring Bridget's cry of surprise as he easily picked the monk up off of the couch and slammed him into the wall, the wallpaper tearing as the drywall crumbled beneath. "You fucking selfish prig," he sneered, enjoying the feel of his anger finally hitting a target. He ignored the fact that Notus pulled at his hand as he pinned the monk by the throat. Older or not, rage gave Fernando greater strength. "Do you realize what you've done?"

"Fernando! Stop!" shouted Bridget. "I've already given him a piece of my mind."

"That's not good enough," spat the Noble. He leaned forward until he was a breath apart from the stunned Chosen. "You've lost the Chosen the only weapon we've ever had against the Vampires and worse you may have turned him against us." He dropped the monk and turned away from him.

"What happened?" Bridget came up to him, horrified concern etched her face. "Fernando. What happened?"

Glancing over his shoulder at Notus who had slid to the floor and was rubbing his quickly healing bruised throat, Fernando replied, "It seems that the Angel is still the Angel, Chosen or not. Not only does he still react adversely to iron but he still fucking controls those fucking demons of his."

Notus' eyes popped wide at the revelation.

Disgusted at the monk, Fernando turned his attention to Bridget. "I found him. And I'll tell you this. I have never seen him so enraged. I tried to convince him to come back, as you wanted, but he would have none of it. The air chilled around us and I could see a fog swirl up around our feet. Needless to say I let him go." Without glancing back at Notus' stunned expression Fernando added, "Well done, monk. Your lies have left us in great danger."

He could feel Fernando's burning gaze on his back as he stalked away. Fury shook him and clenched his pale hands into fists. *How dare he!* he fumed. The thought of going back and seeing that man, let alone talk with him, disgusted and fuelled his rage. Some part knew that Fernando was just trying to help, probably on Bridget's behest, but he could barely keep his anger in check, especially when the Noble grabbed him.

He did not recall ever speaking so to another the way he had done to Fernando. If he was not so hurt at the whole situation he would have felt bad for how he had talked to the Noble. Instead he ignored the glare and was relieved when its presence disappeared. He did not want to hurt the Chosen.

There was no going back, even if he wanted to, which he did not. Instead he strode under the dark canopy of trees, Ontario's capital a red and black monument far away. Everything that he was now gone, stripped from him with the lies from a Chosen who had sought only to control him. That realization burned his heart. Even if Notus came crawling back, begging for forgiveness and offered him the Choice, he would throw it back into that little man's face.

How dare he keep me from my family! he silently raged. His whole existence was a search for belonging and acceptance, to fill the gaping void of loneliness encapsulated his heart. He had only found true release from that existence with Jeanie, but Vampires destroyed that, sending him back into darkness. No doubt remained that Notus would have done everything to ensure she would never be Chosen, even to the extent of erasing her memories of her love and time with him like Notus had done with Tarian's granddaughter. To discover that the Monk purposely kept him away from such connections over and over, especially with his blood family, destroyed all the trust he had ever had in the man. To have it revealed that he had once had a father and a sister was a childhood fantasy come to life, one that Notus would have always know was something he desperately wanted. The fact it came fifteen hundred years too late blurred his eyes with unshed tears. *Geraint, Eira, Auntie, why did you never tell me?*

Because they needed to protect you.

He halted in mid-stride as the chorused voice of the Three Ladies filled his mind. Astonishment turned his anger into a simmer for a brief moment before flaring higher. *Where have you been?* he silently cried.

No answer.

Aren't you going to say anything *to me?* he demanded, staring at the trees above.

Again he was met with silence.

Their abandonment added fuel to the fire. He shuddered in unreleased fury and closed his eyes. The image of his father's sword filled his mind and he knew that no matter what he must get it back from the Vampires. It was the only thing in his life that never let him down. And if he was killed, so what? He had lived long enough to learn that there was nothing left except lies and deception. It was true; cold steel was the only thing a man could trust.

Opening his eyes he allowed the burning anger to cool, stilling his body, until cold wrapped his heart. No longer would he be the tool of someone else's revenge. No longer would he leave life changing choices in another's hand. No longer Chosen, he was released to seek out the Vampires on this continent, to kill as many as would get in the way of recovering what was his, or die trying.

He knew where the Vampires could be found. Now only if he could get one of them to tell him the location of his sword. With long purposeful strides pulling at his broken ribs he continued through the park. He would get his father's sword back, and once he did he would ensure that the damnable Chosen would leave him alone or suffer the same consequences as that of the Vampires.

The sound of a stick breaking behind drew him up short. He turned in time to see a blur dive at him. Centuries of training controlled his movements and with a side step and a flick of his wrist he sent his attacker flying past him to land on his back several metres away.

"You killed Daniel and Thomas." The accusation came from the direction of his attackers launch.

Turning his head, white locks draping his face, he felt hatred's elation at finally finding a target. "I know no Daniel or Thomas," he whispered darkly. Anger's energy flowed up from the ground, filling him with anticipation for a fight. "But I am sure that as Vampires they got what they deserved."

A roar of anger preceded the attack from the one he had thrown. Turning his attention, he grabbed the thrown punch and twisted the arm until he heard the satisfying pop of a dislocated shoulder. Ignoring the scream of pain from his ribs, he kicked the Vampire in the chest, releasing his grip on the creature's incapacitated hand so as to let him fly to the ground.

It was more a feeling than a seeing. The Vampire who had accused him joined the fight. Spinning around, the Angel dropped to let the Vampire's kick fly over him and at the same time he struck the knee with an open hand strike. The sound of crushed bone and gristle accompanied by the man's scream electrified the cold around his heart. Sadistic enjoyment of his revenge gave energy to him as he watched the Vampire hop back.

Unconsciously his hand found a discarded branch from a tree above as he pushed off the damp grass. Just as his first attacker recovered enough from his injuries to attempt another blow, the Angel stepped in and slid the broken wood between immortal ribs to pierce the meat of the Vampire's heart. Surprised grey eyes met his and he delighted in watching them dry and shrivel as the creature succumbed to the effects of the stake in his heart.

Pain erupted down his back, forcing him to release the desiccating form, stick still in its chest. The pain, so similar to what he had endured at the hands of another Vampire, exploded his fury. Spinning around, ignoring his laboured breathing, he struck out on the offensive, uncaring that he was a mortal fighting a preternatural monster.

His clawed hand made contact with the Vampire's face, breaking the jaw and sending a sharp tooth flying. He did not wait for a retaliatory strike as his open right hand impacted the creature's sternum. Again the satisfying sound of crushed bones added to his dark elation. His attacker stumbled back, clearly in pain despite the swift healing. Not waiting to let the Vampire gain the upper hand, the Angel, tasting metal, spun and kicked, imploding the Vampire's chest with its force.

Lifted off his feet, the Vampire's flight came to an abrupt halt against a tree. Realizing that his attacker was stuck on the tree, the tip of a broken branch glistening through the creature's abdomen, the Angel slowly made his way to the Vampire, stopping momentarily to pick up another discarded branch.

The terrorized expression on his would-be assassin's face invoked dark pleasure as he came to stand before it. Cold crimson eyes caught brown. "Where is my sword?" he demanded through clenched teeth.

The Vampire mewled in pain, his jaw slow to heal.

The lack of an answer was too much. He had asked a question and to be denied the truth yet again made it impossible to control his bucking fury. Grabbing thick brown hair, he slammed the Vampire's head against the tree, the sound rang hollow in the glade, and he leaned in close. "Tell me where my sword is and I'll release you." Ice coated his words.

"I–I d–d–don't…" The Vampire tried to shake his head, brown eyes imploring the Angel of Death to believe him.

Ignoring a gaze that would have once, a long time ago, drawn guilt from him, the Angel pressed closer, his long white locks brushing the man's chest as he tilted his head. "You don't know or you don't want to get in trouble with your Master."

"Know!" blurted the terrified Vampire, his jaw almost healed.

Answer received, the Angel stepped back, taking in the full measure of the creature and found disgust twisting his gut. Maybe it was lying. Maybe not. He could not tell.

"You said you'd let me go," demanded the Vampire as it struggled on the broken branch.

Regardless, he could not trust the utterances from the vile

creature. Full white lips slimmed into the feral smile of one having captured its prey. Slamming the large branch into the Vampire's chest, piercing its heart, he whispered into the new made Vampire corpse's ear, "I said I would release you. I did not specify how."

Turning away from the dead Vampire, the Angel did not bother a glance at the dried curled creature on the ground as he walked away. The sharp pain of his broken ribs flared back to life as his vented anger reduced to a simmer. He clutched his side as he walked on to the only place where he would find answers – *The Veil.*

It had not gone as she had planned.

Everything up to Thorn's birth was perfect, if delayed. It was after his consumption of the vagrant that she realized that reality did not match with her expectations. Terry was gone and Thorn did not bestow upon her the adoration she had become accustomed to. Fed and dressed in black jeans, cotton shirt, and worn running shoes, Thorn's swaggering steps were barely contained next to hers.

"This is incredible!" announced Thorn. He turned to face her. "I'm still hungry."

"You're going to have to wait," said Rose, ignoring his pleading blue eyes. What? One old bag lady was not enough? Obviously not.

"I don't want to wait." Anger tinged his tones. It was an emotion Rose had never heard on his soft velvety voice before.

"Well, you'll have to wait," she said tersely. Picking up speed, Rose passed Thorn and was hit with a mixture of relief and annoyance at the sound of his booted footsteps catching up beside hers.

"Why?" he demanded. "There's one over there." He pointed to a homeless man asleep over the subway's venting grate.

Rose halted and pulled Thorn to a stop. "Listen to me." She gripped his arm until he winced and brought his angry gaze down on her. "You are the first of my coterie and you have a lot to learn."

"But–"

"No buts," she snapped, her anger rising. "The first thing is to know when the sun rises, which it will do soon. Or do you wish to die and have the sun's rays give you a true death?" He shook his head, fear creeping into his pale face. "No. I thought not." She resumed walking, not waiting for Thorn. She loved the way his long blond hair swayed in the breeze.

"Where are we going?" Thorn made sure to keep a pace back from his maker as they entered *Queen's Park*.

"Back to the club," answered Rose. Did she see something?

"*The Veil*? Why?"

"That's our home." There it was again. Rose halted, her green eyes going wide. It was Corbie's Angel, the one she had barely escaped from when she stole his sword from the museum. Shushing Thorn's next irritating question, Rose carefully approached, keeping hidden behind a sleeping maple.

She could not believe what she was seeing. Here was a specimen of true beauty as he strode through the dark trees, keeping away from the lighted path. Thorn's prettiness was but a pale reflection. Rose flitted to another tree in an attempt to get closer to the creature that had hunted down and slaughtered the Vampires to near extinction and drove the survivors to this new land. Anger illuminated off the Angel. Corby had given Rose direct orders to stay away from the Angel, but he never said she could not spy on him from afar.

Closer she moved with Thorn on her heels until a sudden burst of speed nailed her to her hiding place. In a split second Rose watched the Angel throw his Vampire attacker as exhilaration sent her senses tingling. Every motion of the Angel appeared a sensuous dance. His white locks whipping about set a craving in her bones. How she wished to feel those silken strands running through her fingers and to have his strong arms encircle her. She knew that he was the sworn enemy of the Vampires but she could not halt her yearning to feel his smooth pale body press against hers again.

Again?

The thought staggered Rose, furrowing her brow. Perplexed, she lowered her gaze away from the Angel and his attackers. It was then that she noticed the strange white mist rising from the ground, ringing the fighters. Confusion evaporated as quickly as the fog rose, obscuring the Angel. In its place dread caught in her throat as ghost like apparitions appeared in the mist, their faces gruesome in their enjoyment of her terror. Strangling a scream Rose fled before one of the white faced demons could devour her, uncaring of the fact that her beautiful Thorn was now in their clutches crying out for her to save him.

XXIX

odfrey's hands trembled despite his white knuckled grip on the steering wheel. Driving into the rising sun he was not looking forward to reporting his failure to his master. It was not that which made him tremble in fear, it was his attempt to persuade the Angel to go back home that turned the coffee in his gut into acid.

After receiving orders to find the Angel, Godfrey went back to his last known location – *Beyond the Veil*. Not surprisingly, the club was already closed for the day. It was a surprise to find the Angel striding down Queen Street. Godfrey pulled over and stepped out of the limousine, removing his cap as he took a shuddering breath. As the Angel approached to pass Godfrey's throat closed up and his heart sped. Fear had tightened its noose, stoppering his voice. Pure unadulterated rage boiled from the Angel as he walked over to a parked motorcycle.

Godfrey decided to try again, seeing the Angel halt and disconnect a locked helmet. Swallowing the ball of fear, he took a step towards the Angel, his intent to be unthreatening as he cleared his throat.

The Angel spun around, his crimson eyes burning. "What do you want?"

Godfrey barely managed not to exclaim his surprise and hold his position. Despite the fury in the Angel's countenance it was clear he had a rough night. The split lip was gruesome evidence to Dr. Thompson's testimony.

"My master sent–" began Godfrey, daring to gaze up at the Angel's face.

Without warning the Angel was a foot away glaring down at him. "You can tell your master that I demand my sword back and until I do I will continue to kill whomever he sends to stop me." Frost coated the Angel's words and he turned back to his motorcycle.

Mouth gone dry Godfrey tried again. Clearly the Angel had him confused with someone else. "I believe you have–"

The Angel turned to face Godfrey. This time Thanatos' servant had the where with all to flee as the sky lightened towards dawn.

Closing himself into the safe confines of the limousine, Godfrey nearly stalled the engine in his attempt to turn it over. He threw the hand gear into drive and tore off down the road ignoring the squealing tires and the scent of burning rubber. Never before had Godfrey felt such terror. A part of him wished that the Angel was still Chosen. That, at least, he could have handled. Now he had to report to his master his failure with the Angel. A new shudder ran up his spine as he tightened his grip on the wheel.

$\boldsymbol{XXX}$

lizabeth startled awake, sending Grimalkin scurrying off her feet, and winced with the realization that she had fallen asleep on the living room couch while she had waited up for her daughter and guest to return. Groaning, she pulled herself to a sitting position and tightened her robe as she stretched out her neck muscles. On the coffee table before her was the paranormal romance novel she had fallen asleep to. Elizabeth was sure she had not placed it there, or the note beside it. She turned on the end table light she was positive had been on when she dozed off and picked up the paper. A smile formed as she read Vee's handwriting informing her mom that she was safe and sound at home and that Karsha was crashing over.

Elizabeth frowned. Gwyn's motorcycle could only hold two. Where was her guest? Climbing to her feet, she went to the front door and finding it unlocked Elizabeth went outside into the brilliant new day. Parked beside her car the Y2K motorcycle was still warm to the touch. Her frown deepened and she turned from the sunlight and entered the dark sleeping home. Quietly, she climbed the stairs and was rewarded with the sound of movement. Someone was awake and using the shower.

The broadloom muffled her steps as she came to the guest bathroom. Light spilled into the hall from the slightly open door, as well as humidity. A gentle tap elicited no response. Elizabeth knew it would not be Vee or Karsha. It could only be one other person. Heart pounding, Elizabeth opened the door. The question of his late arrival and why her daughter came home past curfew died on her lips.

His pale body glistened, water droplets reflecting the light, as he turned off the water and stepped out of the bathtub. The moisture clung to his slim body, emphasising his smooth muscular build, delineating each curve and valley.

"What happened to you?" she blurted, eyes wide at the black and purple bruises along his arms. Elizabeth's mouth dropped open at the gigantic blossom along his side. Eyes roving lower, taking in sights she had only felt, Elizabeth snapped her gaze up to his split lower lip after noting the bruises on his sleek muscular legs. The harsh florescent light illuminated the burn, scars and bruises, making Elizabeth wonder if there was not a part of him that was not damaged in some way. His eyes met hers and she nearly flinched at the anger there. Did his ruby eyes flash? She had no time to follow that thought as he turned away from her to face the fogged mirror and the counter top that held his clothing. Rumpled atop was a wide beige tensor bandage.

"What do you what, Dr. Bowen?"

She had never heard him with anger in his voice and wondered at the regression of her name. It startled her and got her ire up.

"I want to know what happened to you." She closed the bathroom door, not wishing their discussion to wake Vee and her friend. "And I want to know why Vee came home without you."

"You're daughter is safe." He rolled the tensor in preparation for its use. "The rest doesn't matter. I'll be leaving as soon as night falls."

His dismissal of her concern for him drove Elizabeth forward to grasp the bandage from his hands, noticing the blackened cut on his left. She met his glare with one of her own. "Doesn't matter? Of course it matters. I ask you to accompany my daughter and you come back bruised, battered and ready for a fight."

A flicker of guilt momentarily broke his visage before being replaced with a mask of ice. With no reply forthcoming Elizabeth pressed on.

"Do you think you don't matter? That's bullshit. Do you think I open my door and entrust the care of my daughter to just anyone? Do you think I have sex with someone just for the sake of it? I have to consider that person a friend, someone I care about." She jabbed her finger into his damp smooth chest. "I have to trust that person. And stop calling me Dr. Bowen. My name is Elizabeth. Use it."

She could not believe her outburst. Her eyes widened in

surprise before she recovered her indignant glare. It was, therefore, a shock when he grabbed her shoulders and planted the most passionate kiss on her lips she had ever experienced.

He did not plan to kiss Elizabeth and was as surprised as she, but when she opened her mouth to let him enter the pressure from the rage and the hurt from millennia old lies grabbed him. He did not deny Elizabeth's truth and a large part of him pressed its veracity. He darted his tongue into her mouth, luxuriating in the texture and taste until her tongue caressed his and entered his mouth.

She tasted of stale wine as he attempted to devour her. She considered him a friend, but for how long until she too abandoned him?

Mouths still locked onto each other his rage fuelled his desire. Hands finding the ties of her robe, he unknotted the terrycloth and jerked the robe from her body. A part of him registered that she had helped but he did not care as the heat of her body pressed against his. Her hands ran up his chest until fingers interlocked behind his neck, keeping the embrace of lips.

He broke off the kiss, feeling his movements controlled by another. Inches apart, his eyes flicked over Elizabeth's face noting her heavy breathing and dilated blue eyes. He grit his teeth as anger surged forward. He would not be controlled again. Ignoring the pains of his body he bent to kiss her, biting and sucking at her lips, forcing moans from her. His hands reached behind his head, unlocking her grip, as he lowered her arms his hands followed. It was when he felt the firm roundness of her thighs as her hands came to rest on them that he growled, pressing his kisses until she was trapped between the counter and him. His body thrilled as she squirmed, realizing her predicament, and devoured her moan as it vibrated through him. Without another thought he pressed further, his body rigid in its throbbing need. Abruptly, he sat her on the counter and left her pinioned hands to lift and separate her thighs until he was able to slam himself into the hot moist centre of her being.

Her cry and scrabbling to gain purchase broke their kiss, but he did not care. Hand against the mirror and one supporting her rump he pulled out only to penetrate her defences, slamming himself against her inner gates to demand further entrance. She tried to pull away but she was trapped.

Again and again he entered her, aware of the gradual tightening around and through him. All was physical sensation demanding release. Soon her body was slick with sweat and each quickening penetration broke her lips with a cry. He did not want it to end and so he closed his eyes, the heat and wet of her inner being driving him forward until he could not stand it any longer. With a shout that was part growl his body exploded, shuddering its pulsating release until it was mimicked with caresses that promised to drain him to the quick.

An eternity passed before the sounds of rapid heavy breathing opened his eyes. Still conjoined, his eyes met Elizabeth's and the full impact of what he had done made him gasp. Pulling out, he shuddered.

What have I done?

All the rage had been expelled as his body released itself into her. Elizabeth's face was flushed as she attempted to right her uncomfortable position and he turned his back, grabbing the towel hanging on the bar to wrap it around his waist. The stabbing ache in his side returned making every effort to quiet his rampaging breath difficult. He could not believe what he had just done.

Shame and guilt overwhelmed him and he bowed his head, white wet ropes falling to cover his face. How could he have done that after all he had gone through in his life? But he knew. He closed his eyes and took a painful shuddering breath. He wanted to hurt someone, anyone, because he was hurt. He was about to leave when he felt something he had never felt before. His body stiffened and his attention focused on the gentle fingers that traced the silver ridges along his back, the heat of her palms scorching him as they slid along to larger swatches where skin and muscle had been flayed from his body. He stood there, more aware of the damage his body had sustained than ever before.

The hands slid to his sides but did not wrap to embrace him. He winced as her hand brushed the bruised skin over broken ribs until the hands disappeared to be replaced but the smooth flow of warmth as she pressed against him. She was not running away. She was still there beside him. White brows pulled together in confusion. Silence filled the room only to be punctuated by the occasional drip from the shower.

"I'm sorry," he whispered. "I should not have—"

"What happened to you, Gwyn?" she asked. The warmth of

her breath caressed his scarred back.

His frown deepened in the realization of what she was truly asking and it had nothing to do with beating he had taken earlier. "I was never wanted. As a babe I was left to die by a family I never knew, all because of my appearance." He could not believe he was confiding in her like this, but he could not stop the flow of words. "I was raised in secret by a woman who was killed because people found out about me." The band around his heart tightened, proving the ancient scars were still intact. "Throughout my life people have been terrified of me and sought to kill me, or they would want to try and control and use me for their own ends."

"Not everyone," said Elizabeth, incredulously. "What about Paul?"

The name of his former Chooser made him wince. The pain of Notus' betrayal stabbed at the scar in his heart. He slowly nodded, squeezing his eyes shut in an attempt to cut off the flow of tears. It tore his heart to count Notus among those who betrayed and used him.

A vision popped to mind, causing him to gasp. Jeanie's smiling face framed with riotous cinnamon curls accentuating the summer green of her eyes. "There was one," he whispered. "She's dead, because of me."

He felt warm hands on his arms turn him around and he opened his eyes to take in Elizabeth's dishevelled robed appearance. He was surprised to find sadness darkening her bright blue eyes.

"You can't take on the responsibility of someone else's death," stated Elizabeth. "I know. Between my parents when I was a child, my grandfather in my early twenties and my ex-husband to AIDS. I know something about this."

He knew she was trying to help, but natural loss was not the same as violent loss. He shook his head and stared into her eyes. "Jeanie was strong, but I wasn't strong enough to save her. She was murdered because of me, because of who and what I am, and because I believed her safe. I was wrong." He dropped his gaze past Elizabeth's shoulder to the mess of the counter as memories surged forward. "She saved me but I couldn't save her," he murmured.

"Saved you?"

Elizabeth's query brought his attention back to her, panic rising at the memories. "I– I can't." He tried to turn away, to flee.

"Does it have anything to do with your scars?" Elizabeth's

hand alighted over his as he went to turn the doorknob.

He turned back, shocked, to face Elizabeth, reading sympathy and concern in her face. He went to sit on the edge of the bathtub and closed his eyes, lowering his head. She had seen and felt the scars on his flesh. It was more than anyone else had done save Notus and Bridget, but they did not count, they had done so to help them heal. A lovers hand had never touched them before save one – Jeanie.

"Yes," he whispered his voice rough with suppressed emotion. "Throughout my life it was as I told you, but I was always able to escape before the worst could happen. But not that time. Not with Jeanie." He did not know why he was telling Elizabeth, but he could not stop the words from falling out. He heard her sit beside him. "I was led into a trap arranged by a so called friend of Jeanie's. We didn't know it was her until it was too late. Jeanie was captured and I was forced to give myself over or watch Jeanie killed. I submitted."

He felt Elizabeth's hand on his shoulder and he flinched. "No, don't," the words rushed out. Sitting upright, he stared at her shocked expression as she removed her touch. He bore his gaze into hers. "I was tortured because I wouldn't turn my heart from Jeanie. I couldn't even had I wanted to. I don't know how many days I was in that dungeon." He lowered his eyes as shame burned through. "In the end I lied – anything to stop the pain. I don't believe she believed me but she left me alone. Maybe she thought I was dead. I don't recall.

"Some time after – a week or more, I'm not sure – I woke somewhere else. Jeanie was there. She had managed to escape and come back for me. When I confronted those responsible for setting the trap I had thought Jeanie was safe where I had left her. I was supposed to meet her after. We had made plans to spend our lives together. I should have never brought her along but I didn't want her to be in danger, but she was, because she was with me.

"I found Jeanie dead beneath a street lamp." He took a shuddering breath.

Silence crowded the room and he knew Elizabeth was at a loss for words. Standing up, he gazed down on her disconcerted expression. Elizabeth was not pretty like Jeanie, but there was a regal beauty about her that was quite alluring. It was also strangely comforting that she never flinched when their gazes touched, as they did now.

"I'm so sorry for all you have gone through." She stood, but it was her words that made him step back in surprise. "There is no way for me to truly comprehend what you have been through." A half smile lifted her sad expression but did not banish it.

Crimson eyes wide, he could not believe the truth of her sympathy and shame crashed in once again. "I should not have taken it out on you."

Elizabeth stepped forward, a true smile lifting her features, until she was but an inch away. He could feel her warmth penetrating his skin.

"Could've, would've, should've," she said. "There powerful words that bind one to regret and sadness. I don't regret what happened, Gwyn. In fact," a mischievous spark alighted her eyes, "sex with you has been the best I've ever had."

Her admission stunned him and stole the remorse he held, replacing it with a rising heat. He closed his mouth and swallowed, unable to speak. No one had ever said the like to him before. Dumbfounded, all he could do was watch Elizabeth carefully roll the tensor bandage. When she turned back to wrap it around his aching ribs he could not but notice her soft touch nor the caresses of her terrycloth covered arms. Heat flowed downwards until he was distinctly aware of the towel and the robe between them.

Elizabeth secured the tensor with two plastic clasps and noticed the difference in how the towel draped over him. "It's nice to know that even at my age I can still affect a young man," she smiled.

"I'm older than you think," he blurted. He wished that parts of his body would not react so to her. She lifted a slim brown brow and he regretted the utterance. Even though he was a millennium and half older he had no doubt that she discounted his statement. No matter their chronological ages he appeared more of an age with her daughter.

Elizabeth sighed and shook her head, sending short locks swinging. "I don't care about age. I was twenty when I had Vee, twenty-one when I married her father and twenty-four when he came out of the closet and we divorced. Numbers mean nothing. Experience is everything. It wasn't your youth that drew me to you and nor was it the fact that I find you incredibly attractive. It's because despite what you've experienced you are an old soul with a good heart."

The touch of her palm over his heart burned him as her words warmed and confounded him. He did not know what to say and felt a fool with his mouth hanging open.

"It is why I told you no strings," said Elizabeth, taking her hand back. "And I'll say it again if need be. You do not owe me anything. I don't expect a relationship other than friendship unless you desire more, and after what you told me I'll be happy to take whatever you offer."

Gooseflesh flared across his cool skin and he frowned, confused. Breaking his gaze he realized Elizabeth was the first person not to place expectations, requirements or honour bound duties upon him. She was demanding nothing from him and was accepting of whatever he could give. This was unprecedented. Meeting her sadly smiling face he shook his head. "I...I don't know what to say."

She took his injured hand in hers. "There's nothing to say. Just be."

He huffed out a pent up breath and looked at her with the expectation of deceit and received only open honesty, confusing him further. He needed to think, to digest the full implications of what Elizabeth had said despite the fatigue he finally allowed himself to feel. Turning away, he opened the door and halted when she did not release his hand.

"You may want to sleep in something, pyjamas, whatever. Vee has a friend sleeping over," warned Elizabeth.

He nodded his appreciation as her hand slipped from his, allowing him to retreat to the guest room, questions and confusion muddling his mind.

Elizabeth watched him leave the room before she stumbled, catching herself as she grasped the counter in an effort to make the washroom cease to spin. She recognized the sensation and was surprised that it hit without being in Circle with her coven. Then again, she realized, she had not experienced it as she should have. She placed her other hand on her forehead and the room snapped back into reality, causing her to gasp.

You have done well, my daughter, came the chorus of female voices.

Elizabeth knew the sound was inaudible regardless of how it reverberated in her skull, but the reality of whom she heard stole the strength from her legs, forcing her to sit on the closed toilette seat, head in hands. She blew out a shaking breath and grounded and centred herself. Never before had she heard or felt Her presence so strongly before. Then it hit her – everything that had happened this morning had been with Her presence upon Elizabeth. It explained so much, but left incalculable questions racing through her mind. Elizabeth lifted her head and stared out the door her guest had disappeared through moments earlier, the all-prevailing question overriding the others.

Who are you?

No answer replied.

With a shaking inhalation Elizabeth sat back, resting against the tank.

Ever since he had come into her home she felt inexorably drawn to him. She had not lied when she told him that he had been the best sex she had ever had. Never before had she climaxed through penetration alone. The intensity of those waves of pleasure had been greater than what she could give herself. Even now her body thrummed with desire to be taken by him again while her heart wanted nothing more than to save him from more pain and brutality.

Tears flowing down her face Elizabeth realized that she cared deeply for him as her body craved him and for the first time in her life she knew what it was to truly love a man.

The chorus of female voices resonated through the room, *We have chosen well.*

xxxi

He floated between the realms of sleep and the lands of wakefulness as he watched the familiar nightmare blossom the stabbing pain in his side. In alert detachment the fear did not startle him into consciousness as it usually did. Instead he witnessed Jeanie's feasting with a sense of fatalism. A part of his mind rationally recognized the impossibility of such an event, but his heart still ached.

The pain in his side turned into a burning and he looked down to see Geraint's sword impaling him through the abdomen. He knew he should be alarmed at the black snake serpentine up his chest and down his torso but he only had eyes for the black grip, silver pommel and battered guard. Despite the burning weakness he could only smile – it was his father's sword! He had once had a father and a sister!

Darkness crashed down, obscuring the view of the hilt. Jeanie was nowhere to be seen.

"He abandoned you," floated a voice behind his right ear. He recognized the creature and grew angry. "He left you to die."

Denial shook his head, sending white locks floating in the Void.

"Why do you deny it?" The voice slid to the other ear.

He frowned, turning his head away from the voice made of dry leaves. The question echoed unbearably through his soul. Why did he deny the fact that Geraint had left him for dead an never claimed him when he found his son was still alive? Why the pretext of being a teacher of the warrior arts and not be the father he should have been to a boy desperately in need of one?

The answer ricocheted through his being. Because to accept the truth would mean he had found the reason why he was always abandoned, especially by those claiming to love him.

"But that isn't always the case," buzzed the voice in both ears.

Images of others flashed before his eyes. People who had cared and even who had loved him where time and distance separated, flowed like water across his vision. He saw his old master at the Chinese monastery when he was healing from the wound he took in service to King Richard. He saw other teachers, other masters. Visions of Tarian and Tarian's grand-daughter tugged him. Auntie and Geraint and Eira.

Jeanie.

He knew the truth.

It was not only because of how he appeared but because all things had a beginning, a middle and an end, over and over. He was eternal, unchanging.

Until now.

A clatter broke his attention and he saw Geraint's sword suspended in the darkness surrounded by rose petals the colour of blood. He reached out and grabbed its hilt and brought its sparking surface to his face. He was not alone. The sword, as unchanging and eternal as himself, held the memories of those who loved and cared for him. Though they did not claim him, they cared for him. This was the barrier kept others away. It was the fortification that armoured his heart against loss. It was the only gift his family ever gave him that had not succumbed to time and decay.

"But is that enough?" The rasping flowed from above.

"I don't know," he replied. He tightened his grip and lowered the point. The band around his heart squeezed.

"And what of Notus?" The voice floated out of reach.

Hurt and anger flared through him at the mention of the monk's name. Of all the betrayals, of all the pains inflicted upon him both mental and physical, through the ages, this was, by far, the worst. Notus was supposed to be the father he never had, the mentor that had guided him, the one who would never leave him because of the love they shared. They had been eternal together. Now there was no going back, even if Notus begged for forgiveness, which was unlikely. The wound was too new, too raw, and wept red blood.

SHADOW OF DEATH

He fell to his knees in a bed of rose petals and roared his frustration, loss and pain until the darkness vibrated. Tears flowed as he bowed his head, hugging his father's sword to his chest.

Diffused daylight burned his eyes and he blinked back tears, rubbing them away with the back of his hand. It took him a moment to recall that he lay on his good side in the guest bed and closed his eyes as the thought of his hostess evoked memories of what had transpired between them. He could deny it no longer. He was attracted to her, and what she had said to him only made him more confused about his feelings. One thing was painfully obvious as he gingerly rolled onto his back, his ribs protesting, was that parts of him reacted to Elizabeth without his conscious consent. The sudden sensitivity to the duvet's weight and the throbbing pressure between his legs proved it.

A sense that he was being observed made him glance over at the room's entrance to see Vee standing there and glaring at him, her arms crossed over her chest, a dour expression written across her pale face. He could have sworn he had closed the door when he went to bed this morning.

"You left me," stated Vee, angrily.

He winced as he attempted to prop himself up on his forearms, thankful for Elizabeth's wardrobe suggestion when the duvet slipped from his chest to his lap. He was unconcerned with Vee seeing the marks on his arms below the t-shirt. She had already seen those. It was the full extent of his damage that she did not need to see.

"You disappeared, left, and never came back," continued Vee. "I didn't know where you went, and I looked. You were supposed to drive me home too, you know. I was gonna call mum to pick me up but I didn't want her to freak. Shell's car was full. If I hadn't run into Karsha I'd still be stuck downtown. You abandoned me, you asshole."

Vee's growing rant and advancement forced him to sit up on the side of the bed, his sleep dishevelled hair falling to cover half his face. He met her blue sparking eyes, so similar to her mother's, and noted she too did not flinch from his stare. It was what she said at the end with her finger punctuating each word by stabbing it into his white cottoned chest that forced him to avert his eyes.

"Aren't you gonna say anything?" Vee shouted.

He knew she was right. He had abandoned her and left her to find her own way home. It was a feeling he knew full well. At least she had a home to find. It was also a remarkable blessing that no harm had come to Vee in his absence, considering the type of patrons that filled *The Veil*. The full impact of what his selfish move could have caused flashed an image of Vee lying dead beneath a streetlamp, stealing his breath in an airy apology.

"Damned straight you're sorry." Vee uncrossed her arms and turned on her bare heel to leave in a swirl of black and red skirts. "Oh, and mum wants you downstairs. Some sorta police lady's here."

He frowned at Vee's retreating back as he rose to his feet. All thoughts of what he and Elizabeth had done together were dashed to the side. His frown deepened as he closed his door. He raked his hair from his face, sending the fall of long white locks down his back and winced as the movement pulled at his healing ribs.

Walking over to the dresser mirror, he lifted the cotton shirt exposing the swatch of beige across his pale white skin. Above the bandage, peeking over, his damaged ribs leaked black, blue and purple. With a sigh he lowered the shirt and turned to find his black jeans on the floor. Clutching his aching side, he picked them up and slipped on the tight fitting trousers. He walked across the broadloom to the stairs and slowed his pace suddenly unsure of why a police officer would want to see him.

Images of the two fights filled his vision. What if the police found the impaled bodies and traced them back to him? No longer Chosen he could not redirect their investigation.

Quietly he descended the stairs and followed familiar voices into the kitchen until he halted at the sight of Elizabeth sitting at the table sharing coffee with Detective Donaldson. His stomach fell and he suddenly wished that Elizabeth had not drawn the curtain. A hasty retreat would have then been understandable. As it was, it was too late, both women saw him and stood.

"I wasn't sure Vee was going to wake you like I asked," smiled Elizabeth. She turned to the counter, grabbed a plate and poured a mug of coffee, placing them in the empty space at the table. It was clear this was an invitation to join the two women and his stomach agreed at the sight of the sandwich on the plate obviously meant for him.

Unable to shake Detective Donaldson's querulous stare he ignored her as he stepped forward to pull the chair out from the table opposite from her. He matched glares and was surprised as she leaned in closer.

"Get into a lot of fights?" Detective Donaldson canted her head, long corn row braids of black hair brushing the table. She ran her gaze over his healing split lip and the scars on his arms.

"Only when I'm attacked." So this was about the Vampires he had killed. He kept his voice dispassionate, hoping that the mask of the Angel would still be effective now that he was no longer Chosen.

"And why would anyone want to attack you?" It was clear that Detective Donaldson did not believe him.

Relaxing back into the country style wooden chair he glared down upon her midnight skin and hair, her dark chocolate brown eyes pinched in study. The silence between them stretched uncomfortably until he could sense Elizabeth's growing concern. Placing his forearms on the table, the plate between them, he was pleased the detective lowered her gaze but was unhappy as her study resumed on his scarred arms.

"Detective Donaldson." His voice snapped her attention back to him. Did she appear shaken? He could not tell but pressed forward nonetheless. "You are of a racial group where, at one time, just because of what you looked like you would be attacked, thought inhuman and enslaved. Luckily for you this level of bigotry is mostly gone, at least in civilized areas. For me this is not the case. My differences make me stand out no matter where I am. They make me a convenient target. Crying bigotry, though logically applicable, is not something that can be done when all individuals, regardless of their race, view me as different – as other."

The tension in the kitchen evaporated, transforming into uncomfortable embarrassment that sent Detective Donaldson to hastily pull out a manila folder from her black satchel. In his peripheral vision he noticed Elizabeth's posture and turned to look at her. She smiled sadly at him as she blew the steam rising from her coffee before taking a sip and returning her gaze to the detective.

A slight frown pulled at his lips and he picked up his own mug. Staring momentarily at the black contents he followed Elizabeth's motions and blew on the liquid before taking a cautious sip. Heat and bitterness exploded across his palette and he stared at the coffee. It was hotter than blood but it was the taste that threw him. Placing the mug back onto the table he became aware that the two women were watching him.

"Never had coffee before?" queried Elizabeth.

He shook his head.

"There are a lot of things you've never had," she mumbled, as if she had not realized she said the words.

Frowning at the truth, but unable to explain why, he picked up half of the sandwich. He recognized the lettuce and tomato but it was the rest he did not know, probably because he had never eaten a sandwich before.

"Do you want something else?" Annoyed, Elizabeth placed her mug down with a thunk.

It was then he realized he was staring at the sandwich as if it was going to bite him. He bit first, slowly chewing and was surprised at the tastes and textures. Though his mind bucked at the concept of eating, his treacherous stomach joyfully accepted the offering. He turned his attention to what Detective Donaldson was doing, his frown growing.

"As I was telling Dr. Bowen, we've had some success in the recovery of some of the stolen items." Detective Donaldson placed several eight and a half by eleven coloured photos face up on the table.

Elizabeth picked up one portraying a large gold cross with jewels of ruby, amethyst and emeralds encrusted on it. Excitement flowed from her and it was clear that the cross had been part of the exhibit that had been pilfered. "Where was it found?"

"That's partly why I came here," stated the detective. "I have more photos for you to identify. You see, the items turned up in a pawn shop. Luckily the owner recognized the items from the photos we circulated, thanks to you, and he called us. We have officers contacting other shops in case more items can be recovered."

Hope sparked as he swallowed the last half of the sandwich. "My sword?"

"Unfortunately that hasn't surfaced yet." She pulled out another folder containing more photos. These were black and white and she placed them beside his plate. "I was hoping that you'd be able to identify the individuals in these photos."

Both he and Elizabeth picked up the photographs to take a

better look.

"I don't recognize them." Elizabeth shook her head and placed the photo down.

He frowned and felt flush with anger. He recognized the man, if one could call him that, in the black and white still so obviously taken from a security camera that pointed towards the pawnshop's front door. Dressed in dark slacks and button down shirt, the Vampire who had eluded him and stolen his sword smiled maliciously for the sake of the camera. The woman in the short miniskirt and striped blouse could not be identified for the mass of flowing dark curls that obscured her bowed face. It was clear she did not want to be known.

"Do you know who he is?" inquired the detective.

"I don't know *who* he is." He met Detective Donaldson's hungry eyes. "I do know that he is the one who stole my sword."

"And the girl?"

He shook his head. "Her I don't recognize." He placed the photo back down before picking up the cooling mug, taking a sip of the awful tasting liquid.

Detective Donaldson began gathering up the photos. "Thank you very much. That helps us tremendously." She placed the coloured photos into one file folder and the black and whites into another. "Would you be willing to view a line-up?"

"If it will get my sword back, yes." He doubted that he would ever get called. A Vampire in a police line-up would never happen.

"Perfect." Detective Donaldson slipped the files into her satchel and straightened up, holding a photocopy of the photo he identified. "If anything else sparks your memory please call me."

He took her business card and the paper with a nod. He studied the photograph as Elizabeth showed the detective to the door, their voices floating down the hall. There was no need to follow the discussion; he knew they conversed about him. Instead his concentration was drawn to the mysterious woman beside the Vampire. There was no doubt that he did not recognize her, but something about her awakened a sense that he should.

The door to the basement opened the same instant that Elizabeth re-emerged into the kitchen, allowing Vee and another girl to enter.

"And this is the reason why I was lucky to run into you last night," explained Vee, shooting a nasty glare at him before proceeding to the fridge.

Vee's friend halted in her tracks, her eyes wide and mouth open as she saw him. Familiar with such attention he still could not escape the embarrassment and anger that such looks evoked. The taste of the bitter coffee was preferable and a welcomed distraction.

"Karsha, want do you want to eat?" called Vee as she rummaged through the fridge.

He could sense the girl's trepidation as she stepped into the kitchen. He continued to gaze at his coffee. It was better not to see the expression on her face. No matter if it was disgust, fear or even desire, he knew well what emotions his appearance caused in others. He was about to take another sip when the girl halted near him, her hand reaching out to pick up the photo. He followed the upward rise of the paper until he saw her blue-grey eyes studying the image.

She swept her straight brown hair behind her right ear. "Where did you get this photo of Brian and Rose?"

His stomach lurched and his heart raced. Vee's friend knew the culprits. Elizabeth left the washing of the dishes at the same time Vee approached her friend until all were staring at the photo or at Karsha.

"You know who these two are?" asked Elizabeth, incredulously.

Karsha nodded and pointed to the male. That's Brian. Don't you remember him from last night?" The last she directed at Vee.

Vee shook her head. "That's the Brian Shell was going on about?"

"I don't know about that, but that's Brian. I'm sure of it."

His mouth went dry as he asked, "Where do you know him from?"

Karsha jumped at the sound of his voice and quickly met his eyes before sliding them back to the paper. "He's the manager of *Beyond the Veil*."

"And the girl?" he pressed.

"That has to be Rose." Karsha's voice diminished under his scrutiny. "Rumour has it that the owner built the club for her."

His eyes met Elizabeth's and witnessed the worried flicker towards Vee. He did not need Elizabeth to voice the question. He nodded once – yes, that was the man who had threatened Vee's life. Elizabeth paled and turned to lean on the counter. The saving grace was that Vee did not recognize her hostage taker, having never gotten a good look at him.

"Do you know who the owner is?" he asked, bringing his attention back to the girl.

Karsha shook her head. "No one knows, except, I guess, Brian and Rose." She placed the paper down and blushed when she met his gaze.

"C'mon Karsha, there's nothing here for lunch. Let's go over to Mickey D's." Vee grabbed her friend's elbow and steered her out of the kitchen.

"I know he's hot," he over heard Vee say to Karsha. "But he's still an ass!"

He sighed and took another sip as Elizabeth sat beside him, a topped up coffee mug clunking against the wood table top. "Whatever it is, she'll get over it," said Elizabeth.

He frowned and pushed his plate and mug away. "That's not it. You're going to call Detective Donaldson and let her know what Karsha said."

"I will once I speak to Karsha and talk with her parents. Hopefully Vee and Karsha won't be gone too long. The sooner this information gets into police hands the faster the exhibit pieces can be returned to the ROM. And, of course, you get your sword back."

He released a breath he did not know he was holding and stared at the remains of his meal. He knew that Elizabeth was right but the plan he held last night about going to the club to find out where his sword was crystallized. He had recognized the place for what it was but little did he realize at the time that his sword may be there. Having police go in would ruin his chances of recovering the sword. Despite the recent discovery that Geraint had been his father, the sword was his only link to the past, to a time before he was Chosen, to a time when he was cared for before it because the scythe of the Angel of Death. Though he no longer wielded it, the sword was as much part of him as his flesh and blood.

"What is it? What's wrong?" Elizabeth's concerned frown caught his attention.

He was not sure if she would go along with what he had in mind, but nevertheless he had to ask. Cocking his head so as to look at her, he asked with a frown, "Can you hold off calling Detective Donaldson for at least twenty-four hours?"

"What? Why?" She placed her mug down, her blue eyes wide

in surprise. "I would have thought that you of all people would want to get your sword back."

"I do," he sighed, dropping his gaze from her crystal blue eyes. He chewed on his lower lip, doubting she would agree to his request. "I want to try and get it back from them myself," he added in a whisper.

"That doesn't make any sense. Let the police do their job. They'll get your sword and all the other stolen items."

He shook his head. "You don't understand."

"You're right. I don't." Anger heightened Elizabeth's tones. "So explain it to me."

"I can't." He reached out to play with the coffee mug; his long white fingers a slight shade's difference from the porcelain.

"Bullshit." Elizabeth's chair scratched backwards as she stood and came to stand across the table from him. He refused to meet her gaze. "I've been very accommodating and understanding, even forgiving you and letting it slide that for whatever reason my daughter had to catch a ride home with a friend while you were out getting the shit kicked out of you."

He snapped his attention up at her and attempted to form a defence but she barrelled along.

"After what we shared the night before and early this morning I would have thought you would be more open with me, but you've shut down again."

She was right. She had the right to know. It was not just a matter of stolen items; it was about keeping Vee from a Vampire infested nightclub. Yet he could not tell Elizabeth the truth. The last mortal he had allowed knowledge of their world was dead because of it and he was not going to let that happen to either of the Bowens. Resting his chin in his hand, his eyes fell to the photograph. "I didn't lie when I said I recognized the man in the photo. My run in last night after going to *The Veil* made me realized that these people – if you can call them that – are part of the same group that murdered Jeanie and …" He could not bring himself to say the rest, the pain choking off the words.

Elizabeth audibly sucked in a breath. The words left unsaid were written in the scars across his body. She pulled out the chair and sat, the anger blown away. "Mafia? They're Mafia?"

He met her startled sky coloured eyes. "Organized, yes. Criminal, most definitely. Mafia, no."

"How dangerous are they?"

"They make the Yakusa look like boy scouts," he said quietly, returning his gaze to the abandoned dishes on the table.

"Who are they?" Fear filled Elizabeth's voice. "And why steal the objects from the ROM?"

He shook his head, his long white locks brushing the table. "I won't tell you. It's safer that way, but they attacked the museum and stole my sword to get my attention and send me a message. It was not because of the relics." He closed his eyes and shook his head, sending a wash of white swinging.

"What message?"

"That I'm not supposed to be here, that I broke an armistice by coming to North America."

"But why?" she cried. "That makes no sense."

"I wish I could tell you, but I can't," he sighed. "But I will say that there is a long standing feud between them and me, and no I won't tell you about that either. Suffice it to say you already know too much."

Elizabeth leaned across the table and took his injured hand in both of hers. "If they're so dangerous why not let the police do their job? Why go there?"

He pointed to the man in the photograph. "He knew he was being caught on film. He knew the police would bring it to me. It's a challenge, and one I have to accept because if the police go into the club none of them will come out alive."

"That's ludicrous! How can they—"

"They did it in France," he said quietly. He remembered how Hugo, the Master of France, would not allow him to route the Vampires at first. Instead Hugo made an anonymous tip to the constabulary. The resulting massacre left Hugo deeply shaken and immediately called for the Angel.

"Jesus Christ," swore Elizabeth. She pulled back, releasing his hand. "And what's to stop them from killing you?"

He stood up, suddenly weary of all the white lies and explanations and offered a sad smile. "I've survived everything they've thrown at me. That alone makes them fear me."

"Or want to kill you," stated Elizabeth, bluntly, her eyes wide in horror.

"That too," he remarked sadly.

He felt Elizabeth's eyes on his back as he exited the kitchen for his room upstairs. There was a lot to do before he faced Vampires as a mortal.

xxxii

hanatos awoke with a start, something that never happened, his heart filled with dread. Throwing off the down filled duvet and pulling the bed curtains apart he frowned at the ornately decorated room. Something was wrong. Godfrey should be there waiting to attend him, instead he was nowhere to be seen. Stepping down, Thanatos found his robe where he had left it over the footboard and put it on. He thought to call for his manservant but doubted that shouting would work. Slippers ensconced on his feet, Thanatos left his suite for the quiet dark halls of his mansion.

Everything was still, adding to Thanatos' growing anxiety. Normally his home felt warm and full of life. It was one of many reasons that he kept Godfrey and others like him over the ages. It also lightened up Thanatos' dreary existence, but not today. Frowning, he followed the hall runner down the stairs, sliding his hand along the dark polished wooden banister. He left it as he came to a rest at the base of the staircase. All was still and quiet.

His frown deepened, pulling dark brown brows together as he walked across the heated marble tiles to the large oak double front doors. Placing a hand on the ornamental wrought iron he pushed the handle down to find it would not budge. The door was locked. Unfortunately it did not answer the question as to Godfrey's disappearance.

Thanatos dismissed the notion of going room to room and instead thought to search areas that were solely Godfrey's domain. If Godfrey was not where he was supposed to be, then he would not be in areas of the house he had no need to be in.

A horrible thought halted Thanatos in his tracks. *What if Godfrey ran away?*

He shook his head at the preposterous idea and continued on to the kitchen. If Godfrey was not there then the next place to look would be Godfrey's quarters. Thanatos was formulating his next step when he opened the swinging doors and found his servant sitting at the small mahogany kitchen set, staring sadly into a mug. His wrinkled and haggard appearance, not to mention the short growth of new beard, indicated that his major-domo had not slept.

"Godfrey?" queried Thanatos, gently.

At the sound of his name Godfrey's head snapped up in surprise. "Oh sir, I'm so sorry—" He managed to stand, weaving on unsteady legs as Thanatos cut off his apology with a wave of his hand.

Pulling out the opposite chair, Thanatos sat and indicated Godfrey should resume his place. *How many years has it been since we sat like this?* mused Thanatos. An image of a blonde headed youth pouring over textbooks while Thanatos stood over and assisted Godfrey in the study of his university finals filled his mind. The boy he had taken off the street had grown into a brilliant young man who graduated University at the age when most were just entering.

"You need not apologize, Godfrey," said Thanatos. "You are forgiven. After all, you are only human. The only thing I require is an explanation, but be mindful that an explanation is not an excuse."

"Yes, sir." Abashed, Godfrey sat down, hanging his head, unwilling to look at his employer.

Over the next hour and a half Godfrey did exactly as ordered, going over every detail and answering every question until Thanatos nodded. "Thank you, Godfrey. I know this was difficult to do – to admit your failure in convincing the Angel to leave. Believe it or not I would have done the same as you."

"Thank you, sir," sighed Godfrey, his shoulders slumping in relief. "What do you wish me to do now, sir?"

Thanatos stood and gently tucked his chair back into place. "Firstly, I expect you to clean yourself up – a day's growth of beard does not suit – and, if you have not done so yet, I want you to eat something. Coffee is a beverage, not a meal, contrary to what most people believe. When you have properly composed yourself I wish you to meet me in the Parlour."

"Yes, sir." Godfrey stood, receiving his orders. "But what of yourself, sir?"

The kitchen door halted its open swinging motion, Thanatos' hand holding it still as he turned back to his manservant. "I have taken care of myself long before we met, Godfrey. I'm sure I can manage for one night." He turned and took a step out of the kitchen and realized what he had done and called back, "Before you jump into the shower I need you to call into the office and inform them I will not be coming in tonight. Make whatever excuses you deem fit."

"Yes, sir," said Godfrey, enthusiastically as he followed his master into the foyer. "What is the plan for tonight, sir?"

Thanatos halted his first step to take him back to his suite and turned around. "I'm going to do what I should have done in the first place – I'm going to talk to the Angel."

"No one's answering." Fernando placed the cordless phone back into its charging station and turned to face Bridget and Notus. "Are you sure that's the right number?"

Notus closed his eyes and nodded. "I'm sure."

Unable to sleep the day away in Fernando and Bridget's guest room, in the same bed that the boy had been in, with the boy's scent still permeating the bed clothes, Notus was exhausted. It was not so much the lack of sleep put rather the swirling thoughts mingling with guilt and anxiety that had him tossing and turning. He knew he had completely severed his relationship with the boy. It was necessary. What had been unexpected was the boy being awake to hear Notus break millennia old confidences. To be on the receiving end of the boy's unleashed rage was heartbreaking, but understandable. What terrified the monk the most was hearing Fernando's description of the mist the boy had unconsciously summoned.

It was always apparent that the boy was different. All one had to do was look, but Notus had never known the boy before his accidental Choosing. The evidences over the centuries only enhanced what he tried to ignore – the differences that marked the boy for Destruction by the Chosen also singled him out by mortals. Now to find out that these differences were still part of the boy shook the monk. Long buried questions of the boy's true nature filtered up. Notus knew that both Fernando and Bridget were asking the same questions, expecting answers that Notus could not give.

"That is Elizabeth's telephone number," stated Notus, quietly. He did not understand why the Master and Mistress of England could not let the boy go.

"And you're sure that he's staying there?" asked Bridget. She sat on the couch beside him.

He was sure of nothing. His life was no longer the same. He shrugged.

"Well that's a great help!" Fernando walked over to the dinette where a sleek laptop lay open, its screen glowed brightly in the sparsely lit room. "Do you know where she lives?"

Notus frowned. He did not want Elizabeth or her daughter brought into the world of the Chosen. The risk to their lives would be too great.

"Paul, please, we need to talk to him," implored Bridget. "Hopefully he's cooled down."

He shook his head. "He won't talk with me."

Fernando glanced up from his computer and stared at Notus as if the monk had said the stupidest thing he had ever heard. "I don't want you going near the Angel. You incinerated that bridge quite nicely. I don't want you to blow up our chances to possibly regain a valuable asset." He went back to his computer, typing and swivelling the wireless mouse.

"I don't understand," queried Notus.

Fernando sighed and looked over the monitor. "Bridget, you explain it. If I have to be reminded one more time that it is because of Notus that we're in this predicament, I swear, I'm going to strangle him until his head pops off."

Notus' eyes went wide. No doubt remained. The Master of the British Chosen was still furious at him.

"It's clear that the Angel still has the abilities that make him what he is regardless of whether or not he's Chosen," explained Bridget, in a business like tone. "The severing of your ties to him in the callous and hurtful way—"

"Don't forget selfish," interrupted the Noble without looking up from his screen.

"Do you want me to do this or not?" snapped Bridget.

They're both furious with me, thought Notus, sadly. He had not ever been on the receiving end of her whip like anger, but having witnessed others cower under her lash Notus did not relish the prospect that he was next.

Fernando raised his hands. "He's all yours."

Bridget gave a terse nod and redirected her flashing eyes back to the monk. It took what was left of Notus' nerve not to cringe under her imperious glare.

"Yes, well, because of you the Chosen have either lost their greatest protector or have turned that weapon against the Chosen. Fernando and I hope that we can convince the Angel to return to us and not rise against us. It is our deeply held hope that we can, at least, try to repair some of the damage you created. If we can get the Angel back we'll be thrilled. The least we can hope for is that he won't turn on us."

"And you think he would do that?" asked Notus, horrified. "Turn on the Chosen?" *Because of me?* This last thought he smartly kept to himself.

Bridget sighed. "I pray not, but he's been used and abused, and he has every right to be angry."

Notus dropped his gaze to his hands that rested on his thighs. "And if he's turned against the Chosen?"

Bridget's jaw locked, unable to respond. She glanced to Fernando who penetrated the monk's eyes with a gaze that bespoke death.

"There is no way in hell that I'll let a weapon of such destructive capabilities be turned against the Chosen," said the Noble, icily. "If it comes to it I will kill the Angel."

The Master and Mistress ignored Notus' sudden intake of air.

"I found it," stated Fernando looking at the monitor. He quickly scribbled something down on the hotel pad of paper as he stood. Bridget followed suit, leaving the couch for the front door.

Fernando met Bridget there and gave her the paper before turning to face his unwanted guest. "You will stay here. If you are not here by the time we come back I will hunt you down myself and toss you in front of a Grand Council, am I understood?"

The Nobel's imperious tone chilled Notus and he slowly nodded. He watched the two leave without another word. All that was left behind was their anger permeating the suite. Notus closed his eyes and buried his face into his hands.

Dear God, what have I done?

XXXÍÍÍ

o you think there will be any problem with Dr. Bowen remembering us," asked Bridget as she smoothed out the navy blue skirt over her knees.

Fernando shifted the car into greater speed and wished that he had the top down. Unfortunately Bridget insisted it stay up less the wind mess her hair. He shook his head. "I'm just glad that she was home when we arrived." He sifted down again, slowing the BMW as they fell into heavier traffic. The Global Positioning System calmly spoke the next set of directions. "I wouldn't worry about it. The worst case scenario is that the Angel isn't at the club she said he was going to and he heads back to Dr. Bowen's."

"I still don't like it," frowned Bridget. "He's never been one for crowds. Hell, it's like pulling teeth to get him to come over to the house. Now he's off to some nightclub alone. I don't understand and Dr. Bowen seemed relieved that we were going after him."

Shaking his head Fernando followed the GPS' instructions and turned right. "I don't get it either. I could have if I Pushed."

"And have the Angel more furious at us for doing so? I think not." Bridget watched Fernando's dark features tighten with an impending outburst. "You know he'd figure out that one of us Pushed her. It's better that she believes that we're friends who, after finding out what happened between he and Paul, flew over to help mend things between the two."

"I don't care—"

"Yes, you do," snapped Bridget. "That's always been your problem. Don't think to fool me. I've known you far too long.

You care too much."

"Bridget," growled the Noble, not liking the shift in the conversation.

"Fine." Bridget crossed her arms and stared out the passenger window to watch the flowing scene of lit up buildings and passers-by. "Do you have a plan what we're going to say when we find him?"

"Nope. I thought I would leave that to you." He turned onto Queen Street West and slowed the two-seater so they could count the numbers as the GPS counted down the metres. Fernando pulled into a parking spot before the SUV could parallel park into it. He expected to have the driver get out of his car to start something and was surprised to hear some nasty names directed at him before the SUV pulled slowly away in search of another space.

Exiting the BMW, Fernando walked around, opened the passenger door and offered Bridget a hand as she rose from the low riding vehicle. She smoothed out the wrinkles in her skirt as Fernando closed the door and locked the car with the key fob.

"Do you want to guess which the nightclub is?" smirked Bridget.

"Fuck," swore the Noble. "Is he insane?"

The two Chosen stood outside *Beyond The Veil* watching Gothically dressed individuals move in and out the propped open black doors. Two guards stood to either side of the entrance, crossed arms bulging, threatening to rip the tight t-shirts, as they kept a watchful eye. Music pounded out the doors and onto the street, mingling with conversing patrons seeking fresh air or to pollute their lungs with cigarettes. All ignored the security, though on the occasion, someone would find the courage to glance their way. Despite the plethora of mortals pretending to be Vampires it was clear to the Master and Mistress of the Chosen what sort of place this was.

"Why would he come here, of all places?" concern tightened Bridget's voice, sending it higher.

"A death wish perhaps." Fernando walked towards the guards.

Bridget rushed up to her Chosen and grabbed his forearm, stopping the Noble and turning him to face her. "What do you think you're doing?" she hissed, fear widening her eyes.

Fernando glanced over to the guards and noticed their full

attention on him and Bridget. The Noble grasped her arm and pulled her off to the side to stand beside the rundown neighbourhood storefront. "We need to find him and get him out of there before he either gets himself killed or breaks the tenuous truce by killing everyone there," he whispered through clenched teeth.

Bridget worried the inside of her cheek, her gaze running past Fernando to land on the two guards. "But if that place is a— "

"Come on, Bridget," snorted the Noble. "Of course it's a Vampire club. Don't be an idiot. I have three in London alone. They're perfect for finding a willing dinner, especially one that can have their memories appropriately dealt with. You think the Chosen are the only ones to have whorehouses and nightclubs as our versions of restaurants?"

Bridget scowled. "Of course not, but do you think that walking into a Vampire infested club is wise for us?"

"No, but I've done worse." He turned to head towards *The Veil's* entrance.

"Shall I remind you of how you got your nice golden tan?" Bridget looped her arm through his.

"That was because of the Angel allowing me to be captured." Anger darkened Fernando's tone.

"And how is this any different?" asked Bridget in all seriousness.

"Shut up, Bridget," snapped the Noble as they approached the guards.

"I'm sorry but there's a dress code in effect. You're fine but your girlfriend isn't." The guard kept his relaxed stance as he looked down on the couple.

"What do you mean?" fumed Bridget. "I'm impeccably dressed!"

"Yes, you are, miss, but blue is a colour and the dress code is monochromatic and red," replied the guard.

"Bloody hell," she swore. "It's navy. It's so dark that–" She halted realizing to what she spoke to. No mortal would have noticed the difference in the faint light that streamed out of the door and onto the sidewalk.

Fernando stiffened and unhooked his arm from hers as the same realization hit. He was not expecting a run in with a

Vampire quite so quickly and damned himself an idiot. He should have expected it; after all he hired Chosen to act the same part as these two at his clubs. The question now was how to proceed. Fernando being Fernando chose the direct approach. At least if an altercation rose both he and Bridget could have room to manoeuvre.

"Actually we're not here to take part of your fine establishment." Fernando put on the airs that were instilled into him as the last heir of the Fidalgo de Sagres.

The Vampire frowned, confused. "Then why are you here?"

Bridget's eyes widened. The idea of starting a conflict with the Vampires made her blood turn to ice. She was a lover, not a fighter. That she left to Fernando and the Angel. It was more than enough to hear the reports of violent clashes between the Chosen and the Vampires, but here they were woefully outnumbered.

What are you doing? She Sent in a panic.

"Introducing ourselves to the Master," Fernando answered them both, "And looking for the Angel to take him back home."

The two guards lowered their crossed arms, their bored expressions turning hostile. One turned away, speaking into the air and holding his ear. It was then that Fernando noticed the covert communications device on him and realized he may have played his hand too soon. Keeping relaxed so as to appear nonchalant, Fernando scanned about for a possible ambush.

It did not take long to see an average sized man, dressed in black trousers and a black dress shirt, descending down the stairs to halt just before the guards. His short dark blonde hair stirred slightly in the soft breeze, highlighting his handsome features.

"Well, well, well, isn't this a surprise," stated the Vampire. "The Master and Mistress of the British Chosen here on this side of the Pond. Isn't that against our mutual agreement?"

"You have the advantage, sir," bristled Fernando.

"Yes, I do, don't I?" The Vampire smiled smugly. "How's the head? I understand the Thames is not fit for swimming anymore."

"You!" hissed Fernando, his cool countenance broken. He felt Bridget's hand on his, stilling him from pouncing.

"Ah, so you remember." The Vampire flicked his gaze to the growing crowd. "Either get them inside or get rid of them."

"Yes, Mr. Haskell," answered the guard. He went over to the mortals, herding them away from the scene.

"Now that we have a modicum of privacy why are you here?" Mr. Haskell's voice turned threatening.

"We're looking for the Angel," replied Bridget before Fernando could say something ignoble.

Anger emanated from the Vampire, his square jaw clenched and his eyes flashed. "The Angel is here? You sent your–"

"We didn't send him," snapped Fernando.

"So he's snapped his leash," sneered Mr. Haskell. The guards poised themselves for a fight. "I would have thought you'd have more control over your dog. Now you're saying he's here, where neither of you should be unless you wish this war to continue."

"He's not a dog." Bridget's voice grew louder as anger overrode fear.

"We're here to take him back," stated Fernando at the same time.

The Vampire smirked. "And you thought to come here, of all places? Well, he's not here, and if he did show the incredible lack of intelligence to come here he wouldn't be allowed to leave alive. Now, I'm generously offering you fourty-eight hours to leash your pet and drag it home. If you're not on your way back to England, dog in tow or not, we *will* hunt you down and do to you what the Angel *did* to us. Have I made myself clear?"

Both Fernando and Bridget shook with bridled rage. "You do–"

"What?" The blond Vampire took a menacing step forward. "You are not in Europe and the Angel isn't here. You are not in a position to threaten us though the reverse is true. The line is in the sand, Chosen, do not cross it again or you will wish that the Vampires had killed off every disgusting excuse of an immortal you hold dear when my Lady Bastia was still alive."

Bridget and Fernando watched the Vampire turn around and head back into *The Veil*, the two guards closing ranks to block the Chosen from following. They did not need it to be spelled out clearer. Grabbing Bridget's elbow, Fernando steered her away from the scene.

"Why that fucking bastard," swore Bridget once they halted at the car. "How dare he!" Her body shook, her hands balled into fists. "The Angel is not a dog and to threaten us–" Bridget let out a roar and punched the red newspaper box, crushing it down to half its size. Broken glass tinkled to the concrete. "What the fuck are you laughing at?" She whirled around onto her Chosen, her anger reduced but not extinguished.

"Oh, nothing," chuckled the Noble.

"Bullshit." She crossed her arms. "You're taking this all very well. I would have thought you'd be the one tearing up the street."

"And why should I? You're doing such a fine job yourself." Fernando realized his error and caught her open hand before she could make contact with his face. Their eyes locked onto each other and he kissed her, sliding his tongue into her mouth for a moment before breaking apart. "Save it for the hotel."

Bridget gazed up at Fernando, uncaring of what the passers-by thought, her fury rerouted to something more desirable. Using the key fob, Fernando opened her door and gave her a hand before he joined her in the BMW.

"You seen awfully calm," she remarked, buckling herself in.

"I'm not," growled the Noble as he inserted the key and turned. "I want that asshole dead. I want them all dead."

The tires squealed as he tore out of the spot, sending other cars swerving to avoid an accident. Horns blared.

"But I can't. Not on this side of the Atlantic," fumed Fernando. "You heard him. We have fourty-eight hours and Dr. Bowen was wrong. Not to mention Mr. Haskell is not the Master Vampire."

"He's not?"

"No, but he's high up enough for the guards to call him. Probably the Master's right hand." His tanned hands squeezed the steering wheel, indenting it.

"Where are we going?" asked Bridget, her blond brow rising at the sight of the damaged wheel.

"Hunting," replied Fernando matter-of-factly. "I need to kill something before we go back to Dr. Bowen's to wait for the Angel."

"Kill?" Bridget's jaw dropped. "We haven't killed since mortal forensics—"

"I know." Fernando darkly smiled. "If we can't strike at them directly we can strike at them indirectly. Let's see how they fare when cries of vampirism abound through the local newspapers."

Bridget returned her Chosen's smile as she settled into the leather bucket seat. New hunting grounds were always fun.

Brian stood in front of the large plate glass windows overlooking Queen Street. To either side and behind him patrons would occasionally glance at him before returning to their drinks and conversations. He could make out the gossip of what occurred just moments ago. Speculation abounded as to why the manager of *Beyond The Veil* would have to join the two guards in dealing with two foreigners, causing the club to be locked down until he returned. Brian ignored the prattle and the thumping music that came from the back room. Predatory blue-grey eyes stared across the street but it was not the goings on below that held his attention but rather the figure atop the roof opposite to the club. Brian allowed himself a small satisfactory smile before turning away from the scene.

Through the blood scented room Brian walked, making his way across the gyrating dance floor. Vampires danced with prey, nearly nude caged mortals seductively moved, enticing both Vampire and human alike, while the DJ perched on the stage lorded over all. The crowd parted as Brian passed through. They all knew who he was but it was the Vampires that knew he was more, much more. He was the Dominus' right hand man. What none but he and Corbie knew was once, long before either was turned, Brian had been Corbie's slave and lover. Though no longer either, Brian stayed with Corbie for the power and recognition it brought.

Out of the corner of his eye he saw Rose dancing with a new patron. It was a shame her turning of that boy did not work out, but Brian suspected something else happened to Rose's first. It did not matter. If Rose was lucky she would have what she was looking for. Relief flooded through Brian. Everything he and Corbie worked towards would have been dashed to pieces had the two Chosen seen her. Luckily the fates willed it otherwise. Now it was a matter of planning and the information he brought Corbie would determine the next play in this elaborate game.

Brian made a mental note to replace the burnt out bulb as he exited the back door. It did not matter to him, but certain things were necessary when running a business that incorporated mortals. He walked down the thin dark hall until he stood beside the steep staircase descending to Corvus' apartments and the units Brian, Rose and others kept so as to be close to their Dominus. The sound of his shoes clicking against the linoleum rang through the dead space only to confront the soft pounding coming from the club above until only Brian's footsteps filled the air.

Down one flight of stairs, turn, and then down a second set of stairs, Brian followed the route to the end of the hall, past doors to other apartments. Brian could hear the feasting upon willing mortals through closed doors. Only one rule must be followed – do not kill. Killing mortals was frowned upon. Why destroy a good source of food when it can feed you for years and be glad for it? If a death occurred then the Vampire responsible had to properly dispose of the body. If a mortal was killed on premises then Brian had the enjoyable duty of staking the Vampire spread eagled onto the roof to await the rising sun.

Entering the Parlour's audacious decorated confines, Brian's blonde brow rose in surprise. In a high backed black leather recliner the Mayor of Toronto dozed, a satisfied and relaxed countenance making her appear much younger. Brian did not need to see the puncture marks to know his Dominus was entertaining. Dressed in business attire Brian knew where Corvus would feed from. No point creating scars where paparazzi can see.

He stepped to the door that led to Corbie's white room and knocked.

"Come," came the response.

Brian entered the white control room. Beyond was Corbie's sleeping chamber, the door open. Lit by candles Brian could see the sleeping nude figure on the futon that served as his Dominus's bed.

Corbie stepped out of the chamber patting a handkerchief to his mouth. "What is it, Brian?" He walked to his new white oak desk and sat down.

"I have some interesting news." Brian crossed his arms over his muscular chest.

"And this needs to be brought to my attention now? Can't you see I'm in negotiations?" Corbie swept his black hair from his face. "More clubs are required, ones to attract the elite so as to increase our control. Not all of us wish to dine on Goths alone."

"No, definitely not," drawled Brian.

Corbie steepled his fingers before pursed thin lips, surprised at the impertinent tone. "Spill it."

"We had a couple of visitors tonight," stated Brian.

"Who?" Corbie's black brow rose in mild annoyance.

"Fernando de Sagres and his whore, Bridget."

Corbie's reaction to the news was more impressive than Brian expected. It was clear his Dominus had not expected the Master and Mistress of the British Chosen to break the tenuous treaty by crossing the Pond. Once the stunned shock wore off Corbie's face darkened with constrained fury. His body trembling, the Dominus clenched his steepled hands into a single fist and closed his eyes as he pressed his forehead against the white knuckled grip.

"Did they say why they were here?" asked Corbie, his voice a strained whisper.

"They're looking for the Angel to take him back to England," stated Brian matter-of-factly.

"Did they mention the Priest?"

Brian shook his head. The corners of his mouth turned slightly down. The question of Notus' whereabouts remained unsolved.

Corbie unclasped his hands and laid them flat on the table. "And you thought it best to deal with that rogue yourself rather than bringing the situation to my attention first?"

Brian chose to take the statement as a question rather than an accusation. "I believed it prudent to keep your identity from them less that they discover that Valraven still lives and rules the Vampires after having deceived the Chosen as Lady Katherine's right hand man."

Sucking at his upper lip, Corbie leaned back in his chair, the anger gone and nodded his appreciation. "Smart. Did the Chosen see anyone else?"

"They did not see Rose and she did not see them. She was too busy dancing." Brian uncrossed his arms, stuck his hands into his pockets and proceeded to detail the events that transpired between the Chosen and the Vampires, all the while carefully watching his master's face for the tale tell signs of another outburst.

"Well done, Brian." Corbie offered one of his rare tight lipped smiles. "I know you've been eyeing that pretty brunette. I give you my permission to change him."

Brian inclined his head, grateful for the generosity. If the transformation took, then Jacob would make an excellent second before possibly taking control of a small city. Receiving what he had been hoping for Brian decided it was time to deliver the *piece de resistance*. "I have further information."

"Oh?" Corbie leaned forward, arms resting on the desk.

A smile quirked Corbie's second's lips. "The Angel is on the roof across the street."

"What?" Corbie's black eyes snapped wide. "How long has

he been there?"

"Since I went out to deal with the Chosen."

A malicious smile broke the Dominus's face. "Is everyone here?"

"All but Stephanie and Michael. They're out hunting."

"Call them back."

"Sir?"

"It's time."

A true smile split Brian's face, revealing white even teeth in boyish features.

xxxív

He watched the activity at *Beyond The Veil* from his perch across the street, huddled in his black leather long coat in an attempt to escape the spring night's chill. When he arrived he first contemplated going into the club, find the first Vampire he ran into and demand his sword. It was an ill-conceived plan based upon the premise *what would Fernando do in my place?* Instead he fell back into patterns of behaviour etched into his soul for over a thousand years.

The glamour of the Angel fit as comfortably as ever as he parked his Y2K motorcycle down a residential street near the club. At first, standing in front of the closed shop's entrance across from *The Veil* seemed a wise idea. The burnt out bulb offered darkness but the indented entrance was still too visible from the sidewalk and street. The stares and ogling from those out for the night were inhibiting his reconnaissance of the club and its patrons. It was a chance but he left his observation to find an intact external fire escape behind the building. He climbed the rattling iron works, ever careful not to cut himself. His aching ribs screamed in protest as he pulled himself up to the gravel covered roof.

The view was perfect – a snipers paradise. Nothing obscured his line of sight. He stood, with arms crossed, as he watched the patrons, both Vampire and mortal, go in and out of the black building. It also provided a better view through the second floor windows. Lights flashed, silhouetting patrons enjoying the establishment.

The wind whipped his long white locks but he ignored the

strands except for when they crossed to obscure his eyes. Then he would raise his hand to brush the offending hair away without breaking his study of the club. He doubted he would be seen, and if so, only Vampiric sight would penetrate the rooftop darkness. He hoped to catch their attention. It was therefore a surprise when he saw two familiar figures step into the puddle of street lights as they exited the Beemer. Curiosity mixed with growing irritation as he watched Fernando and Bridget walk up to the two guards. *What are they doing here?* he seethed.

Stepping closer to the edge he watched the scene play out. When the Vampire who stole his sword and who posed for the security camera came out to meet the Chosen, did his breath caught and his heart sped up. There was no doubt that his sword lay somewhere in the building.

Worry wiggled its grip around his chest. If the Vampires attacked the Chosen, there was nothing he could do about it. The ramifications of such an act would be tantamount to a declaration of war – a war in which the Angel could not participate. It was, therefore, a relief when he witnessed the Master and Mistress of the Chosen turn and leave.

He stepped back from the edge and frowned. Though he was relieved no violence was done to his friends, he could not stop wondering what Bridget and Fernando were up to. The nagging concern stayed with him even after the Chosen drove away and he resumed his position to watch over *The Veil*.

Time dragged out and he could not shake the feeling that something was wrong. As the club returned to its normal activity he decided that he would approach the sword thieves toward the closing of the club. Hopefully there would be the least number of mortals to potentially end up in harm's way. Then again chances were that there would be more Vampires. It was this that created solid doubt about the wisdom of going up against of Vampires just for a sword.

He knew he was probably irrational about his desire to get his sword back, but he could not deny his desperate attachment to it and what it represented. He had lost too much in his life, many because time and circumstance willed it so, but the recent losses were the most devastating. He needed his sword, his father's sword, no matter the cost. It had never failed him.

The sound of someone climbing the fire escape pulled his attention from the club. It did not take long for a figure clad in black to reveal himself by standing before the metal ladder. Stepping away from the edge of the roof, his body tensed at the sight of the blonde headed Vampire. He knew he should not be surprised, after all he had expected the Vampires to notice him.

Time eked by. The only evidence that the minutes flowed past was the wind whipping the clouds past a swollen moon. They stood, two predators, studying each other for any sign of offence until the Vampire took a cautious sideways step, his expensive shoes shushing over the stones.

"Here we are again," called the Vampire. "I figured it would be better that I come to you since the events that occurred after your brief visit to my establishment. I guess I can assume that Ben and Mitchell's disappearance can be laid at your feet?"

He continued to watch the Vampire through the shifting veil of his white hair, never letting his eyes flicker from the creature. The mention of the two other Vampires did not stir him. Either they were the two that Fernando dispatched or they were the ones he staked in the park. It did not matter except to allow the Vampires to believe he was still Chosen and thus the Angel.

"Do you have nothing to say?" The Vampire opened his arms, pale palms outstretched as if to placate the moonlight that streamed down.

"Where is my sword?" Quiet menace carried his soft spoken words.

The Vampire lowered his hands as the corners of his thin pale lips curled upwards. "Ah, the direct approach. I can appreciate that." He took a step forward and paused when the Angel held his ground.

He allowed the pause to grow, not deigning to response to the creature until he received an answer to his query. Unmoving, he watched the smirk metamorphose into a scowl.

"Okay then," remarked the Vampire. "You want to get to the point – fine. You want your sword back – even better. We'll give it back to you."

The declaration surprised him. It did not make any sense except for one thing. The question he had to ask himself was whether or not it was worth the risk. The answer clutched his heart. "When and where?"

It was the Vampire's turn to be surprised and a smirk pulled his lips. "Do you not want to know what we want in exchange?"

"No," he stated. "I already know."

"Well then, this is a surprise. The Angel of Death expects death," said the Vampire. "If it is ours, you do not get your sword back. If it is yours, why bother?"

The Angel lowered his gaze. Did he truly expect to die? And was the Vampire correct? Did it really matter? He tried to keep the frown from his face and failed. What was the worth of his life now that all he held dear was taken from him? He swallowed and brought his gaze up to stare at the Vampire through a veil of white strands. "I am not afraid of death, are you?"

The Vampire's eyes went wide before tilting his head in a slight nod. "*Beyond The Veil* closes at three. I'll need about an hour or so to clear out the mortals. Meet me at the back of the club. There's a small parking area that the staff uses. Say four-thirty?"

"Fine." His eyes never left the Vampire as the creature moved towards the ladder.

"One other thing," the Vampire turned back from the ladder. "If you even dare to call those damned creatures, if I see one misty swirl, I will not hesitate to shatter your precious sword into pieces. Am I clear?"

"Crystal," he replied, angered by the threat.

Satisfied, the Vampire disappeared over the side.

Alone once more he pulled a white strand away from his mouth and turned back to observe the club.

Death. Was that what he was truly seeking? Was regaining his sword just an excuse? He slowly released a tension filled breath, ignoring the twinge of his broken ribs. He was no longer the Angel as either the Chosen or the Vampires knew him. Centuries of identity was blasted away in an instant leaving the same scared boy that had expected to live his life alone in a cave. Notus had called it existing, not living. The reality was that he never truly lived, except with Jeanie, and that was gone.

It was several hours before the meeting was to take place and the question of what to do in the interim gnawed at him. Taking off the leather coat, he rested it on the gravel to lean against the roofing's bricked edge, removed the two Japanese blades from their hiding places within the fabric, and came to stand in the centre of the roof. The wind plucked at his white linen shirt and hair as if to tell him that this was no place for the Angel. His right hand gently touched his healing ribs. It was going to be uncomfortable, even painful, but it had been too long. He settled into the starting position and began the martial forms that focused his mind and prepared his body.

"Sir, what do you want to do?" Godfrey stifled a yawn as he drove the limousine. "We've been driving all over in hopes of spotting the Angel. We've even gone to *Beyond The Veil* to see if he was there. Nothing."

Thanatos, sitting in the back leather seat, sighed and glanced at his gold Gucci watch. "What time does Corvus' club close?"

"Three, sir." Godfrey turned the limo south.

"From what you've stated, Godfrey, the Angel has been in or about *Beyond The Veil* at least twice.

"Yes, sir, but we were already there tonight."

Thanatos pursed his lips in contemplation. "Go back, Godfrey."

"Sir?" Godfrey glanced at his Master in the rear view mirror.

"A hunch, Godfrey," said the God of Death. "Drive us back to Corvus Valerius' club."

"Yes, sir." With a firm destination in mind Godfrey returned his focus on driving and turned onto Queen Street.

His side stabbed him as he panted from the exertion and the pain three cycles of forms had pulled from his broken ribs. The wind turned the sweat down his chest and back into icy rivers under the cotton shirt, yet another new and unwelcome sensation. Bent over, arm around his chest; his long hair brushed the gravel roof when the wind did not play with it. Carefully straightening to stand, he walked over on burning legs to pick up his jacket, sheathing the swords in the hidden pockets.

Slipping the coat on cut the chill but did little to warm his body. He shivered and hugged the leather tight. Of all the new experiences and sensations being cold evoked the worst memories from the time he was alone and outcast, existing in a cave.

He found the ladder and made his way down the rickety fire escape to stand in the garbage strewn alley. With several hours to go he frowned into the darkness. A grumble emanated from his stomach and he closed his eyes as the hunger for food made its presence known – yet another undesired reminder of his mortal state. It was clear how he would spend part of the time and he pulled out his wallet from the inside jacket pocket. Walking out of the darkness and into the diffuse street light, he checked his cards and hoped Notus had not lied about allowing him continued access to the accounts. He slipped the wallet back into its pocket.

Despite the late hour finding an open eating establishment proved promising. Toronto was a city that never truly slept. The question he had to ask was what he was willing to try, if anything. The thought of sitting under the scrutiny of staff and patrons while he attempted to master knife and fork as he ate unknown food dulled the roar of his stomach. He rounded the corner of the building and back into the main thoroughfare, his eyes landing on *Beyond the Veil's* active entrance.

No sign of the impending confrontation took place. Only the natural late night behaviours of mortals unaware of the dangers they placed themselves in. His jaw tightened to grate his teeth together and he turned away before he did something rash. The time to deal with the Vampires was soon approaching and that had to be enough.

He turned to his left, deciding to walk westward in hopes to find a quiet place to eat and to kill some time. Hands left out of his pockets at the ready it was a surprise when a man leaning against a limousine hailed him.

"Excuse me, sir," came the fear tinged voice.

He halted and turned to face the fair man, the black driver's cap covering most of his corn silk strands. A frown pulled as he recognized the man from earlier this morning. What were the Vampires playing at? "What?" he spat.

The driver recoiled as if hit, blue eyes wide.

"I would appreciate if you would stop scaring my manservant." A short young man with dark curling hair and large brown eyes stepped from the back of the car. For his fancy appearance he looked no older than his mid twenties, but held the bearing of someone much older.

Was there fear in the man's dark eyes? He crossed his arms to glare down at them. "Why are you following me?"

"I – well – uh," stammered the man, flustered at the direct assault. "We need to talk." The words flowed out in a nervous rush.

He cocked his head, narrowing his eyes. "What other conditions do the Vampires place upon me in order to get my sword back?"

"My master isn't—" blurted the driver, finding his courage.

"Still, Godfrey." The man placed a restraining hand on his servant. "It doesn't matter."

The driver looked askance at his employer before relaxing his stance.

"I was hoping we could talk in private." The dark haired man offered the warmth of the back seat of the car by holding the door open, his brown eyes flickering nervously.

He studied the two for a moment before turning on his heel to continue on his way.

"Please wait," called the short man, panic colouring his tones.

He halted but did not turn around. Enough was enough. "I will be back for my sword at the agreed upon time."

He did not wait for a response as he continued down the sidewalk.

Thanatos stood dumbstruck as he watched the Angel's retreating back. There was no doubt that a serious misunderstanding took place. The question left hanging was what exactly did the Angel assume was going on? He frowned and closed the car door. After searching for answers and hoping the Angel was the one to relinquish them, Thanatos had hoped that finally meeting the Angel would have gone differently. To have the Angel react to him so cut deep, but after all the Angel had gone through maybe it was too late to find the answers he sought since before the Angel's birth.

"What do we do now, sir?" Godfrey's question cut to the heart of the matter.

A sigh escaped and Thanatos frowned. "I'm not sure, Godfrey."

"Sir, he took you for a Vampire, why would he do that?"

Thanatos gazed up into hurt blue eyes, saddened by what he saw in his Godfrey's face, and shook his head. There were so many reasons and none that he could tell his most trusted of servants.

"Let's go home, Godfrey," he said, opening the car door for himself. "I don't know what else to do."

Godfrey took the door once his master was seated on the black leather. He had almost closed the door before snatching it open.

"What is it, Godfrey?" Thanatos stared up at the man, surprised by the strange behaviour.

"Sir, the Angel said he'd be back." Godfrey's voice rushed out in excitement.

Thanatos was going to debate that but then nodded, remembering the Angel's last statement.

"He said–"

"He said that he's coming back for his sword as if we knew where it was." In his excitement Godfrey realized his *faux paux.* "Oh, sir! I'm so sorry!"

Perturbed by Godfrey's slip Thanatos dismissed his servant's behaviour with a wave of his hand. "Just so that it doesn't happen again. We will stay here and wait. Corvus is up to something and I *will* find out if he's still dead set on defying me. If the Angel refuses to listen there is nothing to be done about that."

"Yes, sir." Godfrey closed his Master's door and entered the driver's seat, settling his cap more securely upon his head. It was a surprise when the yawn overtook his professional veneer.

"Godfrey," spoke Thanatos, gently. "Take a nap. I will wake you when the time comes."

Appreciative blue eyes met brown through the rear view mirror. "Thank you, sir."

Godfrey slipped his cap low enough to shade his eyes as he relaxed into his seat.

It did not take long before his servant was snoring softly. Quietly, so as not to disturb Godfrey, Thanatos opened the door and stepped out of the limousine to lean against the trunk. His dark brown eyes narrowed as he watched patrons of *Beyond The Veil* exit and enter.

What are you up to, Corvus?

Corbie Vale, Lord of Valraven, once Corvus Valerius Tertius of the Roman legions, caressed the length of the sword laid across his white oak desk and scanned the faces of the Vampires who ruled beneath him. Satisfaction burned through as he named the faces. Some were of Brian's progeny, such as Michael and Stephanie who lounged on the white leather sofa, touching and making eyes at each other. Who knew that two Vampires could love, especially love one another? Disgust warred with astonishment and Corbie slid his study onto Orchid who was speaking with his other flower – Rose. A smile quirked his thin lips, everyone was here to witness Corbie's revenge against the Angel and thus the

Chosen.

No longer would the Chosen be able to cower behind the Angel's skirts. Tonight would usher in a new age of dominance where Corbie would be truly free of the Chosen's threatening presence. He would be able to take back what was rightfully his. It was time to pursue, in full measure, the destruction of the Chosen and the domination of the humans, placing them properly in the food chain. Let the Chosen hide, for the moment, across the Pond. One day soon the Vampires would cross the Atlantic and finish what Bastia had intended – the decimation of the Chosen.

The door opened and Corbie's right hand walked in. Their eyes connected across the room and Brian nodded at the unspoken question. It was time. The room grew still as Corbie stood, all eyes turning to the Dominus.

"You all know why you are here," stated Corbie. Many Vampires nodded while others, like his beautiful Rose, smiled maliciously. "Tonight we humiliate and destroy the creature that sent us fleeing to these untouched shores. For that we thank the Angel by giving back what we took from him. Since he cannot give back what he took from us we will take it from him." Snickers flitted through the room. "It is time to take our destiny into our own hands. Everyone here knows what he or she is to do, let's do it."

Brian opened the door to let the Vampires prepare themselves.

"Not you, Rose," called Corbie.

Rose halted and frowned at her Dominus.

"It's alright, Brian." Corbie raised a stilling hand as his second was about to close the door to stay with Corbie and Rose. "You can go and oversee that everyone is where they are supposed to be."

Brian inclined his head and left, sealing the room behind him. Rose walked over to Corbie and the sword that glittered in the darkness. "Why are you keeping me from this?" she demanded, hands on her green skirted hips.

"I'm not," said Corbie. He stood and walked around the desk to meet her floral green eyes. He loved to see the angry spark flare to life before being extinguished by his generosity. "You are given the honour of presenting the sword to the Angel."

"Really?"

Rose's stunned visage almost made Corbie smile and he nodded. "Most definitely. This is what I want you to do …"

XXXVI

It was nearly time for his meeting with the Vampires and the slice of pizza and can of soda sat like lead in his gut. It had been a quick choice that proved the wrong one. For all the foods he had to consume now that he was mortal this had been, by far, the meal that had made him most crave to be Chosen again.

He rounded the corner and halted, anger tightening is pale features as he saw the dark haired Vampire leaning against the trunk of the black limousine. He would have to find another way around to the back of the club.

Careful not to draw the Vampire's attention he backed up before turning around and was surprised when he bumped into someone. The girl, all dressed in ragged and mismatched clothing, attempted to walk past him but he knew a pick-pocket when being fleeced by one.

He thought about letting her go with his possessions, but it was just one more thing that someone was trying to take from him. Before she could disappear into the night his hand shot out and grabbed her arm, spinning her around.

"Ye'd bedder let me go, or'll scream," she said as she swung about. Whatever else she was about threaten evaporated once she caught sight of her pick. Eyes and mouth wide, fear rippled over her smudged face.

"I believe you have something that belongs to me," he stated coldly.

Her hand shook as she pulled his wallet from the inside of her ratty and stained sweatshirt.

He took the wallet without losing eye contact. "And the rest?"

A shudder ran through the street urchin and she quickly revealed the cash and cards she had hoped to sneak from the wallet.

"In the past I would have dealt with such offences in a more permanent manner." He took the money and plastic, returning them to the wallet. "Count yourself lucky tonight is not one of those nights."

Eyes widening further it took her a moment to realize that she was free to go. Her footpads came quickly together as she fled the fearsome angel.

He watched her retreating back and slipped the wallet into a deeper internal coat pocket. It was ever the same. He sighed and shook his head. Chosen or mortal, people still were either drawn to him or, more often than nought, fearful because of his appearance. He was about to turn around to resume his search for an alternative route to the back of *The Veil* when he noticed that the Vampire and the limousine were no longer there. Frowning, he decided to take up his original course.

It did not take long to find the laneway that ran parallel to the municipal parking lot. A dappling of different coloured cars sprinkled the lot, their windows black and vacant. Widely dispersed street lamps rained puddles of luminescence, throwing some vehicles into sharp relief while others faded into the blackness of deep night. No one stirred as the ricochet of his steps bounced from the brick buildings into the wide open space of the lot. A loud squeak of a rat exiting its hiding space beneath a dumpster was the only warning of its scurry across his path to a garbage bin next to the lot. Disgust warred with awe as he watched the cat sized creature hunt for throwaways. Only when it had achieved its goal of finding a discarded hot dog bun did it flee into the darkness, its prey in its mouth. Swallowing his disgust, he continued his search for the rear of *The Veil*.

There was no doubt he was walking into a trap. He had to get his sword back and he would do almost anything to do so. The likelihood of death was high but he no longer cared. All that was left for him was his sword, nothing else. It was all that mattered, the only thing that never failed him. If necessary he would kill as many Vampires as possible before that eventuality. The only ace in his hole was the fact that the Vampires did not know about his current state of mortality. As to what would happen when they discovered the truth, well, he did not care about that either.

A lone figure stood at the corner of the black bricked wall and he walked up to the Vampire, staring down at the creature of modest height and muscular girth. With short cropped black hair and beard, the Vampire appeared well tailored for the venue in a suit more fitting a hundred years ago. With a nod of the Vampire's head he walked past and stepped into the private parking lot for the club.

He repressed the shiver at seeing so many Vampires standing statuesque and hated having even one of them at his back. He had been told not to invoke creatures he had no access too but he had not been told not to bring any weapons. Placing his hands into his pockets he could feel the pommels of the two Japanese blades in their hidden compartments within the long leather coat. The sensation of cool smooth wood wrapped in silk was a comfort.

He came to stand in the centre of the lot. Two black cars flanked the black painted door. Nervousness evaporated the moisture in his mouth, leaving it dry as ash as numerous Vampires seemed to appear out of nowhere to encircle him. There were more, many more, than he expected. He hoped that keeping his hands gripping the *katana* and *wakizashi* would make him appear nonchalant rather than exhibiting the fear that threatened to fell him.

No sound stirred from the creatures. Only the occasional rat squeak and police siren filled the tense air until the clanging sound of the back door opening drew everyone's attention. The sandy haired Vampire who had stolen his sword, and who had issued the invitation, stepped forward.

"Well, well. You're here." Fake astonishment dripped. "It's not every night that Vampires can stand before the Angel of Death without experiencing his demonic wrath. So nice of you to keep to our bargain."

"And what about your end?" he asked impassively. There was no way he was going to display the fear that filled him. "Where is my sword?"

"It's coming, but first to other matters." The Vampire stepped to the left of the door as it opened once again.

A short man with black hair gelled back from his Romanesque face emerged from the building.

He could not believe who he was seeing. His shock broke his

cold reserve allowing anger in its place. "Valraven!"

"It's nice to be remembered," smiled Corbie, stepping forward. "Does your back itch for my staff, Angel? Or do I need to capture your sire first?"

Rage sent him trembling, his hands and jaw clenched. He would not succumb to the taunts Valraven spewed. He guessed he should not be surprised at Valraven's sudden appearance or that he was a Vampire. After all he had been the right hand of the Vampiress who had not only completely deceived the Chosen, but had enacted their genocide. He would not succumb to the taught and instead stood silent, refusing to take his eyes off the Vampire as others around him chuckled.

"You're the one behind the theft of my sword," he stated coldly. It was tough keeping the mask from slipping.

"How astute of you," smirked the Dominus. Hands clasped behind his back, Corbie rolled onto the balls of his feet before settling back down. Excitement radiated from him.

"Your second said he would give me back my sword." He bore his gaze into Valraven and was pleased that his nonchalance slipped a notch.

"Brian, you didn't, did you?" recovered Corbie, mock surprise widening his dark eyes.

Brian shrugged, his face placid.

Corbie returned his attention to the Angel. "It seems Mr. Haskell doesn't recall such arrangements."

He bristled at the expected statement, his crimson eyes narrowing. It was not a surprise to have the Vampires break their word or to be caught in their machinations. It was disturbing not to know what was next. "Regardless, I am here for my sword."

"And what will you give me if I give you what you want?" Corbie stepped closer to the Angel, but not in immediate striking range.

He was loath to ask. "What could I possibly give you?" *Except a quick death,* he silently added.

A quirk at the corner of the Vampire's thin mouth did not match the sudden darkening of his eyes. "I want you to bring back all the countless Vampires you destroyed." Hatred broiled from Corbie.

It was a ludicrous request designed to be impossible. He matched it with one of his own, taking a step closer to the Vampire. "Only if you bring back all the Chosen you poisoned."

Corbie barked a laugh as he turned around, his arms wide, addressing his audience. "How like the Chosen!" he declared. Corbie turned back to face the Angel. "Of all the things to ask I would have thought the Angel would have asked for something more dear to his heart. But no. It's always about your accursed Chosen. If it wasn't for you and your kind we Vampires would have placed the humans in their proper position - as slaves below us on the food chain like the animals they are!"

Whoots and hollars exploded.

The statement made no sense. Both Chosen and Vampire fed from humans.

"So you wanted to kill the Chosen over food resources." he stated, doing his best to hide his confusion. It was therefore a surprise when Corbie's face fell, dumbfounded.

"You don't know?" asked the Vampire, incredulously.

A measure of his confusion must have broken through his cold mask. He did not know what Valraven was talking about, but he knew he was finally close to the real reason why the Vampires had waged their war against the Chosen.

"You truly don't know?" Corbie began to laugh, his voice ringing against brick until it came to an abrupt end. "The Chosen are called that because they are supposed to be the Chosen of God, or Gods, to be protectors of man! Oh, how low have the Chosen fallen!" Corbie turned to address his Vampires. "Oh, what cruel irony!"

Protectors of man? The thought swirled in his mind. They were the Chosen, but chosen for what? Even Notus did not know, or did he? Was that the reason for his life as a monk? It would explain so much of what Notus did in his life. The pain of thinking of that man cleared his head and focused it onto the task at hand. He took a step closer towards Valraven.

Corbie noticed the threatening position of the Angel and took a retreating step backwards. With a nod of Brian's sandy head he tightened the noose of Vampires.

"I know you are armed, Angel," stated Corbie. "I haven't been around for nearly two thousand years without learning a thing or two."

He relaxed the grips on the hilts yet kept his hands in the pockets.

"I'll make you a trade." Corbie paced, finger tapping his lower lip in contemplation. "Whatever you have in your two coat pockets for the sword you came for. I'll even throw in a small surprise."

"And if I do, how do I know you'll allow me to walk out of here alive?" His eyes narrowed.

"And how do I know that once the exchange is made you won't call your demons to kill us all?" countered Corbie.

He clenched his jaw and whispered, knowing that the Vampires would hear him. "On my honour."

Corbie inclined his head and nodded, contemplation twisting his features. "Well, then. On my honour."

Unsure whether to believe the Vampire, the Angel realized he had little choice as he glanced right and left, taking in the ring of dark figures. Grasping the hilts, he slid the Japanese blades from his coat. He knew he was just moments from violence as he heard the creatures shift to the sudden threat he became. It was a surprise when Valraven stepped forward.

"Ah, what beautiful craftsmanship." Corbie held out his hand indicating to the Angel that he should place the *katana* and *wakizashi* onto the ground.

"I've shown you mine," stated the Angel, refusing to relinquish his weapons. "Now show me yours."

"If you want it that way." Corbie nodded once and Brian went to the black door. The circle of Vampires tightened further.

The black back door to the building opened. Another Vampire, a female, carrying his sword across her two outstretched hands, slowly approached. Even in the darkness he could make out her long curling locks of cinnamon as the breeze tugged it to obscure her face. She halted next to Valraven.

Everything about this Vampiress screamed to him of familiarity. The hair, the voluptuousness of her body dressed in a tight leather mini-skirt, and full breasts rising above a black satin corset cinched over a deep green silk blouse. He recognized her from the police photo, but his body remembered what his mind failed to comprehend. It was only when she lowered his sword point down and brushed the dishevelled locks from her face that the name he denied rushed through his lips.

"Jeanie!"

Her name rushed from his lips as he bounded forward in an attempt to save her, his mind reeling at the impossibility of whom he saw. He was only able to take a single step before crushing pain flared down his left thigh and up into his hip, sending him sprawling onto the concrete. The grip on his blades failed, sending *katana* and *wakizashi* skittering across the ground.

The blow and the fall wrenched his slowly healing ribs and he gasped as he was forcibly hauled to his knees. He was held in place by a couple of Vampires who pinioned his arms behind his back. His eyes flickered over triumphant brown to land on green he had last seen staring blankly into the night. He let out an involuntary sob.

"This is going so much better than I had hoped. 'On my honour.'" snickered Corbie. A true smile brightened his face, his dark eyes filling with sadistic delight. "I bet you're wondering how it is possible for your beloved to be standing here." Corbie stepped closer knowing the Angel was well secure.

"Jeanie, what happened to you?" He implored and was rewarded with a look of confusion before she shook it away. He could not believe who he was seeing. It was impossible. Jeanie was dead. But here she was alive. His heart clutched in joy and pain.

An unknown hand yanked a fist full of his hair, forcing him to match gazes with a Vampire he desperately needed to kill.

"Now, now," clucked Corbie. "How we create Vampires is for Vampires to know, but I'll let you in on a little secret." He leaned in to whisper. "She was so delicious when I kidnapped your sire. Granted it was a little bit more than a taste from her wrist, but when I saw her underneath that lamppost again after you murdered my Lady Bastia, I knew I had to have her, this time all of her. Oh, how intoxicatingly delicious. No wonder you had her. Did you know she came willingly to my embrace?"

"Liar!" he shouted, anger flooding him as he attempted to break from his fleshy bonds. He had known he had walked into a trap. He was even prepared to die. He was not prepared for this.

Corbie jumped back from the Angel's wrath and glanced around, fear flickering across his face. "Your part of the bargain – none of your demons. You call them and her true death lands squarely upon your shoulders."

He did not know what Valraven was talking about until it struck him – Valraven believed he was calling the mists. Seething, he forced himself to calm down, the pain of his ribs and thigh throbbed in time with his racing heart as slowed his breath.

"Good. Good," nodded the Dominus. "I wouldn't want Michael to have to use Subtle Persuasion on you again."

He glanced over his shoulder, past the Vampire who pinned him, to see the Vampire he had met upon entering this nightmare holding a large limestone hammer. Returning his attention to Valraven he glared his compliance. "What now?"

"You get your sword back," said Corbie, nonchalantly. "I am a man of my word. One other thing; a message to the Chosen," his voice hardened. "The Americas – north, south and central – are mine. The Chosen will keep away. *You* will keep away. No matter what you see or hear, the Chosen will not set one foot here. If you do then all out war will be declared and *we* will kill you to the very last like we had hoped to have done a hundred years ago. This time you would fight us *and* the humans.

"I am not Bastia, a High Priestess of Isis, who worked at domination and destruction through the guise and glamour she excelled in. I am Corbie Vale, Lord of Valraven, Corvus Valerius Tertius, Tribuni Praetorian to Invictus Maxentiuns. I was born to lead and trained to rule. I am not interested in destroying the Chosen so long as the Chosen continue to be ignorant to what they are."

Corbie stood inches from the Angel, his face and stance rigid in martial discipline. No fear caught his dark eyes, only deadly purpose as if reciting his full name has brought him back to his true self.

Hands clasped behind his back, Corbie turned and marched back to stand next to Rose. "Give him back his sword," he ordered.

Still held on his knees, his arms wrenched painfully behind him, he watched a shudder run through Jeanie before she lifted his sword and stepped towards him. Nothing about her had changed. She was still the most beautiful woman he had ever seen, and his heart ached at her transformation. His ragged breath caught as she halted a foot in front of him. He did not care about the pleading gaze he sent her. The mask of the Angel was shattered.

She took a moment; head cocked to the side to allow cinnamon falls to run past her shoulders, her pale beautiful face was pinched in contemplation. "When Corbie gave me the honour of giving you back your sword, I was thrilled," she began. "Never before had I seen such beauty in a man, but there you were, standing in that newspaper photo and I just knew."

"Knew what?" he rasped, his heart breaking. Even her

sensuous Highland burr was gone.

"I knew I had to have you," she smiled. She brushed his smooth pale face with the tips of her fingers.

He shuddered at her touch, his eyes closing as he tried to come to terms with what his heart cried and what his mind screamed. "Jeanie," he pleaded. A century of guilt and despair filled him.

"When I saw you as I plucked your sword from its glass coffin I felt something more," she continued. "I thought that by creating Thorn I would satisfy that feeling. It did not. And when I witnessed you slaughter two of my brothers in Queen's Park all I wanted was to be in your arms. Why is that?"

"I–"

"Shhh." She pressed her fingers to his lips.

His breath ran hot around her cold fingers, his eyes swimming in green. This was Jeanie! This was the woman he loved and had wanted to spend eternity with.

Her fingers left his mouth to be replaced with lips as cold as they were familiar. When she pressed him to open his mouth he let her in, tasting copper as he gave in to his desires. Tears sprung to his eyes with the realization of whom he was kissing. When she broke off he was almost grateful for the bonds that kept him from toppling over.

She took a step back, her fingers flying to her mouth, her eyes wide. "You're warm," she susurrated.

Fear stabbed through him and it took all his willpower to push down the rising panic. Jeanie knew he was no longer Chosen.

"Get on with it Rose," called Corbie.

Snapped back to her purpose she renewed the close distance. "Corbie wants me to give you back your sword," she purred. She ran her fingers along his cheek to slide into his silky milk white hair. "He didn't say how."

He knew where this was going. He had lived through it every time he slept since learning he was coming to this accursed land. Therefore it was not a surprise when she grabbed his hair close to the scalp, forcing his head to the side. He gasped in pain.

"Jeanie, you don't have to do this," he panted. Images from reality, his dreams and his past when he was in Violet's clutches swam through his mind, increasing the terror of what was to come. Jeanie moved closer, her mouth open and her canines lengthening.

"Ahh, but I want to."

Her cold breath tickled his neck. Instinct and self preservation kicked in as he struggled to break free of the Vampires who kept him subjugated on his knees. His left arm was almost free when he felt the delicious agony of Jeanie's teeth rip into his exposed jugular. The sound of her suckling accompanied the sensation of his blood being drawn up and out of the wound. It took all of his willpower not to move lest she rip out his throat.

Pain.

Hot searing pain stabbed through him, exacerbating the throbbing of his injured ribs. The taste of blood filled his mouth at the same time nausea forced it out of him, spilling black blood over white lips. Every breath was torture as he fought to breathe, black bubbles popped to dribble down his chin.

Beyond the agony he could tell he was held only by Jeanie. Somewhere his mind registered that she had finished feeding. His eyes met hers and saw horrific realization. Unable to breathe he glanced down at himself, his hands pressing his abdomen. Unsurprisingly his sword was buried nearly to the hilt. He gazed back at Jeanie and saw bloody tears tracking her face. He knew it was not her fault. It was his. He had failed her. He had broken his Oath to her.

"I—I love you," he managed to get out with what was left in his lungs.

His eyes blurred and black tendrils stretched into his vision. Somehow he managed to catch himself with one hand on the concrete as he bent over. His long white hair caught drops of black blood before they could splatter to the ground.

Time moved slowly. Corbie's order rang warped and elongated in his ears.

Excruciating pain tore at his insides as he felt the sudden pressure placed upon the end of the sword until he felt the break deep within his body. Blackness swallowed him, stealing his strength and his consciousness.

XXXVI

The first thing that struck her was how exquisite the Angel's blood tasted. Never before had she imbibed someone so delicious. Each mouthful, each gulp, was pure heaven until she had given him back his sword, sheathing it through him. Then the flavour changed. Bitter, his blood stung her throat and she pulled out to witness blackness creeping up along his skin, marring his perfect paleness. Black blood spluttered from the Angel's full lips, black mingling with white. His ruby eyes filled with shock and pain before he toppled over to catch himself, the length of his blade extruding from his back.

Did she hear that correctly? Did the Angel utter his love for her?

She stumbled as an onslaught of images assaulted her.

Flash!

She saw him sad and distant, always trying to keep apart from her as she tidied his home, her heart yearning for him.

Flash!

She was held captive and then he was there, saving her. The scent of clean linen and something that could only be the Angel encompassed her in strong arms that she had always desired to feel wrapped around her.

Flash!

She was above him as he lay on a bed, their bodies entwined. Her heart soared with fulfilled love before he sat up to penetrate her awaiting neck.

Flash!

Held in his strong arms the world spun as he fiercely defended her. Someone went flying and then the Angel was there, his blood splattered beautiful face filled with concern and love.

Flash!

The Angel suspended, his body burnt, bleeding and damaged because she would not listen. She loved him and her stubbornness killed him.

"Now! Do it now!" The order shocked her. Through bloody tears she saw Michael wield his limestone hammer, swinging it to make contact with the protruding sword. Time halted as she reached out her hand in an impossible attempt to stop the Vampire.

The sound of the hammer rang against metal, drowning the Angel's scream as the force of the blow broke the blade deep within him. She did not realize she had shouted until she witnessed the Vampires staring down at her. Somehow she was at the Angel's side as he lay on the concrete, black blood staining his lips and black tendrils eked across his pale face.

"Get off the ground, Rose. You're embarrassing yourself," snapped the man with black hair.

A shudder of fear ran through her. This was the man who had broken into the Angel's home, kidnapping Notus. This was the man who had held her prisoner until the Angel saved her. This was the Vampire who had killed her while she had waited beneath the light post for her beloved to rescue Father Notus. This was the creature who sat a-top a headstone as she clawed out of the grave to feed upon that poor wrench of a boy.

Memories assaulted her, who she had been and what she had become warred within her. She gazed down at the Angel – no, Gwyn, - the full impact of her actions slamming into her. Tears streaming, her head grasped between her hands, she let out a scream of heart wrenching agony.

"What have I done?" she cried. Her eyes fell upon the Vampire who had been her father, her mentor, her destroyer – the grand manipulator.

"Well, this is quite fascinating." Corbie walked over to her, staring down with surprise on his face.

Brian stepped up beside his master, arms crossed over his muscular chest. "I suppose your message to the Chosen won't be delivered."

"Probably not," commented Corbie. A round of chuckles responded. "He got what he wanted and I got more than I hoped for – the death of the Angel."

"That *will* definitely send a message to the Chosen," said Brian.

A smile lifted Corbie's lips. "Yes. Yes, it will." He gazed around at his Vampires, his smile growing. His power over the Americas was increasing and with the threat of the Angel and his Chosen eliminated it would not be long before he would truly be Imperator.

Corbie returned to the Angel and a possible new problem. He had heard Rose scream and the return of her accent. "Everyone inside, the sun will soon be up, everyone except Rose."

Quizzical Vampires slowly made their way into the building, the sound of the footsteps loud in Jeanie's ears, until all who remained were she, Brian and Corbie. Jeanie trembled as Corbie crouched in front of her.

"You remember who you were?"

His question was more a statement. She nodded.

"Fascinating. It's been a very long time since a Vampire was allowed to recollect, or even could recollect who they were before their true birth," stated Corbie. He stood and gazed imperiously down upon her. "The Angel is dead. My plans fruited better than I expected. You served your purpose, Rose."

"My name is Jeanie," she said, unsure of herself or what was about to happen.

Corbie's gaze rained ice. As if deciding something important, he gave a curt nod and turned around. "Let's go, Brian."

"What about Rose?" asked Brian, following.

"Let the sun have them both."

Jeanie watched the black door close and flinched as she heard the heavy bolt slam into place. She stared at it for a moment and then brought her attention to the man she loved. New tears fell as Jeanie carefully and gently managed to lay his head in her lap, his white hair catching her stained tears. She touched his face, noting the flesh was still warm.

It was all her fault. She wanted to be with him for eternity. It had all been planned a century ago, only to be ruined by her stubbornness. Now he laid dead, his sword felling him.

Sobs wracked her body. She had plunged it through his body. She had killed the only man she had ever loved. Her life as Rose was a sham, one in which shame and guilt stabbed through her. It was Rose who fed off the Angel. It was Rose who impaled the Angel with his own sword. But she was not Rose, was she?

"I'm Jeanie," she said through her tears. "I'm Jeanie. I'm Jeanie!"

She had been forcibly turned into a Vampire, her life and her love ripped from her. This was not how they had planned. She was to be Chosen! She was supposed to spend eternity with the Angel, caring for him, loving him as he loved her.

Glancing up at the lightening sky Jeanie knew dawn was soon approaching and returned her gaze to Gwyn's still form. Using the edge of her sleeve she dabbed the blood from his mouth and smoothed his black lined face with her fingers.

He canna be dead, she thought. He had been through much worse at Violet's hand. *He's Chosen. He's the Angel.*

If she removed the sword them maybe he would recover, but how long would it take? Already Jeanie felt the familiar lassitude of the sun's rise. Soon it would be moot. She would die with him, joining him for eternity, but at least she could make him comfortable.

Carefully, with fading strength and through tear filled eyes, Jeanie grabbed the hilt of his sword and pulled it out. The sound and smell of burning flesh assaulted her senses. Only half the sword came free. A whimper escaped her throat and she tossed the sword aside to ring off the concrete. Now to pull the other end, Jeanie grasped the double edged blade feeling it cut deep until her blood filled the bloodgroove to drip towards the exit wound at his back. It took more effort to yank the metal out, her blood making the task slippery as the blade cut to the bone. Jeanie cried in relief when the blade came free. There was little time left and she tossed the other half of the sword.

Free of the impalement Jeanie was able to turn and lift him until she had his head pressed against her silent chest. She bowed her face until her forehead touched his.

"I love ye, Gwyn. I always will," she whispered into his unresponsive ear. She kissed his soft full lips, savouring his taste.

Darkness and nothingness descended as the sun broke over the horizon.

XXXV

They had waited as long as they could, hopeful of the Angel's return to Dr. Bowen's before Fernando returned them to the hotel. In silence and growing concern they entered the suite. The Angel had not returned here either.

It was close to dawn when they felt it, though what it was was indefinable. Tears sprung from Bridget's eyes and even Fernando could not hold back the sense of loss that overwhelmed him. He had not felt its like in centuries.

It was Bridget who came to the understanding first Fernando held her as she cried.

"He's gone."

In the condo, just before sunrise, Notus stood and stared blindly into the dark emptiness. Nothing could repair the chasm he had wrenched into his heart. No matter how he tried to rationalize his reasons his heart screamed the opposite.

He loved the boy.

He needed the boy.

In every way possible, the boy was his family and Notus had done worse by him because he never wanted to feel the same loss as when he lost his family. This time it was he who took the sword and pierced the heart. Not the Romans.

A gut wrenching pain grasped Notus, springing tears to his eyes.

"It's too late."

Elizabeth woke and glanced at the glowing red numbers. No wonder the sun was not up, it was too early. Releasing an exasperated sigh, she rose knowing she would not get any more sleep. She pulled on her robe and slipped into her bunny slippers before going down the hall. She did not know why but something deep within her sensed wrongness. She frowned at the empty guestroom and decided to look outside.

Nothing stirred as she descended the stairs. Not even Grimalkin opened an eye from his curled position on the couch. The feeling of unease never left her even as she stepped outside.

His motorcycle was not there.

It was then that it hit Elizabeth.

"He's never coming back."

Thanatos sat in his limousine, furious and stunned at what he and Godfrey had witnessed. "Drive up to them, Godfrey," he ordered.

"Yes, sir." Godfrey put the vehicle into gear and slowly rolled the car up to the fallen Angel and the Vampire who slew him.

There were bare moments before the sun's rays would fall upon the two, but would that be enough? Thanatos did not care. He had waited lifetimes to discover the answers he craved. It could not end like this.

"What do you want me to do, sir?" asked Godfrey, staring at his master in the rear view mirror.

Thanatos met his fatigued servant's gaze with determination and gave his order.

epilogue

The Three Ladies stood around the gurgling pool of water. Rounded stones ringed the well that was situated in a grove carpeted with lush emerald green grass. Tall trees where the tops could not be seen for their height and flowers the colours of the rainbow surrounded the grove in a floral embrace. On a flat rock in from of the pool a silver chalice sat, its new chain linking it to an iron ring.

"All is lost," mourned the Lady in Black. Her long black hair hung over sad black eyes as she stared into the pool.

"Nothing is lost forever," consoled her White Sister. "There is always hope." She reached out a long delicate hand to grasp a hand the same in all ways except for the darkness of her skin. The two sisters shared themselves, opposites in colour yet the same in spirit.

The Red Lady took Her Black Sister's other hand and gave a gentle squeeze, Her crimson eyes filled with hope, smiling at the other two. "There is always another way."

"Another choice," said the White Lady.

"Another life," smiled the Black Lady.

One in Three, the Ladies gazed into the well. In the waters Their daughter stood sadly at the door to her home, unaware of the seed that was planted deep within her.

about the author

Karen Dales is the Award Winning Author of the widely acclaimed *The Chosen Chronicles,* having won Siren Books' Award for Best Horror and Best Overall 2010. *The Chosen Chronicles* include *Changeling, Angel of Death* and *Shadow of Death.*

She is currently at work on the next book in *The Chosen Chronicles - Thanatos* as well as a historical fiction novel.

Born in Toronto, Ontario, Canada, she shares her life with her two cats, one son and husband.

Visit her website at www.karendales.com